EZEKIEL & ABRAHIM:

GHOSTS

of

LOST CREEK JUNCTION

Dale Thele

Published by

Fountain Literary Press
a unique approach to publishing

Austin, Texas, USA

ISBN: 979-8-9857557-6-3 (pbk)
ISBN: 979-8-9857557-7-0 (ebook)
ISBN: 979-8-9857557-8-7 (hc)

ASIN: B0DYJWJBS1

First Digest Paperback Edition: February 25, 2025
First Hardcover Edition: March 11, 2025

14 15 16 17 9 23 24 25 26 25

*Dedicated to those who believe in
things that go bump in the night.*

"Trust your instincts and follow your heart—
you never know what delightful surprises await
just around the bend."

~Taylor Stefan Greene~
Ezekiel & Abrahim: Ghosts of Lost Creek Junction

EZEKIEL & ABRAHIM:

GHOSTS

of

LOST
CREEK
JUNCTION

a fictional tale

Dale Thele

DAY ONE

Tuesday, May 15, 2018

On this bright and humid early afternoon, a slender young man, standing at 5'10", steps off a red, white, and blue Trailways bus. Taking his first steps onto an empty gravel lot, he feels nerves fluttering in his stomach like butterflies. The sun beats down relentlessly, making the sun-bleached pebbles shimmer. Heat waves shimmy, rising toward the blue cloudless sky.

Wait a moment. I can already sense your questions—who is this guy? Where did he come from on that bus? What town has he arrived in? And why should I give a flip?

Let me introduce myself—I'm Taylor Greene, and I'm excited to tell you the story of my epic summer vacation I had with three amazing friends and my trusty dog. Buckle up, because the summer was anything but ordinary. Can you imagine spending three whole months filled with laughter, adventure, and memories that'll last a lifetime? Well, that's exactly what we experienced. Not to mention strange noises in the night and being chased by ghosts—every exhilarating moment kept us on our toes.

My story begins two weeks before my college summer break in Austin, Texas, when something unexpected happened. I was about to leave my apartment when the landline phone rang. A man on the other end claimed to be a lawyer and started rambling about some property waiting for me in Lost Creek Junction. Curious, I quickly Googled the location and found out it was a real town situated about one hundred miles northwest of Austin. Right away, my instincts kicked in; it was clearly a scam. Who wouldn't suspect it was one of those sketchy timeshare deals?

I didn't have time for this salesman's nonsense, especially since I was already running late for class at the University of Texas.

Lost Creek Junction—doesn't that name scream *timeshare scam*? You know the routine: a smooth-talking salesperson calls you, promising luxurious amenities and an unforgettable getaway. It sounds appealing, right? But there's always a catch. Before you can enjoy your *free* weekend stay at their so-called resort, you're required to go on a guided tour of an expensive property that's way out of your budget. Just when you think you're off the hook, the high-pressure sales pitch for a timeshare condo begins. It's like being trapped in a never-ending game of sales tag.

It's a familiar yet frustrating story: nothing in this world comes without a price tag. You may think you're getting a great deal, but before you know it, that charming salesman is pressuring you to buy something you never wanted and certainly can't afford. Suddenly, you find yourself leaving the resort financially drained, while he walks away with a hefty down payment check in his pocket. Just like that, you've become the reluctant owner of an overpriced timeshare that you'll likely never use.

Let me tell you, this salesman picked the wrong person to pester that day. First of all, I'm a second-year college student. Secondly, I only had a few dollars in my bank account, and I was already dealing with two years of college loan debt weighing heavily on me, with more to come. I was hardly in a position to entertain any sales pitches. Thirdly, I was already running late for class—talk about adding stress to an already hectic day. Lastly, let's be real: I was not in a receptive mood.

"I'm not interested," I told the man on the phone, my patience wearing thin.

"But hear me out—"

"I said I'm not interested, okay?" I interrupted, trying to end the conversation.

"Please, give me a moment of your time," he insisted, his voice surprisingly urgent. "You have inherited a sizable estate."

Wait, what? Inherited? Did I hear this man correctly?

"I represent the estate of the late Mabel June MacAllister-Blackburn. You are her sole beneficiary, and she has left you a substantial inheritance."

Confused, I replied, "I'm sorry, but I don't know anyone by that name. You must have dialed the wrong number."

The voice continued, "Your name is Taylor Greene, right? And Greene is spelled with three *E*s?"

"Yes," I confirmed hesitantly, "but I assure you, I don't know anyone named Maybelline-Whatever-Whatever-Blackbird."

"Actually, the name is Mabel June MacAllister-Blackburn," he interjected. "She could be a long-lost relative or perhaps a distant cousin you have forgotten."

I paused for a moment to let that sink in. "I honestly doubt that, you see, both my parents passed away in a car accident when I was a sophomore in high school. I don't have any aunts or uncles, and when I turned 16, I moved in with my maternal grandmother. Two years ago, I came to Austin with my best friend to attend classes at the University of Texas. So, I doubt this lady was related to me."

"Are you absolutely certain the name Mabel June MacAllister-Blackburn doesn't sound familiar?" the man asked. "Perhaps she was someone you encountered at some point?"

"I don't think so," I replied, shaking my head. "As I mentioned before, it's just been my grandma and me since my parents passed away."

"Regardless of whether she was family or not, one thing is clear: Mrs. Blackburn left you her entire estate and a house in her will."

There was a long, awkward pause on the phone. What do you say in a moment like this? My mind raced with uncertainty— was this guy for real? I could have used some cash right about then. But again, just my luck: a long-lost relative would suddenly appear and contest the will, snatching it all away from me. I could end up drowning in legal fees instead of swimming in riches. Can you believe it? Just moments after discovering I was an heir, I was turning into a greedy so-and-so, already daydreaming about how I'd spend money that technically wasn't mine yet.

"Mr. Greene, are you still on the line?"

"Yes, I'm here," I replied, trying to clear the whirlwind of thoughts swirling in my mind.

"I would like to finalize the details concerning the Blackburn estate as soon as possible. Can you come to my office in Lost Creek Junction next week? What day and time would work best for you?"

"Sorry, I won't be available to come for at least two weeks. The school term doesn't end until then."

"Can we meet once your summer break starts?"

"I don't see why not," I said to the attorney, intrigued by the promise of an inheritance and a place called Lost Creek Junction. But what if this guy is genuine? The thought of inheriting money—any amount—was just too tempting to ignore. So, call me adventurous (or maybe a little reckless), but I decided to dig deeper into his claims. What's the worst that could happen? I'd lose the price of a bus ticket to some obscure town. That seemed like a small gamble if cash awaited me at the end of it all. Yet, every rational part of me screamed I might be falling for a scam. Still, every reasonable fiber of my being told me I was being played for a fool. But hey, when do we listen to logic when there's money involved?

That's where the story I'm about to share with you begins. It all started with a single phone call—a moment that ignited an unforgettable summer, one I could never have anticipated. I promise you this: I'll tell you the honest truth, without any embellishments. But whether you choose to believe it or not is entirely up to you.

As I step off the bus, which I assume has brought me to Lost

Creek Junction, I drop my backpack and suitcase onto the scorching, sun-baked ground. The sun blazes overhead, transforming the vacant lot into a vast desert of heat—it's as if I'm a lone island adrift in an ocean of sunlight. I squint against the brightness as the bus fades into the distance, leaving behind a swirling cloud of dust that settles around me like a shroud—a stark reminder of my solitude.

Coughing, I squint through the swirling dust enveloping me like a thick fog. Instinctively, I cover my mouth and nose, waiting for the gritty particles to settle before I breathe. As the air clears, I survey my surroundings to realize I've been unceremoniously dropped off in a vast, deserted desert. If it weren't for the hungry vulture giving me a side-eye from a nearby skeletal tree, and tumbleweeds rolling by as if enjoying a leisurely Sunday stroll, I'd feel completely isolated in this scorching expanse of emptiness. In front of me stands a small bus terminal; its peeling paint and rusted benches hint at years of abandonment. Yet, despite its forlorn appearance, it may be my only hope for escape.

Suddenly, a sleek black sedan speeds across the gravel, sending up a massive cloud of dust behind it. It comes racing in from the opposite direction of the bus that just pulled away, and before I realize what's happening, the car skids to a stop—barely missing me by inches.

Dust swirls around like a mini tornado, coating me in dirt and grime and making me feel filthy and gritty. As I brush myself off, I hear the annoyed flapping of a vulture's wings nearby. Is it me, or does the bird seem irritated I won't be its next meal?

The driver's side window slides down, revealing the silhouette of a man, sitting behind the car's steering wheel.

"Are you Taylor Greene?" The figure in silhouette leans closer, his face illuminated by the warm glow from the open passenger window.

"Yes, sir, that's me," I reply, squinting against the sun's relentless glare reflecting off the sleek car and the vast expanse of sun-bleached gravel surrounding us. Dang it, why didn't I bring my sunglasses?

"I'm Mr. Andrews. We briefly spoke on the phone about your inheritance," he says, his voice slicing through the dusty stillness like a knife. The very mention of *inheritance* sends a chill racing down my spine. What could it entail? I can hardly contain my curiosity—what am I about to receive?

"Right," I reply, nodding as I blindly trust this stranger. But what choice do I have? After all, I'm a helpless hostage stranded in this desolate desert.

"Throw your things in the back seat and hop in," Mr. Andrews calls out with a warm smile. His friendly demeanor puts me somewhat at ease and I'm pretty certain he's not a serial killer. I toss my gear into the back and slide into the front passenger seat, grateful for the rush of cool air from the blasting air conditioner—a welcome relief from the scorching heat outside.

"How was your trip?" he asks, glancing over at me as he steps on the accelerator. Mr. Andrews is a middle-aged man, probably in his forties, with an easygoing charm that makes his part of the conversation seem effortless.

As he navigates through the swirling dust storm, the car sways unpredictably, making it difficult to tell if we're looping back or forging ahead. It's like being caught in a tornado and not knowing where it's carrying you.

"I suppose the bus ride was like any other," I finally manage to say, my fingers fumbling as I fasten my seat belt. The driver's reckless driving is making me extremely anxious—it's so bad I might actually become car sick. My white knuckles grip the armrest as I desperately steady myself against this crazy man's driving skills.

"Was this your first time on a bus?" he asks, navigating the car with excessive enthusiasm.

"Yes, sir," I respond, as a charming little town emerges from the swirling dust. "I usually get around Austin on the metro buses, this was my first time taking a commercial bus."

"Oh right, you're from Austin," he replies, nodding in

recognition.

Dust clouds swirl outside, casting a hazy veil over the tiny town I can barely make out. An awkward silence settles between us, heavy like the air just before a storm.

"You're not much of a talker, are you?" he observes, his gaze fixed on the road barely visible through the swirling dirt.

"Well, I'm not exactly sure what to say to a lawyer," I admit with a sheepish grin. "Unless it's about legal matters, but I don't know anything about that." (Just so you know, I tend to ramble when I'm nervous. It's my way of filling the silence.)

"Lawyers are like everyone else," Mr. Andrews chuckles, adjusting his dark sunglasses with a flick of his middle finger. "We put our pants on one leg at a time, just like you do."

I smile at his down-to-earth humor as I glance out the window, watching the scenery change. We've left the vast desert behind and are now rolling into a quaint little town—a town so small it feels like it could fit in the palm of my hand.

What strikes me first is the wonderfully vintage appearance of the buildings. It's like stepping into a time machine. Their old-fashioned charm feels perfectly preserved, transporting me back to the late 1800s or early 1900s.

Mr. Andrews navigates a street of weathered red bricks, meticulously arranged in a basket-weave pattern. Can you believe it? Even though the bricks have seen better days, Mr. Andrews' modern car glides effortlessly over them as if they were freshly laid. It's almost surreal. I imagine what it would be like to ride in a horse and buggy or even a classic Model T instead of this modern vehicle, feeling out of place in this antiquated setting.

Mr. Andrews pulls up in front of a charming four-story building, its stone facade covered in vibrant green ivy, seeming to whisper secrets of the past. As I glance through the large plate glass window of the quaint drugstore on the ground floor, I catch sight of a few curious patrons inside. Our eyes lock for a moment, but as if suddenly caught in the spotlight, they quickly retreat into the shadows, leaving me wondering what's their deal?

I anxiously follow Mr. Andrews up the creaky wooden stairs to the fourth floor. Each step makes me question why there's no elevator. We finally arrive at a plain wood door with a frosted glass window. The words *Simon J. Andrews, Attorney at Law* are stenciled in block letters.

I wonder if the door is his official stamp of approval as a legitimate attorney? After all, who'd bother putting *Attorney at Law* on their door if they aren't the real deal?

The moment I lay eyes on the door, I have the feeling I've stepped into one of my detective novels—classic paperback thrillers where the tension is thick enough to cut it with a knife. You know the plot: someone swings open a door, and Blam! Blam! Blam! Bullets start flying. Honestly, I'm addicted to page-turning detective novels.

Mr. Andrews slips a key in the lock and twists till there's a click. He then grips the doorknob, twisting and pulling with no luck. After a forceful shoulder shove, the door gives way with a reluctant creak and swings open.

I instinctively step aside to let Mr. Andrews enter first—after all, there could be someone waiting inside, machine gun drawn, ready to blow away whoever opens the door. Maybe I should cut back on my detective novels.

"Isn't it fascinating how time shapes a building?" Mr. Andrews muses as we stroll through the outer office. "This place may be old, but it has character. Sure, the stairs teeter a bit, the floors creak like an old ship at sea, and the doors tend to stick—as if they're playing hard to get. But honestly? It's holding up remarkably well for its age."

As we pass by an empty reception desk cloaked in dust, I wonder how long it's been sitting vacant.

"Good help is hard to find these days," he comments with a knowing smile, catching my gaze on the unoccupied desk before opening yet another door.

As I step into what must be his private office, I'm struck by the chaos surrounding me. The room is overflowing with law books, old newspapers, and dog-eared crime novels that have seen better days. The bookshelves are so overloaded they seem to groan under their weight, while stacks of books on the floor create narrow pathways that twist and turn through the clutter. It feels like a scene straight out of my childhood—like an ant farm come to life.

I remember those tiny architects working tirelessly to carve intricate tunnels in the sand. Their determination to navigate from point A to point B was nothing short of inspiring. Much like those ants, this office evokes memories of my childhood ant farm.

Mr. Andrews chuckles softly, his cheeks flushing a shade of crimson as he clears a stack of well-worn paperback crime novels from the leather-upholstered side chair. "Here," he gestures with a warm smile, "make yourself comfortable."

"Thanks," I reply, fully aware once I sink into the chair, I'll leave an indelible butt impression in the layer of dust that's settled there.

Mr. Andrews strolls around his desk and sinks into a plush, high-back swivel chair that creaks under his weight. The office is filled with a musty aroma, as if it hasn't seen fresh air in ages. Stacks of books tower precariously on every surface, each covered in dust—some lightly kissed by time, while others are shrouded in a thick layer, suggesting some haven't been touched for years.

"Give me a moment to get organized," he says with a hint of exasperation, sifting through the chaotic mountain of papers scattered across his cluttered desk. Each movement sends showers of dust particles into the air like confetti at a New Year's party. "Ah, here it is," he exclaims, triumphantly holding up a manila file folder decorated with colorful pastel sticky notes. "As I mentioned during our phone call a few weeks ago —"

"Sorry," I quickly add, "I couldn't make it until summer break began."

"No worries. You're here now, right?" he responds, his voice trailing off as he stares blankly over my shoulder.

I turn to look behind me but see nothing—just specks of dust swirling in a beam of afternoon sunlight. "Excuse me, Mr. Andrews? Is everything alright?"

He shakes his head, as if trying to clear a brain fog. "Oh yes," he replies with a smile that doesn't quite reach his eyes. "Now, where was I?"

"You were about to say, *as you mentioned during our phone call a few weeks ago,*" I gently remind him.

"Ah, yes," he replies, leaning back in his chair, the creak echoing the significance of the moment. "You are the sole beneficiary of Mrs. Blackburn's estate. Can I ask you something personal, son?"

"I suppose so," I respond.

"Can you remind me again how you are related to the late Mrs. Blackburn?"

"Like I mentioned on the phone, sir, I've never heard of anyone named Blackburn until you brought it up. I asked my grandma about it, and she said there's no one by that name in our family tree."

"Could she have been a long-lost relative?" Mr. Andrews inquires.

"Not that I'm aware of," I reply, shaking my head.

"That's strange," Mr. Andrews says, scratching his head in bewilderment. "A complete stranger leaving you prime real estate? Not to mention a substantial sum of money."

In a way, I feel like I'm channeling the spirit of Jimmy Durante and his beloved Mrs. Calabash. *Thank you, Mrs. Blackburn, wherever you are,* I say, casting a wistful gaze toward the heavens. In reality, I'm staring at a grimy, water-stained ceiling that could use a good patch and paint job.

I imagine my benefactor perched on a fluffy celestial cloud, a serene smile lighting up her face as she looks down at me. Or perhaps she's gazing up from the depths below. The truth is, I never had the pleasure of meeting her, nor do I know her final destination—be it celestial or otherwise. Her current afterlife whereabouts remain a mystery to me.

"Are you ready to see what Mrs. Blackburn left you?" Mr. Andrews asks, a twinkle in his eye.

"Absolutely," I reply, excitedly springing from my chair. The prospect of seeing what the widow left me is monumental—like opening a treasure chest filled with secrets waiting to be revealed. In my eagerness, I accidentally kick up a cloud of dust that dances in the sunlight streaming through the window.

Note to self: Never, under any circumstances, move quickly in Mr. Andrews's office.

Mr. Andrews pulls his car into a driveway, which features a stunning path of rectangular blonde clay bricks woven together in an eye-catching basket-weave pattern. The drive leads to a magnificent four-story Victorian house that commands attention with its intricate limestone carvings on the first floor and robust granite adorning the upper levels. Is that an attic peeking out from the top? It's hard to tell. At the end of the driveway sits a detached three-car garage, which might even have an apartment located above it—how cool is that? The garage doors stand firmly shut, guarding whatever secrets lie within.

The garage feels like something straight out of the TV show *Let's Make A Deal*. With three enticing doors to choose from, which one hides the ultimate prize? *Monty Hall I'll take door number two, please.*

"Is this really my house?" I gasp, my breath catching in my throat as I take in the breathtaking enormity of the structure and the sprawling yard that seems to stretch on forever.

"Yes, it is, son," Mr. Andrews replies. "All thanks to the generosity of the late Mrs. Blackburn."

"Well, I'll be darned," I exclaim, hardly able to believe my eyes.

Just then, my cell phone buzzes in my pocket. I pull it out and answer without thinking twice. "Hello?" I say, instantly recognizing the voice on the other end. "Hey, Rye," I greet before hitting mute for a moment.

Turning back to Mr. Andrews, I explain with a grin, "It's my friend." I unmute the call and ask eagerly, "Where are you guys?"

I listen intently to Ryan's voice on the phone. "You're almost here," I encourage him. "Take Main Street until it dead ends. My house is on the right—you can't miss it. It's huge. I can't wait for you guys to see this place. See you in a few minutes." With that, I tuck my phone back into my pants pocket.

Turning to Mr. Andrews, I say, "My friends are coming to stay for the summer."

"That's fantastic," he replies. "Having extra hands around will help you get settled in." He reaches into his pocket and pulls out a ring of keys, handing them to me with a smile. "Here are the keys to your new home. I should probably let you go— your friends will be here before you know it. Remember, if you need anything at all, don't hesitate to call. You have my number."

"Thank you for everything," I say, giving him a firm handshake, genuinely grateful for his support.

"I'll be in touch soon," he replies.

As I swing open the car door and step out of the cool, air-conditioning, I'm immediately body-slammed by the heavy, humid Texas air, making me wish I hadn't left the comfort of the car. "Sounds good," I respond, grabbing my backpack and suitcase from the backseat. "Thanks again for all your help."

At that moment, a cream-colored SUV screeches to a halt at the curb in front of my house, its horn blaring like it's announcing a parade. Arms flailing out of the windows, and from one window, a gigantic dog barks with uncontainable excitement.

"Looks like your friends have arrived," Mr. Andrews chuckles, glancing back at me with a knowing smile. "That's my cue to get out of here."

With that, he revs his car engine and backs out of the driveway.

In an instant, my friends Julie, Ryan, Duncan, and a massive dog scramble out from the SUV. The human trio stand frozen for a moment, mouths gaping and eyes wide with wonder as they take in the sight of my new to me house.

With his sleek black muzzle and big, soulful eyes the huge dog—my Great Dane, Beau, bounds toward me, his tail wagging like it's trying to take flight. He nearly knocks me off my feet as he leaps up to greet me joyfully, his paws resting on my shoulders while he showers me with slobbery kisses. I drop my suitcase and backpack in the driveway, laughing at his enthusiasm. "Beau," I chuckle, "I'm happy to see you too. It's like you think we've been apart for ages. Remember? We hung out for a bit this morning before I left Austin."

"Beau missed his daddy," Ryan teases, pulling the rambunctious dog off me. "Just like I missed you," he adds with a playful grin as he leans in for a quick kiss on my lips.

"Ew!" Ryan grimaces, dramatically spitting and wiping his mouth with the back of his hand. "You've got yucky dog slobber all over your mouth."

"Oh, come on," I tease Ryan. "You've had way worse in that mouth of yours."

"Okay, okay," Ryan concedes, throwing his hands up in surrender. "There's no need to go into detail in front of your friends."

Just then, Beau nudges my leg, clearly trying to get my attention. "I see you, big guy," I say as I squat down to wrap my arms around the gentle giant's neck for a warm hug.

"Wow, is this your house?" Julie asks, her eyes wide with astonishment.

"Yep, welcome to my humble abode," I reply.

"This isn't a house—it's a freakin' mansion," Duncan exclaims, looking around in awe. "And trust me, I know mansions when I see one."

"Wow, look at these twisted old trees. There are so many of them," Julie exclaims, her eyes wide with wonder. "Those curly branches give the impression your house is situated in a haunted forest. No offense, Taylor, but all these trees make your place feel spooky."

"Spooky, really?" Duncan asks. "I was going to say *royaume des fées*."

"What does that mean?" Julie inquires.

"Loosely translated, it means *fairyland*," Duncan explains.

"Okay," Julie nods. "I can see that."

"So, Taylor, what kind of trees are they?" Duncan asks.

"Those are *Live Oaks*," Ryan jumps in. "They're everywhere in Austin—trust me, you've seen them before."

Duncan shakes his head, puzzled. "I don't remember seeing trees like these in Austin."

"Oh, you probably didn't notice them because Austin doesn't have a whole lot of them. And the ones here are definitely older."

"How old do you think these trees are?" Duncan asks.

Ryan rubs his chin thoughtfully. "I'd guess they're at least a hundred years old. They've been here for a long time—there's no doubt about that."

"Hey guys," I chime in, "do you want to check out my house?" I didn't intend to interrupt Ryan's and Duncan's conversation but I'm dying to see the inside of my house.

Julie is curious too, as she eagerly replies, "We totally want to see your house."

"We'll see it together for the first time," I say, leading Julie, Ryan, Duncan, and Beau up the stone stairs. The wrap-around porch stretches out before us, its large blocks of solid sandstone radiate warmth under the afternoon sun.

As we stand in front of the door, which is beautifully adorned with a stained-glass window, I imagine how stunning it must look when the light shines through it. I fumble through the keys Mr. Andrews gave me, and with each key I try, my anticipation builds. After the third attempt, to my surprise, the door creaks open on its own. "Well, it looks like it wasn't locked after all," I chuckle, pushing it wide and inviting my friends inside.

Before going any further with my story, I bet you're wondering why I took the bus instead of riding with my friends in Duncan's SUV.

The reason is that I had an appointment with Mr. Andrews, the attorney, and my friends weren't sure when they would be able to leave Austin. You see, Duncan and Julie had business to wrap up at the university before heading out of town. Surprisingly, they completed everything in record time. If I'd joined them, I'd have cut it too close and risked being late for my meeting.

Honestly, taking the bus turned out to be a blessing in disguise. It gave me a perfect opportunity to catch up on my reading while enjoying the ride. And guess what? I arrived right on time for my appointment with Mr. Andrews.

As soon as we step inside, we're struck by the sheer beauty of this stunning, fully furnished house. It feels like walking into a Victorian museum, with every corner filled with perfectly preserved vintage treasures. While we stand frozen in awe, our mouths agape at the exquisite decor, Beau shows no hesitation in making himself comfortable. With an aggressive leap, he claims the forest green velvet settee as his own, sprawling out luxuriously along its length. His large frame spills over the edges as he rests his head on his paws and lets out a blissful sigh —clearly feeling at home.

"I can hardly believe how fresh and vibrant everything looks —the furniture, the rugs, the curtains, the stunning chandeliers. It's all so captivating. Yet, I have the feeling these furnishings must be over a century old," I say. "There's no way any of this are new reproductions."

Julie nods in agreement, her eyes sparkling with excitement. "It feels like we've stepped into a turn-of-the-century furniture showroom. Everything looks pristine despite its age. How is that even possible?"

"So, Taylor, all of this is a surprise to you?" Duncan asks. "You weren't expecting a fully furnished house?"

I chuckle softly, shaking my head. "Honestly? I had no idea

what to expect. But I definitely didn't anticipate anything this swanky."

Who was Mrs. Blackburn? This question keeps swirling in my mind. Why would a complete stranger leave all of this to me? How did she find me? Did she randomly pick a name from the phone book, and somehow it was me?

It's honestly mind-blowing to think I've inherited something from someone I've never heard of before. How could a total stranger know anything about me? It feels like I'm standing at the edge of an intriguing mystery, just waiting to be unraveled.

Fortunately, with summer vacation stretching ahead of me like an open road, I have the perfect opportunity to find the truth. Who knows what I'll discover as I seek answers and piece together the puzzle of Marabella-Whatever-Whatever-Blackburn?

In the midst of the chaos, with my friends whooping and hollering as they race up the stairs to claim their bedrooms, Beau lifts his head and lets out a startled bark. However, once he realizes no one is in danger, he relaxes with a satisfied sigh and curls up for a well-deserved nap.

Ryan claims the bedroom at the end of the second-floor hallway, and guess what? It's the one he and I'll be sharing. As I step inside, I find him bouncing on the bed like a kid breaking in a new trampoline.

The room exudes a distinctly masculine vibe, thanks to its striking green and gold filigree wallpaper, which adds a touch of elegance. The centerpiece of the room is a massive marble fireplace in deep green, flecked with shimmering gold. Underfoot lies a rich, deep green Oriental rug that perfectly complements the décor. There's also an ornate chandelier overhead, loaded with glistening teardrop crystals that beautifully catch the light. However, the true showstopper is the king-sized four poster bed. It looks like it's never been slept in —everything in the room is spotless and dust-free.

Duncan chooses the bedroom closest to the stairs, which is

next to Julie's room. It's a comfortable arrangement, with our bedrooms lined up in a neat row along the second-floor hallway. There's even an unoccupied room nestled between mine and Julie's.

Stepping into Duncan's room feels like entering a gentleman's retreat from another era. The deep blue wallpaper, adorned with delicate gold floral patterns, sets a striking tone that is both bold and inviting. Can you imagine sinking into his massive bed? With its intricately carved headboard and footboard, it resembles a California King—though that might be a stretch since those didn't exist in Victorian times. It appears to be custom-made.

The furniture complements the bed perfectly; each piece is heavy and beautifully carved, creating an atmosphere of refined elegance. And let's not forget the fabulous burgundy oriental rug that adds warmth to the wood-planked floor. The bed looks freshly made, dressed in creamy linens paired with a matching quilt and pillow shams, inviting one to dive in.

Julie's next-door bedroom is beautifully decorated in a delicate French provincial style. The satiny wallpaper is elegantly accented with cream and gold trim, creating a soft and inviting atmosphere that feels warm and welcoming. Imagine sinking into a bed with a high headboard featuring a luxurious tufted satin inlay—this detail perfectly complements the footboard, making it an elegant focal point in the room.

Every piece of furniture harmonizes beautifully with the serene color palette. The nightstands, makeup table, mirror, and spacious chest of drawers all showcase the delightful off-white and gold design. Additionally, the polished alabaster marble floor gleams underfoot, while a stunning cream and gold oriental rug adds warmth and charm right at the center of the room.

The room feels fresh and welcoming, as if it's just been pampered by a diligent housekeeper. Crisp linens are neatly arranged on the bed, making you wish you could dive in. The only thing missing are mints placed on those fluffy pillows for an extra touch of hospitality.

After selecting their bedrooms, Ryan, Duncan, and Julie hardly contain their excitement. They dash outside to the SUV, eager to bring their luggage into the house. As they animatedly share details about the rooms they picked, I'm happy to see my friends finding their places in my new home away from home.

I join them outside, grabbing my backpack and suitcase from the driveway. The air is filled with laughter and chatter as we head back inside together. It feels like a great start to summer for all of us.

Once everyone settles into their rooms, I turn to Duncan and ask, "Hey, can you take me to the grocery store?" The others perk up, eager to come along for the ride.

As we head out the door, Beau stirs from his self-proclaimed settee bed. His big, soulful eyes look up at me, filled with hope. However, I shake my head. "No, Beau," I say firmly but kindly, making sure he knows I'm serious. "Not this time. You stay here and guard the house, okay, buddy?"

All four of us climb into Duncan's SUV. What do we do now? I don't know where the grocery store is. In a small town like Lost Creek Junction, which has a population of just a couple of hundred, finding the only grocery store turns out to be a piece of cake.

Bounding out of the SUV, the four of us head into the grocery store. "Everyone, just a quick heads-up—we don't need to go overboard with our grocery shopping today," I say, glancing around at the group. "What do you think about having hot dogs for supper and dry cereal for breakfast?" Those seem to be the least expensive options I can think of. It's not about being cheap. I don't have the money for much else.

"Sounds great," Julie beams as she grabs a grocery cart.

"Tomorrow, once we're settled in, we can make a more detailed grocery list," I suggest, hoping for time to figure out how to scrape together the cash for tomorrow's groceries.

"So, if we're having hot dogs for supper," Julie continues, pushing the cart with determination, "we need hot dogs and mustard—"

"Ketchup for me," Duncan chimes in.

"Alright," Julie laughs, tossing both mustard and ketchup into the cart. "Now, we need potato chips—"

"I want corn chips," Ryan pipes up enthusiastically.

"Potato and corn chips," Julie confirms with a nod. "And we need hot dog buns."

"Don't forget the Twinkies," Duncan adds, his voice rising playfully. "No offense, Rye." He gives Ryan a lighthearted pat on the back, accompanied by a cheeky grin.

"Oh, no offense taken," Ryan retorts, shooting Duncan an annoyed glare. This playful banter is a familiar routine between them—Duncan's teasing often skirts the line of homophobic jabs. But to be clear, Duncan isn't actually homophobic—he loves to poke fun at Ryan for kicks.

Duncan flashes a mischievous grin at Ryan as he gleefully tosses canned baked beans, zesty relish, and an assortment of quirky condiments into the shopping cart. Meanwhile, Julie's on her own mission, adding a jumbo pack of paper towels and a super-sized bundle of toilet tissue. I've lost track of everything going in the buggy, and I can picture the receipt tape stretching longer than my arm.

As if that weren't enough, Duncan adds a couple of colorful boxes of breakfast cereal. Ryan tosses in a fresh loaf of bread, creamy butter, a jar of jelly, a gallon of milk, and his favorite brand of breakfast cereal. Julie snags a hefty canister of coffee and loads up on ten pounds of sugar, along with a jar of powdered non-dairy creamer.

While wheeling the overflowing grocery cart into the checkout area, I completely forgot about Beau. He needs to eat too. With a determined sigh, I leave the cart at the register with my friends and head to the pet food aisle, where I grab the largest bag of kibble I can find. As I toss it over my shoulder, an unsettling thought gnaws at me—how will I pay for all this? My checking account only has four dollars, and I've got some loose change in my pocket. That won't even come close to covering the cost of Beau's food, not to mention the cart full of items my friends have collected.

"Hey, Taylor, what's up with you?" Duncan asks as I walk back to the checkout, his eyes scanning my face. "You look like you're about to hurl."

I lean in close and lower my voice. "Honestly, I'm freaking out about how I'm going to pay for all these groceries."

"Relax," he says reassuringly, pulling out a shiny Platinum American Express card like a superhero revealing their secret weapon.

"Wait, do they even accept American Express here?" I ask.

Duncan chuckles and gives me a wink. "Trust me, everyone accepts American Express, right, darling?" Duncan grins at the clerk.

The cashier pauses mid-ring, hands firmly on hips, her expression a mix of disbelief and annoyance. "We don't accept American Express," she states flatly.

"Well, what now, Einstein?" I shoot back at Duncan.

Calmly, he reaches into his wallet, a demeanor that contrasts with the growing tension in the air. He pulls out a sleek platinum Visa card. "Ma'am," he says, waving it proudly like a flag, "do you take Visa?"

Her eyes flicker to the card before she nods and resumes scanning our groceries. A wave of relief washes over all of us as we exhale—thanks to Duncan's wallet full of credit cards.

Duncan and I bag groceries while Julie flips through a grocery tabloid, her eyes scanning the latest celebrity gossip. Meanwhile, Ryan is on a mission at the end-cap display, tossing an eclectic mix of impulse buys into our cart—packages of gum, flashlights, batteries—you name it. It's like watching a kid in a candy store with no spending limit.

As long as I've known Ryan, he's had this peculiar habit of collecting all those tempting little items that catch your eye while you wait in line. Is it just me, or does he have an impulse buy addiction?

"Where y'all stayin'?" the cashier asks, her fingers dancing over the keys of an old-fashioned register as she rings up our groceries. The clinking of keys and the whir of the machine fill the air, creating a nostalgic atmosphere. "I ask 'cause I haven't seen y'all 'round these parts before."

"We're staying at the Widow Blackburn's house," I reply proudly.

The cashier raises an eyebrow. "Y'all know it's illegal to camp on someone else's property, right?"

"Oh," Julie chimes in with a grin, pointing at me. "He's the new owner. The widow gave it to him in her will."

A puzzled look crosses the cashier's face. "Y'all knows that place is haunted?" she asks, her tone shifting from curious to cautionary. "I wouldn't go near that ol' house even if ya paid me a bazillion dollars."

"It's actually very nice inside," I defend, trying to dispel any lingering doubts about my new house.

"Maybe so," she replies sharply, "but it's haunted all the same."

"Are you telling me there are actual ghosts in that house?" Duncan asks, raising his eyebrows in disbelief.

"Absolutely," the cashier replies, her eyes wide with conviction. "It's been haunted by ghosts for as long as I can remember."

Duncan rolls his eyes, a smirk forming on his lips. "Oh, come on. There's no such thing as ghosts," he scoffs, waving a dismissive hand.

The cashier looks at him sternly, nervously fiddling with a silver cross hanging around her neck. "Ya really shouldn't dismiss things ya don't know 'bout," she scolds gentle but firmly.

The four of us exchange puzzled glances, caught between skepticism and curiosity.

"Aha, you almost had us there," Ryan chuckles, a playful glint in his eye. "You're pulling our leg, right?"

The cashier clutches the cross from her necklace as if it's a magic amulet, protecting her from the supernatural and responds thoughtfully, "Heed my warning."

Duncan hands over his credit card, casting a wary glance at her, uncertain whether she's serious or joking about ghosts. As the cashier swipes the sales receipt and Duncan's card through an old manual credit card reader—a relic from another era—he watches her every move, as if it's some sort of magic trick. She hands him the paper copies along with a ballpoint pen.

Duncan examines the receipt with all the enthusiasm of someone inspecting a pile of dog poo. It's possible he's never encountered one of these ancient devices before—he's most likely used to sleek electronic readers where he swipes his credit card.

"Duncan," I say, "you need to sign the top piece of paper."

With a reluctant sigh, he takes the pen and scrawls his signature. The cashier quickly tears off a duplicate receipt and hands it to him.

Duncan looks suspiciously at the tissue receipt then at me.

"That copy is for your records, I explain, trying to reassure him. "Think of it like an ATM receipt—just put it in your wallet."

He looks at me with skepticism, unsure whether to trust my words. After a moment's hesitation, he folds the receipt and tucks it away.

"Thanks, miss," I say to the cashier as we grab our bags of groceries. An awkward silence hangs between the four of us until we reach Duncan's SUV.

"Can you believe that cashier?" Julie exclaims, her eyes wide with disbelief. "Ghosts? Seriously, who actually believes in ghosts these days?"

"Woooo," Ryan moans dramatically, waving his arms above his head like a ghost from a B rated horror movie.

"Come on, Rye, cut it out," Julie says, rolling her eyes and suppressing a smile.

"Admit it, I scared you, didn't I?" Ryan teases, a playful grin spreading across his face.

"No, you didn't," Julie states. "I agree with Duncan—there's no such thing as ghosts."

When we return to the house, there's an unmistakable energy in the air. Julie takes charge of the kitchen like a seasoned captain navigating uncharted waters. "Put that there, and those go in the second cabinet," she directs us confidently, as if she knows every nook and cranny of the kitchen by heart. It's almost as though she has an invisible map guiding her—no one dares to question her instructions.

As the sun dips below the horizon, casting a warm glow over the backyard, Ryan lights a campfire that crackles invitingly. Soon, we're gathered around, skewering hot dogs on makeshift sticks we found in the yard. Julie is in her element, handing out paper plates loaded with baked beans straight from the can—simple but satisfying. Meanwhile, us guys dive into a bag of chips, passing it around making sure everyone gets their fill.

Duncan swings open his ice chest from Austin, revealing a delightful stash of ice-cold canned sodas, glistening in the fading light. The evening unfolds under a tapestry of stars as conversation and laughter fills the air. We joke about the grocery clerk's misguided belief in ghosts. Being college-educated, we know better. But for now, we brush those ridiculous thoughts aside and immerse ourselves in the relaxing moment together. The soothing serenade of crickets adds to our contentment.

"Will you look at all those stars," Ryan exclaims, sprawled out on a comfy quilt spread on the lawn. "We never had this many in Austin. It makes you wonder—where do all the missing stars go?"

"They don't go anywhere, doofus," Duncan chuckles, his fedora tilted low over his face as he rests beside Ryan.

Correction: Beau is nestled comfortably between them.

As Ryan absentmindedly scratches behind Beau's ear, the dog's hind leg twitches—like all pups do when you find that perfect spot. Beau's tail wags in a joyful rhythm, keeping time to a melody only he hears.

"The number of stars you see is influenced by the light pollution from city lights," Duncan explains, adjusting his straw fedora.

A playful grin spreads across Ryan's face. "Even so," he muses, "isn't it cool to imagine the stars playing hide and seek in different towns? It's like they're hiding from us."

Duncan removes his fedora and raises an eyebrow, shooting Ryan a skeptical glance. "Rye, how much pot have you smoked today?"

"Aw, man," Ryan groans dramatically. "I totally forgot to bring my stash. It's still sitting on the coffee table at the apartment in Austin."

Duncan chuckles softly and places his fedora back over his face, shielding his eyes from the nonexistent Texas sun that has already dipped below the horizon.

A long moment of reflective silence stretches between us.

"Listen to that, will you?" Julie breaks the stillness.

"What are you talking about?" I ask.

"Can't you hear it?" she presses on.

"All I hear are millions of crickets," Ryan says, shrugging his shoulders.

"Exactly," Julie exclaims. "There's no traffic, no blaring car horns, no sirens, no loud music."

"Hey, you know what? You're absolutely right," I nod. "I think I could get used to small-town living."

"Taylor," Ryan exclaims with a mix of disbelief, "you've been here for less than a day, and you're already considering making this place your home?"

"Maybe not at this exact moment," I reply with a playful grin. "But it's definitely a nice thought to entertain."

Duncan adds, "So, are you willing to leave all the excitement of Austin for a place like Mayberry to be with folks like Gomer, Goober and Aunt Bee?"

I chuckle at his words. "When you put it like that, it does

sound a bit silly, doesn't it?"

"This small-town stuff isn't my vibe," Ryan pipes up, a hint of frustration in his voice. "I need the hustle and bustle of the city. Honestly, small towns are just too bor-ring for me."

"You're already bored?" Julie asks.

"Yep," Ryan replies with a resigned sigh. "There's literally nothing to do here."

As the conversation dwindles, the soothing serenade of crickets fills the air, their chorus rising and falling like gentle waves lapping against the shore. A soft breeze sends a shiver through Julie, prompting me to wrap my arm around her for warmth. She leans closer, resting her head on my shoulder as her breathing slows. The rhythmic chirping of the crickets lulls me into a peaceful state, making my eyelids grow heavy.

Suddenly, I'm jolted awake, bolting upright with my heart racing, momentarily unaware of my surroundings.

"What's wrong, Taylor?" Julie mumbles, her voice thick with sleep and confusion.

"I must have nodded off," I reply, rubbing the sleep from my eyes. "Honestly, it might be time for bed. Today has felt like a marathon, and I'm wiped out."

"You're so right," Julie exclaims, stretching her arms above her head. "Just thinking about sinking into a soft bed sounds heavenly right now."

Ryan and Duncan gently stir, waking Beau from his nap. He stands up, shakes himself, and stretches before letting out a big yawn. Then he trots into the dark yard to take care of business or chase after elusive fireflies hovering above the grass.

Meanwhile, Duncan casually places his fedora atop his head with a flair that only he can pull off. "Rye," he says with a hint of mischief in his voice, "would you kindly get off the quilt?"

Ryan reluctantly complies.

Duncan grabs the quilt and shakes it vigorously before heading inside.

Ryan stands beside the open door, leaning on the door frame, waiting for Beau to come back inside.

It's been a long day, and I'm sure I'm not the only one feeling the toll it's taken. Today marks the official kickoff of our college summer vacation. After a year filled with late-night study sessions, endless lectures, and those dreaded pop quizzes, we've finally earned this much-needed break. No more alarm clocks blaring at the crack of dawn or rushing to classes—it's time to relax and soak up the sun.

Ryan and I head to our shared bedroom while Julie retreats to her room, and Duncan goes off to his. Meanwhile, Beau claims his spot on the downstairs settee—his temporary throne during our summer vacation in Lost Creek Junction.

As we snuggle into our beds and bid each other goodnight, it feels like a scene straight out of *The Waltons* weekly TV series.

"Good night, Duncan."

"Good night, Julie."

"Good night, Rye."

"Good night, Taylor."

Even Beau chimes in with a hearty bark, eager to be included in the nighttime ritual. That's my lovable goofball—175 pounds of pure, overgrown puppy.

DAY TWO

Wednesday, May 16, 2018

At this point in my story, you know my group of friends by our names, so let me take a moment to briefly introduce everyone. I'll start with myself—after all, this is my story. My name is Taylor Greene. Yes, that's right. I'm the guy with the two last names.

I'm your average run-of-the-mill twenty-year-old college student navigating life at the University of Texas at Austin. Last week, I completed my second year, and while I'm not exactly a prodigy, my grades are good enough to keep those student loans rolling in—thank goodness for that.

I was born and raised in Beaumont, a decent size town in South Texas, near the Louisiana border, about 250 miles southeast of Austin. Growing up there shaped me in ways I'm still discovering. Life in Beaumont was simple but full of character—much like me.

At first glance, I might seem pretty ordinary—just another face in the crowd. I have a medium build, striking dark blue eyes that can light up with emotion, and moderately long ash-blonde hair that's kissed by the sun. Standing at 5 feet 10 inches tall, I blend in enough to keep things interesting.

Life hasn't always been easy for me. When I was sixteen, I faced one of the toughest challenges imaginable: I lost both of my parents in a car accident. This heartbreaking event changed everything for me. For the next two years, I lived with my grandma, who became my rock during those turbulent times. Then, I moved to Austin to share an apartment with my best friend, Ryan Bartlett—you'll get to know more about him in a bit.

My best bud is an irresistibly adorable fawn Great Dane named Beauregard Winston Churchill Greene—quite a regal name, right? But let's be honest—I just call him *Beau* because his full name is a mouthful. I only use his full name when he misbehaves, which is amusing because he knows he's in big trouble at that point. That's when he pulls off his best hide-and-seek moves, darting away as if he thinks I can't find him. Despite his calm demeanor, Beau is surprisingly smart. I still remember the day I got him as a tiny, precious puppy—a Christmas gift from my grandma after I lost my parents. He filled a void I didn't even know existed and has been my best buddy ever since.

There's my boyfriend, Ryan Bartlett. We've been inseparable since elementary school, sharing countless adventures and laughter as next door neighbors for years. However, life took a turn when I lost my parents and had to move in with my grandma across town.

During those challenging times, Ryan and I grew even closer. Despite the distance, we officially became boyfriends.

Ryan has the most captivating emerald green eyes that seem to sparkle with mischief, and his curly coppery-blonde hair adds a touch of warmth to his charming personality. We're the same age and share similar builds, though I have to let you in on a little secret—recently he's started packing a few extra pounds. Don't tell him I told you, but he's developing a tiny tummy roll. Trust me, I know all too well since we share a bed together.

Oh, did I mention Ryan is also a student at the University of Texas? That's why we moved to Austin, where we share an apartment. Living with Ryan is an adventure filled with late-night study sessions and lots of pizza deliveries.

Then there's my friend Duncan Campbell, who hails from the charming city of Charleston, South Carolina. Have you heard of Campbell's soup? Now, I can't say for certain how wealthy Duncan's family is, but rumor has it they are quite loaded. What truly sets Duncan apart isn't his background—it's his incredible generosity and open-mindedness toward others.

We first met in one of my introductory classes at UT, and from that moment on, we clicked. Our friendship has only grown stronger since.

Duncan is a towering figure, standing well over six feet, which makes him noticeably taller than Ryan or me. With his slender frame, you might even mistake him for someone battling anorexia. However, don't be fooled—this guy eats like he has a tapeworm. Seriously, he never seems to gain an ounce. If only I could borrow a bit of his metabolism.

But there's more to Duncan than just his impressive height and enviable eating habits. He's also incredibly good-looking. Imagine this: long, straight black hair cascading over dark, mysterious eyes that seem to hold countless secrets. And let's not forget his signature cheesy cream-colored straw fedora—it's as if he stepped out of a classic black and white movie. Honestly, if he weren't as straight as they come, I could easily see myself falling head over heels for him.

And did I mention he's a genius? We're talking Einstein-level smart. It's just one more reason why Duncan is annoyingly perfect in every way.

Finally, Julie Burris is a wonderful friend I met in the same university class as Duncan. From the moment we connected, it felt like we were destined to be friends—especially since she has always dreamed of having a gay best friend. And guess what? I fit that role perfectly. Now, she proudly refers to me as her *gay bestie*, and I wouldn't have it any other way.

Julie is a striking blonde from Dallas, known for her eye-catching sense of fashion that truly sets her apart. With her shoulder-length hair and mesmerizing blue-gray eyes, she has a look that draws you in.

While some might assume Julie's affluent background affords her a confident, stuck-up attitude, she completely breaks those stereotypes. While her family may not match the wealth of the Campbell's, they come quite close. Her mother has a passion for luxury and showers her only child with extravagant gifts that would make any girl envious. The Burris family fortune comes from a chain of mega sporting goods stores located throughout the southern states.

Now you have something more to go on about my friends. While I have many other college friends, these are the friends staying with me for the summer at Lost Creek Junction.

The sun shines through the windows on this Wednesday morning, while Julie and Ryan are still lost in dreamland. Meanwhile, in the heart of the house—the kitchen—Duncan is hard at work. Wearing his signature fedora and an apron, he's preparing a breakfast feast of fluffy scrambled eggs, crispy bacon, and perfectly toasted bread. And just when you think it couldn't get any better, he fries extra bacon for Beau. Can you believe how he spoils my dog?

The tantalizing aromas drift upstairs like a gentle wake-up call, coaxing Julie and Ryan from their dreams. Downstairs with Duncan, I can hardly contain my excitement as I wait for the coffee to finish brewing. Who knew Duncan had such impressive culinary skills? It's a delightful reminder that sometimes people surprise us in the best ways—after all, it's true what they say: you can't judge a book by its cover.

A little while later, Julie and Ryan, giggling like mischievous children caught by adults, make their way downstairs to the breakfast table. The dining room is larger but feels too formal for our casual needs. Who wants all that formality when the kitchen table is just a few steps away? It's near the stove, refrigerator, and all that delicious food waiting to be devoured.

After a leisurely breakfast, we're gathered around the kitchen table, sipping our morning coffee and enjoying the lazy morning. Everyone's relishing the moment except for Beau, who's outside, busy doing whatever he does when he's outdoors.

Suddenly, Julie interrupts our chatter by setting her mug down with a flourish and holding up a necklace for us to admire. Her eyes shine with excitement as she reveals a skeleton key dangling from a delicate satin ribbon. "Look at this," she exclaims, her voice bubbling with enthusiasm. "I discovered this old key wedged between the wall and the door frame in my bedroom. Isn't it awesome? I decided to wear it as a pendant because it just felt special." As she speaks, she twirls a curl of hair—a telltale sign she's feeling uncertain but eager for our approval.

"Cool," Ryan exclaims, eagerly piling a second helping of scrambled eggs onto his plate.

"What do you think that key unlocks?" Duncan asks, spreading butter on a slice of toast like a plasterer at work.

"It could be a key to anything," I reply, taking a satisfying sip of my coffee.

"I have a hunch it opens something in my room," Julie chimes in, her eyes sparkling with curiosity as she admires the prized key. "Maybe a jewelry box or a locked diary."

"Well, I don't know about the rest of you," Ryan says with a grin, "but we should explore this old house. Who knows what we might uncover?"

"I agree with Rye," Julie adds. "This place is probably full of history. Imagine what we might find."

"Maybe a skeleton or two," Duncan says, imitating Vincent Price's scary voice.

"Stop it, Duncan," Julie giggles, playfully swatting his arm as laughter fills the room.

"There's bound to be all kinds of surprises waiting for us to uncover on this property," Duncan exclaims, setting down his fork and knife with a satisfied clink on his empty breakfast plate.

"I volunteer Taylor and me to check out the detached garage," Ryan jumps in, catching me off guard with his enthusiasm.

"I want to explore the basement," Julie says, playfully nudging Duncan with her elbow. "What do you say?"

Duncan raises an eyebrow, a playful smirk creeping onto his face. "Oh? Are you inviting me along?" he asks, playfully adjusting his fedora.

"Only if you're up for it," Julie replies with a bright smile that lights up her eyes.

After Ryan and I finish our second mugs of coffee, we get up from the table. I stroll over to the back door to check on Beau. As soon as I open the door, he dashes inside like a rocket and makes a beeline for Duncan—probably searching for more bacon. To my surprise, Duncan pulls out a few secret strips he had stashed in a napkin and slyly hands them to Beau.

"Duncan," I tease in a mock scolding tone, "you're going to spoil my dog."

"Taylor," he replies with a grin, "I hate to tell you this, but we're way beyond that point."

I can't argue with that logic and shake my head in playful resignation. Meanwhile, Julie bends down and wraps her arms around Beau's neck, cooing at him in baby talk. Honestly, it's hard to tell whether Beau's tail is wagging in delight from Julie's affection or if he's reveling in the tasty bacon treat from Duncan.

Ryan and I clear the breakfast table, while Julie and Duncan wash dishes. Once the table is cleared, Ryan and I slip out of the house through the side door, with Beau happily trotting between us.

Ryan affectionately scratches behind Beau's ears, and in response, Beau adoringly rubs against Ryan's leg, clearly showing his appreciation. It seems that today, Beau has chosen Ryan as his favorite human, which leaves me feeling a bit like an overlooked shadow. But I know at lunchtime, I'll win back Beau's attention with a bowl of kibble and his favorite treat.

As we approach the garage doors, curiosity gets the better of Beau. He dashes ahead to sniff them intently. I notice how the doors hang from sturdy steel tracks above.

"Taylor, I hope you brought the key," Ryan calls out, shaking a sturdy padlock with a hint of impatience.

"I remembered to grab the set of keys before leaving the house," I reply. As I sift through the jumble of keys Mr. Andrews gave me—none of which are labeled, unfortunately—I test each one against the stubborn lock. After what seems like an eternity, I finally match the correct key that fits the lock. The rusty tracks groan in protest as we wrestle to slide the middle door open.

"Later, I'll grease these tracks so the doors slide easier," Ryan says, wiping sweat from his brow. "But right now? I'm dying to see what's inside this old garage."

Finally, we slide the door open with a determined heave, and sunlight pours in like liquid gold. To my surprise, the garage is in decent shape for its age. It seems newer than the main house, built of red bricks rather than sandstone and granite.

Beau's tail wags with infectious excitement as he dives into the depths of the garage, his curious nose sniffing out every corner. Tools dangle from the walls like forgotten memories, while shelves overflow with vintage items that hold secret tales of the past.

"If only this junk could talk. Can you imagine the stories they'd tell?" Ryan muses, playfully pushing aside rusted tin cans to uncover what lies behind them.

"This place feels like a time capsule—everything's so old," I add, scanning the cluttered space. Suddenly, something catches my attention: a large, mysterious object draped in a dusty tarp in the center of the garage. "What on earth could this be?" I wonder aloud, my hand inching closer to the stained canvas cover.

Suspense hangs thick in the air as Ryan and I pull back the dusty tarp, revealing what lies beneath.

"Oh my goodness," I can hardly contain my excitement—it's all I can do not to squeal like an overly enthusiastic schoolgirl. "Is this what I think it is?"

"Well, I'll be..." Ryan gasps, his eyes wide with disbelief as he inspects the object before us. "It looks like you've got yourself an old Jeep."

"I wonder if it runs?" I ask.

Ryan shakes his head thoughtfully. "It'll take some work," he replies, scrutinizing the Jeep's weathered exterior.

"Where are the tires?" I point out. "It doesn't have tires."

"Looks like someone knew what they were doing when they put the Jeep on blocks before storing it," Ryan observes, his approval evident. "You know what, Taylor?" he continues, a spark of inspiration lighting up his face.

"What?"

"I bet Duncan can have her up and running before the end of summer. That guy is a wizard when it comes to fixing things," Ryan says with a grin.

"Really? You think so?"

"I know how much you've dreamed of having your own wheels. So far, your options have been pretty slim. Just imagine —after this summer, you won't have to squeeze onto the bus or borrow my car anymore. You'll have your very own ride."

"That is… if she's running again," I reply, a hint of skepticism creeping into my voice.

"Hey, don't sweat it," Ryan assures me with a friendly pat on the back. "I'm confident Duncan will have her purring like a kitten in no time."

Finding that old Jeep reminds me of when I was eleven and woke up on Christmas morning. I couldn't believe my eyes— there was a full-size, fire-engine red Schwinn bike with a hand brake next to the Christmas tree. This wasn't just any bike; it was my first full-size bicycle, and honestly, I never thought my parents could pull off such an amazing gift.

Sure, it had its quirks—some minor scratches here and there, and the front fender had been swapped for a black one—but to me, it felt brand new.

After we finished Christmas lunch, my neighbor friend Ryan came to our house. I was practically bursting with excitement to show him my new ride. To my surprise, Dad and Ryan whisked my bike into the garage and told me to wait inside the house.

What were they up to? About an hour later, Dad rolled my bike out of the garage—and wow! They had spray-painted the front fender bright red to match the rest of the bike. But that's not all; they added a front basket perfect for carrying books and even attached a handbell—a surprise gift from Ryan.

These unexpected features completely overjoyed me. I couldn't wait to take it for a spin around the neighborhood to show off my new wheels with Ryan riding his bike beside me.

Five years later, after my parents passed away, I found myself living with my grandma. The transition was difficult for both of us, but I felt the weight of grief more than anyone else. To help me through this challenging time, Grandma surprised me with the most adorable Christmas gift—a puppy.

I named him Beau, and he quickly became my little sidekick. I'd wrap him snugly in a bath towel and tuck him into my bicycle basket. Together, we went on endless adventures, pedaling through the neighborhood for hours. Beau absolutely loved those bike rides. However, as time went on, we faced an unexpected challenge: he grew into a giant Great Dane. Suddenly, our biking trips came to an end.

Even though I couldn't take Beau along anymore, my fire-engine red bike remained one of my prized possessions. Its hand brake, front basket, and shiny handbell symbolized freedom and joy for me. In fact, last semester, I rode it to my college classes.

I can't help but think about that trusty bike sitting in my Austin apartment, waiting patiently for our next adventure together. When summer vacation ends and I return to Austin, we'll ride again.

Enough reminiscing about my bike—let's get back to the story of Ryan, Beau, and me exploring the garage and the upstairs apartment.

"Hey, Taylor. Want to check out the upstairs apartment?" Ryan calls out.

"Absolutely, but where's Beau?" I ask, scanning the area.

"He's already ahead of us," Ryan replies, gesturing toward

Beau, who's bounding up the stairs with his tail wagging.

With each step we take, my curiosity grows. The apartment door is slightly ajar, inviting us in like a secret waiting to be discovered. Beau nudges it open with his snout and trots inside, as if he's been here before.

Stepping inside, I notice the apartment appears newer than the main house. Although the furnishings are old-fashioned, they exude a cozy warmth that makes me feel welcome and encourages relaxation.

An open common area seamlessly combines the kitchen, dining room, and living room, creating an ideal space for a small gathering of friends or a quiet evening at home. At the end of the hall, there are two bedrooms and a bath.

What stands out is the meticulous preparation of the furnished apartment, as if someone anticipated our arrival.

Beau's restlessness quickly gets the better of him as he clomps down the stairs, his impatience echoing through the garage. Ryan and I follow suit, our hearts race as we struggle to shut the garage door once more before returning to the kitchen in the main house.

"Hello?" Ryan calls out, his voice slicing through the silence. The kitchen feels oddly empty, almost eerie.

"Where can everyone be?" I wonder aloud, glancing around for signs of life.

"I have no idea," Ryan shrugs, his brow furrowing in confusion. He raises his voice, calling again, "Hello? Anyone here?"

Suddenly, a muffled response floats in from an open door across the kitchen. "We're down here," says Duncan.

Curious, I peer into the doorway from which Duncan's voice came and see a set of stairs descending into an ominous, pitch-black basement. A chill runs down my spine—dark, confined spaces have never been my thing.

"Come on down," Duncan calls out, sounding like a TV game show host.

"Watch your step on those stairs—they're a little wobbly,"

Julie adds, her warning adding a hint of tension.

With our hearts racing, Ryan and I carefully navigate the creaky steps leading down into a dimly lit basement. As we reach the bottom, Duncan and Julie use their flashlights like searchlights, illuminating an old closet that seems to hold secrets.

"My key," Julie exclaims. "Remember the one I showed you at breakfast? The one I tied to this ribbon? It turns out it unlocked this closet door."

"What is this room, anyway?" Ryan asks, his eyes darting around as he tries to make sense of the shadowy space.

"I think it's what folks used to call a *fruit cellar* or a *root cellar*," Duncan explains with an air of historical authority.

"A fruit cellar?" Ryan echoes, his eyes widening in astonishment as he processes this intriguing revelation.

"During the summer, families gathered their harvests and canned the produce, turning ripe fruits and vegetables into sealed jars of goodness they could savor throughout the winter. Back in those days," Duncan explains, "they couldn't pop into a grocery store for canned goods—they had to make their own from what they grew in their gardens."

"Oh, I get it," Ryan nods. "They kept the sealed jars in this closet."

"Exactly," Duncan replies. "This space was ideal because the temperature remained more consistent than upstairs in the house."

"There's something I don't understand," Julie interjects, wiping grime off an old jar. "These jars seem to be filled with herbs and spices, not fruits or vegetables. I don't recognize the names on the labels."

"So what's your point?" Ryan challenges as he snatches Julie's flashlight and swings it willy-nilly around the dark cellar.

"Give me back my flashlight," Julie demands, reclaiming her light with a firm grip.

"Aren't we touchy today?" Ryan quips with a smirk.

Julie shines the beam directly at the jars, her brow furrowing in confusion. "Seriously, though, these labels look like they're written in some foreign language. What's the deal here?"

"Maybe they are," Duncan adds. "People from all over the world settled in this area. It's possible not everyone spoke English. And we have no idea how long these jars have been sitting on these shelves."

"Check this out," Julie exclaims, her eyes sparkling with excitement as she pulls an ancient leather-bound book from a shelf, sending a cloud of dust swirling into the air.

Ryan, caught off guard by the sudden explosion of particles, lets out an unexpected sneeze, echoing through the musty room like a clap of thunder.

"Next time, could you give me a heads-up before you unleash a dust storm?" he quips, trying to mask his surprise with humor.

"Ew! Rye, you got snot on my arm," Julie gasps, scrunching her nose in exaggerated disgust and holding out her arm for everyone to see. It's a comical scene that has us all stifling laughs.

"Sorry about that," Ryan says sheepishly, wiping his nose with the back of his hand. "I can't help it—I'm really sensitive to dust."

"He's not kidding," I confirm. "Have you ever seen Rye clean house? He's practically an expert at getting someone else to do it for him."

"Is it safe to say you're the one who does all the cleaning?" Duncan teases, a playful sparkle in his eye.

"Guilty as charged," I reply with a grin, nodding in agreement.

"Okay, that's enough about me," Ryan interjects. "I admit I am my favorite topic of conversation, but only when it's flattering."

Suddenly, Beau barks from the top of the stairs, his eager face peering down at us.

"Okay, buddy," I call to him. "I'll be up in a minute."

"Poor Beau," Duncan chuckles. "He's missing his daddy."

"That's my cue to head back upstairs," I announce, turning toward the stairs. As I do, disaster strikes—I accidentally knock over a ceramic container. The lid flies off with a noticeable clink and rolls across the floor. "Oops," I exclaim as I set the container back upright on the shelf.

"Taylor, you're a walking disaster. You know that?" Ryan remarks.

"Ew! What's that awful smell?" Julie interjects, pinching her nose.

"Yeah, seriously, where's that odor coming from?" Duncan asks, glancing around suspiciously. "Rye, did you... you know?"

"Don't look at me," Ryan protests. "I didn't break wind. Maybe it was Beau."

"Are you kidding? Beau's way upstairs," I reply. "Sure, he's known for some pretty stinky ones, but there's no way we could smell one of his from down here."

"Hey, guys," Julie exclaims, lifting the open container I'd moments earlier set upright. "I think the awful smell is coming from the container Taylor knocked over." She inspects it with a furrowed brow, clearly trying to identify the source of the stench.

Duncan, unable to resist, leans in close and takes a whiff. Instantly, he recoils, gagging as if he might throw up. "Gross, I totally agree with you, Julie," he manages to choke out between gags. "For the love of god—put the lid back on."

Taking charge, Julie sweeps her flashlight beam across the floor like a detective on a mission. Her eyes land on the elusive lid, and she snatches it up with determination before quickly securing it back onto the container. With that simple act of closing it, we breathe a collective sigh of relief.

"What on earth was in that container?" Ryan exclaims, his face contorted in disbelief.

"I've no clue," Duncan replies, pinching his nose in an attempt to ward off the foul odor. "But I swear it smells worse than anything I've ever encountered. Just keep that thing far away from me."

With a determined look, Julie carefully places the stinky container on the back of the shelf, ensuring it is well out of reach.

Pinching our noses, we retreat, eager to escape the lingering stench clinging to us like a bad memory. The group rushes back upstairs, relief washing over us as we leave the horrid smell behind. Meanwhile, Julie clutches a leather-bound book under her arm, its cover adorned with odd and intricate designs.

As much as we'd have liked, the day's discoveries don't end with the thrill of finding the Jeep tucked away in the garage, Julie's prize skeleton key or unearthing the foul smelling container in the basement. It didn't stop there. Just before lunch, Duncan enters the kitchen, where Julie, Ryan, and I sit at the table, enjoying freshly squeezed lemonade.

"Hey, does anyone know where there's a hammer?" he asks.

"I think I saw one in a kitchen drawer," Julie replies casually.

"Which drawer?" Duncan shoots back impatiently.

"Oh, really?" Julie retorts, her tone laced with sarcasm as tension grows. "Do I look like I've taken inventory of every drawer in this kitchen?"

"I just thought—" Duncan begins.

"Well, think again, buster. I'm not helping you," Julie interrupts sharply, her refusal hanging heavy in the air like a storm cloud. "Find it yourself."

With mounting frustration, Duncan frantically rummages through the kitchen drawers, slamming each one shut as if hoping to release his pent-up irritation.

"What do you need a hammer for?" Ryan asks.

"Here it is," Duncan exclaims sarcastically, holding up the hammer triumphantly for Julie to see. "Look at that. Found it on my own—no thanks to you."

"Duncan," Ryan interjects, "you haven't answered my question."

"I've got a loose floorboard in my bedroom," Duncan replies, angrily waving the hammer in Ryan's direction.

Ryan nervously ducks to avoid getting hit.

Meanwhile, Duncan, fueled by frustration, storms upstairs with hammer in hand, each stomp echoing his determination.

Moments later, the rhythmic sound of a hammer striking hardwood reverberates through the house—THWACK! THWACK! With each blow, the tension thickens like fog rolling in on a chilly morning. Then, just as abruptly as it began, the hammering ceases, plunging us into an eerie silence.

We exchange anxious glances, then tiptoe up the stairs without saying a word. A sense of dread and curiosity hangs in the air as we gather outside Duncan's slightly ajar bedroom door. Peering inside is tempting yet nerve-wracking. We hesitate, searching each other's faces for answers, we realize we must first unravel the mystery unfolding in Duncan's room.

Our insatiable curiosity drives us to the brink of madness. As if we're connected by an invisible thread, we lean in and peek into the room. It's dimly lit, and dust particles twirl gracefully in the beams of sunlight filtering through the loosely drawn curtains. In the center of the room, an oriental rug lies partially rolled up, revealing worn wooden floorboards beneath. Amid this quiet chaos, Duncan sits cross-legged on the bare floor. He's hunched over a spot where several floorboards have been removed, sifting through old, yellowed papers, as if they hold the key to the world's secrets.

"Duncan?" I ask, breaking the silence. "What are you up to?"

"You won't believe this," Duncan exclaims, his voice buzzing with excitement. "I found an old metal strongbox hidden under a couple of loose floorboards. I used the hammer claw to pry it open, and you'll never guess what I found inside—"

"What?" I ask, eager to know more.

Duncan's eyes widen as he holds up brittle yellow papers. "These are legal documents—stocks, bonds, certificates, and deeds. Taylor, if these papers are legit, you could own a major stake of Lost Creek Junction. In addition, there are valuable stocks and bonds here. If all of this is real, you could be looking at a lot of money."

Overwhelmed by Duncan's shocking news, I find myself in desperate need of time to process everything. Retreating to the bedroom I share with Ryan, I distract myself by tackling the last bits of unpacking. But my mind races—how did I suddenly inherit a sprawling house, a Jeep, and a portion of Lost Creek Junction? I need to visit the attorney soon to ensure everything is legitimate. What if it's all real?

Rummaging through the closet, I run across one of ol' lady Blackburn's hat boxes perched on the shelf. With a gentle nudge, I slide it aside to clear space for my empty backpack. As I do, a faint scent of rose water wafts through the air, likely lingering from the hat box. Her belongings are everywhere in this house—her presence is almost suffocating. The emotional weight of sorting through her possessions is heavy on my heart as I grapple with the unexpected new role as a property owner— a title that still feels foreign and surreal.

I push the hat box aside and discover an old photo album and a leather-bound journal behind it. With a sense of anticipation, I remove both items from the shelf.

As I flip open the photo album, I'm immediately transported to another era. The photographs are aged and charmingly vintage, showcasing people dressed in styles long forgotten. Instead of vibrant colors, they're wrapped in warm shades of tan and sepia that whisper tales of the past. Some images are marred by scratches, while others bear the scars of time with torn edges —each imperfection adding to their allure. It feels as though I'm peering through a window into a distant past, evoking a bittersweet nostalgia that tugs at my heartstrings.

However, what strikes me is the absence of names or dates to anchor these faces in time. Who were they? What stories did they carry? Each photo raises questions that deepen the mystery surrounding the enigmatic ol' lady Blackburn—who was she?

I wonder what secrets the journal I found might hold about the Blackburn family history. As I delicately flip through the fragile, yellowed pages filled with elegant handwriting, I feel a mix of curiosity and unease. Some entries have faded to whispers of their former selves, while others stand out, vibrant and clear.

Starting from the beginning, I carefully turn each brittle page, but my heart sinks as I discover entire sections are missing. Some entries are jumbled up. What happened to the lost pages? What hidden truths might they reveal? The mystery deepens with every turn of the pages.

Earlier today, Beau came across a stick. You might be thinking, *A stick? What's the big deal?* But for him, this seemingly ordinary find is nothing short of a treasure. It got me thinking how everything we encounter can hold significance. So, until we fully understand the history of this house I'm not dismissing or leaving anything we find to chance.

Beau's stick isn't particularly remarkable—just a short piece of tree limb—but it has a shiny, smooth surface he seems to like. He guards his newfound prize fiercely; whenever he leaves the room, he buries it under the settee cushion like a priceless treasure. And when he returns, it's the first thing he digs up. He keeps it close even at night, sleeping with it nestled under his paws.

But watch out. Beau transforms into a fierce protector if anyone dares approach his precious stick. His growl is so deep and menacing I jump back—it sends chills racing down my spine.

It's strange because he's always been laid-back, docile, and generous to share his toys with everyone. However, there is one exception that leaves me scratching my head: his stick. When it comes to that particular piece of wood, he transforms into a fierce guardian, ready to defend it at all costs. This behavior is such a stark contrast to his usual demeanor. What a peculiar dog I have. It might seem odd I'm telling you this, but I felt I should mention it.

During a leisurely late lunch, we share our morning discoveries from exploring the property—it's like a grown-up version of show-and-tell. Instead of preparing an elaborate meal, we delight in the simple joy of peanut butter and jelly sandwiches with a side of corn chips. Just a heads up: PB&J will be our go-to comfort food for the next few months.

Meanwhile, Julie is completely absorbed in a leather-bound book she found on a shelf in the fruit cellar. Although it's handwritten in a foreign language we can't decipher, its pages are filled with intricate sketches resembling recipes—certainly not my Grandma's Betty Crocker cookbook.

Duncan eagerly rummages through the yellowed documents he unearthed from the rusty strongbox. Among his finds are land ownership certificates, stock certificates, ancient bond notes, and—most intriguing—loose pages from a handwritten journal. With a glint of excitement, "Taylor," he says, passing me the papers, "take these. They might be missing pages from that journal you found in your bedroom closet."

An interesting question pops into my head as I sift through the disjointed pages, piecing together fragments of thoughts and stories.

"Guys," I say, "do you think another journal might be hidden somewhere on the property?"

"Anything's possible," Julie nods. "If those additional pages don't align with that journal, I'd be inclined to believe there's another journal somewhere."

Meanwhile, Ryan flips through the pages of an old photo album of sepia-toned photographs of strangers and long-ago businesses. The challenge of identifying anyone who might recognize the faces in these images serves as a poignant reminder of how quickly time slips away from us. However, as Ryan spots some familiar buildings peeking out from behind the people—those iconic landmarks—he's transported back to an era that predates our own lives.

"Hey, Taylor," Ryan calls out with excitement, his eyes sparkling with discovery. "You've got to see this. I found something cool."

"What is it?" I ask.

"You remember that stick Beau found?" Ryan replies.

"Yeah, what about it?" I respond as he hands me an old photo.

"What do you see in this picture?" Ryan asks, pointing to a stick clutched by an elderly woman. Her face is lined with deep wrinkles, and her eyes seem to hold secrets that have been buried for centuries.

"That looks like Beau's stick," I observe, my curiosity growing by the uncanny resemblance.

"Exactly," Ryan exclaims, his tone heavy with the gravity of the discovery. "That isn't just any ordinary find—something's going on here. What do you think?"

"It's just a coincidence," I say, trying to downplay the eerie connection.

"If you ask me," Ryan counters earnestly, "I believe there's more to Beau's stick than meets the eye."

"Rye, you're letting your imagination get the best of you," I chuckle, trying to keep the mood light.

"Think about it for a second. What do we know about that stick?" Ryan counters.

"Rye, come on. It's just a stick," I respond, waving my hand dismissively. "There's nothing extraordinary about it. Just some random piece of wood Beau found—nothing more. That photo is probably over a hundred years old—there's no way it could be the same stick, right?"

"Let's break this down logically," Ryan suggests, leaning forward. "Fact one: Beau loves to sleep on the settee with his precious stick always by his side. Fact two: we assume it's just an ordinary stick with no historical significance. But why is it when he's not lounging on the settee, he buries it under the cushions for safekeeping and digs it out later to protect it again? There's something about that stick we don't know about," he adds.

"Wait a minute," Julie interjects suddenly, her tone shifting as she holds up something intriguing. "Check out this sketch I found in the recipe book—"

She points to a page featuring a rough sketch of an old woman with a wrinkled face, holding a stick like Beau's over a cauldron. The caption beneath the drawing isn't in English.

"Come on, guys," I say. "Let's not get carried away with our imaginations."

"I suppose you have a point," Julie replies. "But don't you think all of this is a bit...odd?"

"Only if you let your mind wander too far," Duncan counters firmly. "Seriously, let's be rational about this. We're in an old house filled with relics from the past. If we start piecing together random bits, we could end up creating a distorted picture instead of uncovering the truth. Who knows how these items are related? This place has undoubtedly seen its fair share of colorful stories, so let's not fabricate one ourselves, alright?"

As always, Duncan is our steadfast voice of reason, providing much-needed stability amid our swirling uncertainties.

In the late afternoon, Duncan's heart races with excitement as he discovers a deed for a gold mine hidden among old legal papers. He quickly powers up his laptop to locate the coordinates listed in the deed. To his astonishment, he finds the mine is not far outside of town. As he delves deeper into his research, Duncan uncovers fascinating stories about the gold rush that once attracted fortune-seekers to this area.

As I sift through the extra loose pages of the journal, I attempt to reconstruct its contents. Despite my best efforts, several sections remain missing. What events occurred during those lost moments? Could they conceal deep, dark secrets about the history of this house and its former occupants?

Meanwhile, Julie is diligently compiling a list of the house's previous owners from the documents she found in the strongbox. With unwavering determination, she pieces together a detailed history of the house and its former residents.

As the sun sets, we gather around the kitchen table for a comforting supper of Hamburger Helper. The atmosphere buzzes with energy—a delightful chaos. Dishes are passed from hand to hand, papers are strewn about, and laptops and legal pads compete for space on every surface. Voices overlap in excitement as everyone tries to make themselves heard amidst the clatter.

To outsiders, we might seem like crazed college kids, but this is how we thrive. We've crammed for exams and pulled all-nighters together, tackling the ups and downs of college life side by side. Yet it's not all stress; we've shared countless moments filled with laughter and joy, too. This lively gathering around the kitchen table feels like home—a familiar echo of those late-night study sessions that brought us closer together.

As the grandfather clock in the hall strikes two in the morning, a wave of realization washes over us—horror of horrors, we've run out of snacks. With this ghastly news, we call it a night. My friends shuffle off to bed one by one, leaving me alone in the kitchen.

Peeking into the parlor, I check on Beau, who's blissfully lost in dreamland. I turn off the downstairs lights and head upstairs to Ryan's and my bedroom. A sudden flash of lightning illuminates the staircase, casting eerie shadows to dance on the walls. A chill runs down my spine—could there be more than just a storm brewing outside? I quicken my pace, racing up the stairs as if they might come alive beneath me.

I jump into bed and pull the sheet over me, comforted to be next to Ryan, who's already fast asleep. I think back to moments ago as I climbed the stairs when that unsettling feeling crept in— what was that all about? Was it the sudden flash of lightning slicing through the darkness, or the wind whispering through the trees? Or maybe it was this eerie, quiet, unfamiliar house that made me anxious.

Another lightning flash briefly brightens the room, casting

eerie, dancing shadows on the walls. I instinctively pull the sheet over my head like a child trying to ward off monsters. The distant rumble of thunder harmonizes with Ryan's soft snoring, a strange lullaby for this restless night.

Unexpectedly, everything goes deathly still. The sounds of the approaching storm cease, leaving only the soothing rhythm of Ryan's breathing. Usually, I'd expect to be lulled by crickets serenading outside, but they too, have gone silent. Tentatively, I lie on my back, staring at the ceiling above me. If we were back in our Austin apartment, I'd be watching the gentle spinning of our ceiling fan. Instead, I gaze up at this centuries-old plaster ceiling—so different yet oddly comforting.

The air hangs heavy and still, carrying a faint hint of sulfur. Suddenly, a blinding flash of lightning erupts outside, brighter than a thousand suns, transforming our bedroom into a scene from an action movie—like a bomb detonating just beyond the window. The atmosphere crackles with electric energy, and for one surreal moment, the room is bathed in an intense white light.

Then comes the thunder—a deafening roar that rattles the very bones of the house.

Ryan stirs awake, his eyes wide with alarm. "What was that?" he mumbles, still half-asleep.

"It's just thunder," I reply.

"Oh," he says, caught in a sleepy haze. He fluffs his pillow and instantly falls back to sleep.

How does he manage to fall asleep so effortlessly? I can never drift off right away—it feels like an endless battle. I toss and turn, experimenting with different positions, searching for that elusive sweet spot. Then there's the eternal dilemma: should the bed sheet be on or off?

I try counting sheep, but I always lose track and have to start over—again and again. My pillow becomes too warm, prompting me to flip it to the cooler side in hopes of finding some comfort. The clock ticks away mercilessly, reminding me sleep remains just out of reach. Tonight is no exception; sleep eludes me once more. Perhaps the storm brewing outside is causing my mind to race.

Another flash of lightning illuminates the room, casting eerie, dancing shadows on the ceiling and walls. I can't decide which is more unsettling: the silence that follows each thunderclap or those bright bursts of light slicing through the darkness. Anticipation coils tight in my chest as I brace myself for the next bolt. Each second stretches into an agonizing eternity.

A flash of lightning slices through the night, illuminating the room with an electrifying burst of energy. Moments later, a thunderous boom rattles the house's very foundation, making my heart skip a beat with each rumble.

The relentless rain pounds against the house in a fierce symphony, showing no signs of letting up. Crawling out of bed, I pull back the sheer curtains to witness the storm's fury—the rain comes down sideways. The wind shifts abruptly, sending sheets of water slamming against the glass panes. I jump at this unforeseen turn in the weather. It seems as though nature itself is tapping on the window panes, begging to come inside.

Please let us in, the pelting rain seems to plead like frightened children, knocking on the windows. *We're scared of the lightning.*

A sudden, jarring bang—like a gunshot—erupts downstairs. My heart races as I wonder what could have caused such a racket. Just then, the bedroom door bursts open with a crash sending my nerves into overdrive. In rushes Beau, diving headfirst into bed and whimpering as he buries himself under the covers next to the peacefully sleeping Ryan. Something has definitely frightened Beau, but what could it be?

Shaking off my initial shock, I grab a flashlight from the nightstand drawer and cautiously make my way down the hall toward the stairs to investigate the noise. As I reach the edge of the staircase, I shine the beam of light back and forth across the first floor below. Everything looks normal—or so it seems.

A sudden chill sweeps through the air, carrying the

unmistakable scent of rain. I'm caught off guard when I notice the kitchen door wide open. Shivering, I rush to close and lock it tight. Just as I'm about to ascend the stairs, a blinding flash of lightning rips through the darkness, revealing an old man's face right in front of me—like he materialized from thin air.

I scream like a nelly queen, but my shriek is swallowed by a thunderous boom that rattles my bones. Another bolt illuminates the room, and for a fleeting moment, I catch glimpse of a man's face just inches away from mine before he vanishes into the night like a phantom. My heart races; I sense he's near by, lurking in the shadows.

"Come out, you son of a bitch!" I shout, my voice shaking as I flick on every light switch in sight. Adrenaline surges through me like wildfire, igniting an unexpected bravado that makes me feel butch, like I can take on anything.

"What's going on down there?" Duncan calls from the top of the stairs.

"We've got an intruder in the house," I shout back over the racket of the storm.

"Are you sure?" Duncan asks.

"I found the kitchen door wide open, and I definitely saw someone," I reply, trying to keep my voice steady despite the rising panic within me.

A blood-curdling scream pierces the night—a harrowing cry so filled with terror it sends tremors through my body.

"That sounds like Julie," Duncan exclaims, his eyes widening in alarm. Without hesitating, he spins around and rushes to her room.

"Julie, are you alright?" Duncan bursts into her bedroom, flipping on the lights as he quickly scans the room.

"There was a man—" she stammers, her finger trembling as she points to a shadowy corner. "He was wrinkly and had a furious glare in his eyes."

"I don't see anyone," Duncan replies, skepticism lacing his tone.

"He was right there," Julie insists, her voice rising urgently as she gestures emphatically at an empty space. Her wide eyes reflecting sheer terror.

"What's going on?" Ryan asks, rushing into the room.

"Julie thinks she saw someone," Duncan explains, still trying to make sense of the situation.

"I swear I saw someone," Julie insists, her eyes wide with urgency. "He was as real as you, standing right in front of me."

"Shhh," Ryan murmurs, settling onto the edge of the bed and wrapping his arm protectively around her shoulders.

"What happened?" I ask as I enter the room.

"Where have you been?" Ryan shoots back at me, suspicion etched on his face.

"I was downstairs," I defend. "The kitchen door was open, so I closed it—"

"Did it blow open by itself, or did someone come inside?" Duncan interrupts.

"I honestly don't know," I reply, trying to piece together the fragments of the recent events. Everything happened so quickly. "I was lying in bed when I heard a loud noise. Naturally, I went downstairs to check it out and found the kitchen door wide open. Rain was blowing in, so I closed and locked the door."

"Then what happened?" Duncan asks, his eyes wide with anticipation.

"I turned around to head back to bed, and that's when I saw him," I reply, my voice steady, though my heart races.

"Who did you see?" Duncan presses.

"A wrinkly old man," I say, the memory making me shiver.

"The man I saw had a wrinkled face, too." Julie's voice trembles like leaves in the wind, and tears glisten on her cheeks as she clings to Ryan for comfort.

Duncan's expression shifts from concern to determination. "I'm calling the cops," he declares. "I won't feel safe until I know it's just the four of us in this house."

In our pajamas, fluffy robes, and comfy house slippers, the four of us huddle together in the parlor, illuminated by all the lights downstairs. At first sight, it looks like a scene straight out of a Hallmark holiday movie. However, we're not in a festive holiday mood. Beau is sprawled on the floor beside me while Julie and Ryan sit on Beau's plush settee. Meanwhile, Duncan paces back and forth like an anxious, caged animal. I'm perched on the edge of a side chair, feeling as tense as a coiled spring ready to snap. My heart races, thumping loudly against my chest. Without warning, we jump at the heavy knock echoing through the stillness.

Duncan, closest to the door, calls out, "Who is it?" directed at the bolted front door.

"Police," comes the response.

Hearing the word *police* sends all of us into a frenzy—yes, even Beau. He leaps to his feet and bolts toward the door, sniffing eagerly around the frame. His tail wags back and forth like the pendulum of the upstairs grandfather clock. But then, something shifts. Suddenly, he growls low in his throat and bares his teeth, as if defending my home from whatever—or whoever—is on the other side of the door.

I grab Beau by the collar, wrestling him away from the door before Duncan can swing it open.

"What's up with Beau?" Julie asks.

"I have no idea," I reply, dragging him into a nearby room and locking the door. As I step away, Beau starts pawing at the door and whimpering pitifully, as if his heart is broken. I know this act all too well—he's trying to appeal to my sympathetic side so I'll let him out. But not this time. I'm not falling for his shenanigans.

"Beauregard Winston Churchill Greene," I say firmly, "I know what you're up to, and it's not working. You stay put and think about your actions. I'll let you out once the cops have gone."

Beau's pitiful whimpering fades as I approach the parlor, where two uniformed police officers stand ready to introduce themselves.

"I'm Sergeant Paul Ackers, and this is Sergeant Stephen

Ramos. We're from the Lost Creek Junction Police Department," Ackers states.

Duncan raises an eyebrow, skepticism clear on his face. "That was a surprisingly quick response after I made the call."

"We were in the area," Ackers replies. "You must be the new owner of this grand old house."

"No, sir," Duncan says politely, tipping his fedora slightly. "That honor goes to him," he adds, gesturing toward me.

"I apologize for my dog, Beau. I have no idea what got into him. For the time being, I put him in another room."

"That's perfectly alright—no harm done," Ackers assures with a calm smile. "So, you had a potential intruder tonight?"

"Yes, both Julie and I saw him," I explain, my heart still racing. "I saw him in the kitchen, while Julie saw him in her bedroom."

"Officers," Duncan interjects, his voice steady but urgent, "could you please search to make sure the house is secure?"

"Not a problem," Ackers replies confidently. "Sergeant Ramos will sweep the house while I gather details from you, young man, and from the little lady."

Without a word, Sergeant Ramos pulls out a long-handled flashlight from his belt. Its bright beam cuts through the darkest corners, creating a tense atmosphere as he goes about searching the house.

Before Ackers begins his report, I take the opportunity to introduce everyone.

"I'm Taylor Greene, and these are my college friends, Julie and Duncan. My boyfriend, Ryan, is beside me, and in the other room is Beau—my Great Dane, who you heard barking earlier. I've had him since he was a puppy."

Ackers raises an eyebrow and asks, "Is this everyone living in the house?"

"Yes, sir, that's all five of us," I respond.

"Pleasure to meet all of you," Ackers says politely, nodding at each of us as if he's taking mental notes.

"Please, take a seat, Sergeant," I offer.

"Thanks, I don't mind if I do," Ackers replies as he settles into the chair opposite Ryan and me. "Now, let's get down to business, shall we? Missy, may I begin with your statement?"

"Sargent, sir, I don't mind going first," Julie interjects. "But I think it would make better sense for you to start with Taylor since everything that happened tonight began with him."

"Alright," Ackers replies, pulling out a pocket notebook and clicking a ballpoint pen. "Taylor, why don't you share your version of events from earlier tonight? Remember, every detail counts—no matter how small or seemingly insignificant."

I applaud you for making it this far in my story. Let me save time and avoid repetition by skipping ahead, without retelling Julie's and my accounts of the night's events. Is that agreeable with you?

Later, Ramos strolls back into the parlor, a hint of curiosity in his eyes. "I didn't find anyone or anything in the house," he informs us. Then, with a slight furrow of his brow, he asks, "Are you aware there's a puddle of water on the kitchen floor near the back door?"

"Yes, sir," I reply, feeling embarrassed. "That's rain. It blew in when I found the back door open. I haven't had a chance to clean it up yet."

Ramos nods thoughtfully as he scribbles in his notebook. He then poses another question: "Did any of you hear the canine bark or growl before or during the events of the night?"

I take a moment to gather my thoughts. "Beau was curled up on the settee where Julie and Ryan are sitting," I explain. "I remember everyone had turned in for the night and I was switching off the lights on my way to Ryan's and my upstairs bedroom."

"Did the canine make any noise during the night?" Ramos asks.

"I don't remember Beau making a sound," I reply, trying to

recall the events from earlier.

"Wait a second. I definitely heard Beau," Ryan interjects suddenly. "It was during the worse part of the storm. He jumped into bed with me. Now that I think about it, Taylor, you weren't there. As Beau crawled under the covers, he was whining. I remember trying to comfort him even though I was half asleep —the poor baby was terrified."

Ramos and Ackers exchange a quick glance but keep their thoughts to themselves.

"Excuse us for a moment, will you?" Ackers says as he and Ramos go to the kitchen.

I shoot Ryan a questioning look. He simply shrugs and remains silent.

A few moments later, the officers return to the parlor, their expressions unreadable.

"Based on what Miss Julie and Mr. Taylor have reported," Ackers begins dismissively, "and what Sergeant Ramos found during his search of the house, it appears there was no intruder at all. What you thought you saw was merely a figment of overactive imaginations."

"I swear to you, I saw a man in the kitchen," I insist, my voice rising with urgency. "His face was wrinkled and gnarled —like a scary character out of a horror movie. He was right in front of me, just as real as you are now."

Ackers raises an eyebrow, his expression calm and collected. "Did you turn on a light when you went to the kitchen?" he asks, almost teasingly.

"No, sir, I didn't," I shake my head vigorously. "I had a flashlight with me."

"Was the flashlight on?" Ackers asks.

"No, sir," I say.

"At any point during the aforementioned events did you turn it on?" Ackers drills.

"No, sir," I answer. "I turned it on when I was at the top of the stairs. I swept the light back and forth across the first floor, then I turned it off."

He leans back in his chair, contemplating my words. "There was a raging storm outside—lightning flashing and thunder rumbling," Ackers explains. "You heard a loud crash and climbed out of bed in a sleepy daze to check it out. That's when you caught a glimpse of a man's face illuminated by the lightning... then poof. He vanished with the next flash."

"But I know what I saw," I protest.

With a patient smile, Ackers replies, "Our minds can play tricks on us when we're half-asleep. I'm not saying you didn't see something. It's just that your imagination could have filled in the gaps during such an intense moment."

"How can you be so sure it was all in my head?" I ask.

"I'll explain in a moment," Ackers replies, his tone measured. "But first, let's take a closer look at what Miss Julie observed."

"I'm absolutely convinced that what I saw was as real as anything," Julie insists, her conviction unwavering.

"Yes, I believe you," Ackers responds thoughtfully. "Earlier, didn't you mention waking up to a sound? Could it have been thunder? When you opened your eyes, did you catch a glimpse of him illuminated by a flash of lightning? Is it possible you weren't fully awake and simply saw a shadow on the wall—a fleeting image lasting for as long as a flash of lightning? Could it have been your imagination playing tricks on you?"

"I'm not sure. I-I-I'm really not sure," Julie stammers, clearly shaken. "You've got me all confused. I don't know what to think anymore."

"Here's something we do know for certain," Ackers states firmly. "Sergeant Ramos didn't find any shoe tracks in the kitchen. If someone had entered the house, they would have left muddy footprints behind—yet there was nothing but clear rainwater on the floor."

"Maybe the rain washed the intruder's shoes clean," Duncan suggests.

"That's highly unlikely," Ramos counters. "There are several inches of thick mud outside the kitchen door. The only way someone could have entered without leaving tracks is if they sprouted wings."

Duncan, ever the challenger, leans forward with a sly grin. "Sergeant Ramos, how did you and Sergeant Ackers manage to enter this house without tracking mud everywhere? Wasn't it pouring rain when you arrived?" He smirks, convinced he has Ramos cornered.

"Aren't you the observant one?" Ramos replies smoothly, confidence radiating from him. "We removed our rubber overshoes and raincoats before stepping inside, leaving them on the front porch. Did you not notice how dry our uniforms are despite the thunderstorm raging outside?" His self-assured demeanor causes Duncan's smirk to falter.

Duncan visibly puffs up, clearly uncomfortable. I've learned from experience he doesn't take kindly to being called out or proven wrong. His discomfort is evident, adding an extra layer of tension to the atmosphere in the house.

"And one more thing," Ackers interjects. "Your canine friend has given us a crucial clue, even if he can't talk. He's provided a key piece of the puzzle."

"What are you getting at?" Duncan snaps back, frustration creeping into his voice.

Ackers leans in, his gaze steady. "Each of you agreed the canine didn't make a sound during last night's events—except for a quick whimper." He pauses for effect. "If there had been an intruder, the canine would have barked or growled, just like when Ramos and I arrived tonight."

"That wasn't like Beau," I jump in to defend my loyal companion. "He's friendly and laid-back."

Ackers raises an eyebrow, unconvinced. "That's what you want to believe," he counters. "However, when challenged, most canines instinctively protect their territory when they sense danger. Since the canine didn't react, and the other evidence doesn't point to an intruder, I'm confident no one broke into this house. The entire scenario? Just a case of overstimulated imaginations running wild."

Let me set you straight (no pun intended), if Sergeants Ackers and Ramos hadn't been wearing badges, four irate college students might have literally kicked them right out of the deceased Widow Blackburn's house. As the resident and new owner of the old mansion, I can assure you the bizarre events that occurred during the storm earlier in the night were not mere figments of our imaginations. A thunderstorm rolled into town as if it had its own agenda, unleashing a series of strange occurrences in the grand ol' house perched atop the hill overlooking Lost Creek Junction.

DAY THREE

Thursday, May 17, 2018

The morning sun spills golden light across the kitchen, the air is crisp and invigorating after last night's storm. However, heavy fatigue lingers in the Blackburn household, where the former widow once lived. Duncan, Ryan, Julie, and I feel the physical aftermath of last night's events. Our bodies ache as if we've run a marathon, and our minds are wrapped in a thick fog. Meanwhile, Beau remains entirely unfazed, blissfully snoozing on the settee. It's almost comical how he manages to fit his large frame into that tiny piece of furniture, with half of him dangling like rising bread dough spilling out of a bowl. What is it about the settee that he's so attached to?

Last night's encounter with the Lost Creek Junction police left us scratching our heads.

"Are we expected to accept their simplistic explanation for what Julie and I witnessed? It simply doesn't add up," I say.

"I for one, refuse to buy into their half-baked notions. As college-educated individuals, we know better than to be misled by those two hick officers," Julie states emphatically.

This morning, breakfast is mostly a quiet affair, filled with the crunching of dry cereal. The four of us gather around the kitchen table, each lost in thoughts, the atmosphere thick with unspoken tension.

"I'd never doubt anything Taylor or Julie say," Duncan declares between spoonfuls of cereal. "I still believe we had an intruder in the house last night."

"I agree," I reply, scooping cereal into my spoon as I

contemplate the situation. "But the cops raised some valid points against that theory."

"Maybe it wasn't an intruder after all," Ryan says, muffled by a mouthful of cereal. "What if the person Taylor and Julie saw was a squatter? This house is huge. It's entirely possible someone could be living here without us knowing."

"Seriously? A squatter? I can't believe it," Duncan exclaims, nearly choking on his cereal. "Sergeant Ramos was crystal clear —the house was secure, and no one but the four of us were here."

"Don't you mean five? You're forgetting Beau," Ryan states.

"Alright, five," Duncan acknowledges.

"I don't know, guys," Julie says, blowing gently on her steaming coffee before taking a sip. "I have this nagging feeling there was someone—or something—lurking in this house last night."

A heavy silence blankets the room as we reflect on the strange events of the previous night.

"Wait a second," Ryan interrupts. "Julie might be onto something."

"Onto what exactly?" Julie says, intrigued but confused.

"We've been looking at this all wrong," Ryan says. "What if what Julie and Taylor saw wasn't a person? What if it was something else entirely?"

"Okay, Rye," Julie replies. "You've completely lost me. What are you talking about?"

"We've been assuming what Julie and Taylor saw last night was a person, but what if it was something else instead?" Ryan suggests.

"Okay, Rye," Julie concedes. "You've completely lost me. I have no idea what you're talking about."

Beau lets out a muffled bark from the next room, causing us to pause. After everything that happened last night, the four of us are definitely on edge, our senses heightened like a cat ready to pounce.

"Hold that thought while I check on Beau," I say as I rise

from my chair and tiptoe toward the parlor. When I peek in, I find Beau sprawled on the settee, lost in his dreams. His head twitches, and his paws paddle the air as if he's chasing something exhilarating—maybe a butterfly or lightning bugs? It's hard not to snicker at his comical dance as I make my way back to the kitchen.

"What's up with Beau?" Julie asks.

"He's sound asleep," I reply, settling back into my chair at the table. "He's probably dreaming about chasing butterflies."

"Rye," Julie interjects, "getting back to what you were saying —"

"Sure," Ryan says. "Do you remember what the cashier at the grocery store said about this house being haunted? She wouldn't step foot inside for any amount of money."

"What does that have to do with our conversation?" Duncan asks.

"Don't you see?" Ryan asks. "What if this house is actually haunted?"

A thick silence blankets the room as we exchange glances, uncertainty swirling like a fog. Julie's eyes widen in disbelief, Duncan's brow furrows, and Ryan shovels cereal into his mouth.

"That's absurd," Julie scoffs. "We know ghosts aren't real... right?"

I hesitate momentarily before responding, "After what I witnessed last night, I might have to rethink my position on ghosts."

"Ghosts?" Julie rolls her eyes dramatically. "Seriously?"

"Does anyone have a better explanation for what happened last night?" I ask.

Duncan strokes his chin thoughtfully. "Alright, let's entertain the idea someone believes in ghosts. How would one go about communicating with them?"

"How about we try a Ouija board?" Ryan suggests, a spark of mischief in his eyes. "I think I saw one in the front hall closet."

Julie glances around at us guys. "Does anyone actually know how to use a Ouija board?"

Ryan shrugs nonchalantly. "How hard can it be? It's just letters and numbers, right?"

I sense the excitement building. "If everyone's up for it, why not try the Ouija board experiment after supper?" I propose.

Duncan shakes his head in disbelief, clearly skeptical about the proposed plan.

As the last rays of sunlight fade and the moon rises to join a myriad of stars in the darkening sky, we gather in the dining room after tidying up the kitchen from supper. With candles flickering to life, their warm glow dances across the polished table, casting reflections in the glossy wood. We have a mission tonight: to summon spirits and uncover answers about the mysterious events that unfolded last night.

In this dimly lit haven, Ryan carefully lays out the Ouija board at the center of our makeshift circle. The four of us settle around it, forming a square instead of a traditional circle—an unconventional choice, but who says we can't bend the rules? We share nervous glances, wondering if our little tweak might alter the outcome of what lies ahead.

Ryan places the plastic pointer on the Ouija board. "Alright, everyone. Here's how it works," he reads from the instruction sheet. "Each player gently places their first and second fingers on the pointer—just a light touch. You want to avoid pressing too hard, or you might accidentally influence its movements." He pauses for dramatic effect, letting the curiosity build. "One individual will ask a question out loud while the other participants focus intently on that question. It doesn't matter if your eyes are open or closed—what matters is the collective energy of all participants. When a spirit connects to the board it will guide the pointer to reveal an answer."

Ryan leans in closer, his voice dropping to a conspiratorial whisper. "Remember—no manipulating the pointer. It's all about allowing whatever forces at play to guide us. Alright, everyone, place your two fingers on the pointer."

"Who's going to kick things off with a question?" Julie asks, her eyes sparkling with curiosity.

"Why not you, Julie?" I suggest.

"Okay, are we ready?" Ryan says, glancing around at all of us.

Everyone nods in agreement.

"Do I ask the question now?" Julie asks.

"Anytime you're ready," Ryan nods.

With a deep breath, Julie says, "Hello, spirits from the great beyond. Can you hear me?"

The room falls into an expectant silence as we hold our breath, waiting for a response. The pointer remains eerily still.

"Nothing's happening," Julie says softly, disappointment creeping into her voice.

"Try asking another question," Ryan suggests.

"Maybe someone else should give it a try," Julie proposes.

"I have a question," Ryan declares. "If there's a ghost in this room, please give us a sign."

As we wait for something—anything—to happen, the atmosphere buzzes with anticipation.

"Wait a minute. I have a question," I say, my voice barely above a whisper. "Widow Blackburn, can you hear me? Please give us a sign." My heart races as I hope for a response.

The atmosphere is thick with tension. The only sounds come from the hissing flames of the candles. Their flickering light casts eerie shadows to gyrate on the walls and ceiling, heightening the suspense of our ghostly endeavor.

"This is ridiculous," Duncan scoffs, rolling his eyes. "It's a silly board game for kids. Clearly, it's either broken or never worked in the first place."

Just then, the candle flames flicker, almost as if they're frightened spirits.

"Did you guys see that?" Ryan asks.

"It was probably a draft," Duncan dismisses, waving his hand. "This old house is drafty as hell."

"Let's ask another question," I suggest, trying to keep the momentum going. "Is there someone here we can't see? Please give us a sign if you're listening."

A long silence falls over us, filled with anticipation that slowly morphs into profound disappointment when no answer comes.

"This is nonsense," Duncan says, lifting his fingers from the plastic pointer in frustration. "It's not getting us anywhere."

"Wait, everyone," Julie interjects. "Since we're all set up, why not ditch the Ouija board and try a séance instead? I've dabbled with my sorority sisters before—just for fun, of course."

"Have you had any success with them?" Ryan asks.

Julie shrugs, a playful grin on her face. "Well, it was hit or miss—mostly miss. But we had a blast. I'm totally game if the rest of you are."

"What do we have to lose?" Ryan asks. "I'm in if everyone else is. We're in this together, right?"

Duncan, our resident skeptic, rolls his eyes and says, "Sure, why not?" His tone drips with disbelief but hints at a flicker of intrigue.

The room is cloaked in dim candlelight. Flickering flames cast eerie shadows resembling ghostly figures. As Ryan stands and clears away the Ouija board, he inadvertently stirs up even more restless shadows, heightening the expectant atmosphere around us.

Julie clears her throat before giving us instructions. "Alright, everyone. Stay seated and place your palms flat on the table," she says. "Touch your pinkie fingers with your neighbors on either side of you and press your thumb tips together."

It's as though we're weaving a thread that connects us all.

"Is everyone ready?" Julie asks, her eyes sparkling with anticipation.

Each of us nods enthusiastically, excitement buzzing in the air.

"Oh, spirits of the great beyond," she begins dramatically, "make yourselves known to us by giving us a sign."

The candles unexpectedly flicker, casting ominous shadows

about the room. At the same time, the rich scent of burning wax envelops us. Suddenly—whoosh!—the room is plunged into darkness as the flames extinguish completely.

We collectively gasp. It's as if time stands still. Then, just when we think it's over, the candles reignite one by one—like trick birthday candles refusing to die. The tension in the room thickens—one could practically cut it with a knife. We inhale sharply, holding our breaths in unison as curiosity washes over us.

We're cloaked in a heavy silence. The only sound breaking through is the whispering wind, creating an eerie contrast to the stillness surrounding us. Suddenly, a flash of lightning illuminates the room, followed by a booming crash of thunder.

"Well, was that it?" Duncan breaks the tension with a hint of sarcasm.

"Sorry, guys," Julie responds sheepishly.

"Don't apologize," I interject with a grin. "That was pretty awesome how the candles flickered and then—bam!—the thunderstorm came up out of nowhere."

"I don't know about you guys," Ryan yawns, "but all this ghost talk has worn me out. I'm beat."

"Same here," I nod in agreement.

We extinguish the candles, plunging the house into darkness. Retreating into our thoughts, we make our way up the stairs to our bedrooms. Occasional flashes of lightning stream through the windows, casting strange shadows on the walls and ceiling —these shapes somehow feel less threatening than they did the night before. The distant rumble of thunder mixes with our weary footsteps, as the ol' house on the hill settles in for the night.

Dale Thele

DAY FOUR

Friday, May 18, 2018

Ryan, Duncan, and I are in the kitchen having breakfast—well, at least Ryan and Duncan are. I'm at the stove flipping pancakes on the griddle using batter from a box while they eagerly devour each fluffy creation as fast as I churn them out.

Suddenly, Julie bursts onto the scene, racing down the stairs as if the house is on fire.

"Guys, you won't believe this," Julie excitedly announces.

Beau barks from the parlor, apparently startled by her unexpected enthusiastic entrance.

"What's up, Julie?" I ask, quickly moving to meet her halfway between the stairs and the kitchen, spatula in hand like a culinary warrior ready for action.

"You won't believe what happened last night," she says, dashing into the kitchen.

"Is everything okay? Are you alright?" I ask, struggling to keep up with Julie's brisk pace. I can't shake the feeling that something is off.

"I'm fine," she replies, her voice bubbling with excitement. "You won't believe what I saw last night."

"What did you see?" Duncan asks, clearly intrigued.

Julie's eyes sparkle, "I saw something—"

"Please don't tell me it was that hideous, wrinkled old man again," I interrupt.

"Nothing like that," Julie shakes her head vigorously. "This was different... I don't even know what it was. Maybe it was a ghost."

"A ghost?" Duncan replies, skepticism dripping from his

voice.

"Maybe? I don't know," Julie responds, her eyes sparkling. "Whatever it was, it was the most incredible thing I've ever seen."

"Are you absolutely sure you weren't dreaming?" Duncan presses.

"No way. This was no dream," Julie insists.

"Why don't you start from the beginning?" Ryan suggests, guiding Julie toward the kitchen table. "And don't leave anything out."

"Well," Julie begins, taking a deep breath to steady herself, "I was asleep in my bed when suddenly I woke up and opened my eyes… there she was."

"Who? She who?" Ryan asks, his brow furrowing with concern as he pours a steaming mug of coffee for Julie.

"Arabella," Julie exclaims, her eyes wide with excitement.

"Who's Arabella?" Ryan asks, handing her a freshly poured mug of coffee.

"The ghost—or whatever," Julie replies, accepting the coffee as if discussing a spectral encounter is perfectly normal despite her earlier skepticism.

"Wait a minute," Ryan interjects, setting the coffee pot down with a clatter. "What did I miss here?"

"Come on, keep up," I chuckle at Ryan's bewilderment, finding humor in his puzzled expression.

Julie's practically bouncing in her seat, so eager her words come out like an intricate puzzle waiting to be solved.

"Okay, okay," Ryan says, looking at Julie with a mix of concern and curiosity. "Take a deep breath, calm down, and start over—slowly this time."

With renewed focus, Julie carefully places her coffee mug down and begins again. "Like I was saying, last night was unlike anything I've ever experienced. I was asleep in bed, when suddenly—I woke up to the most amazing sight. There beside my bed stood a glowing figure—a sweet little girl who looked about eight years old. She wore an old-fashioned nightgown, and her hair was styled in a Gibson Girl up do."

"Are you absolutely sure you weren't dreaming?" Duncan asks, skepticism evident as he peers over the rim of his coffee mug.

"I wasn't dreaming. You have to believe me," Julie insists. "I was completely awake, just like I am right now. This little girl appeared out of nowhere and introduced herself as Arabella. She said she had an urgent message for us."

"What kind of message?" Ryan asks.

"She was being all mysterious and stuff," Julie continues, her voice dropping to a conspiratorial whisper. "She said, *There are others in the house—heed my warning. Two of them mean you harm.* And then… poof! She vanished into thin air."

"Are you sure you didn't imagine this?" I ask gently, trying to gauge her sincerity.

"I swear it wasn't a dream," Julie's voice rises an octave, tinged with frustration. "Why won't you guys believe me?"

Duncan shakes his head slowly. "This—whatever this is—sounds weird. Do you honestly believe this *girl* could have been a ghost?"

"I don't know—maybe it was a ghost, an apparition, or even an angel. Who can say for sure?" Julie shrugs, her eyes sparkling with intrigue. "But I do know it happened, just like I said." She takes a thoughtful sip of her coffee, letting the moment linger.

"Well," Duncan chuckles, his skepticism evident but playful, "if you say it went down like that, then I guess it must've happened."

"Hey, lay off Julie, will you?" Ryan interjects. "It's clear she experienced something, and it's not our place to judge."

"I'm siding with Julie," I declare. "I'm all in on this Abigail's advice."

"Her name is Arabella," Julie corrects me gently as she cradles her mug and takes another sip of coffee.

"Okay, whatever," I reply with a grin. "This is still useful information. The source may be questionable, but who are we to dismiss the possibility of ghosts or anything else? There's so much in this universe that remains a mystery, and maybe we'll never fully understand it all. So why not follow Julie's new friend's advice and see where it leads us? Who's with me?"

Everyone raises their hand in agreement—even Duncan. Though he's skeptical at heart, I'm pretty sure he doesn't want to go against the group. Besides, what if we're onto something? Or worse yet, what if Duncan's right, and this is one colossal joke on all of us?

Once again, we delve into the old papers and journals we've collected. This time, our mission is to unravel the mystery surrounding Arabella and her cryptic message. However, we're puzzled, questioning whether Julie's sighting was a ghostly apparition, a celestial angel, or simply a trick of her imagination. With Julie's claims being our sole insight into this perplexing scenario, our understanding remains limited.

After hours of sifting through old papers and forgotten journals, we hit a dead end. During our lunch break, Ryan speaks up, voicing what we're all thinking. "You know, guys, we've been cooped up in this house for too long. We need a break."

"Absolutely," Julie agrees. "Some fresh air would do us wonders."

"A distraction from all this research is exactly what we need," Duncan adds, nodding in agreement.

"So, what do you have in mind?" Ryan asks, curiosity sparking in his eyes.

"What if we explore my gold mine?" I suggest.

"Hey, yeah," Ryan responds. "That sounds awesome."

"But first," I say, "I need to meet with Mr. Andrews to confirm I actually own the mine. The last thing I want to happen is to accidentally trespass on someone else's property while thinking I'm the rightful owner."

"Smart move," Julie agrees.

"Duncan," I turn to him, "would you mind driving me to the

lawyer's office?"

"No problem," Duncan replies with a smile. "And hey, don't forget to grab those documents I found in that old strongbox along with the deed for the mine."

A little while later, I'm in Mr. Andrews's office, my heart racing with anticipation.

"Son," he begins, his eyes scanning the yellowed deeds, stock certificates, bonds, and various legal documents I've brought with me. "These papers appear to be legitimate. Of course, I'll need time to review them more thoroughly. But for now, let's assume you're a wealthy landowner, and indeed the rightful owner of the gold mine."

Wait—what? As the weight of his words sinks in, a wave of excitement washes over me. Not only do I own a gold mine, but it seems I might also have a stake in some land in Lost Creek Junction. My property holdings could extend beyond Widow Blackburn's hill. Could it be? Have I just struck gold? Cha-ching!

Duncan and I return to my house on the hill to pick up the others. Everyone is excited to explore my old, abandoned mine. We pile into Duncan's SUV—Beau included—and our anticipation bubbles over with every mile we travel, like fizzy soda. Armed with a rough hand-drawn map resembling something out of a treasure hunt, Duncan drives us to a remote location where he says *we'll have to hike the rest of the way.*

We climb out of the SUV and face the rugged terrain ahead. With determination, we set off on foot, pushing through the dry, overgrown brush which seems to whisper secrets we can't quite decipher.

"This is so cool," Duncan exclaims, his voice brimming with enthusiasm as we trudge through waist-high grass that dances in the breeze. We swat away swarms of pesky bugs buzzing around us like they're part of a wild obstacle course.

"Ew!" Julie suddenly shrieks, her face scrunching in disgust as she prances in an incoherent circle. "A bug flew into my mouth!"

"Don't worry, Julie," I laugh. "Those bugs aren't poisonous."

"What are they?" she squawks, frantically wiping her tongue as if trying to erase the experience.

"They're harmless gnats," I explain with a grin. "They swarm together in little floating clouds—it's kind of their thing."

"That's gross, I don't like them," Julie declares defiantly, swatting the air like a person possessed.

"I doubt they're too fond of you either," Duncan teases back, his eyes sparkling with mischief.

After what feels like an eternity of hiking—complete with Julie's constant grumbling about her aversion to flying bugs—we finally arrive at the spot Duncan insists is the entrance to the mine. Honestly, it's not much to look at, just a boarded-up hole in the side of a small hill. The wooden planks seem hastily thrown together to keep out vandals and trespassers. However, it hasn't stopped mischievous souls from tagging it with graffiti.

Driven by our insatiable curiosity to discover what lies inside, we pry apart the nailed boards blocking the entrance, creating an opening large enough for one person to squeeze through. One by one, we slip into the darkness, our hearts racing with excitement and anticipation. It's only when we're inside, enveloped by shadows, we realize we forgot to bring flashlights. Recognizing the potential danger, we quickly retreat, our hearts still pounding from the experience.

As Ryan and I wait our turns to crawl through the narrow gap meant to keep us out, he suddenly exclaims, "Hey, Taylor, check this out." He holds up a dazzling rock that sparkles brilliantly in the afternoon sun filtering through the remaining boards covering the mine's entrance.

"Where did you find that?" I ask.

"It was lying on the ground," Ryan replies, wincing as he shifts his weight. "I stubbed my toe on it."

"You're lucky you didn't step on it and roll your ankle," I

remark, my voice echoing off the walls of the cavernous mine. "Hey, if you're lucky, that could be a genuine gold nugget," I tease with a grin.

"Really? Genuine gold, you say?" Ryan's eyes widen with excitement.

"I wouldn't get your hopes up too high if I were you," I tell Ryan while Duncan helps me climb out of the mine.

Ryan shoves the fist-sized rock into his pants pocket before following me back into the sunlight.

Later, as we gather around the kitchen table for a casual supper of juicy hamburgers and crunchy potato chips, Ryan pulls a rock from his pants pocket. Excitedly, he passes it around for everyone to inspect.

"Check this out. I stubbed my toe on it," Ryan exclaims, grinning. "At first, I thought it was just an ordinary rock. But then I picked it up and noticed how it sparkled in the light coming through the boards covering the mine entrance."

Duncan raises an eyebrow, "How many times are you going to tell us that same tired story?"

Ryan's face falls as he replies, "Sorry, I didn't mean to bore you."

I add with a playful nudge, "Come on, Rye. How many times have you shared that story since you found that rock?"

"Hey, guys, don't be so hard on him," Julie quickly defends him. "He's excited about something special that happened to him. Who else is he going to tell his story to but us?"

Julie's words hang in the air, inviting us to pause and reflect for a moment.

"This might interest you, Rye," Duncan muses as he deftly assembles his second hamburger. "Have you heard about the Texas gold rush of 1853?"

Ryan sulks, his silence speaks volumes.

"I had no idea Texas had a gold rush," Julie exclaims as she passes a bag of chips to me.

Duncan leans in, eager to engage Ryan. "Oh, absolutely. It

took place right here around the upper Colorado River—now known as the Texas Hill Country." He continues enthusiastically, "Lost Creek Junction is believed to be where it all began."

"Wait... are you suggesting Taylor's mine could actually have gold?" Julie's eyes sparkle at the thought of treasures and dollar signs dance in her imagination.

Ryan shakes off his gloom and perks up at this new possibility.

"According to Texas history," Duncan says, "this area was at the very heart of the original Texas gold rush."

Suddenly, Ryan bursts out with joy, "We're rich!" He dances about in the kitchen. His excitement is infectious, luring Beau to join in the fun with enthusiastic barks and leaps into the air alongside Ryan.

"Unbelievable, can you imagine it? The thought of us being wealthy feels like a dream," I exclaim, shaking my head in disbelief.

Ryan chuckles, "It's no big deal for Julie and Duncan. They're already rich."

Julie shrugs. "Sure, we're comfortable, thanks to our parents' money."

"But now you and Duncan can be wealthy in your own right," Ryan says excitedly. "And all of this started with my lucky gold nugget." He kisses the shiny rock as if it's a treasure from a fairy tale.

"Hold up, everyone," Duncan interjects, typing on his laptop. "We need to get Ryan's rock certified by a gemologist first."

"Good point. But where do we find one?" Julie asks.

"I found a gemologist online. He's located in Ballinger," Duncan replies. "It's about an hour's drive."

"What are we waiting for?" Ryan shouts. "Let's hit the road."

"It's too late tonight," Duncan replies, a hint of reluctance in his voice. "But how about we head out tomorrow morning if everyone's on board?"

"Absolutely, tomorrow, I'm going to be rich!" Ryan exclaims, his eyes sparkling with excitement.

"Whoa there, Rye. Let's not get carried away," I interject, trying to temper his enthusiasm. "What if your rock turns out to be fool's gold?"

A heavy silence fills the kitchen. I didn't mean to spoil everyone's mood, but Ryan's treasure could be a mirage. We won't know until we go to Ballinger in the morning.

Dale Thele

DAY FIVE

Saturday, May 19, 2018

"Come on, let's get moving," Duncan urges as we hurry through breakfast. The thrill of adventure is in the air, and even Beau can sense it—his ears perked up at the mention of *road trip*. Those two words are like magic to him. Ever since I got him as a puppy, he's been a car enthusiast at heart, especially after he outgrew that basket on my bike.

"What should we do with the breakfast dishes?" Julie asks, glancing at the dishes stacked in the sink.

"Leave them—we'll get to them when we get back," I reply with a wave of my hand, eager to keep things moving.

Meanwhile, Duncan grows more impatient by the second—his SUV's engine roars to life while he insistently blasts the horn.

"Duncan's getting antsy," I state. "Let's not keep him waiting any longer."

"Okay, I'm coming," Julie calls back with urgency and excitement.

"Where's Beau?" I ask, my eyes darting around the parlor. "Beau!" I call out, my voice echoing through the house.

"You know him—he's probably off exploring the backyard," Julie replies nonchalantly, her fingers rummaging through her handbag as if digging for valuables.

"He's in the SUV with Duncan," Ryan calls from the open front door.

With that, Ryan, Julie, and I dash outside, excitement bubbling as we scramble into the vehicle.

"Is everyone present and accounted for?" Duncan asks, his

tone playful yet serious. "Count off—Duncan, present," he declares, waving his hand like a kid eager to be noticed.

"Julie, here, sir," she responds with a giggle, raising her hand.

"Ryan, here," he states confidently, lifting his arm enthusiastically.

"Taylor, here," I chime in, waving my arm.

A moment of suspense hangs in the air as we glance around at each other expectantly.

"Beau? Are you present?" Duncan calls out, breaking the silence.

Only the sound of the SUV's engine answers him.

"Beauregard Winston Churchill Greene! Are you present?" Duncan tries again, casting a challenging look at Beau through the rearview mirror.

Beau springs into action, responding with an enthusiastic bark sending us into fits of laughter.

"All right. Everyone's present and accounted for," Duncan announces triumphantly before hitting the gas pedal.

And just like that, we're off to Ballinger to see a gemologist about Ryan's rock.

Anticipation crackles in the air as we wait outside the gemologist's office. The small reception room is filled with the rich scent of polished stones and an air of silence. Duncan paces back and forth like a windup toy soldier, his anxiety discernible. Meanwhile, Julie flips through brochures with fervor, setting one down only to pick up another. I sit beside Julie, my legs vibrating with pent-up energy while Beau snoozes peacefully at my feet. We're all on edge, our nerves frayed as we await the verdict on Ryan's rock.

"What's taking so long?" Julie asks, her foot tapping rhythmically against the cool tile floor. "This suspense is killing me."

"If Rye's rock turns out to be genuine gold, it could change everything for us," I muse aloud, letting my imagination run wild with visions of untold riches.

Duncan, ever the realist, shakes his head. "I wouldn't count your chickens before they hatch," he warns. "We still don't know if that rock is truly gold."

"I just know it is," Julie insists. "It has to be real gold. I can feel it in my bones."

The gemologist's office door swings open, and Ryan steps out, looking visibly disheartened. He stares at the ground, seemingly searching for answers among the scuffs on his trainers. His body language radiates disappointment, suggesting that the news he brings is far from what we had hoped. Our dreams of striking it rich appear to dry up and vanish like sand in the wind. Just when we think our luck couldn't get any worse, Ryan suddenly announces, "It's real gold!" A radiant smile spreads across his face, and his demeanor shifts instantly from gloomy to gleeful.

Julie playfully elbows him and quips, "You're such a tease. You had us believing you got bad news."

With a grin that lights up the room, Ryan replies, "The gemologist said my rock is a fairly pure specimen, and it's valuable." The excitement in his voice is contagious. But there's more—Ryan shares the gemologist's tantalizing suggestion: *This discovery suggests the possibility of a gold vein within the mine.* The mere thought of unearthing future treasures sweeps us aboard the gold rush train.

"Since we're already here, why not take the opportunity to shop, sightsee, and explore what Ballinger has to offer?" Duncan suggests with a grin. "Honestly, I don't know about the rest of you, but I'm way too excited to head back to Lost Creek Junction just yet. So, how about we have some fun?"

"You know what, Duncan? You absolutely nailed it," Julie exclaims, her eyes sparkling with enthusiasm. "We definitely deserve a little fun. After all, this is our summer vacation."

"I can't wait to see what Ballinger has in store for us. What's our first stop?" Ryan adds, his excitement stirring a tourist spark in everyone.

"While at the gemologist's office, I snagged a brochure filled with things to do in Ballinger," Julie shares.

"I'm curious—what does the brochure recommend we see first?" I ask.

"It says the Olde Park Hotel is the number one place to visit in the area," Julie exclaims, her eyes sparkling with excitement as she reads from the brochure. "This place dates back to the 1800s and is said to be haunted by thirty different souls. Sounds like something right up your alley, Duncan."

"Ha, ha," Duncan replies with his signature sarcasm while rolling his eyes.

While we didn't encounter any ghostly apparitions during our tour of the hotel—just a few creaky floorboards and some old portraits—Duncan, our resident skeptic, certainly wasn't expecting anything supernatural. His playful disbelief added a fun twist to our excursion.

Our day in Ballinger ended with an unforgettable outdoor Mexican fiesta in the town square. The vibrant atmosphere was infectious as Beau and the rest of us savored mouthwatering authentic Mexican tacos and burritos from various food vendors. With colorful decorations fluttering in the breeze and lively Mariachi music filling the air, it was impossible not to get swept up in the celebration—even if we did invest a little too much on souvenirs.

It's well past midnight when we finally roll back into Lost Creek Junction, our hearts still buzzing from an unforgettable day. We're completely exhausted after indulging in delicious food, exploring unique shops, and dancing the night away at a vibrant Mexican celebration. Yet, despite our fatigue, excitement bubbles beneath the surface as we dream about reopening the mine.

"I don't know about the rest of you, but I'm beat," Julie says, fighting back a yawn.

"Same here," Duncan adds, stretching his arms overhead.

"Me three," Ryan says playfully, a grin spreading across his face.

"Count me in as well," I say, chuckling at our collective weariness.

Exhausted, we drag ourselves—and the many souvenirs we picked up in Ballinger—up the creaky stairs as we prepare for bed. Before long, the lights flicker off in the old house, and one by one, we drift into a restful sleep filled with dreams of adventure and fortune.

I've been drifting in and out of sleep for what feels like ages when suddenly, I'm jolted awake by the unmistakable sound of heavy footsteps echoing in the hall just outside the bedroom Ryan and I share. "Duncan, is that you?" I whisper, expecting him to be up to one of his usual pranks.

Silence hangs in the air like a thick fog.

"Come on. Enough already. I know it's you. Go back to bed," I call out, directing my words at what I assume is Duncan lurking just beyond the closed door.

Still, there's no response. But wait—what if it isn't Duncan?

The noise grows louder. Each thud of heavy boots reverberates against the floorboards, sending a chill down my spine.

I nudge Ryan, who's blissfully snoring, but he doesn't budge. With a little more force, I jab him again with my elbow, and he finally stirs.

"Hey, what's the big idea?" he mumbles, still half-asleep and barely opening his eyes.

"I heard something in the hall," I reply, my heart racing like a wild drumbeat.

"It's probably just the house settling," he shrugs, rolling over to face away from me. "Go back to sleep."

"I know I heard something," I insist, shaking him gently.

"Then get up and see what it is," he grumbles, punching his pillow into submission before burying his head in it. "Leave me alone. I want to sleep."

Suddenly, a loud bang erupts from the hall outside our bedroom door.

Ryan bolts upright in bed, eyes wide with panic. "What the —?" he gasps, his breath quickening as fear overtakes him.

"You heard that too, right? It came from outside our door." My heart pounds, each beat echoing in my ears. "Aren't you going to check it out?"

"Not a chance," he retorts. "It's most likely Duncan trying to scare us."

"It's not Duncan. I swear it's something else," I plead.

"What's going on over there?" Julie's voice cuts through the quiet from her bedroom.

"We don't know," I shout back, my heart racing. "Ryan's too scared to check it out."

"Why don't *you* take a look?" Julie yells back impatiently.

"I'm too scared," I admit, glancing nervously at the door.

"Well, someone better find out what that noise was," Duncan chimes in angrily from his room.

"See? I told you it wasn't Duncan making all that racket," I say to Ryan, trying to make my earlier point.

Just then, another loud bang echoes through the hall, followed by hurried footsteps. My pulse quickens as our bedroom door bursts open, slamming against the wall.

Ryan and I squeal, clutching each other as if we're facing a monster.

Something heavy lands on our bed with a thud before burrowing under the covers between us. Terrified and filled with adrenaline, we scramble over each other in a frantic attempt to escape from whatever has taken over our bed.

Then Ryan snickers.

"What's so funny?" I ask.

"It's Beau. He jumped into our bed like a total scaredy-cat," he chuckles, pointing at my dog, quivering beneath the blankets.

With nervous laughter bubbling up inside us, we dive back under the covers as if they will shield us from monsters lurking in the hall or protect us from the floor transforming into molten lava—lingering childhood fears creeping back to haunt us.

"Whatever's out there," I whisper, my voice trembling as I pull the bed sheet up to my chin, "has scared Beau half to death."

Ryan glances at me, his expression a mix of concern and annoyance. "One of us should go find out what's making that noise."

"I'll go if you come with me," I reply, my heart racing.

"Do I have to?" Ryan whines.

"If I'm going, you're coming too," I insist.

With a resigned sigh, Ryan climbs out of bed, grumbling under his breath, "Alright, let's get this over with."

As we approach the open bedroom door, my white knuckles grip a baseball bat like it's a lifeline.

"What do you plan to do with that bat?" Ryan raises an eyebrow.

"I'm protecting myself," I shoot back. "If we run into someone... well, let's just say they won't know what hit 'em."

"Oh, for heaven's sake," Ryan shakes his head in disbelief, as a grin crosses his face.

Together, we creep stealthily through the pitch-black hallway, the darkness swallowing our every move. Each step echoes ominously in the silence—what could be lurking just out of sight?

A blinding flash of lightning from an approaching storm slices through the gloom, transforming the corridor into a stark, eerie landscape. Shadows dance on the walls, floor, and ceiling, morphing into ominous shapes resembling claws, reaching out to tear us to shreds. With every cautious step we take, we draw closer to an unknown danger hiding in the shadows. Is it a rabid creature waiting to pounce, or perhaps an evil spirit poised to frighten us? The anticipation is almost unbearable.

Ryan suddenly stops and squeals sending me crashing into him. My startled, high-pitched nelly shriek pierces the air, followed by a bone-chilling scream from an unseen third entity.

"Why are you guys sneaking around in the dark?" Julie's voice cuts through the silence, and suddenly, her flashlight beam reveals her questioning expression.

"We're checking out the noises," I manage to say, my breath coming in heavy gasps as adrenaline surges through me. My heart racing like a drum in my chest.

"Seriously? Why don't you guys have flashlights?" Julie raises a curious eyebrow.

Ryan shifts nervously in front of me. "We don't want to see what's causing those sounds," he admits, his voice barely above a whisper.

Julie rolls her eyes. "Oh, for Christ's sake, you guys are such wusses. Get behind me, and we'll figure this out together."

Trembling with fear, Ryan and I fall into step behind her, our footsteps echoing eerily in the stillness as we make our way toward the stairs. Julie's flashlight cuts through the darkness ahead of us. As we descend the stairs, the lower floor looks undisturbed and quiet.

Once we reach the kitchen, I flick the light switch. But instead of brightening our surroundings, the room stubbornly remains cloaked in darkness. I try again—nothing happens.

"Come on, stop fooling around and turn on the light already," Julie urges, her voice tinged with anxiety.

"I tried, but the switch isn't working," I reply, my heart racing.

"I really don't like this," Julie admits, her unease apparent in her tone.

"We'll be fine as long as we stick together," I say nervously, trying to reassure her, myself and Ryan. But deep down, doubt creeps in like the shadows around us.

Suddenly, ice-cold fingers wrap tight like a vise around my wrist.

I scream—an instinctive reaction sending shock waves through the room, triggering Julie and Ryan to also scream. The grip releases my wrist. Panic sets in, and my heart pounds in my chest, making it hard to breathe.

"Why did you scream?" Ryan demands, his voice shaky.

"S-s-something cold and c-c-clammy grabbed my wrist," I manage to stammer, shivering at the memory of the chilling touch.

Ryan gasps and pulls me close. His grip, fueled by fear, tightens around my arm. His fingers dig into my flesh—a reminder we're experiencing this terror together.

In a flash of blinding lightning, I see what Ryan sees: the twisted face of an angry old man, his features contorted in a grotesque grimace. The image is so nightmarish it sends chills racing down my spine.

We scream as one, our hearts pounding as if caught in the climax of a slasher movie. Our terrified cries blend with the rolling thunder outside.

Another flash of lightning, and the old man is no longer as if he vanished into the pitch-black darkness surrounding us.

"D-d-did you guys see that?" I manage to ask, breathless with fear.

"I did," Ryan confirms, his voice quivering.

"That's the man who was in my bedroom a couple of nights ago," Julie says, her eyes wide with recognition. "I'd know that face anywhere." She turns to me and asks, "Taylor, was that him? The man you saw a couple of nights ago?"

"To be perfectly honest," I admit, "I only caught a glimpse of him in the flash of light."

"Could it have been him?" Julie presses on.

"It's possible," I concede reluctantly, "but honestly? I don't know."

"Do you guys remember Arabella's warning?" Julie asks, her voice barely audible over the howling wind. "She said, *There are others in the house, and two of them mean to harm.*" Her words hang in the air like an empty noose, sending chills down our spines as we stand frozen in the darkness.

The storm outside rages on—a blinding flash of lightning briefly illuminates the room, followed by a deafening clap of thunder shaking us to our core. Rain lashes against the windows like a barrage of pebbles, while the wind screams like a wounded animal, rattling the panes and raising goosebumps on our skin.

Julie breaks the tenseness in the air, her voice trembling just above a whisper. "What if the face we just saw belongs to one of those who want to harm us?"

"What did we do to provoke a ghost into wanting to hurt us?" I ask, my mind racing with possibilities.

"I need to reach out to Arabella again after the stuff that's happened tonight," Julie insists. "And we should dig deeper into those journals—there might be hidden clues."

"Where's Duncan?" I suddenly realize, scanning for him.

"I thought he was with you guys," Julie replies.

"Nope, he wasn't with us," Ryan chimes in.

"He couldn't have slept through this crazy storm," I exclaim.

As we exchange worried glances, it becomes clear: something's not right.

"I'll go check on him," Ryan exclaims, urgently dashing upstairs. He flicks on every light switch along the way, and to our surprise, the lights spring to life.

Julie and I exchange worried glances as we wait anxiously at the base of the stairs for Ryan's report. The air is thick with tension and the smell of rain.

Suddenly, Ryan's excited voice comes from upstairs. "Guys, Duncan's not in his room. It looks like his bed has been slept in, but he's nowhere to be found. His keys and wallet are on the nightstand. Where could he be?"

DAY SIX
(very early)

Sunday, May 20, 2018

Dumbfounded, I scratch my head, trying to make sense of the situation. "Duncan has to be around here somewhere," I insist, glancing nervously out the window at the raging thunderstorm. "People don't vanish into thin air, especially not during an intense storm like this."

"I don't know," Ryan replies. "Weird things have been happening ever since we stepped foot inside this house."

"Maybe it's the house causing all this chaos," Julie adds, her eyes wide with intrigue.

"Come on, guys," I say, rolling my eyes. "Do you honestly believe there's something supernatural about this old place?"

"Look at the evidence," Ryan counters. "We've seen what could be ghosts—Julie even had a conversation with one. We've heard strange noises echoing throughout the house, and now Duncan is missing? What more do you need to believe this house might be haunted or cursed?"

"Cursed?" I echo incredulously. "Who said anything about curses?"

"Enough, boys," Julie interjects, stepping boldly between Ryan and me. "Right now, our top priority is finding Duncan."

Ryan nods in agreement, his expression shifting from frustration to focus. "You're right," he says.

"Absolutely, but how do we best approach this?" I ask.

"Should we split up to search for him?" Ryan's suggestion hangs in the air.

Julie shakes her head thoughtfully. "I'm not sure splitting up is the best idea," she counters. "Given the circumstances, it might be safer for us to stick together. We have no idea why Duncan is missing, and staying close could protect all of us."

"Honestly, I think you guys are overreacting," Ryan says. "Duncan's probably hiding somewhere, waiting to jump out to scare us. You know how he loves his pranks."

"I have a strange feeling that's not the case," Julie says.

"What do you think is going on?" Ryan asks.

"I'm not entirely sure," Julie admits, her voice tinged with concern. "But something feels off... as if there's more to this than just a prank."

"Alright, team, it's time to stop standing around and start searching for Duncan," I say. "Talking isn't getting us anywhere."

"Where do we even begin?" Julie asks.

"How about we tackle this from the bottom up? Let's start in the basement and work our way to the attic," I suggest.

"Sounds like a solid plan," Ryan agrees.

"Wait a minute—shouldn't we grab more flashlights first?" Julie proposes.

"Great idea," I reply. "Considering this storm, there's a good chance the power might go out again. We need to be prepared just in case."

Cautiously, we descend the rickety, creaking stairs into the shadowy bowels of the musty basement. Our flashlight beams crisscross like frantic searchlights, scanning the darkness for Duncan. The air is thick with an unsettling mix of decay and the lingering odor from the ceramic container I accidentally knocked over earlier—seriously, how can something smell so bad for so long? The only sounds breaking the oppressive silence are the groaning wood of the stairs under our weight, and the howling wind of the storm outside.

After a fruitless search of the cellar, we return to the first floor. Every room searched feels like a new opportunity, but our hearts race urgently as we call out for Duncan. Where can he possibly be?

"He's got to be around here somewhere," Ryan insists, his voice tinged with worry.

"We still have several more floors to check," Julie replies, her optimism ringing through the parlor like a beacon of hope.

It's unusual to see the settee unoccupied—Beau claimed it as his personal throne when we first arrived. I picture him curled up under the blankets on Ryan's and my bed, looking cozy and content. Earlier, however, he seemed rattled, as if he'd seen a ghost. Could it be he caught a glimpse of something otherworldly lurking in the house? There are times when I wish he could talk—this is one of those times.

After searching every room of the house, we make our way to the attic. I let out a silent sigh of relief upon discovering the bats that usually call this place home are out on their nightly feeding —I guess they feed even when it rains. Since moving in, I hadn't spotted any of these winged creatures. Still, the unmistakable scent of their droppings hit me like a wave of nostalgia, reminding me of the carefree days spent under the bridge by the woods where Ryan and I used to play as kids.

Countless bats hanging by their feet snoozing during the day beneath that bridge. Ryan loved to tease me back then, claiming those bats were vampires waiting to swoop down at any moment. How gullible did he think I was? Did he really believe I'd confuse bats with bloodsucking vampires?

Standing here now, surrounded by memories and echoes of laughter, it's hard not to smile at how easily we fell for each other's jokes back then.

Alright, enough strolling down memory lane. Let's get back to the search for Duncan, shall we?

"Ew! What's that horrible smell?" Julie gasps, quickly pulling her nightgown over her nose in a futile attempt to shield herself from the heavy stench.

"It's probably nothing," I reply nonchalantly, secretly praying she won't freak out when she discovers my little secret—I have bats in my belfry.

"But it smells awful," Julie insists, her face twisting in pure disgust. "You should call someone to find out what's causing that smell."

"Oh, it's just bat droppings," Ryan casually comments.

Thanks a lot, Rye, I think to myself. I wanted to keep this under wraps, and now he's gone and spilled the beans. Surprisingly, Julie handles the news better than I anticipated. I sigh in silent relief as she maintains her composure amidst this smelly predicament.

"Wait—Rye—did you say bats? As in rats with wings?" Julie exclaims, flailing her arms as if swatting at invisible creatures flapping about her hair.

Oops, maybe I spoke too soon.

"There's no way I'm staying in the same house as those disgusting flying creatures," she proclaims with a dramatic flair.

"So, where do you plan on sleeping?" I chuckle. "In Duncan's SUV?"

"I'll move my things into the garage apartment," Julie retorts.

"Hold on a second," Ryan interjects, raising a serious eyebrow. "We haven't searched the apartment."

"That's right," I nod in agreement.

Ryan and I have been to the garage apartment before, but this is Julie's first time stepping inside. As we enter, she gasps, "Wow, this place is nice. It's so much cozier than the house."

"I couldn't agree more," Ryan replies with a smile.

Just then, I hear a faint knocking sound. "Hey, do you guys hear that?" I ask.

"I don't hear anything," Ryan says.

"What are we listening for?" Julie asks.

"Be quiet and listen," I insist.

In the anxious silence I tilt my head to listen closely. The tension in the air thickens as we strain our ears to pinpoint the source of the sound.

Ryan walks over to the first bedroom door and bravely opens

it, only to find the room empty—no sign of anything unusual. But when he swings open the second door, we gasp, our hearts race at what we see: Duncan is on the bed with bulging eyes, bound by ropes and his mouth sealed shut with duct tape.

"Oh my gosh," Julie gasps, her eyes wide with disbelief as Ryan and I quickly free Duncan from his restraints.

"Duncan, listen up," I say, trying to keep the mood light despite the tension. "I'm going to count to three, and then I'm ripping off this duct tape. Ready? One... two... three."

"JesusFreakingChrist!" Duncan yells, his hands cup his face. "That hurt like a mother..."

"I'm really sorry about that, Duncan," I reply sheepishly. "Duct tape and a day's worth of beard growth, don't exactly go well together."

"Who did this to you?" Julie asks.

"I have no idea," Duncan mutters, rubbing his red wrists where the rope had been tightly knotted.

"How long have you been here?" Ryan asks.

"Honestly, I don't know," Duncan admits, confusion in his voice.

"How did you end up here?" Ryan presses.

"I'm clueless about that too," Duncan replies, rubbing his temples as if trying to massage away the fog clouding his mind.

"Do you need an aspirin?" Julie asks, concern flickering in her eyes.

"No, I'm fine," Duncan assures her, continuing to knead his temples. "I can't remember what happened. Everything's a blur —it's like I blanked out or something."

"Don't worry about it," Julie says as she sits beside him, gently clasping his hands. "What matters is that we found you and you're okay."

"Thanks, guys, for coming to my rescue," Duncan replies with a weak smile. "By the way, where am I, anyway?"

"Oh right, you haven't been here before," I say. "You're in the apartment above the garage."

"Funny," Duncan responds. "I don't remember coming out

here."

"You must have had the key because it was still in the keyhole," Ryan points out.

"What key?" Duncan replies. "I don't know anything about a key."

Perplexed, a wave of bewilderment washes over us as Ryan, Julie, and I exchange uncertain glances.

"But we saw the key in the door," I insist, trying to make sense of the situation. "Rye even mentioned it being in the lock when we arrived. We were surprised to find it there."

Duncan shakes his head vigorously. "I'm sorry, but I honestly don't know anything about a key."

"Well, it's not important," I say. "We'll figure it out eventually."

Ryan's stomach growls loudly, breaking the tension. "I don't know about you guys," he declares dramatically, "but after all that searching, I've worked up an appetite."

Julie rolls her eyes. "Rye," she scolds, her tone more teasing than serious, "you're always hungry. Don't you ever think about anything other than food?"

"Honestly," I interject with a playful grin, "Rye can't seem to fit anything else into that tiny brain of his—there isn't enough room for more than one thought at a time."

"Ha ha," Ryan shoots back sarcastically, "that's so hilarious —I forgot to laugh."

Everyone bursts into laughter—except for Ryan.

"Now that Rye has brought it up," I say, "I could go for some breakfast, too."

As we stroll back to the main house, I can't help but wonder what's next for us. I have a sneaking suspicion we've only experienced the tip of the iceberg. I'm afraid we're in for more unexplained drama in the coming days and nights. But for now, I'm putting tonight's drama aside and enjoying the moment, admiring the dawn breaking across the eastern sky. The remnants of last night's storm have painted the horizon with delicate streaks of silver-lined pink and gray clouds. The air is refreshingly crisp and cool, hinting at a fresh start and a brand-new day here in the house on the hill overlooking Lost Creek Junction.

Dale Thele

DAY SIX
(later)

Sunday, May 20, 2018

Seated around the kitchen table, we're wrapped in the warm, inviting aroma of freshly brewed coffee. The harrowing night may be behind us, but an unsettling feeling still clings to me. Why us? What actually happened with Duncan—was it sleepwalking, a ghostly abduction, or something beyond my comprehension? I'm desperate for answers, yearning to unravel this mystery. Did we inadvertently offend the spirits? How can we make amends? These questions swirl in my head like a restless storm.

"Funny isn't it? Just a few days ago, we were staunch skeptics when it came to ghosts, and now look at us," Ryan muses, shaking his head in disbelief.

"I'm not entirely convinced ghosts are behind what's been happening," Duncan counters.

"Do you have a better explanation?" Julie interjects, peering over her coffee mug.

"Alright, for argument's sake, let's say it's ghosts. But I'm not jumping to conclusions until we have more proof," Duncan insists.

"Ghosts. It's amusing how quickly our perspectives can shift," Julie chuckles as she sets her mug down on the table. "I'm dying to know what triggered whatever happened last night. Was it an angry ghost, or maybe multiple spirits? What did Duncan do to deserve this?" Julie's curiosity surfaces as she studies Duncan's face. "Duncan, are you feeling alright?"

"I'm fine," Duncan replies, seemingly lost in thought. "But

something I read in that old journal Taylor found has me concerned."

"Concerned?" I ask. "What can a two-hundred-year-old journal have to do with what we're dealing with right now?"

Duncan leans forward, his eyes bright with intensity. "I think it might shed light on our current situation."

Ryan chimes in, echoing my confusion. "Really? How is that even possible?"

"What we're experiencing could be the consequences from events that took place two centuries ago," Duncan explains.

Julie's expression shifts from curiosity to confusion. "You've lost me."

"I might be able to clarify this," Duncan says as he stands up, determination etched on his face. "Taylor, where did you put that old journal?"

"It's on my nightstand, why?" I ask.

"Do you mind if I get it?" Duncan asks.

"No, not at all, help yourself," I tell him.

"Don't anyone move, I'll be right back, let me grab the journal from Taylor's room." He heads upstairs, leaving us in a swirl of uncertainty.

Ryan crosses his arms. "Are you starting to think Duncan's lost a few marbles after whatever happened to him last night? He's not making sense."

"I think we owe it to him to hear him out," Julie counters. "After all, he's the smartest one among us. Who knows—he might have come across something important."

"Even so," Ryan retorts, shaking his head doubtfully, "he's not acting like the Duncan we know."

"Alright then, Mr. Rational. How would you act after being abducted by what could have been a ghost?" Julie challenges.

Ryan shrugs but falls silent, clearly still wrestling with doubt.

As we wait for Duncan's return, I wonder: Could the past actually hold answers for our present?

Duncan strides back into the kitchen, clutching the journal in his hands, excitement shining on his face. "Check this out," he exclaims, flipping through the worn pages with an eager grin. "I found something intriguing here. Let me read a passage, and I'd appreciate your thoughts."

He pauses to scan the text before continuing, "This section doesn't have a date, which makes me think some pages might be missing—there are definitely gaps in the story. It's like piecing together a puzzle. I suspect this entry was written sometime in the mid-1800s because it resembles the Texas Gold Rush era. This is what it says:

> "In the year 1853, two of the most irritable and cantankerous gold miners in all of Sacramento Valley, California, packed their gear and headed to Texas, where gold had reportedly been discovered. Ezekiel and Abrahim originally settled in Sacramento Valley during the California Gold Rush of 1848. Upon hearing the news of gold in Texas, the two old-timers packed up and set their sights southeast in search of their fortune. They eventually settled near the Colorado River in what would later become the township of Lost Creek."

"Wait, what?" Ryan asks. "What does that have to do with us?"

Duncan leans in, his eyes sparkling with excitement. "Don't you see? Their story is more than just history—it's a lesson for us today."

Ryan shakes his head, still puzzled. "I mean, seriously, I don't understand how a pair of miners from two hundred years ago is relevant to us now."

"Hang tight," Duncan insists. "Trust me—it'll all make sense soon. You'll see. Listen to this:

> "Years went by as Ezekiel and Abrahim labored in the gold mine owned by the Widow Scruggs. The mine yielded only modest deposits, with no significant finds. Nevertheless, the two men remained steadfast in their belief their fortune

would eventually come from the Scruggs Lost Creek mine.

"At this point, more pages are missing," Duncan remarks. "But the story gets interesting when it resumes after the missing pages." He continues reading:

"There was an accident at the mine that resulted in the deaths of both Ezekiel and Abrahim when a portion of the mine collapsed. Days later, the townspeople retrieved the bodies of the two men from the rubble. However, the following day, as preparations were being made for their burial, the bodies went missing. The townsfolk claimed Widow Scruggs, who lived in a large stone castle on the hill was rumored to be a witch, had stolen the bodies during the night. According to the tale, the witch extracted the souls of Ezekiel and Abrahim, cursed them, and imprisoned them in a ceramic jar, which she placed on the back shelf of her fruit cellar.

"Is any of this starting to sound familiar?" Duncan asks, his gaze piercing as he scans each of us.

"On top of a hill?" Ryan echoes, furrowing his brow. "In a stone castle?"

Julie swallows hard, her voice shaky. "If you ask me, that sounds somewhat like this house."

I feel tension rising in my throat as I join the conversation. "What about that ceramic jar? I knocked over a ceramic container on a shelf in the fruit cellar just the other day." My words tumble out, and suddenly, my mouth feels parched.

As we exchange glances filled with uncertainty and intrigue, it becomes clear something eerie is unfolding around us.

Duncan continues reading:

"The curse placed on Ezekiel and Abrahim by the witch could only be broken if someone disturbed the ceramic jar. Breaking the seal of the jar would set the souls of Ezekiel and Abrahim free to haunt the living."

"Um," Julie starts, her voice filled with uncertainty, "Taylor, did you release the souls of those two miners?"

"I swear I didn't see anything spill from the container," I plead, my heart racing. "Sure, the basement was dark, but I'm pretty sure the jar was empty—except for that awful smell."

Duncan raises an eyebrow. "You know, if you guys want to put your faith in a two-hundred-year-old journal about witches, curses, and ghosts—"

"No way," Ryan interrupts. "This is a load of crap. It has to be local folklore."

"But think about it, Rye," Julie counters. "This so-called folklore could be our key to unraveling the bizarre happenings in this house. We can't brush aside these eerie similarities."

"I'm not buying into some flimsy fairy tale to explain the strange things going on here," Ryan insists.

As tension hangs in the air like a kite trapped in the wind, one thing becomes clear: whether it's ghostly legends or mere coincidence, something unsettling is at play within these walls.

Duncan continues to read:

"Additionally, the witch cast a curse on Lost Creek, creating an invisible barrier around the town's borders preventing ghosts from escaping, forever trapping their spirits inside its limits."

"Don't stop now," I urge. "Keep reading—this is getting interesting."

Duncan shakes his head, disappointment flickering in his eyes. "That's all there is," he replies, flipping the journal open to reveal no more pages. "This journal captures moments from the past. It's not a magical crystal ball predicting what's coming next."

Frustration builds within me as I come to terms with the limitations of our current resources. There must be something we can do. Then, I get an idea:

"Julie, can you contact that girl ghost?" I ask.

"You mean Arabella?" Julie responds.

"Yeah, that's her," I confirm. "Do you think she can shed some light on this mystery? Maybe she could help us figure out what we're up against?"

"I can certainly try," Julie replies with determination. "I can't promise anything, though."

As the sun dips below the horizon and the stars begin to twinkle, we gather in the dining room, filled with the warm glow of flickering candles. The air is infused with their sweet scent, while the soft rustling of the drapes adds a gentle backdrop to our gathering. We form a circle around the table, fingers intertwined, our hearts racing with anticipation as we prepare for what lies ahead—a séance intended to connect us with Arabella.

"Arabella," Julie's voice cuts through the candlelit ambiance like a whispering breeze, "we invoke your presence, unseen one. Reveal yourself and share your wisdom with us." Her words hang in the air, thick with mystery and possibility.

Ryan leans in close to me and whispers, "*Invoke your presence?* Seriously? Where did she pick up this weird lingo?" His words mirror the skepticism I feel as well.

"Shh!" I hiss at Ryan, fully aware of Julie's commanding aura as her intense gaze sweeps over us like an eagle surveying its territory. "I didn't start it," I protest. "It was Rye. I swear."

Julie shoots me a look so icy it could freeze molten lava.

Ryan snickers.

With every fiber of my being, I want to slap the crap out of him for embarrassing me.

"Arabella," Julie calls out again, her voice laced with urgency. "Can you hear me?"

Only the flickering candles respond, their flames dancing in the dim light.

"Arabella," she repeats, a hint of desperation creeping into her tone.

"Yes," comes a soft, breathy voice from the shadows. "I hear you."

With bated breath, Julie presses on. "Arabella, please tell us —are we being haunted by ghosts named Ezekiel and Abrahim?"

A pause hangs in the air before Arabella's small voice answers, "Yes."

Julie's heart races as she continues, "But why do they haunt us?"

Arabella explains in a child-like whisper, sending cold chills through our bones, "Ezekiel and Abrahim have yet to realize they have been imprisoned for two centuries. Together, they seek vengeance against the one who confined them in a container hidden within the shadows of the root cellar."

Dale Thele

DAY EIGHT

Tuesday, May 22, 2018

Over a leisurely breakfast filled with copious amounts of caffeine, we make a pact to leave yesterday's chaos behind. Goodbye to curses, angry spirits, and spells—hello to the glittering promise of a gold mine and dreams of striking it rich.

"How do we go about reopening a gold mine that's been closed for ages?" Ryan asks.

"I'm guessing it'll take quite a bit of equipment," Julie suggests, absentmindedly twirling a lock of her hair as she considers the challenges ahead.

"Yeah, but the kind of gear we need doesn't come cheap," Ryan counters. "We're talking serious cash—money we don't have. Unless…" He shoots an eyebrow-raising glance at both Julie and Duncan.

"No way am I asking my parents for that kind of money," Julie replies, shaking her head. "I can already hear daddy's response—it wouldn't be pretty."

"My ol' man wouldn't put up money for something as uncertain as a gold mine," Duncan states. "He only invests in sure bets."

"Couldn't we manually mine the gold until we save enough to buy the necessary equipment?" Julie suggests, letting go of her hair and leaning forward with renewed enthusiasm.

"Digging up that much gold by hand would take forever," Ryan exclaims, absentmindedly tracing his finger around the rim of his coffee mug.

Duncan, however, seems completely absorbed in his laptop screen.

"What are you working on?" I ask.

"I'm researching something," he replies, his fingers flying over the keys.

"What kind of research?" I press, leaning closer to catch a glimpse of the screen which has him so captivated.

Duncan raises his head, though his eyes remain glued to the screen. "Well," he starts, "I have some news that might not sit well with you guys."

"What do you mean?" Ryan's finger halts mid-circle around the mug, a hint of concern creeping into his voice.

"I've come across something interesting," Duncan continues. "The journal mentions a gold discovery right here in this area. But... my online findings suggest otherwise. This could be a problem."

Duncan reads aloud from the Internet:

"In 1853, a brief one-column article published in the New York Times reported the discovery of gold in the newly established state of Texas. This single article was enough to ignite a surge of prospectors hoping to strike it rich, launching what would later be known as the Texas Gold Rush. However, no further documentation was produced regarding the discovery of gold in Texas. According to unofficial reports, there were stories of small gold nuggets found in the Texas Hill Country along the Colorado River, but these claims were never substantiated."

"What do you mean by *substantiated*?" Julie asks, her brow furrowed in confusion.

"Well," Duncan replies with a sigh, "the claims about the gold were never properly vetted or verified."

Julie's eyes narrow. "Are you saying our gold mine is a dud?"

Before Duncan can respond, Ryan jumps in, visibly agitated. "First of all, the gold mine doesn't belong to *us*—it belongs to Taylor," he points out.

"Duly noted," Julie nods in agreement.

Duncan continues, "And here's the kicker: I've found some information online suggesting the entire Texas Gold Rush might have been a fabrication. The New York Times reported on it as if it were gospel truth, but it seems people flocked to Texas based on hype rather than hard facts. So, Taylor's gold mine may not be everything we dreamed it would be."

Julie's eyes widen in disbelief, while Ryan's face falls in disappointment as the weight of Duncan's words sinks in. It's hard for all of us to wrap our heads around this shocking news.

"But what about the gold nugget I found in the mine?" Ryan pleads, clinging to hope.

"Small gold nuggets have been turning up in this part of Texas for years," Duncan shares. "But there's never been any record of a significant gold vein discovered here, which suggests a vein might not exist after all."

"Aw, man," Julie sighs. "I thought we were onto something big, you know?"

"Well," I add, "the dream was exciting while it lasted."

"I'm sorry, Taylor," Julie says.

"Hey," I reassure her, "I came here with nothing. Now look at what I've got—a spacious house, some land to call my own, and even a Jeep (okay, so it's not running yet). Plus, I've got spending money in my pocket. How is that disappointing?"

"I guess when you put it that way, it's not so bad," Julie concedes.

"And don't worry about the Jeep," Ryan jumps in. "We'll have it purring like a kitten before summer's over. By August, you'll be cruising back to Austin in style—you can count on it."

"*We'll have it running?*" Duncan raises an eyebrow at Ryan's enthusiasm, clearly skeptical of his friend's capabilities.

"Alright, I stand corrected," Ryan relents with a nervous chuckle. "Duncan, you're officially in charge of getting Taylor's Jeep up and running."

"Duncan," I ask, "have you found any more details online about the gold rush?"

"I've scoured countless websites, but they all seem to tell the same story. In the mid-1800s, many people—us included—were led to believe Texas was rich in gold, just waiting to be discovered," Duncan explains.

"But what could motivate someone to publish an article like that, especially knowing it wasn't true?" Julie asks.

"There are several reasons why the reporter might not have questioned the credibility of their source," Duncan explains. "In those days, verifying information from distant places was no easy task. Newspapers were under immense pressure to deliver fresh news quickly. This often meant sacrificing accuracy for speed, which was a risky gamble. Sometimes, it was more advantageous for them to publish an unverified story and correct it later rather than wait weeks for confirmation."

"Or maybe that article was a clever ploy to boost newspaper sales?" I suggest.

Ryan enthusiastically replies, "An article like that would definitely make me buy a paper."

"Rye, you fall for anything that promises easy money," Duncan teases.

"I do not," Ryan protests.

"Alright, boys, let's dial it down a notch," Julie interjects. "It's almost lunchtime. What's everyone craving?"

"I'm in the mood for peanut butter and jelly sandwiches," Ryan announces with a satisfied grin.

Julie raises an eyebrow, clearly amused. "Don't you ever get tired of PB&J? It seems like every time I turn around, you're making another PB&J sandwich."

"Hey now," Ryan retorts, "What's wrong with that? I love PB&J. They're quick to make and don't leave a mess—what's not to love?"

"You know what?" Duncan jumps in. "You've convinced me —I could go for a PB&J too."

Julie chuckles and shakes her head. "See what you started, Rye? Taylor, you're the independent thinker here—don't let them sway you. What do you want for lunch?"

With a cheeky smile, I reply, "PB&J sounds great to me."

Julie throws her hands up in exasperation. "You boys are incorrigible! Absolutely incorrigible!" she laughs as she walks away.

As the sun begins to set, we gather on the front porch in wicker chairs, soaking in the evening's magic. The air is thick with anticipation, and a cool breeze occasionally sweeps by, carrying the earthy scent of rain. The warm glow of the setting sun bathes us in golden light, creating a cozy atmosphere that feels almost like a warm hug. In the distance, dark storm clouds build in the southern sky, their ominous presence contrasting sharply with the fading warmth. Fiery lightning tentacles dance between the clouds, illuminating the scene with an electric energy.

"Hey, guys," Julie calls out, her gaze fixed on the crossword puzzle in her hands. "I could really use your help."

"Absolutely," Ryan responds. "What's got you stuck?"

"I'm totally stumped on this crossword," Julie sighs.

"How many letters does it have?" Ryan asks.

"Five letters," Julie replies, chewing the pencil eraser in thought.

"And what's the clue?" Ryan inquires.

"*I can be solid or I can be liquid. What am I?*" Julie reads aloud, her voice filled with anticipation.

Silence hangs in the air as Ryan scratches his head and Julie chews on her pencil, both deep in concentration.

Duncan pipes up from across the porch, still absorbed in his magazine. "Water."

Ryan turns to him. "What did you say?"

Duncan looks up with a smirk. "Water. It's the answer to Julie's crossword."

Julie beams and replies, "Hey, that works. Thanks a ton."

"Hold on there, Mr. Smarty Pants," Ryan challenges. "How can water be solid?"

Duncan chuckles and confidently replies, "Easy—when it's frozen."

Ryan shoots a menacing scowl at Duncan, who shrugs it off

with a smirk, engrossed in his magazine as if the world around him has faded away.

Meanwhile, the birds chatter in their whimsical language, filling the treetops with playful nonsense. As the sun dips below the horizon, their chatter gradually subsides. In their place, crickets emerge to serenade us with their soothing evening melody—a rhythmic song which ebbs and flows like the breath of a sleeping baby in a crib.

Then, without warning, everything shifts. The cheerful chirping of the crickets abruptly ceases; even the leaves seem to hold their breath. The cool breeze that once danced around us vanishes, replaced by an unsettling heaviness which lingers in the air, as if nature itself has pressed pause on our peaceful evening.

"Is this what they mean by *the calm before the storm*?" Ryan wonders aloud, glancing nervously at the ominous clouds gathering overhead.

"Guys, maybe we should think about going inside," Julie suggests, her eyes wide with concern as she tracks the darkening sky. "That storm is getting dangerously close."

"Yeah, that's probably a good idea," Duncan agrees, echoing Julie's worry while still trying to maintain his laid-back demeanor.

Urgent energy propels us from our wicker chairs, and Beau follows, leaving his spot on the porch floor. Together, we scurry indoors, leaving behind the eerie stillness of what had earlier been a serene evening.

Suddenly, a fierce southern wind sends dirt and leaves swirling like a violently shaken snow globe. We slam the door shut behind us, sealing ourselves off from the approaching storm. Outside, the wind transforms into a relentless howl, hurling grains of sand and leaves against the window panes in a merciless assault. The sky churns with ominous storm clouds— dark and seething—boiling with a malevolent energy that feels almost alive. A sickly green glow engulfs everything in its path. Inside the house, it's still and stuffy.

"Where on earth did that wind come from?" Ryan exclaims, disbelief lacing his voice as he flicks on a table lamp. "It came out of nowhere."

"That was absolutely insane," Julie adds, sinking into a plush parlor chair seeking refuge from the tempest outside. She reaches for a lamp on the end table, further illuminating the room in light amid the brewing storm.

Just then, another gust of wind slams against the house, bringing with it an unmistakable scent of rain and the sound of crackling thunder.

With an air of casual relief, Beau clumsily hops onto the settee, which creaks under his weight as he searches beneath the cushions for his favorite stick. His eyes light up when he finds it. He settles down, contentedly holding the stick under his front paws and letting out a deep sigh of satisfaction. The rest of us find our places in various empty chairs around the room—our sanctuary amid nature's fury outside.

"It's called an outflow boundary," Duncan says, not looking up from the magazine he's reading.

"What are you mumbling about?" Ryan replies, looking puzzled at Duncan.

"Dude, you asked where that sudden gust of wind came from," Duncan explains, his tone casual yet informative. "It's a wall of wind created by a strong thunderstorm dumping rain."

As he speaks, the lights flicker ominously, and the wicker chairs on the porch jostle against each other like bumper cars in an amusement park ride. The storm's fierce winds send the chairs crashing to the far end of the porch, their clattering drowned by the howling tempest outside.

I get up from my chair and go to the window. My breath fogs the glass pane as I take in nature's fury. "By golly, it's really coming down out there," I exclaim.

Suddenly, a blinding flash of lightning illuminates the living room like a strobe light at a concert, causing everyone to jump. The tension is thick; we're all on edge as the storm rages on.

"One thousand one," I count aloud, my voice barely rising

above the rumble of thunder. "One thousand two. One thousand three—"

Suddenly, a deafening thunder clash shakes the entire house, rattling the windows. "Whoa, that was close," I exclaim, glancing at my friends with wide eyes. "I'd say that lightning bolt was about three miles away."

"How do you know that?" Julie asks.

"It's simple," Ryan jumps in. "You count the seconds after you see the lightning flash. The number of seconds between the lightning and the thunder gives you a pretty good idea of how far away the lightning struck."

Duncan raises a skeptical eyebrow. "I'm not sure that's accurate or even scientific."

Ryan shrugs. "Well, it's more of a game than anything else."

I nod in agreement, memories flooding back. "As kids, Rye and I played that game during thunderstorms all the time. It helped take our minds off the severity of the storm."

Outside, rain pounds fiercely against the house like an army assaulting its fortress, water pelting from every direction as if trying to break through to our safe haven.

"Wow," I marvel, listening to nature's angry symphony. "Can you believe how hard it's coming down?"

Ryan strolls over to the window, curiosity lighting up his face. He pulls back the sheer drapes and peers outside. "Hey, guys," he exclaims. "That's not rain hitting the house—it's hail. And it's coming down like crazy."

The unexpected change in the weather catches everyone off guard.

Julie and I spring to our feet, eager to catch a glimpse of the spectacle unfolding outside. My lawn is transforming into a winter wonderland, with ice balls tumbling from the sky and bouncing like super balls on the grass.

"Careful near the windows," Duncan calls out with a grin. "Those hailstones sound pretty big. You wouldn't want to be on the receiving end if one of them crashes through the glass."

Taking Duncan's warning to heart, we step back, allowing the drapes to fall into place. A sudden thunderclap startles us, causing us to jump into the safety of our chairs, as if the music has suddenly stopped in a game of musical chairs.

The lights flicker momentarily.

"I don't know about all of you," Duncan says, stretching his arms wide and letting out an exaggerated yawn. "But I'm officially calling it a night."

"I'm right behind you," Julie says, glancing outside at the relentless storm. "This weather doesn't seem to be in any hurry to ease up."

"It's odd, though," I interject. "This is the first storm we've had since arriving in Lost Creek Junction that's hit before nightfall."

"Now that you mention it, you're absolutely right," Julie nods. "All the previous storms happened late at night."

"Storms don't distinguish between day and night," Duncan shrugs.

"I was just agreeing with Taylor's observation," Julie retorts, her tone laced with frustration.

Just then, the lights flicker before going out, plunging the house into darkness.

"Taylor, are you ready to call it a night?" Ryan asks, his voice rising above the rumble of the storm. "There's not much we can do in the dark."

"I can light some candles," Julie suggests.

"Nah," I reply, giving Ryan's leg a gentle pat. "I think I'm ready to call it a day."

Beau lifts his head briefly, eyes heavy with sleep as he lets out a soft sigh before settling back down—subtly signaling time for everyone to shut up and go to bed.

Waking up in the middle of the night, I'm jolted from my dreams by what I initially think is a clap of thunder. But as I blink into the darkness, it becomes clear the storm has passed. Only distant flashes of lightning flicker faintly against the walls, and the occasional muffled rumble of thunder rolls in from afar

—so softly it hardly seems loud enough to have stirred me. Whatever disrupted my sleep must not have been too alarming after all. I snuggle closer to Ryan, who mumbles something incoherent in his sleep—a comforting sound making me feel safe and warm.

Just as I'm about to drift back into dreamland, a loud crash echoes from the hallway outside our closed bedroom door.

"What was that?" a half-asleep Ryan demands, springing up in bed like a tightly wound jack-in-the-box.

"I don't know," I reply, my heart pounding.

A scratching sound at the door sends a chill through us, as if the gnarled fingers of an evil spirit are trying to claw their way in. We freeze, our hearts pounding like drums in our chests. The air is thick with dread, and each breath feels like an uphill battle as we brace ourselves for whatever horror might come next.

Suddenly, an anxious bark shatters the tension, followed by frantic pawing on the other side of the closed door.

I recognize the bark, "Oh, it's just Beau," relief washing over me.

Ryan climbs out of bed and opens the door just enough for Beau to rush in. Beau enthusiastically pushes the door wider, knocking Ryan to the floor. In an instant, he leaps onto the bed and burrows beneath the covers, whimpering like a scared child.

Meanwhile, Ryan is left stunned on the floor. "What's gotten into *your* dog?" he nearly yells as he scrambles back to his feet. It's amusing how he always refers to Beau as *my dog* when he's annoyed.

"Something must have spooked him," I say, gently stroking Beau's trembling hindquarters protruding from beneath the blankets.

Just then—out of nowhere—Ryan is flung across the room as if an invisible giant picks him up and tosses him aside. He lands heavy on the far end of the room.

A chilling, hideous laugh reverberates through our bedroom, sending shivers down my spine. Suddenly, a greenish, glowing head of an old man floats ominously in the air between Ryan and me. I'm frozen in fear, too terrified to scream. My heart races in my throat, and my breath comes in frantic gasps.

Panicking, Ryan dives under a heavy table, seeking refuge from the eerie, cackling apparition.

"What's going on in there?" Duncan's groggy voice cuts through the tension as he approaches our open bedroom door from the hall.

Before I can respond, the bedroom door slams shut with a deafening thud, rattling the framed pictures on the walls.

"Are you guys alright?" Duncan calls out from behind the closed door, his voice laced with anxiety as he tries to open it. But it won't budge. "Unlock the door," Duncan orders.

"The door isn't locked," I barely manage to whisper, my voice trembling as the floating head bursts into laughter. It drifts ever closer until it's inches from my face. Its glowing eyes stare into mine. Nose to nose, I feel its glowing orange-red gaze bore into my soul. I can't move—I'm frozen in place, paralyzed by fear. The head bellows loudly, and then—poof!—it vanishes without a trace, just as abruptly as it appeared.

"Step away from the door," Duncan declares with determination. "I'm going to kick it down."

To everyone's surprise, the door swings open on its own without any help from Ryan or me. Duncan stands awkwardly in the open doorway, ready for action but caught off guard. From beneath the table, Ryan emerges like a frightened rabbit, his eyes wide with terror.

"What's going on?" Julie asks, joining Duncan in the hall. She takes in the scene: a bewildered Duncan in a frozen Karate Kid pose, a terrified Ryan crawling across the floor like a frightened toddler, and me—too embarrassed to leave my bed after wetting my pajamas.

"J-J-Julie," I stammer, "I'm not entirely sure what just happened, but I think we may have been visited by either Ezekiel or Abrahim. Whoever it was didn't seem too happy with us." My heart races as I continue, "It felt like it was trying to scare us. Something—or someone—definitely wants us out of this house."

"Does this mean we're going back to Austin?" Julie asks.

"Not if I have anything to say about it. This is my house, and I refuse to let some cheesy ghostly tricks scare me away. Who's with me?" I ask.

"You can count on me. I've got your back," Duncan assures me with a confident nod.

"Taylor, since I rode here in Duncan's SUV, I guess I'm stuck here for now," Ryan adds.

"Count me in too, guys," Julie adds.

Beau pokes his head out from under the bed covers and barks, as if to say, *I'm in. We're in this together.*

DAY NINE

Wednesday, May 23, 2018

Ryan slumps at the kitchen table, his bleary eyes locked onto an empty cereal bowl that seems to mock him. Sighing, he reaches for the box of Captain Crinkle breakfast cereal. The box is a riot of whimsy, a delightful cacophony of colors and shapes, featuring a vibrant illustration of grainy circular-shaped cereal sprinkled with playful, multi-colored marshmallow chunks fashioned in pirate themes: a glimmering treasure chest, a swashbuckling ship, a cheeky parrot, and even a jaunty pirate hat. Ryan tilts the box, envisioning his favorite cereal cascading into the bowl like Niagara Falls. But nothing happens. He tilts it again—still nothing. Frustration bubbles up as he leans in closer to inspect the empty depths of the box. "Who ate all my cereal?" he growls, shooting a suspicious glare at Duncan across the table.

"Honestly," Duncan replies with an exaggerated shake of his head, "I can't understand how you can eat such sugary crap. That stuff will rot your teeth."

"I'll have you know I've been eating this cereal since I was a kid," Ryan shoots back.

"Clearly, you haven't outgrown that phase," Duncan quips with a smirk.

"Who pissed in your Cheerios?" Ryan retorts.

"My cereal is perfectly fine, thank you very much," Duncan responds before scooping up a generous spoonful of his breakfast—milk dripping enticingly from the edges—and offers it to Ryan like a peace offering.

After refilling my coffee mug, I plop into my chair between

Ryan and Duncan. Ryan looks utterly defeated—his head is buried in his hands, elbows resting on the table as he gazes miserably into his empty cereal bowl.

"What's up, Rye? You look as if you've lost your best friend," I say.

"I might as well have," Ryan replies, his voice quivering with emotion. "I'm out of Captain Crinkle cereal."

"Oh, is that all?" I chuckle, reaching for the Cheerios box. "Don't worry—we'll grab more Captain Crinkle when we go into town today."

"Did someone mention *going to town?*" Julie asks as she breezes into the kitchen.

"If I can convince my good ol' pal and buddy Duncan to drive us," I stroke Duncan's ego.

"What's the occasion?" Julie asks.

"Rye's facing a cereal emergency," I joke. "He's out of Captain Crinkle."

"Seriously?" Julie laughs. "That's the big emergency?"

"Yes, that and I want to pay Mr. Andrews a visit," I explain. "I have a feeling he knows more about this house's history than he's let on."

"Good idea," Duncan nods. "Maybe he can shed some light on what's been going on around here."

"It's definitely worth a shot," I add.

Our mornings usually begin in a familiar way, but today is different—Ryan is in a foul mood because he can't have his favorite cereal for breakfast. It's funny how something as trivial as breakfast cereal can completely turn someone's day upside down. Meanwhile, Duncan, our little escape artist, has vanished again. Sometimes I consider tying a bell around his neck just to keep track of him.

As the kitchen buzzes with activity, Beau saunters in, yawning before heading for the back door. He gently paws at it, and I open the door like his personal doorman. But then he pauses at the threshold, staring intently at the dewy lawn outside. He glances back at me and then at the wet grass, clearly torn—will he step out or retreat? With a determined shake of his head, he gingerly ventures onto the dew covered grass, carefully lifting each paw as if he's a tightrope walker. As his confidence grows and his paws get soggier, he suddenly bolts toward a tree in the yard. It seems nature's call outweighs any aversion of getting his paws wet. I chuckle at his antics; it's such an entertaining blend of caution and determination.

Next comes Julie and our post-breakfast routine. She washes while I dry—it's like we've choreographed a little dance in the kitchen. We've developed a comforting rhythm that allows us to work seamlessly as a team.

Later in the morning, the four of us are sitting in the waiting room of Mr. Andrews' downtown law office. It's a familiar place, but this time there's something different—a receptionist sits at the previously vacant desk. She seems as if she's recently stepped out of a drill sergeant's training camp. Her cranky demeanor is evident; she'd rather be anywhere else than dealing with clients.

"Alright, Mr. Greene," she barks, her gravelly smokers voice cuts through the stillness like a hatchet. "Mr. Andrews will see you now."

With that announcement, we rise to go into Mr. Andrews' office.

"Excuse me. I specifically said *Mr. Greene* may go in," she adds sharply, her tone reminiscent of a strict schoolmarm wielding a wooden ruler ready to enforce discipline. I half-expect her to rap our knuckles and sentence us to a week of detention.

Julie, Duncan, and Ryan exchange glances filled with disappointment and mild annoyance as they reluctantly return to their chairs. I gently tap on Mr. Andrews' office door.

"Come in," a voice calls from within. As I step inside, I'm greeted by Mr. Andrews' warm smile—his eyes twinkling with recognition as if he's eagerly awaiting my arrival. Instantly, I feel at ease under his welcoming gaze.

"Hello, my boy," he says, extending his hand toward me like an old friend ready for an embrace. "How can I help you today?"

Our handshake feels solid and reassuring—just what I need before I dive into the concerns that have brought us together again.

"Well," I begin, "I was hoping you could tell me some history about my house."

Mr. Andrews raises an eyebrow, his curiosity piqued. "What specifically interests you?" he asks.

Taking a deep breath, I jump into the core of the issue. "Strange things have been happening—things that defy explanation." I pause to gauge his reaction. "There are strange sounds at night, objects moving on their own, and eerie shadows which seem to dance around corners... It's all a bit much." I choose my words carefully; revealing too much might make me sound irrational.

Mr. Andrews' face drains of color, and his gaze darts nervously around the room. "Um," he stutters, tugging at his shirt collar as if trying to loosen an invisible noose. "Could you provide more details?"

I decide to lay it all out. "I think my house is haunted," I say earnestly. "I've heard whispers in the dead of night and seen shadows shifting where there shouldn't be any. It feels like I'm the main target of whatever this is. But honestly? I have no idea what might have stirred up this negative energy."

Sitting in silence, I feel the weight of my words hanging in the air.

Visibly shaken, Mr. Andrews returns to his chair behind the desk, the wood and leather creak beneath him as he settles in. The sound rings through the room like a warning bell. He clears his throat and takes a nervous sip from the glass perched on his cluttered mahogany desk, wiping beads of sweat from his brow with a monogrammed handkerchief.

Something about Mr. Andrews suggests he knows more than

he's letting on. But why all the secrecy?

After another sip of water, he finally begins to speak. "My boy, you must understand your house has a rich and tumultuous history dating back two centuries," he states, placing the drinking glass down on his desk.

"That raises the question—why does it look so well-preserved?" I interject, unable to contain my curiosity. "The house seems practically new as if this were the 19th century. This question has been gnawing at me."

"I can explain," Mr. Andrews replies, nervously wiping sweat from his neck while glancing around as if searching for an escape route.

"I lean back, arms crossed. "I'm all ears," I challenge. I'm not leaving this office until I uncover every last detail of the mysteries surrounding my house. The truth is out there, and I'm determined to find it.

"Okay," Mr. Andrews concedes after quickly gulping the rest of his water. He pauses for a moment before refilling his glass from the pitcher on the desk. "Where do I begin?"

"Most people agree the beginning is a good place to start," I say.

Mr. Andrews shifts uncomfortably, his unease evident as he struggles to maintain his composure. My questions seem to have struck a nerve, creating more discomfort for him. After a moment's hesitation, he finally responds, "You're an outsider, and outsiders aren't privy to certain things."

"But I'm a homeowner," I counter. "That no longer makes me an outsider."

"True enough," he concedes. "But the information you're asking for is reserved exclusively for longtime residents." He dabs his neck with a damp handkerchief he dipped into his drinking glass—an odd gesture adding to the tension in the air.

"Excuse me," I assert, feeling empowered by my status as a property owner. "I may not have lived here long, but being a resident grants me access to this so-called privileged information, doesn't it?"

He hesitates before replying, "I suppose you have a point... But you must promise never to tell anyone I shared this information with you. Some of what I'm about to reveal is meant only for established residents of Lost Creek Junction." His eyes dart around as if checking for eavesdroppers. "There are listening ears everywhere," he warns in a hushed tone. "You never know who might be listening or who they might report back to."

"Thank you," I reply, my curiosity growing as I eagerly await Mr. Andrews to reveal this so-called privileged information.

"*The House on the Hill,*" Mr. Andrews begins, "is what locals have affectionately called your home for the past two centuries. It was built by retired Navy General Samuel T. Scruggs during the Texas Gold Rush—a time when Lost Creek was merely a tent city filled with hopeful prospectors chasing their dreams of gold. After dedicating his life to service, the General and his wife sought to retire in what would eventually become known as *The Texas Hill Country.*"

"Where did they live before moving to Texas?" I inquire.

"The Scruggs family originally hailed from Boston, Massachusetts," he explains. "There, the General oversaw operations at the Boston Naval Yard. Upon retirement, he and his wife decided to settle in Texas and he commissioned the construction of their dream home on a parcel of land purchased from a Yankee solicitor. The house was crafted from granite hauled in from Austin and native sandstone quarried right from the hill where the magnificent four-story mansion still stands today."

"The stonework alone must have taken forever," I exclaim, imagining the hard work required to build such an impressive structure, which is now my house.

"Your house stands as a testament to artistry and perseverance. Its intricate masonry carvings took three painstaking years to complete. However, that was just the beginning. After another two years of meticulous work, the interior was only half finished when the General and his wife left their home in Massachusetts for a new life in Texas. With their belongings packed onto horse-drawn wagons, they set off for their journey. Yet fate had other plans. Barely one week into their travels, tragedy struck when the General was bitten by a rattlesnake. Despite desperate attempts to save him, he passed away, days later, leaving his wife a widow. This sudden loss cast a heavy shadow over her journey. However, even amidst her grief, the General's widow demonstrated incredible resilience as she continued on to Texas."

"Women in those days were strong individuals," I remark.

"Yes, they were remarkable," Mr. Andrews agrees with a nod. "When she finally arrived at her new home, she was still in mourning. Following the customs of her time, the widow wore all black—complete with a heavy veil beneath a wide-brimmed hat obscuring her face. Rarely did she step outside—instead, she relied on servants to run errands and handle chores. The grand house was eerily quiet, void of lively parties or afternoon teas. The draperies remained tightly drawn both day and night, shrouding the lady of the house in mystery for everyone in Lost Creek. Whispers and rumors swirled around town like autumn leaves caught in the wind, but the widow never bothered to address them or reveal herself."

"Did she remain a recluse?" I ask.

"Yes, to the best of my knowledge," Mr. Andrews replies. "As time passed, the stories surrounding her grew more elaborate and sensational. By the time of her passing, the townsfolk had made her out to be a figure that legends are made of—a witch rumored to dabble in the dark arts. According to local lore, not long before her death, she had a fierce disagreement with two old miners over the rights to her Lost Creek gold mine. It is said she cursed the mine in retaliation, causing it to collapse and entomb those two unfortunate miners who dared to cross her."

"That was quite a dramatic turn of events," I remark.

Mr. Andrews leans in closer and drops his voice to a conspiratorial whisper. "The miners perished in the mine collapse, and it was several days before their bodies were recovered. When the townsfolk went to give them a proper burial, their bodies were nowhere to be found. Legend has it that a witch placed a curse on their souls, trapping them within a ceramic jar to prevent further disturbances. Imagine their spirits confined until someone dares to open or break that jar—only then would they be free to haunt the living."

He continues with an air of mystery, "To ensure that these restless spirits wouldn't wander too far if released, the witch cast one final spell—an invisible barrier preventing all Lost Creek souls of the dead from crossing beyond the township's borders. This spell effectively traps all ghostly entities within the city limits for eternity."

"I have to say, that's a lot more information than I expected," I exclaim.

"Well," Mr. Andrews replies with a knowing smile, "there's a wealth of history tucked away in that old house of yours—more than I can possibly share in just one morning."

I can't resist sharing our own discovery with him. "We found an old handwritten journal in the house telling a story strikingly similar to what you've just described. Do you think there's any truth to the legend?"

Mr. Andrews leans back thoughtfully and says, "Son, I wasn't around in the 1800s to witness those events firsthand. But imagine if there is a kernel of truth hidden within those tales. What are the chances a ceramic jar actually existed? And if the seal is broken, what if it released two ghosts?"

I nod earnestly. "There is indeed a jar."

His eyes widen in disbelief, "Did I hear you correctly? Are you saying there's an actual jar?"

"Yes," I confirm, recalling the moment vividly. "I accidentally knocked it off a shelf in the cellar, and the lid came off."

"Did anything spill from the jar?" Mr. Andrews asks.

"I didn't see anything, but there was a terrible odor that came from the open container."

Mr. Andrews raises an eyebrow, intrigued. "Can I ask, when did the strange happenings in your house start?"

"That very night after I knocked over the jar," I reply.

He leans closer, urgency creeping into his voice. "Did you notice anything odd before the seal was broken? Like unexplained things happening in the house?"

"No, sir, nothing at all," I assure him.

"Since breaking the seal," Mr. Andrews probes further, "have you encountered any apparitions?"

"Are you asking if we've seen ghosts?" I clarify with a hint of nervous laughter.

Mr. Andrews nods, his expression serious yet curious.

"Yes, sir, we've seen two old men who might be ghosts. And Julie summoned a little girl during a séance," I say, noticing the worry etched on Mr. Andrews' face.

"I'd wager my last dollar," Mr. Andrews replies, "those two elderly gentlemen are the souls of those two miners trapped in that ceramic container by the General's widow. They're rumored to be Ezekiel and Abraham—known for their deceitful ways and cantankerous dispositions. And let's not forget about the widow —she wasn't exactly a saint either. Legend says before the miners met their tragic fate, she sold them the gold mine. That's why they were working there when disaster struck. But according to the story, after sealing their souls away, the widow slyly put her own name back on the deed."

"What a sneaky bitch," I mutter under my breath.

Mr. Andrews leans closer, his expression grave. "I'm sharing this with you because it might explain why these ghosts have taken an interest in you."

My mind spins with confusion. "I'm not sure I follow," I admit.

His eyes widen as he connects the dots. "Don't you get it? The ghosts don't realize they've been trapped in that ceramic container for two centuries. To them, it's still the 1800s, and in their eyes, ol' lady Scruggs is their enemy."

"So, are you saying the ghosts of those two dead miners have a grudge against Mrs. Scruggs?"

Mr. Andrews nods gravely, his expression serious. "I strongly advise caution if I were in your position, they may believe that you and your friends are protecting the Scruggs lady" he says, his words hanging in the air. "Angry ghosts should not be taken lightly."

"I'm not afraid of ghosts," I scoff, trying to mask my unease with false bravado. "What harm can they do to me?" I ask as a rhetorical question, not wanting an answer.

His tone shifts, becoming more intense. "Son, if I were you, I'd watch my back. Angered spirits can perform extraordinary feats."

My blood suddenly runs cold as the hair on my arms stands on end. "Like... kidnapping someone?"

"That wouldn't surprise me one bit," Mr. Andrews replies cautiously. "Angry ghosts are unpredictable and unstable—you never know what they might do next." He leans in closer and asks, "Son, have any of your friends gone missing?"

"No—absolutely not, sir," I exclaim, shaking my head fervently, not wanting him to know about Duncan's disappearance to the garage apartment.

"I mentioned kidnapping as an example. I didn't mean anything by it," I say.

I have to tread carefully around Mr. Andrews—he has an uncanny ability to read me like an open book. There's no way I'm revealing I've witnessed firsthand what angry ghosts are capable of—those experiences are mine alone.

"Earlier," Mr. Andrews continues thoughtfully, "didn't you ask something about your house and how it stays looking so new?"

"Absolutely, sir," I reply. "What's the story behind that?"

Mr. Andrews leans in, his eyes sparkling with intrigue. "Remember when I told you about how people flocked to Lost Creek in search of gold?"

"Yes, sir, I remember," I confirm.

"Well, buckle up because I'm about to take you on a journey

back to the 1800s—when Lost Creek was a thriving mining town. This place was once alive with the hustle and bustle of miners seeking their fortunes. But it wasn't all gold and glory—tragedy often struck, as numerous mining accidents claimed lives. The unfortunate souls who perished were buried nearby, but here's where the legend comes in: when these spirits attempted to cross over into the afterlife, they found themselves trapped at the town limits due to a curse. As a result, Lost Creek became a haven of restless ghosts—so many they began colliding into one another. Imagine a town overflowing with wandering spirits."

"Oh my," I exclaim, captivated by this haunting narrative.

"One night, long ago, Mr. Andrews continues dramatically, "the townsfolk gathered for an extended town meeting where they delved deeply into discussions about these spectral residents. As the hours ticked by into dawn, they finally reached a pivotal decision altering the destinies of both the living and the dead in Lost Creek."

"What happened next?" I ask.

"During that meeting, a surprising revelation emerged: the ghosts of Lost Creek cherished their town just as much as the living residents did. This shared affection inspired the spirits to take on a unique commitment—to help maintain and care for Lost Creek. They agreed to handle essential repairs and upkeep, ensuring the buildings' interiors and exteriors remained in excellent condition. The female ghosts volunteered for domestic duties, tackling chores like making beds, washing dishes, sweeping, dusting, and more. Thanks to their ghostly assistance, the living residents had extra time to enjoy with family and friends. It was a win-win situation for everyone involved—the dearly departed and those still living in Lost Creek."

"What?" I exclaim in disbelief. "Are you suggesting there could be hundreds, if not thousands, of ghosts haunting Lost Creek Junction? The only spirits I've encountered are maybe those two you mentioned—Ezekiel and Abraham. Trust me—they were anything but friendly. And there's that girl ghost...

Adriana or something like that—Julie's ghost friend."

In the quaint town of Lost Creek Junction, where history whispers through the streets and friendly spirits roam, Mr. Andrews offers a fascinating glimpse into its supernatural charm. "Most ghosts here are quite amiable," he shares with a knowing smile. "Of course, like any community, there are a few bad apples lurking about." He continues, "While these benevolent spirits are always around us, they won't reveal themselves unless you invite them to do so."

Intrigued, I connect the dots. "That explains how the ghosts keep everything looking so pristine," I muse aloud. "Just look at the widow's house—it's perfectly preserved as if we've stepped back in time."

However, Mr. Andrews raises a cautionary finger. "You should know that the locals fiercely protect their unique bond with these resident ghosts. They tend to discourage tourists from poking around and are often tight-lipped about their spectral inhabitants, considering them an essential part of their cultural heritage."

Nodding in understanding, I realize what he meant by *privileged information*—the town's ghostly secrets. "When we first arrived in town," I recall, "the grocery clerk warned my house was haunted. She claimed she wouldn't step inside my house for any amount of money. At the time, it felt like an attempt to scare us off since we were staunch non-believers. But maybe things have changed..."

Mr. Andrews shifts in his chair, his expression turning serious. "There's one more thing you need to know: the town's financial situation is teetering on the brink of disaster. Without new residents and businesses moving in, Lost Creek Junction could face a grim future that might see it become a ghost town in every sense of the word. In the not so distant future, residents may have no choice but to leave their homes."

"What will become of the ghosts?" I ask.

"They will be stuck here," Mr. Andrews replies. "Trapped within the town's limits, they will become prisoners in a true ghost town—a fate none of us would wish on our worst enemy."

Dale Thele

DAY NINE
(later)

Wednesday, May 23, 2018

Back at the house, during a late lunch, I'm barely able to contain my excitement as I share Mr. Andrews's incredible insights about my house and the history of Lost Creek Junction with my friends. "Guess what? Mr. Andrews told me about the origins of this house," I announce, practically bouncing in my seat. "This was the very first house built in Lost Creek Junction."

"Wait, are you saying this house is actually two hundred years old?" Julie gasps.

"Exactly," I confirm with an enthusiastic nod.

"I know it's old, but I never imagined it's actually two hundred years old. I thought *two hundred years* was a joke—a random number because the house is old," Julie says, shaking her head in disbelief.

"Did Mr. Andrews say anything about why ghosts haunt this house?" Ryan asks.

"Oh, he definitely did," I reply.

"Well, what are you waiting for?" Ryan asks. "What did he say?"

I take a deep breath and reveal, "Mr. Andrews mentioned two specific spirits named Ezekiel and Abrahim." As I continue, my friend's faces light up with intrigue. "It turns out they have unresolved issues they're determined to settle."

"You mean like a grudge?" Julie asks.

"Hold on. Let me start from the beginning," I say, eager to weave together the threads of this haunting tale. "What I'm about to tell you will explain everything that's happened in this house since we arrived."

"You have our full attention," Ryan assures me.

"Before this house even existed," I begin, "there was just a sprawling tent city where hopeful souls gathered to chase their dreams during the Texas Gold Rush."

"So," Ryan turns to Duncan, "there really was a Texas Gold Rush."

"Did you think I made it up?" Duncan replies. "Of course there was a Texas Gold Rush."

"Alright, I believe you," Ryan concedes.

"Can I get back to my story now?" I ask, glancing between them for approval.

"The floor is yours," Ryan says with an encouraging nod.

"Go ahead, man," Duncan adds.

I continue, "There was once a retired Navy General named Scruggs who lived in Massachusetts. One day, he came across a newspaper article about the discovery of gold in Texas and became captivated by the idea of moving here."

"Was he rich?" Ryan asks.

"It seems this Scruggs fellow managed to accumulate quite a nest egg during his time working for the Navy," I say, recalling Mr. Andrews' captivating tale. While I might not remember every detail, I can't help but add a bit of flair as I share the story. After all, it's unlikely my friends will catch on to my creative embellishments. A little imagination never hurt anyone, right? Just between you and me, let's keep this our little secret.

"With his hard-earned savings, General Scruggs made a bold move and purchased a sprawling piece of land that would eventually be known as Lost Creek Junction. He bought it sight unseen from a solicitor in Boston. Once he secured the property, he commissioned an impressive mansion to be built at the crest of a hill. The contractor estimated it would take five years to complete this grand project."

"Five years? Isn't that a long time to build a house?" Julie interjects.

"Back then, things took longer to build," Ryan replies matter-of-factly.

"If you guys don't mind," Duncan chimes in, "will you let Taylor tell his story?"

"As the mansion neared completion," I continue, "Scruggs and his wife packed their belongings into horse-drawn wagons and set off for Texas. But fate had other plans—tragically, halfway through their journey, the retired general was bitten by a rattlesnake and died before they reached their new home. Despite her heart-wrenching loss, Mrs. Scruggs was determined to honor her late husband's dream. She pressed on to Lost Creek with unwavering resolve, intent on spending her remaining years in the magnificent mansion he had built for her."

"Broads were sure gutsy back in those days," Ryan remarks, a hint of admiration in his voice.

"You know what?" I say. "I said something similar to Mr. Andrews."

Julie shakes her head and counters, "I think it was less about being gutsy and more about sheer necessity."

"What makes you say that?" Ryan asks.

"Think about her situation," Julie begins. "When her husband passed away, she found herself without a roof over her head. There she was, on the endless plains, exposed to the elements, with wild animals, thieves and hostile Indians as potential threats. But if she completed the journey to Texas and settled into the house her husband had built, she'd find refuge in a growing town where supplies were within reach. Moving to Texas wasn't just a choice—it was her best chance at survival."

Ryan nods in understanding. "That definitely puts things into perspective."

"So she moved into that grand mansion commissioned by her late husband," I say.

"And she lived happily ever after," Duncan smirks. "The end."

"Not so fast," I interject. "This story is just beginning."

"What do you mean by that?" Duncan asks.

"There's more to the story," I explain.

"Tell us, did the widow find love again in Lost Creek? Did she remarry?" Julie asks.

I chuckle at her curiosity. "Would you stop trying to turn this into a Harlequin Romance? Let me finish the story. As a widow, she wore the traditional black—complete with a thick veil and a wide-brimmed hat—leading locals to whisper she was some sort of witch. She kept her window curtains drawn tight, avoided social gatherings like they were the plague, and relied on her staff for errands and supplies. The townsfolk never saw the widow in person, only her shadow moving in the upstairs windows."

"What an eccentric old lady," Duncan acknowledges.

"According to Mr. Andrews," I continue, "she was no ordinary widow—she was a shrewd businesswoman with a talent for making deals. Take her gold mine, for instance, which was fully operational but hadn't turned a profit. She cleverly managed to swindle two dubious miners, Ezekiel and Abrahim, into buying it from her. These miners were not only suspicious characters but also inseparable as Siamese twins, always seen together as if they were connected at the hip."

Duncan chuckles, "If you ask me, the widow and those two miners were quite the trio—they were made for each other."

But I shake my head solemnly. "Believe it or not, things took a dark turn nobody saw coming. After the sale of the mine, disaster struck when it collapsed, trapping Ezekiel and Abrahim inside. The townspeople banded together like heroes in a storybook, digging tirelessly through the rubble to rescue them —even though those miners weren't exactly adored figures in town. Tragically, when they finally unearthed the miners' bodies, it was too late—they'd already perished. Plans for a proper burial were underway when shock rippled through the community—the bodies mysteriously vanished before they could be laid to rest."

"What happened to the bodies?" Julie asks.

"Well," I reply, leaning in as if sharing a secret, "Mr.

Andrews claims the widow took them for herself. She didn't just decapitate the bodies—she extracted their souls, cursed them, and somehow trapped those very souls inside a small ceramic container. And get this—she hid it deep within her fruit cellar. Legend has it that their bodies were never found."

"Oh my gosh," Julie gasps, her eyes wide with disbelief. "She actually was a witch."

"With the two dead miners out of the way," I say, "she cleverly changed the deed of the gold mine back into her name while pocketing the dead miners' money."

"What a horrible woman," Julie exclaims, shaking her head in disgust.

"I thought so too," I say. "But that's just scratching the surface of this tale."

"What else happened?" Julie leans closer, eager for more.

"The witch cast another curse on the town itself," I explain. "She created an invisible barrier around Lost Creek that prevented any ghosts from crossing over to the other side— trapping all spirits inside forever."

Julie's expression shifts to one of realization.

"If what you're saying is true," Ryan interjects thoughtfully, "then Widow Scruggs ensured Ezekiel and Abrahim could never escape Lost Creek—even if they somehow broke free from that ceramic prison."

"Exactly," Julie adds, piecing it together. "So no ghost can ever escape this curse... right?"

"That's my understanding," I affirm.

"Is there any way to break the curse placed on the miners?" Duncan asks.

I pause for a moment, recalling Mr. Andrews' words. "If the seal on the ceramic container holding the trapped souls of Ezekiel and Abrahim is ever broken," I explain, "they'd be freed —but only within the city limits of Lost Creek Junction. They can't venture beyond that."

"Holy crap," Julie exclaims, her eyes widening in disbelief. "Do you realize what you just said? It's almost identical to what

Duncan read to us from that old journal."

"Exactly. Thank you for catching on, Julie," I reply, relieved someone else sees the connection.

"But wait—do you realize what's going on?" Julie asks.

"What's going on?" Ryan asks.

Julie's eyes grow wide as she claps her hands over her mouth in realization. "We're now part of the story—"

"That's right," I confirm. "I'm the one who broke the seal on that ceramic container and unleashed the spirits of Ezekiel and Abrahim."

"You didn't do it on purpose," Ryan reassures me. "It was an accident."

"Accident or not, the fact remains I broke the seal," I admit, a knot tightening in my stomach. "I'm responsible for Ezekiel and Abrahim haunting my house and putting all of us at danger."

"Alright, so what's our next move?" Ryan asks.

"Well," I begin, glancing around as if the walls might be listening and lowering my voice, "Mr. Andrews believes Ezekiel and Abrahim are out for revenge against the Scruggs witch and they might think we're protecting her from them." I take a deep breath before continuing. "Those two spirits have been trapped in that ceramic container for centuries. Things could get serious once they realize what century it is—and discover I now own the mine."

"How much time do you think we have before they catch on?" Duncan asks, his brow furrowed with worry.

"That's hard to say," I reply, shaking my head. "They may already have an inkling of what's going on, but I suspect they don't fully understand it yet. They could be trying to scare us into leaving so they can go after Mrs. Scruggs without interference from us."

"Do you agree with the lawyer the ghosts believe we're protecting her?" Julie asks.

"I'm inclined to go along with Mr. Andrews," I respond.

"I think we might still have time before they figure everything out," Duncan interjects. "I don't think they understand what's going on just yet."

"Guys," Julie suddenly says, her voice trembling slightly, "this whole situation is giving me the creeps."

"You and me both, sister," Ryan agrees, echoing Julie's sentiment. "You and me both."

Julie and I clear the kitchen table after enjoying our *gourmet* meal of bologna sandwiches, crispy potato chips, and hearty pork and beans served on plain white paper plates.

"That stuff you told us about the history of this house was quite interesting," Julie says as she places the condiment jars back in the fridge. "Did Mr. Andrews mention anything else?"

"Actually, he did," I reply, a thrill of excitement coursing through me, mingling with a twinge of hesitation. "During lunch, I wrestled with whether to reveal the entirety of what Mr. Andrews confided in me. After some reflection, I realize it would be prudent to share everything I know with the whole gang."

"Hey, guys," Julie calls from the kitchen, her voice echoing through the house. "Taylor has more to tell us from his meeting with the lawyer."

Duncan strolls in, exuding his signature laid-back vibe as he adjusts his fedora like a character from a classic film. "What's up?" he asks.

"I'm not sure," Julie responds. "Taylor's keeping things under wraps until we're all present."

Ryan strides into the room, "I'm here. What have I missed?"

"For once, nothing at all," Julie snickers. "Would anyone like iced tea?"

Me! Me! Me!" us guys chime in like we're the Bee Gees on tour.

Julie strolls to the counter to prepare iced tea for everyone. Even though her back is to us, she hears every word.

"What's on your mind, Taylor?" Ryan asks.

"Well," I begin, feeling the anticipation in the air, "it has to do with something Mr. Andrews told me—I think you all need to hear this."

"Why do we all need to be here?" Duncan asks.

"It has to do with Lost Creek Junction," I say gravely. "The town is nearly broke."

Ryan frowns. "What does that have to do with us?"

"Plenty," I reply. "If the town goes under, there won't be any businesses left—like a grocery store, for example. Without a grocer there won't be any more Captain Crunch cereal for you, Rye."

"Oh," Ryan exclaims, suddenly enlightened. "I see your point."

"Did Mr. Andrews say why the town is struggling financially?" Duncan asks.

"Yes," I confirm. "The townspeople are resistant to let new businesses move into town, and they drive away potential new residents."

"Just like that cashier at the grocery store who tried her darnedest to scare us off when we first arrived," Julie interjects as she serves glasses of iced tea.

"Exactly," I nod in agreement, taking a glass from Julie.

"But why push away strangers?" Ryan wonders aloud. "What do they gain from it?"

"It all boils down to... ghosts," I reveal.

"Ghosts?" Ryan echoes. "You mean there are more than just the ones we've seen in this house?"

"Rye," Julie says, "weren't you paying attention earlier? Taylor told us about the curse on this town and how those ghosts are trapped here."

"I thought that was a legend," Ryan protests.

"Pull your head out and pay attention," Duncan shoots back.

"We know of at least three ghosts in this house—Ezekiel, Abrahim, and Julie's little friend—but there could be many more lurking around we don't know about," I explain.

"I must be losing my mind," Duncan exclaims in disbelief. "Just days ago, I didn't believe in ghosts. And now you're telling me there could be bunches of them roaming around?"

"Think about it for a moment," I say. "If Mrs. Scruggs cursed this town to keep ghosts from leaving—"

"That means there are tons of ghosts stuck here," Julie adds, wide-eyed.

"Do you remember the first time we stepped foot in this house?" I ask. "Didn't it seem strange how everything was move-in ready? There wasn't any dust on the furniture, the beds were perfectly made with fresh sheets, and even the bathrooms had crisp laundered towels waiting for us."

"Now that you mention it—" Julie replies, her brow furrowing in thought.

"Mr. Andrews must have had a make-ready crew come in before we arrived," Duncan suggests.

"But he didn't know you were coming," I counter. "Not until you guys pulled up in the SUV."

"Honestly, we didn't know we were coming until the last minute, Julie adds."

"So, did this make-ready crew scrub all the windows, repaint and wallpaper every room, clean the rugs, and polish the floors?" I ask. "Everything here feels almost brand new, even though it's two hundred years old. Doesn't any of this seem odd to you?"

Duncan chuckles and concedes, "Okay, you've made your point."

"Wait, are you telling me ghosts actually prepared this house for us?" Julie muses, her eyes darting around the room for spectral visitors. "If that's true, do they stay around to keep things tidy?"

"Maybe, I don't know," I answer. "According to Mr. Andrews, there are hundreds—maybe even thousands—of these spirits. No one knows for sure how many there are. They look after this town and its people, cherishing it as much, if not more, than the living residents do."

"So, let me get this straight," Julie presses. "Are you saying, aside from the occasional glimpses of Ezekiel and Abrahim here in the house, there's an army of invisible ghosts responsible for keeping Lost Creek Junction looking like it hasn't aged a day in two hundred years?"

Ryan grins. "The folks in Lost Creek Junction have it made in the shade. Do these ghosts do everything from mowing lawns to raking leaves and even cleaning gutters?"

"Apparently so," I confirm with a nod.

"With so many trapped spirits floating around," Ryan adds with a chuckle, "this town takes on an entirely new meaning of *ghost town.*"

Julie nods thoughtfully. "It's mind-blowing to think ghosts are maintaining the town, keeping Lost Creek Junction so beautifully preserved."

"What happens to the ghosts if the town goes bankrupt and everyone has to leave?" Duncan asks.

I pause for a moment before responding. "That's a great question. Unless someone can break the curse that's binding them here, those ghosts will likely remain trapped within the city limits."

"Isn't it heartbreaking the ghosts must stay behind?" Julie says, her eyes reflecting disappointment.

"Unfortunately, according to Mr. Andrews, the town has no plan to save Lost Creek Junction, and I was looking forward to spending my summer breaks here," I reply.

Everyone pauses to reflect, or at least I do.

"What's wrong with you guys? We've never backed down from a challenge. If we work together, we can come up with a way to save the town," Julie encourages with a pep talk.

Unified, we brainstorm ideas to rescue Lost Creek Junction. During our discussion, we explore various strategies, each presenting a potential solution for saving the town. As day turns to night, we compile a list of actionable steps which could help restore the town.

Here's a rough draft of what we came up with:

1. Attract tourists to Lost Creek Junction by highlighting its

rich history as an honest-to-goodness ghost town.

2. Offer visitors the chance to experience the excitement of mining for their own gold nuggets in a designated area of the mine.

3. Create engaging attractions that will captivate tourists and encourage them to spend money during their stay.

4. Instead of waiting for a motel to be built, utilize the charm of local residents' homes by transforming them into cozy bed-and-breakfast establishments. This personal touch will provide a more intimate and relaxing experience compared to traditional chain motels.

5. A potential concern is whether the ghosts of Lost Creek will support our efforts. Will they be willing to participate in our plans?

6. Generate excitement for the grand opening by inviting renowned ghost hunters to investigate paranormal activity in Lost Creek Junction. Capture any ghostly encounters on film to promote the town as a genuine ghostly destination.

7. Enhance the visitor experience by partnering with a traveling carnival to provide thrilling rides, games, and delicious carnival food. Establish a long-term agreement to ensure nightly entertainment for tourists.

The next challenge is to persuade the townspeople and resident ghosts to support our unconventional plan for revitalizing their cherished town.

Dale Thele

DAY FIFTEEN

Tuesday, May 29, 2018

It's hard to believe it's been a week since we first came up with our proposal to save Lost Creek Junction. Time has flown as we've polished our presentation in preparation for tonight's pivotal town meeting. I have a lot riding on this proposal—my house, my land, and even a gold mine. If Lost Creek Junction falters, everything I own will slip through my fingers. This isn't just a personal battle; it's a defining moment for all of us in the community. Tonight's public decision will determine whether we stay and fight for this town or pack up and leave everything behind.

Surprisingly, the atmosphere in the house has been relaxed lately. We haven't felt the presence of Ezekiel and Abrahim—the two notorious ghosts who have haunted us—leading us to wonder: what are those two spirits up to? Are they plotting something? We're keeping our eyes peeled, just in case.

Entering the town hall for the urgently called town meeting, we're greeted by a strange sight: the room is packed with living residents and their ghostly counterparts. The spirits, dressed in vintage attire and shimmering like wisps of smoke, create an undeniably eerie atmosphere.

"Holy cow, will you look at the size of this crowd?" Julie exclaims, her eyes darting around the bustling room. "It seems everyone from town is here."

"And all the ghosts, too," Ryan adds, his voice tinged with nervousness. "They're literally everywhere."

"There's no need to be scared," I assure him, trying to keep my own unease at bay.

"How would you know?" Ryan shoots back. "How much experience do you have with ghosts?"

I give him a pointed look which communicates more than words ever could.

"Oh right," he concedes with a sheepish grin. "I guess we've all had our fair share of ghostly encounters since arriving in this town."

"Did any ghost actually hurt us?" I ask.

"Well..." Ryan hesitates, scratching his head. "Remember when I got thrown across the room? My tailbone was sore for days. Since that night, I'm not exactly a fan of ghosts."

"Come on, Rye. It happened one time," I explain. "That ghost wanted us out of the house for its own selfish reasons. The spirits in this room? They have no grudge against us."

Of course, I've neglected to mention to my friends I have an ulterior motive for attending this meeting. While I'm excited to pitch our brilliant idea to save the town, there's another reason has me buzzing with anticipation: I'm hoping to encounter the ghost of the Widow Blackburn. I want to understand the connection we share and why she chose to give me her house. Why me, of all people?

I have so many questions swirling in my mind, and I'm keeping an open mind about the possibility of meeting her spirit. Will she be a friendly ghost like Casper, ready to lend a helping hand? Or will she be more like Scrooge—grumpy and reluctant? Either way, it promises to be quite the adventure. However, let's hope she's not one of those angry spirits like Ezekiel or Abrahim; I'd prefer a chatty ghost over an angry one any day. Here's to hoping for an intriguing encounter that can shed light on both our pasts.

"Will everyone please settle down and grab a seat or find a spot to hover?" A short, rotund man with receding gray hair declares, wielding a gavel like a conductor's baton. He must be the mayor.

The room buzzes with an eclectic mix of living townsfolk and ethereal spirits, all gathered for this urgently called town meeting.

"Did he really just say, *grab a seat or a spot to hover?*" Julie chuckles, her eyes sparkling with mischief.

"I think the latter was for the ghosts' benefit," I reply, barely able to stifle my laughter. "Have you noticed the ghosts hovering against the wall? Their feet don't touch the floor. They're floating about a foot off the ground," I gesture toward the wall where several translucent figures linger.

"By golly, you're right," Julie giggles.

"What in Sam Hill has gotten into you two?" Duncan shoots us an incredulous look, his eyebrows raised in disapproval.

"Oh, it's nothing," I whisper, stifling a snicker.

"Well, you two best zip it. The meeting is starting," Duncan warns in a stern but hushed tone.

"Yes, sir," I respond playfully to Duncan while giving him an exaggerated military hand salute.

"Order! Order!" The portly man at the front of the room bangs his gavel on the table with authority. "I hereby call this meeting of Lost Creek Junction residents—living and deceased —to order."

The room falls dead silent—no pun intended.

"As you all are aware," the Mayor begins, his voice steady but filled with urgency, "our beloved town is facing serious financial difficulties. If we don't act quickly, Lost Creek Junction could lose its status as a legally incorporated town. If that happens, we will all be forced to leave, and our once struggling community will become nothing more than a literal ghost town."

A woman in the crowd raises a hand, "What will happen to the ghosts?"

The Mayor's expression darkens. "Unfortunately," he replies, "the curse cast by the witch means the ghosts are trapped within our town's borders. If Lost Creek Junction ceases to exist, they'll still remain here—lost souls in an empty shell of a town."

Some angered spirits hovering near the walls start swirling restlessly. Their mournful wails fill the air as others swoop above us in a chaotic dance of despair.

"That's not fair to them," someone shouts from the audience.

The Mayor sucks in a deep breath before responding, "No one ever said life—or death—was fair."

Another voice chimes in from the back: "Is it really so hopeless? Is there nothing we can do?"

"There might be hope yet," the Mayor says, his tone shifting. "We have a new resident named Taylor Greene—"

"You mean that big-city kid who moved into the Widow Blackburn's house?" interrupts an irate man from the crowd.

This remark ignites the assembled mass, causing them to grumble among themselves. As tension builds and hangs thick in the air, whispers ripple through the audience, hinting at displeasure of an outsider.

"Dadgummit, hold your horses, folks," the Mayor exclaims, banging his gavel like he's driving a nail into hard lumber. "Before anyone gets all high and mighty and jumps to conclusions, let's give this young man and his friends a chance to speak their piece."

"What if we don't wanna listen to some outsiders?" an angry man in the audience retorts, rising from his chair as if he's about to storm out of the meeting.

"That's your gall-darn prerogative," the Mayor replies, his face flushing with indignation. "But unless you've got a plan to save our town, I strongly suggest you sit down, shut up, and listen to what these kids have to say. This goes for anyone else who might be thinking through their ass or who's too stubborn to listen to four college-educated young people. In my humble opinion, they've come up with a well thought out, practical solution that could make a big difference for our town. So unless you've got something better up your sleeve, I suggest you shut your traps."

A hush falls over the crowd.

"Like I was sayin' before I was so rudely interrupted," the

Mayor continues, glaring at the dissenting man. The man briefly meets the Mayor's gaze before looking down at his worn shoes.

"Let's give a rousing welcome to Taylor Greene and his friends from the University of Texas as they present their innovative idea on how we can save our town," the Mayor announces with enthusiasm that sharply contrasts with the audience's reluctance. He applauds energetically, urging others to join him in applause. But no one joins in.

"Like I said, let's give these young people a warm welcome to Lost Creek Junction," the Mayor insists, his voice filled with frustration as he scans the crowd with a disapproving glare. A few scattered claps echo through the room, but they're weak and lackluster—just enough to cause the Mayor's face to turn a deep shade of crimson. It's clear he's feeling the sting of embarrassment from his constituents' tepid response, especially with me and my friends in attendance.

As Julie, Duncan, Ryan, and I head toward the table at the front of the room, I sense the hostility in the air. The indifference feels heavy, as if I'm anxiously waiting my turn at the gallows.

I swallow hard as I prepare to speak. "Thank you," I begin, my voice squeaky and an octave higher than I prefer. Clearing my throat, I try again. "Thank you, Mr. Mayor and residents of Lost Creek Junction, for having us here tonight." I pause, expecting applause—but all I get in return is the lonely chirp of a cricket in the back of the room. I cough lightly to clear my scratchy throat and take a sip of water. Winning over this tough crowd isn't going to be an easy task. This isn't going like how I'd practiced.

"My name is Taylor Greene," I continue with renewed determination. "I'm a new resident eager to make your lovely town my second home. With two years left until I finish college —unless my career choice requires additional education—I'm excited about what Lost Creek Junction has to offer." I'm bombing and feeling sick to my stomach.

Ryan jumps in like a poolside lifeguard rescuing me from

drowning. "What Taylor means is that we genuinely love this town. Hi everyone, I'm Ryan Bartlett. I'm here alongside my friends Julie Burris and Duncan Campbell because we care deeply about ensuring only good things come for Lost Creek Junction."

Hey, what do you know? Ryan's high school speech classes are certainly paying off.

"Good evening, everyone. My name is Duncan Campbell, and we've developed a plan to ensure Lost Creek Junction doesn't become an asterisked footnote in Texas history books," Duncan states.

"Hi there, I'm Julie Burris," she interjects enthusiastically. "We've come up with a plan that calls for the collaboration of all residents—yes, even those from beyond the grave—to bring this vision to life." She leans forward, her voice steady. "Your involvement is crucial. So before you jump to conclusions, please keep an open mind as we walk you through our ideas."

Suddenly, a voice calls out from the crowd, "When are ya gonna start the presentation? So far, there's been nothin' but a lot of jaw-flappin'."

I nod appreciatively at his eagerness. "Thank you for your patience. Let's dive into our presentation, shall we?" I take a deep breath. "What makes Lost Creek Junction unique? What sets this town apart from any other place on Earth?"

Silence hangs in the air. I feel like I'm speaking into a void.

"Well, I, uh, understand—some of you might be skeptical, and that's perfectly okay." My heart races as I try to connect with the audience. "But I urge you to give me just a moment to share our plan. Think about it—what if this is your last chance to save your town?" I pause again, searching for any signs of engagement in the audience's faces. "So let me ask again: what truly makes Lost Creek Junction special? What gives it its unique charm and character?"

I stand before an unresponsive audience, hoping my words will spark some interest or ignite something—anything.

"Ghosts," I say, breaking the silence by answering my own

question. "You have a genuine ghost town here, complete with real ghosts. Why not embrace that one-of-a-kind charm? All the so-called *ghost towns* I've been to are crumbling relics of the past—empty, falling down buildings with no ghosts in sight. But your town has the incredible potential to transform into a bustling tourist destination, showcasing authentic ghosts. This living ghost town could attract visitors and their open wallets.

"But wait," someone from the audience calls out, skepticism evident in their tone. "Are you suggesting we exploit our ghosts? That doesn't seem right."

"Our plan isn't about taking advantage of them—it's about giving them the freedom to be the playful spirits they truly are." I continue, "You've been holding them back, stifling their natural instinct to spook and delight. Ghosts thrive on scaring people—it's what they do best."

A woman sitting in the front row interjects, her brow furrowed with concern. "But wouldn't scaring visitors defeat our purpose?"

"On the contrary," Duncan adds. "Tourists will flock to Lost Creek Junction expecting a thrill—an encounter with the supernatural. They'll pay good money for a taste of haunting entertainment. Embracing the ghosts will enhance their experience and attract even more visitors. It's a win-win situation for everyone involved."

"You kids make it sound so easy," a man in the crowd interjects, his voice tinged with skepticism.

"To turn this vision into a reality," the Mayor passionately asserts, "we need every community member on board, yes, even our spectral residents."

I take a breath and continue, "But there's more to our proposal. We want to attract tourists to Lost Creek Junction, and step two is keeping them here to spend their money."

A man raises his hand and asks, "How do we do that? Hogtie 'em?"

There's a few giggles from the crowd.

"We don't have nothin' here to make tourists want to stick

around," he continues.

"Oh, but that's where you're mistaken," Duncan chimes in with enthusiasm. "First off, we need places for tourists to stay —"

"That's easier said than done," a woman mutters skeptically. "We don't have no hotel no more."

The audience nods in agreement, their expressions reflecting doubt.

"Wait just a moment. Let me break it down for you," Duncan says. "How many of you have at least one bedroom filled with stuff you never use?"

Slowly but surely, a dozen or so hands rise into the air.

"And how many of you who just raised your hands would be open to welcoming a friend or family member to spent a night or two if that room were cleaned up and presentable?"

All previous hands shoot up.

"Now imagine earning extra cash money by renting out your spare room to tourists. Your solution for tourist lodging is turning those spare rooms into cozy bed-and-breakfasts. Just think about the tax revenue Lost Creek Junction could generate, not to mention the extra money in your pocket."

The atmosphere shifts dramatically; frowns transform into smiles as chatter fills the room with renewed energy.

"But wait, there's more," I exclaim, channeling my inner infomercial host as I work the crowd. "Now, let's explore how we can attract tourists to spend their time and money here in Lost Creek Junction."

"What if we offered rental canoes on the lake?" a man suggests, his eyes sparkling with enthusiasm.

"I could make space in the drugstore for ghost-themed souvenirs," the pharmacist adds.

"I already envision shelves filled with spooky trinkets," I say.

"How about showing the *Ghostbusters* movie at the movie theater?" a shy boy timidly proposes, his voice barely above a whisper.

Laughter erupts around him, and he sadly ducks his head in

embarrassment.

Julie comes to the boy's rescue, "Actually, screening *Ghostbusters* and other ghost themed movies is a great idea."

Thundering applause and cheers erupt, as the little boy's face lights up with joy. I bet his face hurt to smile the next day.

"Why not host a street fair?" a man suggests. "Think carnival rides, games of chance, and all that delicious carnival food."

"I could open part of my gold mine for tourists to try their hand at gold mining," I declare, getting swept up in the momentum.

Another wave of applause washes over the room as excitement buzzes through the crowd. People chat and laugh while happy ghosts flit about overhead, celebrating the ideas.

"People," the Mayor pleads, pounding his gavel with authority. "People, please, let's come to order."

The chatter subsides, and a hush blankets the hall.

"Before proceeding with tonight's proposal, we must first take a vote," he announces with conviction.

A robust man in the crowd bellows, "I make a motion we vote." His voice resonates like thunder.

"I second that motion," another voice agrees.

"The motion carries. Now, let's see where we stand," the Mayor proclaims. "If you're in favor of moving forward with this proposal, please raise your hand."

Instantly, every hand shoots up across the room—Julie's, Ryan's, Duncan's—even all the ghosts—everyone is on board, including the Mayor himself.

"Those opposing the proposal," the Mayor continues, "please raise your hand."

Suddenly, the room goes silent, growing frosty cold as a chilling spectacle unfolds: two ghastly severed heads materialize above the audience—glowing greenish-yellow and floating ominously. The sight sends shivers down spines—gasps ripple through the crowd as fear takes hold. Mothers instinctively pull their children close to their bosoms while others turn away in horror or disgust. Even friendly ghosts at the meeting retreat into shadowy corners, seeking safe refuge.

"We flatly oppose this proposition," one of the floating ghostly heads declares with a booming voice echoing throughout the town hall.

I can't shake the feeling the floating heads, with their ghostly translucence and unsettling glow, must belong to Ezekiel and Abrahim. As for who is who, I honestly can't tell you—I haven't had the pleasure of a proper introduction. I'd be more than happy if they'd disappear for good and never come back.

"Two votes *against* the proposal," the Mayor announces, his voice quivering with nerves. "However, the majority rules," he declares, "the proposal passes." He brings down his gavel with a resounding bang.

In an instant, those furious floating heads dissolve into thin air.

The Mayor clears his throat, gathering himself for what comes next. "First thing in the morning, we'll establish a committee to turn tonight's suggestions into an actionable plan. Is there any other business?" He scans the room for any dissenting voices.

"I make a motion to adjourn," calls a man from the back of the room.

"I second that," another voice calls out, stirring up a wave of enthusiasm.

"The motion carries. I hereby adjourn this town meeting until a later date," the Mayor declares, bringing his gavel down with a satisfying thud.

Suddenly, the hall erupts in a flurry of activity as people engage in animated conversations. Some rush to the front of the room to congratulate us on our proposal, their faces beaming with excitement. Others warmly welcome us to Lost Creek Junction, eager to share their community spirit. A few offer spare bedrooms and their skills to help bring our vision to life. This outpouring of support feels like a breath of fresh air compared to the tense atmosphere we faced at the start of the meeting.

Later in the evening, the four of us gather around the kitchen table at my house. The warm glow of the lights creates a cozy ambiance as we sip our sodas. The conversation buzzes over the evening's events.

"We actually pulled it off," Ryan exclaims, as he takes several gulps from his glass soda bottle.

"*We* didn't pull off anything," Duncan interjects. "It's up to the people of Lost Creek Junction to implement our proposal. We simply got the ball rolling for some much-needed changes around here."

"Hey, that's more than they had before the meeting," Ryan shoots back.

"True," I nod in agreement, but my mind is elsewhere. "Still, I can't shake the bad feeling I have about Ezekiel and Abrahim attending the meeting. That genuinely worries me."

"It's especially concerning they were the only two who opposed the proposition," Julie says.

Duncan shakes his head. "I fear we haven't seen the last of those two. I sense retaliation is coming."

"Why do you say that?" Julie asks.

"I just have this gut feeling," Duncan replies, "those ghostly figures are furious about the mine and won't share their gold with anyone—especially not outsiders like tourists. Isn't that reason enough to be worried? They could sabotage our plan to save this town."

"But they don't own the mine," Ryan points out. "Besides, that mine stuff happened two hundred years ago."

"The past has a way of shaping the present," Duncan remarks, his voice heavy with thought. "They may not own the mine anymore, but their anger and hatred still linger."

"Duncan, they have no idea about the mine's true history," Julie adds. "They've been trapped in a suspended state for two hundred years. When they finally escaped the ceramic container, they probably thought it was just a quick nap and were eager to return to their mine. But here's the kicker—they don't realize it's no longer theirs. That misunderstanding lies at the heart of their discontent—they resent the strangers intruding on what they still believe to be theirs."

"So," I interject, "are you saying once they learn the real story behind the mine, I'll become their next target?"

"What makes you think they haven't already figured it out?" Duncan shoots back, his tone sharp.

"Are you serious?" I ask.

"From where I'm standing," he replies, "it looks like you have a big red X on your back."

"We'll need to stay vigilant to ensure those two decapitated ghost heads don't mess with Taylor," Ryan adds.

Suddenly, I remember Mr. Andrews saying something along those same lines.

A thick silence envelops us as we absorb the weight of our situation.

"Something I don't understand is why on earth would those two ghosts want the mine?" Ryan exclaims, scratching his head in confusion. "They've got heads but no bodies or arms to do the work. What's going on there?"

"I remember those old journal entries mentioning ol' lady Scruggs decapitated those miners after their lifeless bodies were dragged from the mine," Duncan adds.

"Well,"Julie nods thoughtfully, "that explains the heads, at least."

"But why are they just heads?" I ask.

"Maybe the witch needed to attach their souls to a body part," Julie suggests with a shrug.

"But real heads didn't come from that ceramic container," I point out. "They wouldn't have fit."

Duncan sighs, looking contemplative. "We may never fully understand why those ghosts are just heads or what happened to their bodies. All we know is that these ghostly noggins have been snoozing for nearly two hundred years."

"I doubt there'd be much left of their remains after all this time," Julie adds, shaking her head.

"But all this talk doesn't answer my original question," Ryan interjects again, clearly frustrated. "How can those ghost heads operate a mine without arms and legs?"

"They could hire people to work the mine for them," I suggest.

"That makes sense," Ryan replies, furrowing his brow in thought.

"Not to change the subject," Duncan says, "but starting tomorrow morning, we have a lot of work ahead of us—especially with the Mayor and whoever he appoints to the planning committee."

"We should probably get some sleep," Julie adds. "Before we know it, morning will be here."

"Julie's right," Duncan nods in agreement. "We need to be sharp for tomorrow's planning session. See you all bright and early in the morning." With a tip of his fedora, he strides out of the kitchen and heads toward the stairs.

Julie and Ryan follow suit while I head to the parlor to check on Beau before turning in for the night.

"Beau," I call out, "do you need to potty?"

Leaping from the settee like a spring-loaded toy, Beau bolts through the parlor and kitchen as if he's been zapped by lightning. Watching him almost makes me laugh. He's always been good about doing his business outdoors, and I take pride in how quickly he learned to be house-trained as a puppy. The only challenge? Getting him to come back inside afterward. It seems like every weed and bush calls out to him—not to mention those twinkling fireflies he can't resist chasing.

"Come back inside, Beau," I call softly, careful not to disturb the others who are getting ready for bed.

Beau lumbers in, heading straight for his settee. First, he paws at the cushions, burying his snout deep within them while his hindquarters stick up in the air and his tail wags cautiously. Suddenly, his face pops up, proudly displaying his prize stick clutched tightly in his mouth. With a happy plop, he settles down on the settee, sliding the stick beneath his front paws and resting his head on them. A big, drawn-out yawn escapes him.

"Good boy," I praise Beau.

Have you ever wondered why we humans praise our dogs for something as simple as yawning? It's not like they've conquered a mountain or solved a complex puzzle. Yet here we are, rewarding their sleepy antics with cheerful phrases like *Good Boy* or *Good Girl*.

Beau lets out a long sigh echoing my own sense of relief; he's settled in for the night. I shut and lock the back door with a soft click, turn off the lights one by one, and navigate through the darkened house toward the stairs leading to my bed. The air is thick with the earthy scent of damp soil after rain—a reminder of nature's presence—and my breathing feels almost too loud against the stillness surrounding me.

I'm halfway up the familiar stairs, when an eerie moan pierces through the silence—a sound so chilling it seeps through the walls and sends shivers racing up my spine. It lingers in the air like an unsettling ghostly whisper refusing to be ignored.

Beau lets out a high-pitched whine, startling me more than the unexplained moan. He nearly sends me tumbling as he bolts past me, propelled by sheer panic. He races up the stairs, taking them three at a time. Once he reaches the second floor, he sprints straight to Ryan's and my bedroom. In one swift motion, he leaps nose-first onto the bed and burrows under the sheets like a frightened little rabbit, shivering and whining with obvious fear.

"Taylor?" Ryan grumbles irritably, still half-asleep. "What's up with *your dog*?"

"Didn't you hear that moaning?" I shoot back. "At first, I thought it was the wind howling outside, but now I'm not so sure."

"I was in the middle of an awesome dream until *your dog* woke me up," Ryan mutters, clearly annoyed and still sounding groggy. It's classic Ryan—always referring to Beau as *my dog* when he's in one of his moods.

"Go back to sleep," I reply as I climb into bed beside him.

Beau quivers under the sheets at the foot of our bed.

Thankfully, he's stopped whining. I can almost guarantee he'll drift off soon, and then comes the duet.

A duet, you ask? Well, both Ryan and Beau snore like there's no tomorrow. Somehow, they never wake each other—it's like they've formed their own snoring club. Meanwhile, I'm left listening to them snore in perfect harmony all night long.

However, it's not the snoring that's keeping me awake tonight —it's the eerie moaning Beau and I heard earlier. Where did it come from? What could have made that noise? Should I muster the courage to investigate, or is it better to let it slide for now? Since settling into bed, the sound has stopped, but my mind races with possibilities. I'm snug beside Ryan, and honestly, sleep sounds far more appealing than chasing down ghostly noises. As Duncan always says, *It's probably air in the pipes or the wind whistling through the trees.* Right now, though, I'm too tired to care about anything other than sleep.

As I pull the sheet up to my neck for extra protection against whatever might be lurking about, I lie on my back and stare at the shadows dancing ominously on the ceiling—they seem almost sinister. Will I make it through this night unscathed? I wonder. It's moments like these that make me wish I'd made out a will.

Dale Thele

DAY SIXTEEN

Wednesday, May 30, 2018

Julie runs up and down the hall outside our bedrooms like a whirlwind, her voice echoing as she shouts, "Everyone, wake up! We've overslept! We're late! Get dressed! Shake a leg! We need to go!"

I groggily roll over in bed, squinting at the alarm clock through my bleary eyes. My heart sinks when I see the time— it's 11:32. Panic sets in. I leap out of bed and shake Ryan, desperate to rouse him from his sleep, but he remains unresponsive.

"Rye, get up," I urge. "We've overslept. We're late!"

"Five more minutes," Ryan mumbles, still lost in his dreams.

"There's no time," I insist, shaking him harder. "Get up!"

Sitting up in bed, he wipes the sleep from his eyes, and asks drowsily, "What's all the fuss about? It's not like our being a few minutes late will matter."

"Rye," I say, "you don't get it—it's 11:32!"

Ryan freezes mid-yawn, caught between consciousness and dreamland. The realization hits him like a bucket of cold water. "11:32?!" His voice cracks with disbelief, and his eyes widen in horror. "How could you let me sleep so late?"

"I just woke up myself," I reply.

In an instant, Ryan springs out of bed like a coiled spring released—his movements are a blur as he throws on his clothes. The urgency is clear—we both need to move fast.

Beau peeks out from under the bed sheets, watching Ryan and me frantically get dressed. To him, we probably look like a scene from a Charlie Chaplin movie. Not that I've ever seen

Beau watch a Chaplin film, but it seems like the best way to describe the chaotic situation.

Dressed but still half-asleep, Ryan and I rush down the stairs to find Julie and Duncan sitting calmly at the kitchen table, sipping coffee.

"Why on earth are you just sitting there?" I demand. "We're really late!"

Julie giggles.

"What's the matter with you guys?" I insist, my voice rising an octave. "I said we're late!"

"Look at the wall clock," Duncan says.

"It shows 11:32," I exclaim. "But wait, that can't be right."

"Well, it seems your electric alarm clock and the electric kitchen wall clock are in cahoots," Julie quips with a playful smirk.

"It's possible someone may have had a little fun with the breaker switch during the night," Duncan chuckles, his eyes sparkling mischievously.

"You purposely let Rye and me think we were late?" I ask, glaring at Julie and Duncan.

"Let's say we took advantage of the situation to prank you," Julie snickers.

"So, what time is it?" I ask.

Duncan glances at his wristwatch, his eyes widening. "Oh crap, it's 11:58."

For a split second, I freak out, then realize Duncan's milking this prank for all it's worth.

"Alright," I say, "you guys win. So, what time is it really?"

"You've got plenty of time before we leave for the meeting," Duncan replies.

"It's 7:15," says Julie, her voice filled with amusement. "You guys have time for showers and breakfast. And Taylor, can you try to find *two matching* shoes?"

Looking down at my mismatched shoes, I blush.

It's late evening when we return to the house after a seemingly endless day.

"I have to hand it to the Mayor—that planning meeting was long but surprisingly productive," I comment as we step into the parlor, the familiar scent of home wrapping around us like a soft blanket.

"An all-day meeting without a lunch break," Ryan grumbles, his voice tinged with fatigue.

Julie rolls her eyes. "What do you call the fried chicken, potato salad, chocolate cake, and iced tea brought in by the local ladies?" she counters with a grin.

"Yeah, but we still worked through lunch," Ryan sighs, flopping onto the nearest chair.

"I didn't think this day would ever end," Julie exclaims, collapsing into a chair like a marionette whose strings have been cut. With an exhausted exhale, she slips off her shoes and rubs her swollen feet, attempting to ease the ache caused by a long day spent in the wrong type of footwear.

"If you ask me, I'd have preferred sitting through a professor's lecture," Ryan muses. "At least during a lecture, you know it'll end by a certain time."

"What are you complaining about?" I ask. "We got a lot accomplished."

"You're right, Taylor," Ryan concedes.

"Now it's up to the townspeople to pull their weight," Duncan adds.

"But we have our work cut out for us too," I remind them. "We need to get this house ready to become a bed-and-breakfast."

"Taylor, may I say something?" Julie interjects. "I think Beau's trying to get your attention."

Beau nudges my leg and whines.

"Oh my gosh," I exclaim, leaping from my chair in alarm. "Beau hasn't been let outside all day. Don't anyone say anything or move until I get back."

Beau and I dash to the kitchen door. As I swing it open, he bolts outside like a furry rocket. Instead of racing to his favorite tree, he squats just barely outside the door and relieves himself. Feeling guilty for not getting him outside sooner, I grab some of his favorite treats as a peace offering. When he comes back inside, tail wagging furiously, I shower him with rewards. Just like that, our bond feels strong again—like nothing ever happened.

"What have I missed?" I ask, stepping into the parlor with a relieved Beau trotting happily at my side.

"We were brainstorming ideas on how to best turn your house into a bed-and-breakfast," Julie replies.

"I'm all ears," I say, encouraging everyone to share their thoughts.

"How about we move into the garage apartment?" Julie suggests. "That way, we can free up three bedrooms and increase our revenue."

"That's actually a great idea," I nod in agreement, impressed by her creativity.

"But is the garage apartment big enough for all four of us?" Ryan interjects.

"The apartment has two bedrooms. One is a decent size, while the other is a bit smaller. Julie takes the smaller room, and us guys share the larger one. It's a practical solution, don't you think?"

Duncan raises an eyebrow, clearly puzzled. "Wait, are you saying all three of us guys will sleep in one bed?"

I chuckle at his confusion. "No way. Rye and I'll share the bed, and we'll set up a roll-away for you, Duncan."

"I suppose that will work," he nods.

Julie jumps in, curiosity sparkling in her eyes. "So, Taylor, how many bedrooms are on the third floor?"

"There are four bedrooms on the second floor," I explain. "And the layout on the third floor is identical to the second, we're looking at a total of eight bedrooms."

"Eight bedrooms? Wow, that's more than I expected," Julie exclaims.

"How is Julie going to keep up with eight bedrooms?" Ryan

asks.

"*Julie* won't," Julie replies. "Weren't you at today's meeting?"

"Yes, of course I was," Ryan retorts with exaggerated sarcasm.

"The ghosts in this house will help out," I say. "And it wouldn't hurt us to lend a hand too."

"I don't trust Ezekiel or Abrahim," Ryan says, shaking his head with skepticism.

"There are more ghosts in this house than just those two," Julie responds.

"Julie," I interject, "since you've already connected with that little girl ghost—"

"You mean Arabella?" Julie asks, her eyes lighting up.

"That's her," I confirm. "Could you contact her to help sort out the ghost's housekeeping details?"

"I'll try," Julie replies, though uncertainty lingers in her voice. "I've only spoken to her twice, and both times were brief."

"Hey, that's more experience than any of us have had," I encourage her.

"Like I said, I'll try," she assures with a nod.

"Thanks, Julie," I reply. "While you handle the housekeeping with Arabella, us guys will focus on making the front section of the mine safe for tourists."

"Do you truly think letting tourists dig for gold in that old mine is a good idea?" Duncan asks.

I shrug and explain, "I don't see why not. For starters, they won't be *digging* for gold like the miners did in the past. They'll use small hand tools to scrape the walls for tiny flecks of gold— nothing serious. Plus, they'll only venture a short distance inside —we'll block access to the tunnels to keep them safe from potential cave-ins."

"Can someone please remind me why we're opening the mine?" Ryan asks.

"It's my way of giving back to the local economy," I explain. "By creating a unique entertainment experience, we can entice tourists to stay longer in town. My mine has the potential to boost business."

"Why would anyone want to get dirty exploring that old mine?" Ryan questions.

"For the same reason you went into the mine—to find gold," Duncan chimes in.

"Oh, right," Ryan replies, a flicker of realization crossing his face. Sometimes I wonder how many brain cells he's lost from all that pot smoking.

"Hey, is anyone besides me hungry?" Duncan suddenly changes the subject, eager for a distraction related to food.

"Don't look at me," Julie sighs. "I'm too tired to cook anything."

"Julie, you don't have to lift a finger. It's all taken care of," Duncan assures her with a grin.

Julie shoots him a curious look.

"I brought leftover fried chicken and potato salad from today's meeting. It's waiting for us in the back of the SUV."

"Well then," Ryan adds, "what are we waiting for? Bring on the grub."

Later, we're sitting around the kitchen table, stuffed with cold fried chicken and potato salad leftovers.

"I'm so tired—I think I could sleep standing up," Julie says with a dramatic yawn, her eyes barely open.

"Same here," Ryan adds, wiping the remnants of chicken grease from his face with a crumpled paper napkin.

"It's been quite the day," Duncan states, leaning back in his chair and rubbing his stomach.

"If you all pitch in to help me clean up this mess," I suggest with a grin, "we can all hit the hay sooner."

Us guys toss the stripped chicken bones and greasy paper plates into the trash. Julie wipes down the table top. Once our cleanup operation is complete, we head off to our respective beds for the night.

As the lights go out, a silence falls over the house perched on the hill overlooking Lost Creek Junction. But the peace is short-lived. Soon enough, all I hear are Beau and Ryan's simultaneous snores echoing through the quiet house—loud enough to keep me wide awake as I lie in bed, staring at the ceiling—counting those darn sheep. One. Two. Three...

Dale Thele

DAY SEVENTEEN

Thursday, May 31, 2018

It's a gorgeous morning. The sun is shining, the birds are softly chirping, and there isn't a cloud in the sky. I stand by the bedroom window, holding the drapes apart and enjoying the stunning view. Ryan is peacefully sleeping, without his usual snoring—a rare occurrence I'm savoring. I appreciate the profound tranquility of the moment, occasionally interrupted by the creaks and groans of my two-hundred-year-old house.

Suddenly, I'm startled from my peaceful contemplation by the sound of rattling pots and pans coming from the kitchen downstairs. I assume Julie's making breakfast. After dressing, I pad downstairs in my stocking feet.

"Good morning, Duncan," I greet with a cheerful smile.

"Hey," he replies, pouring himself a mug of coffee.

"Where's Julie?" I ask, scanning the kitchen.

"I haven't seen her this morning," he responds.

"That's strange," I comment. "She's usually the first one up."

"I know," Duncan agrees. "It's not like her to sleep in."

"Should I go check on her?" I suggest, pausing before pouring coffee into my mug.

"Nah, let her sleep a bit longer," Duncan advises. "By the way, where's your other half?"

"Still asleep," I answer, taking a seat at the kitchen table.

"Maybe we should start calling Rye *Rip Van Winkle*," Duncan jokes, a playful glint in his eye.

Suddenly, Beau bounds into the kitchen, his paws pattering against the floor and tail wagging like a flag in the breeze. He stops beside the table, looking up at Duncan and me with big, hopeful eyes.

"Speaking of Rip Van Winkle," Duncan chuckles, "your dog deserves an award for being the champion sleeper."

I chuckle and scratch behind Beau's ear. "Don't mind Uncle Duncan—he's jealous he can't sleep like you can."

Beau seems to understand our banter and lets out a contented sigh as if in agreement. But then, without warning, he erupts into a bark loud enough to wake the dead. The sudden commotion shatters the peaceful ambiance of the kitchen.

"If you ask me, I'd say someone's eager to go outside," Duncan says with a grin that lights up a room.

"Excuse us, Uncle Duncan," I reply, following Beau to the back door. With a swift motion, I swing the door open, and Beau dashes past me like a rocket. He leaps into the dewy morning air, barking and chasing after a butterfly that flits about.

Ryan stumbles into the kitchen, looking disheveled and sporting an impressive case of bedhead. He's still half-asleep and barely coherent. "Coffee," Ryan groans, treating it more like a plea than a request.

"Rough night?" Duncan teases, a mischievous grin plastered across his face.

Ryan shoots him an annoyed glare and a low growl in response.

I shake my head internally, wishing those two would find some common ground.

"Easy there, *Simba*, settle down," Duncan snickers while handing Ryan a steaming mug of coffee.

With an exaggerated sigh of relief, Ryan flops into a chair, cradling his mug like it's made of gold.

"Duncan?" Ryan mutters through sleepy eyes. "Was that *Simba* remark some kind of Disney dig?"

"Let it go already, Rye," I suggest.

Duncan remains unfazed by Ryan's irritated glares, adjusting his fedora with an amused smirk.

Sensing the rising tension in the air, I strategically slide into my seat at the table, positioning myself as a referee between

Ryan and Duncan.

"Where's Julie?" Ryan asks, scanning the room with a puzzled expression.

"I suppose she's still sleeping," I reply.

"That's not at all like her," Ryan yawns, rubbing his eyes. "Julie's usually the first one up, doing stuff in the kitchen." Her absence feels as strange as an Arctic blizzard sweeping through Texas in August.

"We were discussing that before you came downstairs," Duncan says.

Ryan raises an eyebrow. "Okay, I see what's going on. You guys want me to go upstairs and check on her. I have to do everything around here. It's not fair, I tell you," he concludes his mini rant, pushing back his chair and clutching his mug of coffee like a lifeline. With drowsy determination, Ryan trudges up the stairs. Each step echoing through the quiet house—a sequence of heavy thuds shattering the morning silence. Finally, he disappears from view, heading toward Julie's bedroom.

Meanwhile, Beau barks excitedly in the backyard—probably chasing a pesky butterfly that's teasing him. I can't see him from where I'm sitting. Honestly, I'm too lazy to get up to investigate. Besides, he's a big boy. He can handle himself without constant supervision.

"Guys," Ryan rushes down the stairs. "Julie's not in her room."

"Are you sure?" I ask.

"I knocked on her door—there was no answer," Ryan explains, his voice urgent. "I opened it and called for her—nothing. I even went inside to check around. She's definitely not there."

"Where could she be?" Duncan asks." Was her bed slept in?"

"Probably," Ryan replies. "The bed isn't made, if that's what you're asking."

"Alright then," I say. "Let's search the house." I walk over to the open kitchen door and scan the yard. "Beau!" I call out, my voice echoing across the lawn. "Come here, boy!"

I expect him to come bounding toward me like he always does, tail wagging with excitement—but today is different. He doesn't appear.

"Beau!" I call again, my tone growing more insistent. "Come on, boy!"

Still nothing.

"Beauregard Winston Churchill Greene," I call sternly, "you get inside this house this minute!"

Once more, my usually obedient dog is nowhere in sight.

"I don't understand," I say in disbelief as I return to the kitchen table, where Ryan and Duncan are finishing their morning coffee. "Beau always comes running when I call him."

"I wouldn't worry too much," Duncan suggests, a hint of reassurance in his voice. "He's probably wandered too far to hear you. After all, the yard isn't fenced."

"But he's never strayed off before," I remind him.

"He's in a new town—a whole new world for him," Ryan adds. "Let him explore. I'm sure he'll find his way back. Beau's one smart dog."

"I'll make you a deal—if he doesn't turn up by this afternoon, we'll go look for him," Duncan adds with a nod. "Besides, Lost Creek Junction isn't exactly a sprawling metropolis. There aren't many places for a dog his size to hide."

"Alright," I concede, but my worry for Beau weighs heavily on my mind.

"Right now, though, we've got a bigger issue at hand," Ryan interjects. "Where's Julie?"

"She must be somewhere in the house," Duncan assures us. "We'll track her down."

"I'm worried she might be hurt or unable to call for help," Ryan says.

"We need to get started," Duncan urges. "Rye, you start in the attic and work your way down to the second floor. Taylor, you check this floor and the basement."

"What about you?" Ryan asks Duncan.

"I'll check the garage and the garage apartment," Duncan

declares. "Let's regroup here—in the kitchen—let's say, in about thirty minutes."

A half hour later, it feels like an eternity as I return to the kitchen, still empty-handed when it comes to finding Julie. The silence is unsettling. Where can she be? I open the back door, hoping Beau will greet me with wagging excitement, but instead, there's only emptiness outside. Where can both of them have gone? Can this morning possibly get any worse?

Duncan enters the house through the side door from the garage, his face reflecting my rising anxiety.

"Any sign of her?" I ask.

"Nothing," he replies, shaking his head as if to dispel the dread hanging in the air. "Not a trace."

Ryan barrels down from the second floor, urgency etches across his features. "Have you guys found Julie?" he demands.

Duncan and I shake our heads and I feel the weight of frustration settle over us like a heavy quilt.

"I don't know where else to look," Duncan admits, his tone laced with desperation.

"I'm starting to get worried," I confess, glancing around as if expecting Julie to walk through the back door. "She didn't vanish without a trace. There has to be a logical explanation."

"But where can she be?" Ryan ponders aloud, combing fingers through his hair in exasperation. "You don't suppose she was—"

"Hey, let's not jump to conclusions," Duncan interjects, trying to steady our nerves amidst our confusion.

Suddenly, something catches my attention. "Do you guys hear that?" I ask, straining to focus on one specific sound.

"What is it, Taylor?" Duncan questions, concern flickering in his eyes.

"Shh," I urge, focusing intently on a distant sound. I try to block out the rhythmic ticking of the kitchen wall clock and the soft hum of the fridge, which mingle with the mechanical whir of the grandfather clock upstairs. Tilting my head to listen more intently, I shut out all distractions, my heart racing with each passing second. "There it is again," I say.

"There's what again?" Ryan asks, a hint of confusion in his voice.

"It's Beau," I exclaim, my excitement bubbling over. "Can't you hear him barking?" With adrenaline surging through me, I rush out of the kitchen and dash through the parlor. Flinging open the front door, I race onto the porch, scanning the street for my dog.

Duncan and Ryan trail closely behind me. "Are you sure it was Beau?" Duncan questions, concern etched on his brow.

"I definitely heard him," I insist, my eyes darting around in search of my baby. Then I see him—a few blocks away, Beau is sprinting toward us as if he's running a race. His fur glistening in the sunlight while he barks excitedly. As he bounds into the yard, I step off the porch to greet him. He nearly knocks me over with his enthusiasm, putting his front paws on my shoulders and showering me with slobbery kisses.

"Hey there, boy," I say, tears of happiness welling up in my eyes as I wrap my arms around his neck. "I'm glad to see you too." He then breaks free from my hug and starts running in tight circles while barking like crazy.

"Wow," Ryan marvels. "Beau is thrilled to see you—look at him go."

"I've never seen him act like this before," I reply.

"Do you think he's trying to tell us something?" Duncan suggests.

Beau dashes over to Duncan's SUV and begins pawing at the door, barking even louder while spinning around in circles again.

"Boy," I call out, "do you want to show us something? Does this have something to do with Julie?"

Beau barks excitedly, his tail wagging like a propeller. It's as if he understands every word we say and seems to be on a mission.

"Duncan?" I ask. "Do you have your keys?"

"Yup, I've got them right here," Duncan replies, holding them up and giving them a jingle.

"What are we waiting for? Let's get in the SUV and see what Beau wants to show us," I suggest.

As us guys clamor into the vehicle, Beau dashes ahead, barking excitedly as he races in front of the SUV. It's clear he's eager for us to follow him.

As Duncan starts the engine, Beau leads the way. We occasionally lose sight of him, but he circles back to check on us. Meanwhile, Duncan revs the engine to keep pace. To our astonishment, we find ourselves at my old boarded up gold mine.

We jump out of Duncan's SUV.

Beau barks furiously, scratching at the ground beneath the wood planks covering the entrance, as if trying to tunnel under the boards.

"Beau, what's gotten into you?" I ask.

He ignores me and continues to dig.

"I don't know about you guys," Duncan says, concern etched on his brow as he glances between us and the ominous entrance, "but I think he wants to show us something inside."

"What are we waiting for?" Ryan urges, excitement in his voice. "Let's do this."

We spring into action. Ryan and I pry apart the boards at the entrance, creating an opening large enough for Duncan to shimmy through. He's our best bet for this mission—he's the slimmest among us. As soon as Duncan vanishes into the shadows of the mine, Beau barks incessantly at the mine entrance.

Ryan and I wait outside. Waiting is the hardest part. My mind races with questions: What lies beyond those boards meant to keep people out? What is Duncan facing in there? What's got Beau so excited? The minutes drag on like hours, each tick of the clock amplifying my anxiety. Suddenly, a flicker of movement catches my eye between the slats. Ryan and I quickly pry apart more boards, our hearts pounding with anticipation.

We expect to see Duncan, but instead, it's Julie. Disheveled and wearing a dirty nightgown without shoes, looking like an escapee from a nightmare. We hurriedly help her squeeze through the narrow opening, desperate to get her to safety. Beau quiets down and lies down beside the SUV. Moments later, Duncan emerges from the darkness, stumbling and falling as his pant leg snags on a rusty nail. I quickly free him and pull him out of the foreboding mine.

Julie breaks down in tears on Ryan's shoulder—not tears of sadness, but overwhelming relief. "I thought I'd never get out," she whispers between sobs.

"I found her tied up and gagged just inside the mine entrance," Duncan explains as he catches his breath.

Ryan gently wipes away Julie's tears with his handkerchief.

"Julie?" I ask. "How did you end up inside the mine?"

Through her sobs, she manages to explain, "I don't know how I got here. The last thing I remember was climbing into bed last night. When I woke up this morning, I was tied up inside this dark mine."

As we try to piece together this puzzle, with many pieces missing, we suspect either Ezekiel or Abrahim abducted Julie. It has their names written all over it. A chilling message—an unmistakable threat to hand over control of my gold mine or face dire consequences. Dread settles in my stomach like lead, and I can't shake the feeling of being trapped in a game we never signed up for—a dangerous chess match where our lives are at stake. What lies ahead for us?

DAY TWENTY-THREE

Wednesday, June 6, 2018

In my dream, I'm on an unforgettable date with none other than Tom Cruise. Picture this: We're seated at an exquisite restaurant, a hidden gem where the ambiance is as rich as the gourmet food. The flickering candlelight dances around us, creating an intimate atmosphere that feels straight out of a blockbuster romance movie.

As we share laughter and delicious dishes, I'm experiencing what it's like to be in the presence of a Hollywood icon. My heart races with excitement, and I'm lost in the moment, forgetting the reality of our differences. Our chemistry is electric, and every moment is exhilarating.

After dinner, we head to a luxurious hotel room which exudes style and sophistication. The anticipation builds as we step inside, the room a perfect blend of comfort and luxury. It's just him and me in this lavish escape. In an instant, passion ignites, and in the thrill of the moment—clothes come off as we embrace each other with unbridled passion.

Suddenly, a cold, wet nose presses against my face, jolting me from my dream. "Go away, Beau," I mumble, keeping my eyes shut because I know it's him. If he sees the whites of my eyes, he'll know I'm awake.

With renewed enthusiasm, he nudges me again, his wet nose now a persistent little alarm clock. "Beau, please, just ten more minutes," I plead. I have to admit, Beau is a good dog, but expecting him to patiently wait by the bed while I sleep for ten additional minutes is a stretch. And let's face it, I've never given him a wristwatch, so I doubt he's mastered the art of telling time. Sure, he's clever in his way, but not *that* clever.

So here I am, caught in a battle of wills with my furry *child*. Will I give in to his adorable persistence, or will I manage to snag those precious extra minutes of sleep? The struggle is real.

Beau lets out a quick semi-bark—just enough to grab my attention without the jolt of a full-on bark. It's like having a built-in snooze alarm. This sound is one of his many clever tricks in his arsenal to coax me out of bed.

I slowly crack open one eye, still grasping the remnants of a dream I wish could linger a bit longer. The room is filled with soft morning light, casting a warm glow, and Beau's eager face is gazing at me. In my sleepy haze, it almost seems as if Beau has an angelic aura about him, like a radiant halo.

Sitting, his tail thumps against the floor like a drum, and there's no escaping—I'm caught. He knows I'm only half-awake, and there he is, perched at the edge of the bed, pawing at my pillow with those irresistible puppy eyes.

"Alright, buddy, you win," I chuckle, unable to resist his enthusiasm. "But you have to be quiet—Rye's still sleeping." Not that it matters—honestly, hardly anything will wake him.

With a burst of energy, Beau starts dancing in happy circles around the room, excited I'm finally awake.

As I swing open the bedroom door, Beau bursts out like a furry cannonball, his big paws thudding rhythmically down the hall and bounding down the stairs. Full of energy and excitement, he's ready to seize the day.

Meanwhile, I'm still in a sleepy haze, not entirely motivated to join the world of the living. With a yawn, I slowly descend the stairs, gripping the handrail for support.

As I step onto the first floor, there he is—Beau, my furry bundle of joy, waiting by the kitchen door, his tail wagging like a little metronome of excitement.

"Hold your horses, will ya? I'm on my way." I chuckle, amused by his boundless enthusiasm.

As I swing open the door, Beau bursts like a missile, racing into the backyard with uncontainable elation. He's a whirlwind of energy, darting and leaping in a playful chase after a delicate butterfly fluttering just out of reach.

Watching Beau frolic in the yard is like stepping back in time to his playful puppy days. I remember when he'd spend hours darting after flying bugs in Grandma's yard. Although he never quite managed to catch one—at least, not that I ever witnessed —if he did catch one, I picture him gulping it down whole, blissfully unaware of the tiny creature's fate.

Since moving into the Austin apartment with Ryan, I've noticed Beau seems to have lost some of his usual spark. Could he miss the sprawling yard at Grandma's where he could romp freely? Or is it simply a sign he's maturing?

Now that we're in Lost Creek Junction, there's no shortage of open space for him to explore. He can run around, chase butterflies, and hunt for bugs to his heart's content. It's a whole new adventure waiting for him.

"Good morning, Taylor," Julie greets me, her voice laced with sleep as she shuffles into the kitchen, rubbing her eyes. "Why are you standing in the open doorway?"

"I let Beau outside—you know, for his morning business," I reply, watching my happy pup at play.

"Usually, you open the door and then go about your day," Julie points out. "What's different about this morning?"

"I guess I was reminiscing about when Beau was a puppy and how much he's grown," I explain.

"Ah, Doggy Daddy memories," Julie chimes in, her voice light and playful. "Should I get out the family photo album?"

"Cut it out, will you?" I laugh, shaking my head as I move toward the kitchen table.

"You're such a softy when it comes to Beau," Julie teases, a playful sparkle dancing in her eyes as she busies herself with the morning coffee ritual. Honestly, none of us guys can match the magic of Julie's brew. We follow her instructions to the letter, but somehow, our attempts always end up as a sad pot of disappointment—except for Duncan, who makes a decent cup of joe.

"Good morning, everyone," Duncan cheerfully greets as he settles into his favorite spot at the kitchen table. "Is the magic elixir of life ready?" he asks, a playful nod to Julie's incredible coffee.

"Almost there," Julie replies with a smile. "By the way, I'm feeling extra generous this morning. What do you want me to whip up for breakfast?"

Surprise washes over Duncan and me, our eyes widening and jaws dropping in unison. We exchange glances, trying to process Julie's unforeseen generosity.

"Come on, guys," Julie exclaims in a playful yet surprisingly serious tone. "It's not like I haven't cooked breakfast before." Her words, though familiar, hang in the air with an unexpected weight, leaving us momentarily stunned.

"We know," Duncan chuckles, a teasing lilt in his voice. "But willingly offering to make the breakfast of our choosing isn't like you. That's a whole new level of generosity."

Curious, I approach Julie, pressing my hand against her forehead to check for a fever.

"She's not running a temperature," I assure Duncan, my voice light and teasing. I lock eyes with her, a playful smirk creeping onto my face. "What have you done with our Julie? Seriously, bring her back right now."

"Hold on a second," Duncan says, his eyes sparkling with mischief. "Let's not rush into anything. How about we get *our* Julie back—after *this* version whips up our breakfasts.

The three of us burst into a hearty laugh when Ryan strolls into the kitchen, his eyes wide with curiosity and anticipation. "What's so funny?" he asks, scanning our faces as if searching for clues to a secret joke.

Duncan shrugs, a playful grin spreading across his face. "Oh, nothing important," he replies, enjoying the moment.

"Why do you guys always do this to me?" Ryan questions, narrowing his eyes at us.

Before anything else can unfold, Beau barks from behind the partially closed kitchen door.

I swing the door open, curiously asking, "What's going on, Beau? The door's already half-open—just give it a little push," I say, playfully encouraging him to come inside.

With his head held high and a swagger rivaling any royal, Beau struts into the house like he owns the place. His paws making satisfying thumps against the floor, echoing his confidence. Before we know it, he's vanished into the parlor, his *personal* sanctuary. I can picture him heading straight for his precious settee—with his favorite stick hidden snugly beneath the plush cushions.

Moments later, a long, contented sigh emanates from the parlor, confirming what we all know—Beau is right where he wants to be, like a pampered prince in his little kingdom.

Back in the kitchen, I'm helping Julie by flipping pancakes on the griddle, the sweet aroma wafting through the air. The sizzle of frying bacon adds a mouthwatering soundtrack to our morning.

"What's on the agenda for today?" Julie asks the question of the day.

"Well," I grin, "I thought we could go to the gold mine. I figure it's time to check out what we must do to make it safe for tourists.

"Why don't you and Rye go?" Duncan suggests. "We don't all need to evaluate the situation. Plus, I kind of planned on working on your Jeep."

"In that case, can Taylor and I take your SUV up to the mine?" Ryan asks with a bit too much enthusiasm.

"Sure, no problem," Duncan grins, his eyes sparkling with mischief. "Just so long as Taylor is behind the wheel."

"Hey, what gives?" Ryan interjects. "Why do you never let me drive? I promise I won't crash your car."

"Like I said, so long as Taylor drives," Duncan chuckles, shaking his head.

Julie snickers at the banter, enjoying the rivalry between friends.

"No one was talking to you, missy," Ryan snaps at Julie, his voice sharp enough to cut through the laughter surrounding him. Everyone else bursts into giggles, leaving Ryan fuming.

"Ha. Ha," he huffs, rolling his eyes dramatically. "I'm always the butt of your jokes. Just wait—one day, you'll see..."

But honestly, who has time to wait for Ryan's moment of glory? Not us and not today.

Sometime later, Julie's busy scrubbing dishes in the kitchen, Duncan's tinkering with my Jeep in the garage, and Ryan and I pile into Duncan's SUV to head to the mine. Guess who's behind the wheel? Yep, you guessed correctly, it's me.

After driving for a while, I park the SUV beside the barricaded mine entrance, feeling adventurous. After countless trips here, Duncan's SUV has carved out a well-worn path in the dry grass, making it easy for us to pull up to the mine entrance—no more trekking for an extra half hour to get here.

"I was thinking," I start, my mind racing with possibilities.

"Oh, brother," Ryan groans, rolling his eyes. "Here we go again. Every time you start thinking—"

"Wait, hear me out for a second," I cut him off. "Have you ever wondered if there's another way into the mine?"

"You mean like a back entrance?" Ryan asks.

"Exactly," I reply. "What if we look for another way in or out of the mine?" Who knows what we might find?"

"Why are you suddenly interested in finding a back way into the mine?" Ryan asks.

"Well," I start. "Hasn't it bothered you how Julie's kidnapper —or kidnappers—managed to get her into the mine? I mean, they didn't remove any of the boards sealing off the entrance. It's like they knew of a secret way in."

Ryan raises an eyebrow, a spark of realization lighting up his face. "You might be onto something. Why are we just standing here? Let's go hunt down that hidden entrance to your mine."

Sometime later, "Whoa, Taylor, hold up," Ryan exclaims, his breath coming in short, ragged gasps as he struggles to keep himself upright. "How long have we been trudging through this tall grass?"

"Oh, I suspect it's been about an hour," I say, glancing at my wristwatch.

"Phew, I'm totally wiped out. Can we please take a break?" Ryan exclaims, his voice heavy with exhaustion. He flops down onto a massive boulder, sighing relief as he wipes the sweat from his brow with a bandanna. Grabbing his trusty childhood Boy Scout canteen, he takes a long draw of water—to find it doesn't quench his thirst.

"Taylor? Can we please go home now? There's no other way into the mine," Ryan whines, his voice tinged with exhaustion.

"I'm beginning to agree with you," I confess, taking a swig from my canteen, the water refreshing against my parched throat. After securing the lid, I glance around to get my bearings in this desolate landscape.

Ryan's slumped beside me on a boulder, looking like a ghost of his former self—lost in thought and staring blankly into the distance. It's hard to believe how much he's changed since our carefree days as kids in Beaumont. Back in those days, we were unstoppable—now it feels like he's running on empty. As I watch him drift further away from reality, I wonder—what happened to that adventurous spirit he once had?

"Hey, Rye, look over there!" I call out, excitement bubbling as I point to something a few yards away.

Ryan squints, trying to see what's captured my attention. "I don't see anything," he replies.

I gesture more emphatically toward a clump of tall vegetation. "That patch of weeds—there's something there—I feel it."

We push through the sun dried grass and wild shrubs—a sense of hope grows with each step. "Hey, Rye, can you give me a hand with this brush?" I call out.

"Are you sure about this?" he replies, pausing momentarily

as if weighing the risks before plunging into clearing away the overgrowth.

"Look at this," I exclaim, pointing toward an unexpected sight—a rusty steel track peeking through the underbrush, identical to the one at the mine's entrance.

"Could this be the track they used to haul gold out of the mine?" Ryan asks, his eyes sparkling with curiosity.

"Could be," I reply. "That is if any gold was ever actually found."

"Do you think this opening is the backdoor entrance to your mine?" Ryan questions.

"Why not?" I shrug. I can't shake the feeling we've discovered the hidden entrance.

"Man, am I ever bushed," Ryan exclaims as we return by foot to the front entrance of the mine.

"We still have a lot of work ahead of us," I remind him. "We must figure out how to make this place safe for tourists. The clock is ticking. Remember, I promised everyone at the town meeting I'd open the mine to the public. I can't go against my word."

With a reluctant nod, Ryan joins me as we rip down the boards blocking the entrance so we can assess the situation from the inside.

As I enter the shadows of the mine with my flashlight, I turn to Ryan and exclaim, "Wow, check this place out. Can you believe how dark it gets the further in I go? It's like stepping into another world."

Still lingering at the entrance where the sunlight pours in, Ryan chuckles nervous-like. "I'm perfectly fine right here, thank you very much. Who needs darkness when there's light?"

"Aw, is *scaredy-cat* Rye afraid of the dark?" I tease.

But Ryan's tone turns serious as he insists, "I don't think you should go any further. It could be dangerous."

"Come on," I urge, my flashlight slicing through the darkness of the mine tunnel like a beacon. "Where's your sense of adventure?"

"I left it back in Austin," Ryan retorts, his voice echoing off the cool walls. "Seriously, will you stop fooling around and get out of there?"

"This is incredible," I exclaim as I venture deeper into the shadows, leaving Ryan behind. Glancing back, I see a tiny speck of light from the entrance—a fragile glimmer in an ocean of darkness.

"Rye, you absolutely *have* to check out this place," I shout into the darkness, my voice ricocheting off the walls like a bouncing tennis ball.

Suddenly, a familiar, throaty laugh echoes behind me. I whip around, and my flashlight beam lands on an all too familiar wrinkly face bringing back unpleasant memories.

My flashlight suddenly flickers and goes dark. Panicking, I smack it against my palm, praying it's a loose battery connection. But nope—still nothing. As the darkness closes in around me, I feel the grip of anxiety tightening in my chest, my heart pounds like a drum with every tick of the clock. I turn in circles, in vain, trying to make out anything in the dark tunnel.

An old man's crackly voice slices through the darkness like dry leaves crunching underfoot. "Say your prayers—your time is up," he cackles, his sinister laugh echoing in the dark.

But wait, who is this sketchy figure? Is it Ezekiel or Abrahim? The ghost's identity remains a mystery, leaving me even further on edge.

As the tension thickens, one thing is clear—this moment is anything but ordinary.

Suddenly, the ground beneath me trembles, sending vibrations through the soles of my tennis shoes. The shaking intensifies, and I hear rocks tumbling around me, their clatter growing louder by the second. In a quick, instinctive survival move, I hunker down and cover my head with my arms. The impact of falling rocks echoes all around me.

In the pitch dark, I can't see a thing—just the overwhelming darkness swallowing everything whole. An avalanche of rocks and boulders crashes down like thunder, each impact sending chills down my spine. It's a stark reminder that life is fragile and unpredictable. Then, I'm struck on the head...

My mind is foggy. Where am I? But wait. Is that music? The soft, ethereal sound of a harp fills the air—a haunting melody feels both comforting and surreal. I spin around, searching for its source, and see a white light in the far distance. The silhouette of a person stands beside it, but they're too far away to make out any details.

"Rye, is that you?" I call out, my voice echoing into the silence. But there's no reply, just a heavy stillness hanging in the air. As I move closer to the bright white light ahead, curiosity pulls me in like a moth to a flame. Part of me is drawn toward its warmth and brilliance, while another part whispers warnings, urging me to turn back. I'm torn as to what to do.

"Step into the light," a voice beacons, drawing me in.

But here I am, caught in a whirlwind of choices and doubts. What lies beyond that glowing light? Is it safety, clarity, or something entirely different?

"Do not be afraid," the voice urges.

Waking up in complete darkness, I'm disoriented from a strange dream and unsure of my surroundings. As I shake the dream from my mind, memories slowly return, and a sinking feeling settles in—I realize I'm trapped in my own mine. But there's one saving grace—I'm alive, for now.

"Can anyone hear me?" I call out, my throat parched and the air thick with dust. A wave of fear crawls up my spine, making my voice tremble. My pleading call echoes, bouncing back at me.

Desperation tightens its grip on my chest as I wonder if anyone is beyond the rocks that imprison me. "Please, someone, anyone, help!" I cry out, my voice breaking with urgency. I cough, expelling the dust filling my lungs.

The silence is deafening as my words bounce back to me like a cruel joke. Desperation grips my chest tighter than ever, and I wonder if there's anyone out there beyond the rocks that trap me.

"Please, someone! Anyone! Help!" I cry out, urgency cracking my voice like fragile glass. In this moment of isolation, every second feels like an eternity.

I make out a faint, familiar voice calling out, "We're trapped. Please, help us!" My heart races as I decipher who it could be— Ezekiel or Abrahim? Are they stuck behind another rock wall? It feels surreal as if my mind is playing tricks on me. Am I imagining this because of a head injury? Or could they genuinely be in trouble? I'm caught in a whirlwind of emotions, torn between instinct and indifference. Honestly, I have no obligation to them. Part of me wishes they rot where they are. After all, I've got no sympathy for those two old miners. As far as I'm concerned, it's each man—or ghost—for himself.

I wake up again, jolted by a strange sound—scraping, like metal grating against concrete. What on earth is that?

"Hello?" I call out, my hoarse dry voice muted in the darkness. "Is someone there?"

To my relief, Ryan's muffled voice filters through the thick stone wall separating us. "Taylor, are you okay?"

"I'm trapped," I shout back, panic creeping into my voice. "There's a rock on top of my right leg." As the reality of my situation sinks in, I can't help but wonder: How did I end up here? And will I get out alive?

"Hold on. We're almost there," Ryan's steady and reassuring voice cuts through the darkness. I can sense his worry, even through the wall of rocks separating us.

"Please hurry!" My desperate plea escapes hoarsely, trembling with fear. The air feels thin in this suffocating space. What if they don't make it in time? The thought terrifies me.

Suddenly, I hear what I suspect is the sound of a boulder being pushed aside—its weight scraping against the ground like nails on a chalkboard. I cough as dust overtakes the air and I hear pebbles cascading around me. Bright flashlight beams cut through the dust and into my eyes, blinding me. I squint against the harsh light, my heart racing as I realize I'm being rescued.

"Are you hurt?"

"Can you move?"

"Are you bleeding?"

I'm overwhelmed by questions coming from all directions, each one more urgent than the last, highlighting the seriousness of the situation. As more boulders are removed, the wall that traps me starts to crumble, piece by piece. With every rock that falls, a glimmer of hope shines through—I can feel the fresh air calling me from beyond the rubble.

"Taylor, can you move?" Ryan's voice cuts through the chaos.

"No. My right leg is stuck under a rock," I answer.

Suddenly, beams from countless flashlights converge on the boulder, pinning me to the ground. The weight feels suffocating, but then—relief. The pressure starts to ease as Ryan and others work together to free me. As the boulder rises, I finally feel my leg again. With a determined tug, I pull it free.

I'm immediately lifted from the small, confined space I'd been trapped in. The moment I'm out, Ryan wraps his arms around me in a tight embrace. His hot tears soak into my neck as he sobs, "I didn't think I'd ever see you again."

Before I catch my breath, Ryan and I are yanked apart. Suddenly, I'm laid on my back, staring at the dark mine ceiling. My heart races as my leg is wrapped in a splint. Is it broken, I wonder?

All of a sudden, two paramedics appear like heroes out of a live action movie, lifting me onto a board with practiced efficiency. As they carry me out of the mine, the hot afternoon sun hits my face as we emerge into the daylight, and I cover my eyes from the bright light stinging my eyes.

Everything's happening so fast.

Suddenly, I'm hoisted inside an ambulance—just like the

ones I've seen on TV shows. It's surreal—I've never been in a real ambulance before, and I feel a curious mix of fear and fascination.

Every detail around me—the paramedic's focused demeanor and the high-tech equipment—feels new and intriguing. A second or third paramedic (I've lost count) hops in and shuts the door with a firm thud. The siren wails to life, cutting through the air as we speed off into the unknown. I'm bound to a gurney while the first paramedic checks my vitals, and I notice he's pretty cute for an older guy—maybe in his thirties? No wedding ring? My heart does a little happy dance at the thought.

"Where are you taking me?" I ask, my voice barely audible through the oxygen mask clinging to my face.

"Ballinger," the paramedic replies, his tone calm and reassuring. "It's the closest hospital."

"Hospital? But I'm not seriously injured," I protest. "I just have a few cuts and bruises." As the siren wails and the lights flash outside, I can't help but wonder—is this absolutely necessary?

"You need to get that leg and the bump on your head checked out," the paramedic insists, his voice steady and firm.

"But what about my boy—my friend back at the mine?" I catch myself mid-sentence, hesitating to refer to Ryan as my *boyfriend*. This part of Texas can be quite conservative, after all. "He won't know where to find me," I add, referring to Ryan.

"You've got nothing to worry about," the paramedic assures me. "Your boy—friend is right behind us, driving an SUV."

It's the dead of night when Ryan and I roll up to my house in Duncan's SUV, the headlights slicing through the night and illuminating my driveway like a spotlight on a stage. Julie, Duncan, and Beau burst out of the front door of my house, their anxious faces glowing under the vehicle's interior light. Their concern is focused solely on me, completely ignoring Ryan.

Julie rushes to my side, outstretching her arm to help me out of the SUV. Meanwhile, Duncan wrestles with my overzealous dog. "Beau, stay down. You might hurt your daddy—he's been in an accident," he cautions.

Beau whimpers softly, his big eyes filled with concern as he trails us into the house. I swear I saw tears of worry in his eyes.

"Christ, Taylor," Duncan exclaims, shaking his head. "We heard about the cave-in—it sounded serious."

"News travels fast in a small town," Julie states. "Not much goes on in Lost Creek Junction, so when something happens, the news spreads like wildfire."

"Hello?" Ryan interjects, waving his arms in the air to get everyone's attention. "Does anyone care to know how I'm doing?"

"Oh, hello, Rye. I didn't see you there," Julie replies, momentarily distracted as she helps me settle into a plush armchair in the parlor. The soft, velvety fabric wraps around me like a warm hug, instantly making me feel at home.

"Taylor?" Duncan asks, concern etched across his face. "Are you sure you shouldn't have stayed overnight at the hospital?"

I chuckle, shaking my head. "An overnight stay for a few cuts and a bruised leg? Come on, Duncan. I wasn't that seriously hurt."

Duncan raises an eyebrow, his expression serious. "Well," he replies, "you never know. There might be something more serious that you're not aware of."

"I highly doubt that," I insist, "especially after all the tests they ran. I wish I could fill you in on all the details, but I'm wiped out."

"Taylor's been given a sedative, so he's not himself right now," Ryan adds.

"Of course," Julie replies. "We can talk more tomorrow."

"Goodnight, everyone," I call out as Ryan helps me navigate the stairs. Before reaching the second step, he suddenly stops, turns around, and flashes a mischievous grin at Duncan while tossing him the keys to the SUV.

"Just so you know," Ryan smirks, "I've driven much nicer SUVs."

Rye, couldn't you leave well enough alone? I think to myself, shaking my head while trying not to grin.

Dale Thele

DAY THIRTY

Wednesday, June 13, 2018

As I descend the stairs from the second floor, I notice Julie busy in the kitchen.

"Good morning, Julie," I wave at her.

"Hey there," she replies with a smile.

I continue walking toward the parlor to wake up Beau for his morning constitutional.

Beau must have heard me, as he comes barreling around the corner like a furry torpedo, almost knocking me over.

"Looks like someone's excited to go outside," I chuckle, watching him zoom past me. He's already at the back door, tail wagging like crazy and eyes sparkling with anticipation.

I fling open the door, and Beau bursts out, barking and bounding like he's just been paroled from prison.

"That Beau is definitely one of a kind," I snicker, shaking my head in amusement.

"Come on, admit it—without Beau, you'd be completely lost," Julie playfully nudges me with a grin.

"I guess you have a point there," I smile, sliding into my seat at the table.

"How about some coffee to kick-start your day?" she asks, presenting me with a steaming mug that fills the air with its rich aroma.

"You read my mind," I reply, accepting the warm mug.

"What's up with that dog of yours?" Duncan asks, strolling into the kitchen with a curious grin. "He's acting like he just hit the jackpot or something."

"I'm sorry," I reply. "Did Beau wake you?"

"Nah, it's not your fault," Duncan assures me as he settles into his seat at the table. "Beau's just an excitable pup."

"Pup?" Julie chimes in, her eyebrow raised in disbelief. "Are we talking about the same dog? Have you seen how enormous that so-called *pup* is?" She uses air quotes to emphasize her point. "He's practically the size of a small horse."

"Come on, Julie. Beau's not *that* big," I counter, shaking my head with a grin. "When I measured him before leaving Austin, he stood at 32 inches and weighed in at only 170 pounds."

"Like I said, he's one big pup," Julie chuckles as she hands Duncan a steaming mug of coffee. "You should put a saddle on him and enter him in the rodeo."

Duncan and I burst into laughter at Julie's humorous exaggeration.

"What's so funny?" Ryan asks, rubbing the sleep from his eyes as he shuffles into the kitchen, his bedhead hair sticking out in every direction like a wild nest.

"We were talking about how big Beau has gotten," Julie replies.

"Speaking of Beau," Ryan says while pouring himself a mug of coffee, "what's his deal this morning?"

"Sorry for disturbing you, he was excited about going outside," I say.

"What's outside?" Ryan asks.

"His butterfly friends were waiting for him," I say.

"Oh," Ryan exclaims, a look of bewilderment crossing his face as he settles into his seat at the table. "Wait—did you say *butterfly friends*?"

Julie chuckles, her eyes sparkling with amusement as she takes a sip of coffee. "Rye, it's much too early in the day for your brain to unravel the mysteries of Beau's life. Just sit back, don't overthink things, and enjoy your coffee."

Ryan sips his coffee in silence, casting a curious eye at us from over the rim of his mug.

Just then, Beau lets out a quick bark from outside the door.

"Speaking of the devil," Duncan chuckles, a grin spreading

across his face. "Looks like someone's eager to come back inside."

"Hold your horses, Beau," I snicker, walking to the door. "I'm coming, I'm coming."

I swing open the door just as Beau bursts inside, his excitement radiating from him. His paws patter against the floor like tiny drumbeats as he dashes straight for his water bowl, tail wagging furiously in anticipation.

After quenching his thirst and creating a mini flood on the floor, Beau lifts his head and vigorously shakes it. Water droplets spray in the air, like a yard sprinkler in full swing, sending water flying everywhere. He then turns to his food bowl, crunching his kibble with the same gusto.

As the sun peeks through the kitchen window, casting a warm glow over our cozy morning ritual, Julie, Duncan, and I savor our steaming cups of coffee. It's one of those tranquil moments where time seems to stand still—until Ryan begins his signature breakfast routine. With a satisfying grin, he grabs the box of Captain Crinkle cereal and pours himself a generous bowl. The sound of cereal cascading into the bowl is much like when I pour Beau's kibble. After Ryan adds a splash of milk that swirls like clouds in the sky, he scoops up a spoonful and shovels it into his mouth.

I snicker at the sight of Beau and Ryan diving into their breakfasts with such enthusiasm. It's a comical scene making me wonder—who's copying whom? Are they mirroring each other's breakfast habits, or is it just a coincidence?

"I see the family resemblance," Duncan snickers, catching on to my amusement.

"What's up?" Ryan cocks his head and asks Duncan, as milk dribbles down his chin.

"Oh, nothing," Duncan chuckles, a mischievous glint in his eye. "Just a little observation, that's all."

Ryan shrugs nonchalantly and goes back to devouring his breakfast as if it's the day's most important task, as Beau does the same.

"What's on everyone's plates today?" I ask, trying to steer the conversation in a new direction.

"You and I," Duncan replies, "are going to take your Jeep out for a test drive."

"You've got her running?" I ask Duncan, with a little too much enthusiasm.

"Purring like a kitten," he replies with a wink. "So tell me, how long will it take you to be ready to hit the road and feel the wind in your hair?"

The thought of cruising around in my Jeep sends a thrill through me.

"Sorry, Duncan, not today," I say with regret. "I've already made plans."

"Cancel them," he insists, his tone almost pleading.

"I can't," I reply, feeling the weight of my commitment.

"What's so important you can't put it off for one day?" Duncan presses, curiosity sparking in his eyes.

"Someone's picking me up," I say, trying to sound upbeat. "We're going to the mine to permanently seal it up."

"Are you sure you're up for that?" Julie raises an eyebrow, concern etched on her face.

"I'm totally fine, Julie," I reassure her with a smile. "You know what they say, *when you fall off a horse, you've got to get back in the saddle*."

"I always thought the saying was *save a horse—ride a cowboy*," Ryan snickers.

Julie rolls her eyes, clearly unimpressed. "Ryan Reginald Bartlett," she says with a serious tone, using his full name for emphasis (I didn't know she knew his full name), "get your filthy mind out of the gutter."

"Yes, ma'am," Ryan responds with a sheepish grin, ducking his head.

"Hey, Taylor, just be careful out there. Okay?" Duncan warns, concern etched on his face.

"I'll be fine," I brush off his worry with a wave of my hand. "Seriously, I've got this."

"Still..." Julie chimes in, her brow furrowing slightly.

"Do any of you want to come with me? We could use extra hands on this one," I suggest, hoping to rally my friends. "The more, the merrier, right?"

"Nah, I think I'll stick around here and tinker with your Jeep a bit more," Duncan shakes his head.

"What are your plans for today?" I ask Julie.

"I'll be busy preparing the house for our bed-and-breakfast guests," she replies. "There's a lot to do, but I'm ready to take on the challenge."

"And what about you, Rye? What's on your agenda for the day?" I inquire, eager to hear his response.

"Well, you know, someone has to stay and keep an eye on— on—Beau," Ryan replies, looking at my dog, as if he just this moment remembered something.

Beau looks up at Ryan from his food dish and burps loudly, as if saying, *Yeah, right, when hell freezes over.*

I chuckle, shaking my head in amusement. "Looks like Beau thinks he's perfectly capable of holding down the fort without a sitter."

"If anyone needs supervision around here, it's probably you, Rye," Duncan quips.

With that cheeky thought lingering in the air, Beau returns to his bowl, happily lapping up water as if he's the king of the castle.

"Alright, fine," Ryan huffs, rolling his eyes. "I guess I'll just take a nap while keeping an eye on Beau."

But Beau has other ideas. With a playful bark that seems to say, *No thanks, human*, he prances to his settee in the parlor.

"Don't worry about a thing," Julie assures with a smile. "I'll get Rye to pitch in around here."

Ryan shoots her a look that's anything but pleasant—more like a mix of disbelief and annoyance.

Julie giggles at Ryan's expression, then turns to me with a curious glint. "By the way, what time is your ride picking you up?"

"Around 9," I reply.

"It's almost 9 now," Duncan announces.

"Yikes, I better get myself pulled together," I exclaim, rising from the table while gulping down the last of my coffee. "Duncan, can I borrow your work boots?"

"I suppose so. They're in my bedroom closet," he responds with a shrug. "But they're probably too big for you."

"Thanks," I say as I make my way up the stairs. "I'll make do."

A truck horn blares outside, cutting through the morning calm.

"I'll let 'em know you're on your way," Duncan shouts as he rises from the table.

I study Duncan's work boots, which are monstrously big but somehow calling to me. With a determined grin, I slide my feet into them like a kid trying on adult shoes. I layer on thick socks and tuck in an insole to make them fit better. Who knew Duncan had such huge feet?

Beau's sharp barks slice through the commotion, reminding me someone's waiting outside.

"Alright, alright, I hear you, Beau," I call back, my voice echoing as I descend the stairs. Crossing through the parlor to the front door, Duncan's boots thud against the floor.

Stepping onto the porch, the morning sun casts a warm glow over everything, and I spot Herb lounging in his red pickup truck parked on the street. He's deep in conversation with Duncan, who's leaning casually through the open passenger window. I take a moment to soak it all in before plopping down on the porch step. With a quick tug, I tie the laces of the boots I borrowed from Duncan.

"Just a sec, Herb," I shout, ringing through the pleasant morning air.

Herb is that cool older guy everyone loves—a true jack of all trades. He's the go-to fix-it man of Lost Creek Junction, with almost magical skills. Need carpentry? Plumbing? Air conditioning or heating repairs? You name it, and he tackles it like a pro.

From the moment we hatched our plan to save the town, Herb has been one of our staunchest supporters. Today, he's behind the wheel, taking me to the mine where we'll meet up with other townsfolk in a united effort to seal it up for good—before the tourists start rolling in. Last week's cave-in was a wake-up call, reminding me how unsafe the mine is. Who wants to explore a mine that could collapse at any moment? Let's face it—this town deserves better than a risky attraction that puts lives in danger.

"Good morning, Herb," I greet him with a smile as I approach the truck.

"See you later, Herb," Duncan says as he opens the passenger door for me.

I slide into the cab of the truck. "Thanks, Duncan," I reply as he closes the door. "And thank you, Herb, for picking me up," I add.

"My pleasure," he replies with a warm grin as he turns the key in the ignition. But then his expression shifts slightly, concern creeping in. "Are you sure you're up for this? I heard about your accident last week."

"I'm fine," I reassure him. "It wasn't as bad as everyone is making it out to be."

"Alright, if you say so," Herb responds, though his brow still furrows slightly with worry.

Herb's truck might not be the latest model, but you wouldn't know it by looking at how he maintains it. Even though I'm no car aficionado, I can spot a Ford from a mile away—thanks to those four letters embedded on the tailgate.

This beauty is painted a striking red, with a sleek white stripe running gracefully along its sides, perfectly complemented by classic whitewall tires. Inside, the truck boasts an inviting interior adorned with rich red vinyl upholstery and crisp white piping accents. The dashboard ties everything together beautifully, creating a cohesive look that's hard to ignore.

Dang, maybe I'm more knowledgeable about trucks than I give myself credit for. But when it comes to technical specs like engines or horsepower? Well, that's where my expertise fizzles out. Give me a drag show or Barbra Streisand show tunes, now that's where I excel.

Let's get back to Herb, shall we? Have you ever met someone whose kindness shines through even in the quietest moments? That's Herb, his full name is Herbert (I don't know his last name), and while he may not be the chattiest person around, get him talking about mechanical stuff, and you can't shut him up.

Herb is a gentle soul with a past that tugs at the heartstrings. He was married once but tragically lost his wife shortly after they tied the knot in Colorado. I've not asked for details—some stories are best left untouched—but it's clear the experience shaped him into the compassionate person he is today.

What stands out about Herb is his unwavering honesty and genuine nature. In a world where trust can sometimes be hard to come by, he's one of those rare gems who makes you feel safe and valued.

"So, today, we're closing the mine for good?" Herb asks.

"Yes, sir," I reply, taking a deep breath, "after last week's cave-in, I've come to the decision we need to seal up the mine permanently. At first, I was excited about the idea of opening the front part of the mine to tourists eager to try their hand at gold mining. Who wouldn't want to experience that thrill? But after encountering the collapse firsthand, it hit me hard—it's not safe for anyone."

"I completely agree," Herb nods. "That mine is old and, let's face it, definitely not very stable. And honestly, who are we kidding? There's no gold to be found around these parts."

"Hold on a second," I interject. "Just the other day, Rye found a genuine gold nugget in the mine. Can you believe that?"

"Well, I'll be darned," Herb replies, shaking his head in disbelief.

"There may not be a ton of gold down there, but just the possibility of finding some could excite tourists—it gave me and my friends gold fever," I explain. "It's like planting the seed for a gold rush."

"That's pretty much how the Texas Gold Rush of the 1800s started," Herb nods.

"Where do you think I got the idea from?" I ask with a playful grin. "At first, my plan was pretty straightforward—charge a small fee for an unforgettable experience, sprinkle in a brief history lesson about the Texas Gold Rush, and provide visitors with essential tools and safety gear to try their hand at gold mining. Picture this—guests would have a whole hour to dig for gold, and if luck smiled upon them and they struck gold, they could either keep their treasure or sell it for cash to the mining boss in the office.

"And there'd be a bonus, too. Everyone who paid the mining fee would walk away with a certificate proclaiming they'd mined for gold in the legendary Lost Creek Junction Gold Mine. How cool would that have been?"

"That's too bad—it sounds like it was a good idea," Herb says with a hint of disappointment.

"Whether it was a good idea or not, after being trapped inside the mine during the cave-in," I explain, "I realized how dangerous it is. I also have a strange feeling the cave-in wasn't an accident, which makes the mine even more dangerous."

"What are you getting at? You think someone intentionally caused the cave-in?" Herb asks, raising an eyebrow in disbelief.

"Absolutely," I reply with a nod. "I'm pretty sure it was the work of the ghosts of Ezekiel and/or Abrahim."

"Ezekiel and Abrahim?" Herb echoes in disbelief. "You mean those legendary prospectors who vanished two hundred years ago? They weren't real people—they're part of a local legend."

"Herb," I start, "those stories of Ezekiel and Abrahim are more than tales spun around campfires. Those guys were real men who lost their lives in a mine accident right outside of town. After their bodies were recovered, the mysterious Widow Scruggs cast a spell on them, trapping their spirits inside a container. She then sealed it tight and hid it away in the root cellar of my house. When Julie, Duncan, Ryan, and I explored my cellar one day—I accidentally knocked over that very container and broke its seal. We had no clue about the spell or what I'd unleashed at that moment. But soon enough, we found ourselves haunted by none other than the ghosts of Ezekiel and Abrahim."

"I don't want to sound disrespectful, but I'm struggling to wrap my head around this. Are you absolutely sure those apparitions are actually Ezekiel and Abrahim?" Herb inquires, a hint of skepticism in his voice.

I lean in closer, eager to share what I and my friends have uncovered. "You know, the key to unraveling the mystery surrounding Ezekiel and Abrahim lies within an old journal we found in the house. It's packed with detailed accounts of their lives and the tangled history of the gold mine ownership."

I pause for emphasis before continuing, "And it's not just us speculating here—Mr. Andrews, my attorney, has confirmed everything we read in that journal is factual. Everything makes sense when you put all the pieces together. It explains the predicament we're in."

"What *predicament* are you talking about here?" Herb inquires.

"According to the journal, the widow Scruggs sold the mine to the two prospectors. Tragically, the prospectors later lost their lives in a cave-in. The widow Scruggs allegedly destroyed the bill of sale, making it seem as though she never sold the mine. It was easy for her to do since the prospectors hadn't filed the necessary paperwork with the authorities to prove the transfer of ownership," I clarify.

"So, you believe the ghosts of these dead prospectors are haunting your house?" Herb asks.

"Absolutely," I reply with a nod. "Imagine this—the ghosts of long-lost prospectors, stirred from their centuries-old slumber, suddenly awaken to a world they barely recognize. Can you picture their shock? Their first instinct was to reclaim what they believe is rightfully theirs—their precious gold mine. As they uncover the circumstances surrounding their mine ownership, fury ignites within them. And guess what? I've become their primary target because now, the mine belongs to me. I'm not safe no matter where I go, not even in my own mine."

"Are you suggesting these two ghosts trapped you in the mine and caused that cave-in?" Herb asks, his eyes wide with disbelief.

I nod slowly, feeling a chill run down my spine. "Yeah, one of them appeared to me right before the collapse," I reply. "I'm convinced they had a hand in the whole thing. When I was stuck under all those rocks, I heard one of them just beyond the rubble. It sounded like they were trapped, too—just deeper inside the mine. This is the first I've told anyone about seeing and hearing them."

"Why do you suspect both ghosts are trapped?" Herb asks.

"Because the journal mentioned they were *always together, as if joined at the hip,*" I explain.

"What do you suppose happened to them in the mine? Do you reckon they're still trapped in there?" Herb asks.

"I have no idea, but as far as I'm concerned, they can rot in that mine for all I care," I reply.

"But can ghosts be trapped in a mine?" Herb asks.

"I don't know," I say. "Hey, wait a minute, isn't the mine located outside the city limits?"

"I'm not following. What does that have to do with the ghosts?" Herb questions.

"There's a curse keeping the ghosts trapped within the city limits," I explain. "How can those ghosts be outside of the city limits?"

"Not necessarily," Herb counters. "Back in the late 1800s, the town charter was amended to place the mine within the city limits for tax purposes."

"Was the city map ever updated?" I ask.

"I'm not sure," Herb replies. "Even if it hasn't been updated, the mine is probably still within the city limits."

"This raises an intriguing question," I say. "Why haven't the ghosts left the mine? I haven't seen them since the cave-in last week."

"That's an interesting observation," Herb acknowledges. Suddenly, he stops the truck and makes an unexpected U-turn without explanation, leaving me surprised and curious about his sudden action. "I've got something to show you," he announces with a sly grin.

As we drive back through the swirling cloud of dust kicked up by the truck and approach the Lost Creek Junction business district from this new angle, something catches my eye—a deserted building which seems to have emerged from a forgotten past.

The structure is cloaked in a wild tangle of weeds and shrubs as if nature itself is reclaiming what was lost. It's intriguing to think about the stories that place could tell if only its walls could talk.

Herb brings the truck to a gentle halt, dust swirling around us as he steps out. I follow suit.

"Hey, what's that building over there?" I ask, gesturing toward the shadowy outline of a structure looming in the distance.

"Ah, the Lost Creek Junction Hotel and Hungry Man Cafe," Herb says. "Once upon a time, that place was the heart of the town, alive with the laughter and chatter of tourists. Can you imagine? The hotel was always fully booked up. Folks said that if you didn't make a reservation at the cafe ahead of time, you could find yourself waiting an hour—or more—for a table. And that's if you were lucky. But now? Well, it's a different story. The hotel and cafe stand empty and forgotten, their doors closed to the world."

"What happened?" I ask, eager to hear more.

Herb chuckles softly, shaking his head. "You won't believe this. The locals came up with this wild idea—they no longer wanted outsiders in their town." He leans in closer, lowering his voice as if sharing a secret. "They were genuinely worried their ghosts might pack up and leave."

"Wait, what about the curse keeping the ghosts trapped within the city limits?" I ask.

"Curse or no curse, have you ever seen a peaceful town turned upside down by a single person? That's what happened here." Herb shakes his head, recalling the tale of the day a rabble-rouser strolled into the quiet little community. "He stirred things up in the worst way," he says, frustration evident in his voice.

"People began to ignore the truth, choosing instead to swallow every tall tale that lousy con artist spun. Once-friendly neighbors became suspicious of one another and questioned everything they once knew. The atmosphere shifted dramatically —it was no longer a friendly, welcoming town. The townsfolk hung on to that stranger's every word, pushing away tourists and outsiders who once brought life to these streets. And then, one fateful night—well, that's where things took a turn. What happened next left the whole town rattled."

"Well? What happened?" I ask, my heart racing with anticipation.

Herb leans in, his eyes sparkling with intrigue. "That con artist? He packed his stuff and lots of things that didn't belong to him and vanished one night—never to be seen or heard from again."

I shake my head at the absurdity of it all.

But then Herb continues, "You know what? This town is a tough old bird. She's weathered storms far worse than that and still stands tall. Sure, she never fully bounced back from those dark days in her history, but look at her now—she's still here, ain't she? Barely hanging on, though."

"Yes, but how much longer can Lost Creek Junction hold on amidst these financial challenges?

Herb falls silent, his gaze drifting down to the ground.

Following his eyes, I spot a thin stream of crystal-clear water quietly meandering through the tangled weeds. It flows effortlessly over smooth rocks and vibrant pebbles of every hue

—a serene oasis hidden beneath the overgrowth.

"Ever wonder how Lost Creek Junction got her name?" Herb asks, ignoring my earlier question.

"Absolutely," I respond. "I've been curious about that."

"Have you ever come across a hidden gem in nature? Well, you're looking at one right now—this charming little stream is called *Lost Creek*," Herb explains with a twinkle in his eye. "It's a tributary of the mighty Colorado River—Lost Creek has a fascinating secret. As you follow its winding path upstream, you'll notice something curious—the creek takes an unexpected turn away from the river and seems to vanish. But don't be fooled—this isn't just any disappearing act. The water plunges into an underground cave, only to reemerge several miles downstream as a bubbling spring. That's how the creek got its name—it got lost on its way here. Eventually finding its way, this enchanting stream flows through Lost Creek Junction before feeding into the serene waters of Lost Creek Lake."

"Interesting," I say. "But how does *Junction* fit into the town's name?"

"Great question," Herb exclaims, his eyes lighting up with enthusiasm. "Since moving here, have you heard of *The Junction*?"

"No, I can't say I have," I reply.

"It's a fascinating spot of land downstream on the outskirts of town, where the creek forks into two distinct directions. One side flows into the shimmering lake. At the same time, the other veers into mysterious territory—uncharted waters no one has dared to explore.

"Locals affectionately dubbed this fork in the stream *The Junction* for good reason. Picture a lovely, flat, triangular patch of lush green grass adorned with towering shade trees—it's an ideal setting for lazy afternoon outings. Families used to flock there on weekends for delightful picnics—believe it or not, many still do.

"During the early 1900s, this charming spot was a magnet for folks from all around who came to enjoy their weekends and holidays under the sun. Over time, they began to associate *Junction* with our town's name, giving rise to what we now know as Lost Creek Junction. Some of the old-timers claim *The Junction* inspired Georges Seurat to paint his famous painting *Sunday Afternoon On Island Of La Grande Jatte.* I suppose you have to take the claim with a grain of salt, since there's no one still around to corroborate the story."

"That's so cool," I say.

"It is, isn't it?" Herb nods in agreement, a smile spreading across his face.

"So, Herb," I continue, "whatever happened to that shuttered hotel and cafe you showed me earlier?"

"Unfortunately, they had to close down due to a lack of business," Herb replies.

"They must have closed somewhat recently," I remark, noticing how well-preserved the building looks even from this distance.

Herb shakes his head slowly. "They've actually been closed for at least fifty years," he says with a wistful sigh. "So, I've been told. They were closed when I moved here."

"But wait a minute," I say, still grappling with disbelief, "the building looks like it's in great shape."

Herb nods knowingly. "That's because the ghosts of the owners and former employees have kept it just as pristine as when they were open for business. They haven't bothered to tidy up the grounds, though."

"So, if I'm understanding you, both the hotel and cafe could potentially open their doors tomorrow?" I ask.

Herb chuckles. "Well, not exactly tomorrow. The place could definitely use some plumbing and electrical upgrades. But with the right resources? They could be ready to welcome guests in a couple of weeks."

"Thanks, Herb, for showing me the hotel and cafe. Those are definitely two businesses we need to look into getting up and running," I say, expressing my gratitude for Herb's support.

Herb chuckles, removing his cap and wiping the sweat from

his bald head with a bandanna. "Well, I brought you out here for another reason. What if you or someone else tapped into the Texas Gold Rush spirit? Imagine charging tourists to pan for gold right here in this here creek. Picture it—families splashing around, kids squealing with delight as they discover shiny nuggets. Of course, the creek would need to be cleared of brush and weeds—"

"What a fantastic idea," I exclaim.

"Just so you know, there's no real gold in this stream," Herb says. "But rumor has it folks have frequently found fool's gold in this body of water."

"Fool's gold, you say? That's absolutely perfect," I reply, my imagination racing at the thought of tourists flocking here to pan for treasure. I imagine families laughing as they sift through the water, hoping to strike it rich—even if it's nothing more than specks of iron pyrite.

Herb and I find ourselves racing against time as the sun dips below the horizon. We don't make it to the mine, but that doesn't dampen our spirits. Instead, Herb drives me home as darkness overtakes the landscape.

His ideas are like sparks in a dry forest, igniting a whirlwind of plans in my mind. What if we can turn these thoughts into something genuinely impactful? I can't wait to share everything I've learned today with Julie, Duncan, and Ryan. Imagine the possibilities.

Stepping through the front door of my house, a wave of excitement washes over me at the sight of Beau, my furbaby, after being away most of the day. "Did you think I'd abandoned you?" He eagerly rubs against my leg as I kneel down to hug him around the neck. "I'm home now," I assure him with a smile.

The familiar sights and smells of home wrap around me like a cozy blanket, instantly lifting my spirits. The warmth of this space feels like a welcome hug, reminding me why there's no place quite like home.

(Cue up swelling tear-jerking cinematic music and Judy Garland saying, *There's no place like home.*)

"Taylor? Is that you?" Ryan's voice echoes from somewhere in the house, pulling me out of my thoughts.

"I just this minute walked in," I announce. "Where is everyone?"

"We're in the kitchen."

I follow a familiar aroma, something I haven't experienced since leaving Austin.

Entering the kitchen, I'm met with a mouthwatering scene— my friends are happily devouring pizza, laughter filling the air. The countertops are a chaotic display of empty frozen pizza boxes—evidence of the evening feast.

It's during moments like this, I crave something truly special —a pizza delivery from Flying Submarine Subs and Pizzeria in Austin. Have you ever had one of their thick-crust super-duper supreme pizzas? They're an absolute game-changer. Imagine biting into layers of pepperoni, Canadian sausage, mushrooms, black olives, three varieties of bell peppers, onions, and gooey melted mozzarella cheese—all coming together perfectly. It's pure heaven for the taste buds.

"Hey, Taylor, are you going to stand there drooling, or are you joining us?" Duncan teases, a string of mozzarella cheese dangling from the corner of his mouth like a badge of honor.

Honestly, living in a town where the closest pizzeria is miles away, even frozen pizza feels like a gourmet feast. I pull up a chair and settle in with my friends, the sight of cheesy goodness is instantly comforting. After skipping lunch, my stomach growls in protest—who knew hunger could hit this hard? At this point, I care less I'm about to devour a frozen pizza straight from its cardboard prison. It's all about good company and satisfying cravings.

"So, did you and Herb manage to seal up the mine?" Julie asks.

"Come on, will ya? Give Taylor a break," Ryan jumps in, his

protective instincts kicking in. "Can't you see he's starving? Let him enjoy a proper meal. I bet he hasn't eaten since breakfast."

Julie glances at me, concern etched on her face as she waits for my reply.

"Yeah, that's right," I mumble through a mouthful of sausage pizza. "Herb and I didn't break for lunch."

With his head nestled on my lap, Beau looks up at me with those big, soulful eyes that melt the coldest of hearts. Seriously, how can I say no to him?

"Alright, buddy," I grin, "you can have one slice—only one."

In an instant, he devours a slice of hamburger pizza like it's the best thing he's ever tasted before scampering back to the parlor.

I turn to my friends around the table and ask, "Okay, guys, be honest with me—how much pizza has Beau managed to scam out of you?" I scan their faces, eager for confessions.

"Maybe a slice from me," Julie admits with a guilty giggle, her eyes darting away from mine.

I turn to Ryan, anticipating his response.

"Okay, fine, I might have given him a slice," Ryan confesses.

"A slice?" Duncan chimes in, raising an eyebrow. "I distinctly saw you slip him at least three slices."

Ryan smirks back, "Well, you gave him two yourself."

"Alright, alright. Enough already," I laugh. "We all know Beau can be incredibly persuasive when he flashes those puppy dog eyes."

"You're telling me," Julie nods, wiping her mouth with a paper towel. "Those eyes get me every time."

The kitchen falls quiet except for the crunching of pizza crusts, the subtle fizz of carbonated drinks, the gentle hum of the refrigerator and the ticking of the wall clock.

I look around the table, feeling grateful to be home with my best friends, even if they eat like pigs.

"Hey, Taylor," Julie breaks the silence, her voice laced with curiosity. "What did you and Herb do today?"

I sigh, feeling the day's weight settle heavily on my

shoulders. "Honestly, I'm pretty beat," I confess. As much as I'd love to give her a run down of my day, something tells me it's best to keep it under wraps for now. "Can we save this discussion for later? I could use some rest."

"Sure," Julie replies, her brow knitting together in concern as she studies my face. It's surprising how she's letting me off the hook without pressing for more information—she has a knack for digging deeper when she wants to know something. But I'm not taking any chances—sensing an opportunity, I swiftly change the subject.

"Come on, Beau," I call out, pushing my chair back from the table. "Time to go potty."

As I swing open the back door, Beau shoots through the kitchen like a fired bullet, his nails tapping rhythmically against the floor. The fresh scent of damp grass fills the air, mingling with the soothing symphony of crickets serenading the evening.

Leaning against the door frame watching Beau chase fireflies, I relish the cool breeze brushing against my skin. It's a moment of peace amidst a full day with Herb. I yawn—realizing I'm more tired than I thought.

"Why don't you go to bed?" Duncan suggests, his arm draping comfortingly over my shoulder. "I'll keep an eye out for Beau."

As I turn, Ryan's waiting with a warm smile, his hand outstretched toward me. Without hesitation, I intertwine my fingers with his, and we go up the stairs together. The world around us fades as I rest my head on his shoulder, feeling safe and connected. Our gripped hands tighten with each step we take—an unspoken promise we're in this together.

I'm reminded of when Ryan and I were kids. I can't help but smile when I think back to those carefree summer days. We weren't just kids in those days—we were adventurers on a quest for fun.

Those golden days were packed with classic childhood escapades that turned ordinary moments into extraordinary memories. From catching crawdads in the cool, bubbling creek to scaling trees as if we were conquering mountains, every second was an adventure waiting to unfold. And let's not forget our bike rides—how we'd race each other for miles, laughter echoing behind us like music in the wind.

Each morning started with Ryan eagerly awaiting my arrival outside my house. The moment breakfast was done, it was game on. Who could pedal faster? Who could find the biggest tree to climb? Those simple joys filled our hearts with pure happiness and forged a bond that felt unbreakable.

Our days were nothing short of magical—an endless adventure brimming with new discoveries and lessons waiting to be uncovered. Each moment felt like a treasure chest overflowing with knowledge, and our curiosity was insatiable.

As the sun dipped below the horizon and the streetlights flickered to life, we'd glide our bikes down the street, our shadows dancing behind us. The air buzzed with excitement as lightning bugs hovered and twinkled above the lawns, sending out their secret signals adding a sprinkle of enchantment to our evenings.

As we strolled down the quiet street, the warm glow of lights began to flicker in the houses around us, casting a cozy ambiance feeling almost magical. The sounds of families bustling about, preparing their evening meals, filled the air— laughter mingling with the clatter of pots and pans. Shoulder to shoulder with Ryan, I felt my stomach rumbling in protest—it was a familiar growl signaling my growing hunger. After all, I hadn't eaten since breakfast. Those wild berries Ryan and I found and snacked on earlier? They were more a sweet treat than a proper meal.

Before long, we'd find ourselves back at our respective homes, where the comforting rituals of family life awaited us. The only part of the day when Ryan and I were apart. After a refreshing bath and a hearty supper with Mom and Dad, we'd gather in the living room to unwind together. There was something magical about those evenings spent watching our favorite TV shows.

I vividly recall one particular evening when we'd settled in to watch *Mister Ed, the Talking Horse.* Can you imagine my surprise when Mr. Ed opened his mouth and started talking? I was utterly baffled. How on earth did they train that horse to have such witty conversations?

Growing up with Ryan as my best friend was nothing short of a wild adventure. I still remember the day we stumbled upon several empty cardboard appliance boxes on the curb. Can you imagine our excitement? We dragged those massive boxes to our favorite clearing in the woods. That afternoon was pure magic as we transformed those humble boxes into an epic clubhouse.

For an entire week, our mornings were spent lounging in our secret hideout, plotting grand adventures, and sharing secrets. When the Texas sun blazed down and the heat became too much to handle, we'd leave our clubhouse and escape into the cooler embrace of the woods. We always reassured ourselves there was no need to worry—after all, what dangerous animals could lurk in such a familiar place? No tigers, bears, or rhinoceroses here, right?

Our afternoons turned into explorations filled with wonder as we flipped over decaying tree logs and large rocks, revealing all sorts of creepy crawlies hiding beneath them. Each discovery felt like unearthing hidden treasures.

About a week later, after Ryan and I wrapped up an epic day of exploring, and in the comfort of our respective homes, something wild happened. A massive thunderstorm rolled in, turning the skies dark and dramatic. The rain came down like a waterfall, lightning danced across the horizon, and the wind howled fiercely—like a pack of wolves on the hunt. It was one of those storms that simultaneously made you feel exhilarated and a little scared. The rain poured in sheets, so heavy it seemed to come from every direction at once. But then, just as suddenly as it arrived, the storm passed.

The next morning greeted us with a stunning clear blue sky

that seemed almost too perfect to be real. The air was fresh and invigorating, filled with the scent of wet earth after a rain. And oh, how sweet it was to hear birds chirping cheerfully again.

Like most mornings, we hopped on our bikes, racing to our clubhouse with the excitement befitting a summer day. But nothing prepared us for the sight that awaited us. Our cherished sanctuary, once a vibrant hub of laughter and adventure, lay in ruins—completely destroyed by the storm. The sight of our clubhouse reduced to a soggy heap of smelly cardboard hit us like a ton of bricks.

A few days later, it was as if the clubhouse had been only in our minds, overshadowed by the thrill of new adventures. Isn't it amazing how, as kids, we quickly adapt to change? One moment, we're laughing and playing in our cardboard clubhouse, and the next, we're off exploring uncharted territories—like the mysterious woods behind my house or the secret hideouts at the park.

Shaking away childhood memories, I realize Ryan and I are older now, climbing the stairs to our bedroom in my house in Lost Creek Junction. However, one last memory trickles back to me. When Ryan and I were kids, we used to stroll side by side under the glow of the streetlights at the end of each day. Our minds buzzed with laughter and adventure and the fun we'd shared. We didn't need to talk—we walked in silence, a simple yet profound expression of our deep friendship. Sometimes, words can't capture the love you feel for someone. Silence—a powerful non-verbal communication—speaks volumes in those moments, strengthening bonds even further.

In our quiet moment on the stairs leading to our bedroom, I gently squeeze Ryan's hand. It's a simple gesture, but it speaks volumes. He returns the squeeze with a warm smile, and we climb the steps side by side together.

As I glance at him, I notice how he radiates joy—like a proud peacock flaunting its vibrant feathers. His happiness is infectious, lighting up the dimly lit staircase and warming my heart.

Dale Thele

DAY THIRTY-EIGHT

Thursday, June 21, 2018

Gathered around the breakfast table, the essence of coffee and fried bacon lingers in the air, a perfect complement to the delicious meal we've just enjoyed.

"Can you believe it?" Ryan shakes his head in disbelief. "Who would've thought we could pull off such a massive project in such a short amount of time?"

"Hey," Duncan jumps in, "we didn't do it alone—the entire town rallied together to make this happen."

"True," I add, "but while the town might be ready to welcome visitors, have we done enough to ensure we'll raise the funds to save the town?"

"You guys worry too much," Julie interjects with a reassuring smile. "Have faith—everything will work out, you'll see."

"Julie," Duncan playfully nudges, "you've been reading too many of those motivational books."

I chuckle and add, "Books aside, I hope Julie's onto something here. There are so many things that could still go wrong."

"Like what?" Julie asks.

"The weather, for instance," I reply. "What if it rains incessantly all summer? The weather has been unusually erratic since we arrived."

"I agree the weather has been unpredictable lately," Duncan says. "But honestly, once Mother Nature works these late spring storms out of her system, we'll be lucky to see even a light sprinkle. Texas Hill Country summers are typically bone-dry. I Googled it."

"I suppose you're right," I concede, feeling more at ease. "Still, so many other things could go wrong."

"Name one," Ryan challenges, a smirk playing on his lips.

"I can name two—Ezekiel and Abrahim," I reply. "What if they come back and stir up trouble? They could mess up everything we're trying to do."

"Maybe they got pissed off during the town meeting and left town," Ryan suggests with a casual shrug.

"How could they do that with the curse hanging over this town?" I counter. "Even if they wanted to escape, they can't go beyond the city limits—they're ghosts, remember? Besides, have you forgotten they showed up at the town meeting?"

"Ah, that's right," Ryan admits.

"Honestly, if you ask me," Julie says, "I think you're making this into something more than it is—a classic case of making a mountain out of a molehill."

"I agree with Julie," Ryan says, nodding with a satisfied grin.

Just then, Beau saunters into the kitchen, his eyes glued to the closed door as if he's expecting it to magically swing open—like those sleek electric sliding doors at the mall. You can practically feel his eagerness radiating off him—he's absolutely itching to go outside.

As I push away from the table, the chair legs screech against the floor, breaking the momentary silence with a squeal that echoes around us. At the sound, Beau whirls around and starts barking excitedly, his playful yelps filling the kitchen like the morning sun streaming in the windows.

"Alright, alright," I call to Beau, rolling my eyes. "I'm coming—hold your horses."

Man, talk about impatient, I grumble to myself as I release the latch and swing open the door.

Beau bolts through like a bull in a china shop. His burst of energy completely catches me off guard. Before I know it, his wagging tail disappears out the door, and I'm left sprawled on the floor, dazed and trying to wrap my head around what just happened.

Julie, Duncan, and Ryan burst out laughing at my expense. It's like I've become the star of my own shtick comedy show.

Duncan rises from his chair and offers a hand to help me back on my feet.

"Are you okay?" he asks with genuine concern. "You took quite a spill."

"I'm fine," I respond, getting back on my feet and rubbing my stunned tailbone.

"You have to admit," Julie says with a grin, "there's never a dull moment when Beau is around."

"Not to change the subject," Ryan adds, "but doesn't Beau have a birthday soon?"

"Actually, my birthday comes before his," I chuckle, "and it's still a couple of months away."

"Oh, right," Ryan nods sheepishly. "I knew someone had a birthday coming up."

"What great friends I have," I tease. "You guys remember my dog's birthday but not mine."

"That's because Beau has way more personality," Julie giggles, her eyes sparkling with mischief.

"And let's be honest—he's definitely cuter than you," Duncan adds with a playful smirk.

I turn to Ryan, raising an eyebrow. "Rye," I warn, "you'd best keep that mouth of yours zipped if you don't want to share the parlor settee with Beau for the rest of our summer break."

Ryan dramatically pretends to zip his lips shut.

I can't help but smile. It's moments like this that remind me how well I've trained him.

There was a time as kids when Ryan and I transformed my backyard into a bustling pretend circus. Ryan played a ferocious lion while I strutted around as his ever-determined trainer. Armed with a sturdy tree branch and a thick string tied to its end, I'd crack the branch like a whip to coax him into performing for our imaginary audience.

But let's be real—Ryan wasn't the most obedient lion out

there. He'd often stubbornly ignore my commands until I swatted him on the rear with my makeshift whip one day after having enough of his disobedience. Talk about instant results. From that moment on, he did everything I instructed him to do. Sometimes, you have to crack the whip to get your boyfriend to act right, am I right?

Enough with the childhood memories. Let's return to the present day as my friends and I prep the house for our first bed-and-breakfast guests.

"Chop. Chop. We need to get moving," Julie exclaims, rising from her chair with a sense of urgency. "Our very first guests are checking in today, and we must be at our best to welcome them. There's so much to do before they arrive."

"What can I do to help?" Ryan asks, ready to pitch in.

"First things first," Julie explains, her eyes sparkling with determination. "Move all our clothes and belongings to the garage apartment. My stuff is already packed and sitting on my bed. Can you take them over for me? And please—be extra careful with the fragile items. We definitely don't want anything getting broken."

"Taylor's all set—his bags are packed and ready to go," Ryan says with a grin. "It won't take me long to pack."

Julie looks over at Duncan, her voice bright and urgent. "Duncan, can you be a dear and lend Rye a hand with moving our stuff to the apartment?"

"Absolutely," Duncan replies, springing into action.

"Hey, Taylor," Julie says cheerfully, "could you please double-check we haven't missed anything? The housekeeping ghosts will change the bed linens and put out fresh towels for our guests, but it's not their responsibility to keep track of our forgotten items."

Ryan raises an eyebrow and asks, "So, what will you be doing?"

"I'll be cleaning the kitchen," Julie replies with a casual shrug. "Oh, and Taylor," she adds, "could you give me a lift to the grocery store in a bit? I need to pick up a couple of things before our guests arrive."

"Sure, it's not a problem," I respond. "Beau needs kibble anyway."

"This will be my first ride in your Jeep since Duncan got it running," Julie giggles, her eyes sparkling with anticipation. "I can't wait."

Meanwhile, Beau saunters into the kitchen after being outside, his paws cheerfully thumping against the floor. He goes straight to his water bowl, takes several big slurps, and vigorously shakes his head, spraying water in every direction. The sunlight streaming through the window catches those droplets just right, creating a dazzling rainbow effect to dance across the kitchen walls.

"Taylor," Julie growls, her tone leaving no room for debate. "Get Beau out of here and take his water and food bowls to the garage. He and his bowls can't stay in the house, not with guests arriving."

"Yes, ma'am," I reply, mock saluting while clicking my Nike trainers together like an obedient soldier.

With a gentle coaxing, I lead Beau out of the kitchen and into the garage—his new home for the remainder of our summer vacation. As I set down his bowls, I feel guilty kicking him out of the house.

When I return to the kitchen, it's eerily quiet—only Julie remains.

"Where's everyone?" I ask, scanning the empty space.

"Rye and Duncan are carrying out their assignments," she replies matter-of-factly. "Are you ready to take me to the grocery store?"

A little while later, Julie and I pull into the driveway after our grocery run.

"Thanks for the lift to the store," she says, unloading bags of fresh produce and foodstuff from the back of my Jeep.

"No problem," I reply, balancing grocery bags in my arms.

"By the way," Julie grins, "Duncan did an amazing job fixing your Jeep."

"He did, didn't he?" I smile as I think about how great it feels to finally have my own wheels.

"I think your Jeep is pretty cool," Julie remarks, her eyes sparkling.

"Hey there, I was starting to worry I'd need to organize a search party for you two," Duncan quips with a playful grin as he steps out of the side door of the house.

"Seriously, Duncan?" Julie giggles as she hands her grocery bags to him. "We weren't gone that long—just a quick trip to the grocery store."

As we step inside the house, I struggle to balance my bags, realizing no one is offering to help me.

"Where do you want these?" Duncan asks Julie, motioning his head at the full bags in his arms.

"Just set them on the kitchen table for now," she says. "I've got to sort out what stays in the house and what goes to the apartment."

Duncan furrows his brow, looking clearly confused. "I'm not following," he admits.

"It's simple," Julie smiles, happy to explain. "Some of these groceries are for the breakfasts we'll prepare for our guests in the house, while the other items will be for our lunches and suppers in the apartment."

"Oh, I see now," Duncan nods in understanding.

"By the way," I interject, "have you made a schedule for who'll make and serve breakfast for our guests and on which days?"

"It's simple," Julie replies while sorting groceries. "All four of us will make and serve breakfast, together."

"What? Really?" Duncan asks, looking puzzled.

"Absolutely. It's only fair we share the breakfast responsibilities," Julie asserts with a smile. "We'll have our breakfasts here in the house after our guests have had theirs. And don't forget—someone has to wash and dry the dishes afterward."

"I feel like us guys got stuck with the short end of the stick," Duncan sighs.

"Who got stuck with what?" Ryan asks, strolling into the kitchen with a curious look.

"Here," Julie chimes in, handing Ryan a couple of bags of groceries. "Take these to the apartment."

"Why am I always getting roped into doing things around here?" Ryan grumbles, raising an eyebrow as he accepts the load.

"Because this time, you're closest to the door," Julie snickers, her eyes sparkling with mischief.

Ryan exits through the side door with a huff, grocery bags in tow. He mutters something under his breath—it's probably best we don't know what he's saying.

"Alrighty," Julie exclaims, a satisfied smile spreading across her face as she takes in the sparkling, clean kitchen. "We're ready to welcome our first guests."

Just then, a knock echoes from the front door, breaking the moment of tranquility.

The three of us exchange curious glances, our eyebrows rise in anticipation.

"Who do you suppose that could be?" Duncan asks. "Our first guests aren't expected to arrive until later this afternoon."

"Standing around like fools isn't getting us anywhere," Julie replies with a grin, "let's go see who it is."

Filled with excitement and a touch of nervousness, Julie and I follow Duncan as he confidently strides toward the front door. With a swift motion, he swings the door open, revealing our very first guests from Dallas—the ghost hunters' tech crew. They've arrived several hours earlier than expected, but it's not a big deal—we're ready for them. Their task is to set up equipment before tomorrow when their bosses and the ghost investigators arrive.

The tech crew are an odd group of nerds (excuse my bluntness) They consist of three men and one woman—who expertly maneuver trunk after trunk of equipment into the house, accompanied by an impressive array of electronics, tangled cables, and sleek laptops. Who knew behind-the-scenes operations requires such an overwhelming amount of gear?

Julie and Duncan show our guests to their rooms and then move out of the way, allowing the crew to begin setting up their high-tech arsenal.

With a flutter of nerves and excitement bubbling in my stomach, I go to the bed-and-breakfast check-in desk in the parlor for my first shift as the official on-duty desk clerk.

"If you need anything—anything at all—just let me know. I'll be right here at the check-in desk," I call out to the crew, but they're engrossed in their tasks, it's as if I'm not even here.

DAY THIRTY-NINE

Friday, June 22, 2018

Today is an exciting day for ghost enthusiasts and the curious alike. Paranormal investigators from all over the country are gathering in Lost Creek Junction, ready to uncover the mysteries hidden within this fascinating town. TV news crews are prepared to broadcast any ghost findings live across the nation, creating an atmosphere of anticipation.

Imagine if everything goes smoothly and the spirits choose to cooperate—Lost Creek Junction could become the ultimate hotspot for ghost fans everywhere. Just picture it—a place where stories of ghosts and spooks come to life, attracting visitors eager to experience the supernatural. The potential impact on our little town's future is enormous.

Julie and I are bustling around the kitchen, whipping up a scrumptious breakfast for our group of four tech-savvy guests. This weekend is our exciting dress rehearsal before we officially open our doors to paying guests at the bed-and-breakfast. Today, paranormal and media crews will be arriving to delve into the mysteries of Lost Creek Junction and uncover verifiable ghostly presences. If all goes well and the buzz is favorable, we could welcome our very first paying guests in just a week.

Can you imagine the tantalizing aromas filling the air? Fresh coffee is brewing, biscuits are rising in the oven, and bacon is sizzling to perfection. It's the perfect start to a whirlwind day, especially with four paranormal investigators and a couple of TV news crews set to arrive later. It's going to be a thrilling and busy day ahead.

Meanwhile, Ryan is putting the finishing touches on the dining room table to ensure everything's just right for our guests. With plates set and silverware shining, it's shaping up to be quite a breakfast spread.

The three guys from the tech crew bound down the stairs from their third-floor bedrooms, buzzing with excitement. You can feel their energy in the air.

"Listen up, this place is definitely a paranormal hotspot," one of them exclaims into his cell phone. Meanwhile, his friends nod enthusiastically in agreement. "Last night, Jake claims he saw an apparition, Ted picked up some weird presence on his monitor, and I swear I saw a chair move all by itself—no joke. You've got to get here as soon as you can."

A crew member leans in with a playful grin and offers a lighthearted apology for his overly enthusiastic friend as they settle into their seats at the table. "Just ignore him," he chuckles, gesturing toward the guy engrossed in a phone call. "He's giving the morning report to the boss in Dallas."

"So, how did you sleep last night?" I ask while pouring freshly brewed coffee into our guests' cups.

"It was a bizarre night," one crew member chuckles, shaking his head in disbelief.

"You can say that again," another chimes in, eyes wide with excitement.

Once the guy finishes his cell phone call, the tech team erupts into a whirlwind of chatter, sharing their strange experiences from the night.

"Did you hear those weird sounds?" one exclaims. "They seemed to come from everywhere."

"What was that?"

"Could it have been a draft blowing through the house?"

"Too loud. Maybe air in the pipes?"

"The sounds came from too many directions simultaneously."

"And what about that flickering lamp?" adds another, leaning in closer as if sharing a secret. "I figured it was a faulty wire or bad bulb, and when I checked—the table lamp was unplugged from the wall outlet."

"Was the lamp battery operated?"

"Nope, I checked, the ceramic base, it was hollow inside."

Each story is more captivating than the last—the crew felt a spine-tingling sensation of being watched. "It's as if unseen eyes are observing our every move," a crew member says.

Ryan is on the verge of breaking into laughter. His face is contorted in a heroic effort to maintain a straight face, but the signs are unmistakable. His shoulders shake with barely suppressed giggles, his cheeks bulge as if he's trying to hold back a balloon, and his eyes? They glisten with tears—evidence an outburst of laughter is just moments away.

Listening to the excited skeptics who analyze everything through a scientific lens is quite a spectacle. Their animated descriptions of what they've witnessed make me want to chuckle, but I manage to keep a smug smile in check. After all, there's no scientific explanation for the bizarre happenings in this house—unless one believes in the existence of ghosts.

One crew member, blissfully unaware of the house's haunted reputation, innocently asks, "Have you guys ever seen ghosts in this house?"

"Oh," Julie replies with a playful smirk, casually waving her hand as she doles out fresh biscuits from the oven. "Maybe on rare occasions."

That's the final straw for Ryan. He bolts to the parlor like a man on fire and buries his face in a decorative throw pillow as he erupts in a fit of uncontrollable laughter.

The female crew member enters the dining room as if in a trance. Her distant, unfocused eyes seem to gaze beyond our reality, and her movements are slow and deliberate, almost dreamlike. With an air of mystery, she takes her seat at the table, her wide-eyed stare fixed on something invisible to the rest of us.

"Did you sleep well?" Julie asks.

"Uh-uh. Sort of," she replies in a distant voice, nodding with a blank expression. "Last night. I think I saw a ghost. No. I'm certain—I definitely saw a ghost," she insists, her voice quivering under the weight of her eerie revelation.

Julie suppresses a chuckle as she pours a steaming cup of coffee for the bewildered crew member.

If the experiences of these four crew members are any indication, Lost Creek Junction could be on the verge of becoming the next big tourist destination. Who wouldn't want to visit a place with real ghosts and strange things that go bump in the night?

Shortly after lunch, the Dallas paranormal investigative team—a tight-knit crew of three enthusiastic men and one fearless woman, arrive ready to plunge into their work. Julie, the ever thoughtful host, whips up some delicious sandwiches for them, which they gratefully devour before immersing themselves into the videotapes, recordings, and notes the tech crew provides for their review. Eager to collect all the details about the spine-chilling encounters the tech crew reports from last night, they focus intently on the materials at hand.

After the Dallas paranormal investigative team begins their initial work, news crews from NBC5 Dallas-Fort Worth News and KWTV Oklahoma City arrive and check into their respective rooms. Overnight, Lost Creek Junction has become a hub of paranormal activity, bustling with various investigative teams and news outlets from cities such as Philadelphia, Las Vegas, Seattle, and even New York City.

Everywhere you look, haunted bed-and-breakfasts and the recently reopened hotel are filled with curious organizations eager to explore the supernatural. Main Street is a sight to behold, lined with TV news trailers equipped with large satellite dishes on their roofs, each set to broadcast this significant event live.

This weekend isn't just an ordinary weekend—it's a pivotal moment for Lost Creek Junction. The stakes are high for both the living residents and the spirits inhabiting this town. Every resident hopes the visiting paranormal investigators will confirm

Lost Creek Junction's reputation as an authentic ghost town. The very future of the town rests on the outcome of this weekend.

Dale Thele

DAY FORTY

Saturday, June 23, 2018

The sun is beginning to rise, casting a mellow glow upon the hill overlooking Lost Creek Junction. Last night, Julie, Ryan, Beau, and I stayed in the garage apartment to give our bed-and-breakfast guests their privacy. Meanwhile, Duncan worked the overnight shift at the check-in desk in the parlor. He must still be asleep at his post because we haven't seen him yet this morning.

So here we are—Julie, Ryan and myself—pacing the floor, eagerly awaiting the overnight report from the paranormal investigators. The suspense is almost unbearable.

As the paranormal investigation team descends the stairs, a buzz of excitement fills the air. This eclectic mix of seasoned ghost hunters and tech-savvy experts hardly contain their enthusiasm as they settle into the dining room.

"Shew, what a night," exclaims one of the tech crew members, his eyes wide with wonder. "It felt like a roller coaster ride of paranormal activity. Seriously, we couldn't keep up with everything going on in this house. It's as if this place is a living, breathing entity."

"Did you hear those footsteps in the attic?" one techie asks, eyes wide with disbelief. "But here's the kicker—the attic cameras didn't capture anyone or anything to explain those eerie sounds."

Another techie jumps in, adding fuel to the fire. "And what about those floating objects on the second floor? I swear on my grandmother's grave, I saw chairs and books gliding through the air like they were possessed. It's like something straight out of a science fiction movie, defying every law of physics we know."

"Can you believe it? We actually encountered a real paranormal apparition in the second-floor hall," exclaims the lead paranormal investigator, his eyes sparkling with excitement as he quickly sips his coffee. "In my professional career as a ghost hunter, this is the first time I've come across an apparition that actively interacted with us. It introduced itself as Ezekiel and said it lived during the 1800s. What's even more impressive is that we captured the entire spine-tingling experience on video."

"Hold on, did I hear you correctly? You have video proof of a ghost?" The reporter from NBC5 Dallas-Fort Worth News steps into the dining room, his eyes wide with curiosity.

"Yes, my team certainly does," the paranormal investigator proudly replies.

"Can my TV station have exclusive rights to that footage?" the reporter pleads, excited to share this once-in-a-lifetime scoop with viewers. The tape may garner him an Emmy and a promotion.

"Absolutely, why not?" the paranormal investigator replies with a grin, excitement shining in his eyes.

Gathered around the table, the paranormal crew buzzes with energy as they share their astonishing experiences from the previous night. Each story is more thrilling than the last, captivating their peers and the eager TV news crews who are documenting every spine-tingling moment.

Ezekiel's sudden reappearance has put me on edge—it feels like a giant red flag. The last time he was around was during that disastrous mine collapse, the one I'm sure he caused. So, why is he back now? What's his angle? His presence could seriously interfere with our plans to save Lost Creek Junction.

"Ezekiel is a volatile spirit," the lead investigator states matter-of-factly. "His demeanor radiates angry hostility, and honestly, there's no telling what he might do next."

"What makes you say that?" I ask.

"Well," he replies, leaning in closer as if sharing a thrilling secret. "It's all about the erratic behavior—jerky movements and those intimidating facial expressions. It's like trying to predict a storm—you never know when it will hit or how fierce it will be."

"Did Ezekiel try to harm you?" Julie asks.

The lead investigator chuckles and shakes his head. "Oh, he can't physically harm anyone," he explains, waving a dismissive hand. "You see, he's the spirit of a man who died over two hundred years ago. He doesn't have the physical ability to interact with our three-dimensional world. He's a two-dimensional, floating talking head—no body at all, for reasons we can only speculate about."

I can't help but think to myself, *Don't get too cocky, Mr. Paranormal Investigator—you might be underestimating what Ezekiel is capable of doing.*

Under the shade of the twisted Live Oak trees in my front yard, the paranormal investigators take center stage at a thrilling televised news conference, revealing their spine-tingling discoveries in the afternoon heat. They boldly announce—over the screaming cicadas—to news crews that the grand old house perched on the hill is home to multiple spirits.

As reporters and camera operators gather around, the investigators share jaw-dropping video clips showcasing the eerie events that unfolded during their overnight investigation in my very own house. The clips, which include flickering lights and unexplained whispers, leave everyone on the edge of their seats.

This event is not just a win for the investigators; it also shines a significant spotlight on Lost Creek Junction.

Armed with their intriguing discoveries, paranormal investigators invite reporters and camera crews to join them for their final night of exploration inside my haunted house. While this is happening at my house, other haunted bed-and-breakfasts across Lost Creek Junction are extending similar invitations, making our little town a hub of ghostly intrigue.

This town is buzzing like never before, attracting attention across television, radio, newspapers, and social media platforms. YouTube videos featuring paranormal investigators and their eerie adventures are garnering a significant number of views and sparking online discussions. As a delightful result, my bed-and-breakfast is experiencing an extraordinary deluge of reservations. With nearly all our rooms booked for the upcoming year in just one afternoon, we even had to create a waiting list.

This newfound fame is thrilling and promises to significantly boost the Lost Creek Junction economy—hopefully enough to save the town from demise.

DAY FORTY-SIX

Friday, June 29, 2018

Ryan stands before us, practically bubbling with energy. "Are we all set for today?" he asks, sounding overly enthusiastic—almost like a high school cheerleader.

"It's our first official public ghost town weekend," I announce proudly, feeling the thrill in the air. I hope the ghosts are ready to entertain our first paying bed-and-breakfast guests and don't let us down.

"Can you believe the flood of reservations we've received since those paranormal investigators featured our ghosts on TV?" Julie exclaims, her eyes sparkling with excitement. "We're fully booked for the next year and beyond."

Duncan nods, a hint of nervousness creeping into his voice. "Well, the real test will be this weekend. Let's hope we can meet our guests' expectations."

Ryan chimes in with a grin, "Correction. Don't you mean let's hope the ghosts deliver? They're the main attraction, after all."

"Alright, everyone. It's time to wrap up breakfast so I can clean the kitchen," Julie announces, her apron dusted with flour and her hair pulled into a messy bun.

"Hey Julie, is there any more toast?" Ryan asks, his eyes hopeful.

"What did I just say?" Julie responds sharply, giving him a pointed look while placing her hands firmly on her hips.

"Okay, okay," Ryan concedes, throwing his hands up. "No need to have a conniption."

"Julie, how can I help?" I offer.

"Count me in," Duncan adds. "Let us know we can do."

There's a sudden knock at the front door, causing us to exchange curious glances.

"Oh no, they're here already," Julie gasps, her eyes wide with panic. "Goodness gracious, look at me. I'm a total mess." In a flurry of activity, she rips off her apron and hurriedly pulls her hair out of its bun, strands flying in every direction.

"Should we see who's at the door?" I ask.

"What are you waiting for, an engraved invitation?" Julie snaps. "Let's answer the door."

I lead the procession to the front door, my friends trailing closely behind—it's like déjà vu.

"How do I look?" Julie asks, her fingers combing through her hair. A hint of nervousness lingers in her voice.

"You look terrific," Ryan replies, although there's a slight hesitation in his words.

As I swing open the door, I'm met by a young couple standing before us, their smiles bright and warm, like the sunshine on a perfect day.

"We're the Jackson's," the man exclaims, his tall frame casting a shadow over his shorter petite wife. His voice is filled with contagious excitement which instantly draws me in. "I'm James, and this is my lovely wife, Georgina. We have a reservation."

Despite their excitement, the Jackson's nervous energy is apparent, stirring a sense of sympathy in me. It feels as if they've never ventured beyond the familiar streets of their small Midwestern town—or at least that's how I imagine them.

Georgina's cheeks flush a delightful shade of pink as she shyly admits, "This is our first time staying at a bed-and-breakfast."

"Don't worry. This is our first time hosting one," Julie admits.

After a moment of awkward silence, we all burst into nervous laughter.

"Silly me, where are my manners? Please, come in," I say. "Can I help you with your bags?"

With a grateful nod, Georgina hands her suitcase over to me

and in turn, I hand it over to Duncan.

"I'm Taylor," I say with a warm smile. "And these are my friends Julie, Ryan, and Duncan. We're thrilled to be your hosts during your stay."

"Oh my goodness," Georgina gasps, her eyes sparkling as she enters the parlor. "This room, it's spectacular. It's so Victorian. Isn't this place absolutely lovely, Jimmy?"

"It's like we've stepped into a time capsule," James muses, his voice filled with awe. "I feel like a bull in a china shop, fearing I might accidentally break something. Everything looks so... expensive."

"Relax," Julie chuckles. "You'll get used to this place in no time. It's not as intimidating as it seems."

"Let me show you to your room," Duncan offers, leading toward the staircase.

"Jimmy, you have to see this. The hand-carved wooden railing on the staircase is absolutely stunning," Georgina exclaims, her eyes sparkling with excitement.

"I think she's officially a fan of this house," I whisper to Julie.

Julie nods and smiles back.

There's a knock at the door.

As Ryan swings open the door, he greets the newcomers with a bright smile. "Welcome to Blackburn House Bed-and-Breakfast."

"We're the Morrison's," the man standing at the threshold replies with a smile. "We have a reservation."

"Come in, come in," Ryan gestures invitingly. "I'm Ryan—this is Julie and Taylor. Duncan is currently helping other guests settle in but will join us shortly. We're thrilled to be your hosts during your stay."

Mr. Morrison steps forward, his eyes sparkling with excitement. "I'm Charles, and this lovely lady beside me is my better half, Millie."

"May I show you to your room?" I offer.

"Charlie, check out this incredible vintage house," Millie

exclaims as she enters the parlor. Her eyes sparkle like stars on a clear night. She twirls in place, radiating the pure joy of a child on Christmas morning. "I can already feel vibrations from another dimension." With her eyes closed and arms outstretched, she looks like a kid playing pin the tail on the donkey, completely immersed in her magical make-believe world. "I sense the presence of friendly spirits here. They're giving me chills. Can you feel them too, Charlie? Can you?"

"Okay, let's not overdo it, Millie. We don't want you wearing yourself out," Charles says with a forced smile, gently guiding his wife toward the stairs. His voice is filled with genuine concern for her well-being.

"This weekend is going to be absolutely amazing. I feel it. Can't you feel it, Charlie? Can't you?" Millie exclaims, practically bouncing with excitement and anticipation.

"You'll have to forgive my wife," Charles nervously chuckles. "She's a self-proclaimed medium who would probably faint at the sight of a real ghost. This trip is to indulge her passion and hopefully get this hocus-pocus out of her system."

"Yes, sir," I reply as I guide the Morrison's up the stairs.

Additional guests arrive, and among them is Wilhelmina Klumpt—a vivacious woman who seems to have stepped out of a glamorous high-society gala. She commands attention with every click of her high-heeled pumps against the polished floor. Her sparkling jewelry glimmers like stars in the night sky, while a flamboyant, flower-adorned hat adds an enchanting touch to her outfit.

The air around her is infused with the intoxicating scent of exotic flowers. When she speaks, her thick German accent wraps around her words like a mystery waiting to be unraveled. Is she truly an aristocrat? I wonder how someone so refined ended up in Lost Creek Junction, after all, this quaint little town isn't exactly known for having five-star luxury hotels.

Perhaps that's what makes her presence all the more intriguing. In a place where simplicity reigns supreme, Wilhelmina brings a splash of elegance and flair leaving us curious about her story. What adventures led her here? What secrets does she hold?

Next up is Mr. Simon S. Smith—a curious figure whose name raises a question: is it truly his, or merely a clever disguise? Picture a middle-aged man with slicked-back dark hair that may or may not be a toupee. He stands tall and lanky, wearing a gray mole-hair sports jacket with suede elbow patches, giving him an air of intellectual charm, easily leading one to mistake him for a learned college professor.

But there's more to Mr. Smith than meets the eye. As he puffs on his Sherlock Holmes-style pipe filled with cherry tobacco, you can't help but wonder what stories lie behind those mysterious eyes. Is he a scholar of hidden knowledge or perhaps an eccentric detective on the hunt for the next great mystery to solve?

Meet the fabulous duo, William (Billy) Boyd and Carlyle (Carl) Kravis. This charmingly quirky couple of middle-aged gay men proves love knows no bounds—nor fashion rules.

Billy is a vibrant force of nature with an eye for style effortlessly mixing men's and women's clothing. He isn't shy about wearing bold makeup, and his spontaneous outbursts of random screams never fail to catch those around him off guard.

On the flip side, we have Carl, whose sophisticated style tells a different story. With his iconic porn-style mustache, luxurious silk smoking jacket, and dapper satin ascot, he exudes an air of classic elegance. Picture him elegantly chain-smoking clove cigarettes from a chic holder—he certainly makes a statement.

Despite their contrasting styles, one thing remains crystal clear—their love and respect for each other shine brighter than the outlandish outfits they wear. They are an entertaining sight that won't fail to amuse our other guests.

Last but certainly not least, we have the enchanting Lady Douché (French, pronounced *dew-shay*)—a true vision of glamour. Draped in a snug-fitting evening gown accentuating her curves perfectly and sporting high-coiffed hair reminiscent of classic 60s movie stars, she's truly a sight to behold. Her regal grace is heightened by her playful habit of calling everyone *darlin.*' Can you imagine how that single word rolls over her pouty, sensual glossy red lips? It adds an almost scandalous touch to her charm.

Duncan is captivated by her beauty and charisma. She's not just a pretty face—she embodies allure in every sense of the word. So, tell me, what red-blooded heterosexual man wouldn't be drawn to her magnetic presence?

"Is Lady Douché a drag queen?" Julie leans in, whispering into my ear, eyes sparkling with mischief.

"What makes you ask?" I question, intrigued by her sudden curiosity.

With a cheeky grin, she replies, "Real women don't have Adam's apples."

I chuckle at the thought. Could it be we've welcomed our very first guest drag queen?

"Whatever you do," I tell Julie, "don't let Duncan know. It'll crush him."

The both of us giggle at the idea.

Julie, Duncan, Ryan, and I are fully committed to running the check-in desk which Duncan carefully crafted in the parlor. This isn't just any desk—it's the hub of activity and the heart of our operation.

We take turns manning the desk, handling various tasks like answering phone calls, managing reservations, and tackling any business matters that may pop up. But let's be real—we're here to assist our guests. Do they need directions? Are they looking for fun local activities? Or maybe they need extra towels? Whatever it is, we've got our guests' backs.

The desk is open 24/7—even on weekends—because we believe in being available whenever our guests need us. We're all about quality guest service. And don't worry about us burning out—we have a cozy little space in the back where our overnight attendant can catch some Zs when things get quiet at night.

Duncan takes over at the desk for me as the clock strikes six in the evening, relieving me of my eight-hour shift. I slip out of the house through the side door and head to the garage apartment. We've just completed our first full day as an officially licensed, insured, and bonded bed-and-breakfast. Can you believe it? With no major hiccups, I can't help but feel a swell of pride for what we've accomplished. It's not just about running a business—it's about creating a welcoming home away from home for our guests. Here's to many more successful days ahead.

Dale Thele

DAY FORTY-SEVEN

Saturday, June 30, 2018

Julie and I sneak into the house through the side entrance, making sure to keep our footsteps light. The peaceful atmosphere suggests all our guests are tucked away in their beds, lost in their dreams. While Julie heads off to the kitchen to start preparing a delicious breakfast for our guests, I go to the parlor, eager to let in some morning light by drawing back the curtains.

But wait—what's this? To my surprise, I spot Billy sitting alone in the dark parlor. He's fully dressed but looks utterly distraught. It's an unexpected scene for such an early hour.

"Billy, you startled me. Why are you sitting in the dark? Didn't you ring the desk bell for assistance?"

"I didn't want to disturb anyone," he replies.

"I'm here now. Is there something I can do for you?" I ask.

"Yes, you can. Please call me a taxi. I will not spend another minute in this dreadful house," he exclaims, his frustration evident as he loudly blows his nose into a lace-trimmed handkerchief.

Next to him sits a suitcase, packed, ready for escape.

"Have we done something to upset you?" I inquire.

"Yes, you have," he snaps back. "You should have warned us about the real ghosts haunting this place."

I raise an eyebrow and respond, "Well, we thought it was pretty clear this is a haunted bed-and-breakfast."

"Honestly, I was expecting mediocre amusement park pranks and flashy visual effects, not real, actual ghosts," Billy exclaims, his eyes wide with disbelief.

"Did any of the ghosts try to harm you?" I ask.

"Thankfully, no," Billy replies, relief washing over his face. "But just the very thought is enough to send shivers down my spine. I'm ready to leave as soon as you call me a taxi."

"What about Carl?" I inquire, wanting to know if his friend had a similar experience.

"Forget about him," Billy waves a dismissive hand. "He's sound asleep. My husband found last night's madness absolutely intriguing. Now he wants a pet ghost. Can you believe it?"

I stifle a smile and reply, "Well, I'm afraid it doesn't work that way with ghosts."

Billy's expression changes to one of urgency. "Please, call a taxi right away so I can leave immediately."

"Wouldn't you like to have some breakfast before you go?" I offer.

He pauses, clearly conflicted. "Well," he hesitates, "is that coffee I smell? It smells delightful. I suppose one cup wouldn't hurt. That is, if I could have two sugars and a splash of cream?"

"You got it," I say.

"That sounds heavenly," Billy says. "Alright, you twisted my arm into staying—just for one cup of coffee, mind you, then I'm leaving."

I escort Billy into the dining room, where the aroma of breakfast fills the air.

"Good morning, Mr. Billy," Julie says as she approaches with a thermal coffee pot. "Would you like some coffee to start your day?"

"Heavens, yes. That sounds exquisite—two sugars and a splash of cream, if you please," Billy replies, settling comfortably at the table.

With a grand flourish rivaling any cooking show host, Julie announces, "This morning's breakfast is truly a feast fit for royalty. We have eggs cooked just the way you like them, irresistible bacon crackling with flavor, fresh buttermilk biscuits straight from the oven begging to be slathered in butter, and a vibrant cup of mixed seasonal fruit to refresh your palate."

Julie, can we tone it down a bit? I think to myself.

"Everything sounds absolutely scrumptious," Billy exclaims, his wide grin revealing his eagerness as he rubs his hands together in anticipation.

At that moment, the atmosphere changes with the entrance of Wilhelmina Klumpt and Millie Morrison, who are impeccably dressed and radiating elegance. Their laughter fills the air like two giddy schoolgirls sharing delightful secrets. Their joy is contagious, and their beaming smiles light up the room.

"Did you see last night's show? It was nothing short of spectacular," Wilhelmina enthusiastically declares in her thick German accent.

"It was truly out of this world," Millie adds, her eyes sparkling with excitement as she emphasizes her words with dramatic hand gestures.

"How on earth did you manage to pull off those incredible flying acrobatics?" Wilhelmina asks of me, her eyes sparkling with curiosity.

"I'm sorry, but I'm not sure I understand what you mean," I reply.

"Oh, come now. You're just being modest," she teases, playfully waving away my response with a napkin before spreading it across her lap.

Just then, the atmosphere shifts again as Georgina Jackson strolls into the dining room with her husband in tow. "Good morning, everyone," she chirps.

"Looks like it's going to be another scorcher today," Jimmy Jackson adds, wiping the sweat from his brow. "My wife and I aren't used to this sort of humidity—we're from upper New England, you know?"

There goes my Midwestern theory right out the window, I think to myself.

"Did you sleep well?" Millie asks, her voice light and friendly as she turns to the Jackson's.

"Oh, yes, we did. Thank you for asking," Jimmy Jackson replies politely.

However, his wife begins to speak, "To be perfectly honest —"

She's swiftly interrupted by Jimmy's interjection. "Let's not, shall we?" he says softly, glancing at his wife while giving her hand a gentle pat.

The air thickens with unspoken tension, as if everyone senses the weight of what remains unsaid.

"Let's not what?" Georgina challenges sharply, her eyes narrowing. "Let's not discuss the elephant in the room?"

"Good morning, my *darlin's*," Lady Douché announces with a flourish as she glides into the dining room, her presence commanding immediate attention. "Please, don't let me interrupt your discussion."

"Ah, excuse my wife—it was nothing important," Jimmy Jackson replies with a strained smile, pulling out a chair for Lady Douché as if it were the most natural thing in the world. "Just a minor family matter," he adds.

Georgina shoots her husband a glare that could cut through steel—if daggers could kill, Jimmy would be lying on the floor in a pool of his own blood.

"Pleasant morning to everyone," Simon S. Smith chimes cheerfully as he strolls into the room, puffing on his pipe filled with rich cherry tobacco. Wisps of fragrant smoke twirl gracefully in the soft morning light. He takes a seat beside Lady Douché and subtly nudges his chair closer to hers.

In a surprising twist, Lady Douché shifts her chair a few inches away from Simon S. Smith—clearly she doesn't subscribe to his fan club.

Two vacant chairs remain as tensions simmer around the dining table. With a warm smile, Julie pours coffee into the guests' cups while I pass around freshly baked biscuits and locally sourced jam.

"Good morning! Good morning! Good morning!" Ryan exclaims as he bursts into the dining room, his bright smile and cheerful voice ringing like a joyful song. This leaves us waiting for Duncan, who has yet to show up. He worked the guest desk overnight, so he must still be sleeping on the cot in the cubbyhole behind the desk.

Carl Kravis and Charlie Morrison enter the dining room, laughing as if one of them told the world's funniest joke.

"Look who I ran into in the hall—none other than Carl Kravis," Charlie says as he takes a seat next to his wife.

"Good morning, Mr. Kravis," Millie politely acknowledges.

Carl plops into the vacant chair with a grandiose gesture, demanding attention. With a voice that cuts through the morning chatter, he addresses Billy as if his partner is the only person in the room. "Billy, where's your suitcase? And why weren't you in our room?"

Billy fumbles for words, stammering like a kid caught with his hand in the cookie jar. "Well, I, um…"

"Thank you for that concise and provocative answer, that definitely clears things up," Carl retorts, his glare sharp enough to make everyone squirm.

"Carl, can we not clear our dirty laundry in front of everyone, please?" Billy replies, tucking his chin and avoiding Carl's piercing gaze.

"First off," Carl interjects with a smirk, "the phrase is *air one's dirty laundry*, not *clear it*. And second," he continues with a dismissive wave of his hand, "you're making much too much of what happened last night."

A heavy silence settles over the room. Intrigued, the guests lean in closer, their breakfasts ignored as they become engrossed in the unfolding domestic squabble.

Billy lets out a piercing shriek, hitting a perfect high C which startles the guests. "Alright, you got me. The ghosts scared me. Is that what you want to hear? I want to go home, Carl. Home, I tell you," he sobs into a delicate lace handkerchief.

"Ghosts?" Wilhelmina gasps, shock is evident as her eyes widen like saucers.

"Are you saying actual ghosts live in this house? So what we saw last night wasn't a techno show?" Georgina exclaims, her expression a mix of shock and intrigue. "You mean to say there were no actors or puppets—everything we experienced was real?"

"I'm almost hesitant to tell you," I reply cautiously. "But I assure you, whatever you witnessed last night wasn't orchestrated by Julie, Duncan, Ryan, or me. There are indeed honest-to-goodness ghosts haunting this house."

Right on cue, a flower vase on the table suddenly lifts off the surface, defying gravity as it floats gracefully in mid-air. The air around it crackles with an electrifying energy.

Julie dashes over, her instincts kicking in as she grabs the vase and guides it back onto the tabletop.

"Charles? What just happened?" Millie Morrison gasps, her eyes wide as she clutches her husband's arm. "Did you see that? There are real ghosts in this house. They're actually real." Her voice trembles.

"Alright, spirits," Julie announces firmly, her tone steady despite the chaos. "You can show yourselves."

In response to her challenge, transparent human figures begin to materialize before us. Their ghostly forms drift into view, casting an eerie glow enveloping the dining room in a chilling atmosphere. Our guests exchange nervous glances with each other.

Billy lets out a blood-curdling scream, eyes squeezed shut as he nervously recites the Lord's Prayer, crossing himself with fervor. I expect he'll collapse from the vapors at any moment.

Meanwhile, Charles Morrison sits frozen in place, his mouth opening and closing like a fish stranded on dry land—utterly speechless. Wilhelmina holds her cheeks in disbelief, wide eyes reflecting the horror of someone trapped in a waking nightmare.

Then there's Simon S. Smith, who remains eerily still and rigid like a statue, with cherry smoke curling from his pipe like signals summoning reinforcements. A stunned Lady Douché clutches her pearls tightly, her heavily mascaraed false eyelashes don't flutter, making the whites of her eyes seem even larger. All of our guests are too frightened to move a muscle, except for Carl who's unfazed by the madness surrounding him.

He's enjoying his breakfast in peace.

Once the guests recover from the initial shock of discovering our bed-and-breakfast is genuinely haunted by friendly and harmless ghosts, they find enjoyment in the playful antics of our spectral residents. These supernatural beings pose no threat and ensure a safe and comfortable experience for our guests. Instead of evoking fear, their spooky behaviors are seen as entertaining, adding a unique charm not found anywhere else.

A delightful breeze fills the air as the sun sets below the horizon, wrapping the city in twilight. We escort our guests to the excitement of our downtown street fair.

At this vibrant event, inhibitions fade as laughter and joy take center stage. Picture thrilling carnival rides sending your heart racing, alongside mouthwatering food vendors tempting your taste buds with everything from savory bites to sweet treats. Live music gets your feet tapping, creating an infectious atmosphere.

With a dazzling array of booths offering everything from games of chance to mystical fortune-telling, there's something for everyone. Whether you're riding carousel ponies, savoring fluffy pink cotton candy, or daringly sinking your teeth into a crunchy candy apple, each moment is filled with priceless joy and laughter—no matter one's age.

Dale Thele

DAY FORTY-NINE

Monday, July 2, 2018

It's mid-afternoon as I park my Jeep on the street because there's no room in the driveway due to guests' cars. After stepping out of the vehicle, I grab the bundles from the back seat and approach the house from the side door.

Let me bring you up to speed. This week is a significant occasion for Lost Creek Junction, as the Fourth of July celebrations have been minimal in recent years, limited to a few firecrackers and handheld sparklers. This year, Lost Creek Junction is going all out, hosting various festivities over four consecutive days and nights. The celebration kicks off with a spectacular fireworks display on the Fourth, followed by a hot dog eating contest and the street fair which has become a staple for visitors. With such a wide variety of activities, there's something for everyone to enjoy, promising an exciting and memorable celebration.

In the evenings after the Fourth of July and for the next three nights, Lost Creek Junction will come alive with a vibrant array of events and dazzling aerial fireworks lighting up the night sky. Every available accommodation is fully booked, and additional tourists will set up tents, travel trailers, and campers along the scenic shores of the lake.

The appeal of the ghosts, combined with our genuine Texas hospitality, attracts visitors from far and wide. One couple even traveled all the way from the UK to experience the unique supernatural charms of Lost Creek Junction. With its recognition as one of the country's most desirable tourist destinations, Lost Creek Junction has established itself as a must-visit location, right up there with Disney World in Orlando.

That brings me back to the armload of bundles I'm carrying into the house.

"Taylor? Is that you?" Julie calls from the kitchen.

"Yup, it's me, I answer, entering the kitchen.

"Did you pick up the bunting like I asked?" Julie says without looking up at me.

"Here they are, like you asked," I reply, dumping the packaged bundles on the kitchen table.

"Awesome, you and the guys can start hanging them outside," she replies, focusing on the cinnamon rolls she's preparing. The sweet aroma fills the room, making my mouth water. Although I know they are for our guests and not us.

"Sure, I'll get the guys on it," I say. "Remind me again where you want this bunting hung?"

"Hang some from the front porch eave, over all the outside windows, and from the garage apartment eaves. I want the house decorated in red, white, and blue for the four-day Fourth of July holiday event. It's going to be a blast."

"Taylor," Ryan calls out as he enters the kitchen holding an envelope. "You've got a letter. The Post Office forwarded it from our apartment in Austin. It looks important," he says.

"Who's it from?" I ask, unwrapping the bundles of bunting.

"Check this out. It's from the National Collegiate Chess Organization," Ryan says. "Weren't you a contestant in one of their tournaments?"

"Yeah," I reply, pausing for a moment from unfolding the colorful bunting. "But I was just an alternate. You know how it goes—alternates are rarely called to play. It's like waiting for a train that never arrives—no one ever drops out of qualifying national competition."

"Well, whatever, here's your letter," Ryan says as he slips the envelope into my hand.

I stare at the sealed envelope, my heart racing. "Honestly, Julie, I'm too nervous to open it," I confess, feeling a knot tighten in my stomach as anticipation builds.

"Come on," Julie says, her eyes sparkling with curiosity. "Open it already. We're dying to know what's inside."

"I don't know if I can," I admit, my hands trembling with anxiety. The anticipation is almost unbearable. What if it's bad news? What if it's another rejection? The thought of facing that disappointment again is overwhelming.

"Here," Julie says, her voice steady as she reaches for the envelope. "Let me take a look."

I hand the envelope to her, and she tears it open with eager fingers, unfolding the paper like a fragile promise. Her eyes dart across the letter, and suddenly, a radiant smile spreads across her face. "Taylor," she practically shouts, excitement bubbling over like soda fizzing in a glass. "You've been invited to compete in the Qualifying National Collegiate Chess Tournament in New Orleans!"

Julie and I squeal with delight, bouncing up and down like kids on Christmas morning after seeing the gifts Santa brought. "I can't believe it," I shout, my voice a mix of disbelief and pure joy. "I'm going to New Orleans."

Ryan takes the letter from Julie, eyes scanning the words as he reads silently. A small, bittersweet smile tugs at the corners of his mouth. "Uh, guys," he interjects, his tone shifting to something more serious. "The tournament starts this weekend, and they want you in New Orleans on Wednesday."

I snatch the letter from Ryan's hand to read it myself.

Mr. Greene,

We are pleased to inform you that you have been selected to compete in the Qualifying National Collegiate Chess Tournament in New Orleans. We look forward to seeing you at the opening ceremonies on Wednesday. Competition commences on Friday. You will be staying at the sponsor hotel, with all expenses paid. Please keep your travel receipts, as we will reimburse you for your travel costs.

Respectfully,
Reginald T. Whittenhouse
President
National Collegiate Chess Organization

"This doesn't leave much time to decide," Ryan points out, his tone filled with urgency.

"What's there to decide? You're going, right?" Julie asks, her eyes sparkling with excitement.

"I honestly don't know," I reply, sinking into a kitchen chair as the weight of my responsibilities settles on me. "This week is crucial here in town. There's so much to do to prepare for the celebration."

"Taylor," Julie interjects, leaning in closer with an intensity that makes me pause. "This tournament is a once-in-a-lifetime opportunity. It might not come around again."

"Before we came to Lost Creek Junction," Ryan reminds me, "all you talked about was this competition—until you found out you weren't selected to compete. Well, guess what? This is your second chance." His words hit home, stirring up a rush of memories.

"There's nothing for you to worry about," Julie says, her voice steady and assuring. "If you're concerned about us and the house, don't be. We'll be fine. Go enjoy New Orleans. We can manage everything here without you for a few days."

I hesitate, glancing between them. "But Julie," I protest, anxiety creeping in, "I'll be away for at least a week. What if something happens while I'm gone?"

"If something should happen, we'll deal with it," she insists confidently.

"Taylor," Ryan chimes in, lowering his head, "do you realize we've never been apart for more than a couple of days, until now?"

"Hey, what's up?" Duncan strolls into the kitchen, his eyes scanning the room. "Why the long faces?"

Julie perks up, her voice a mix of excitement and uncertainty as she shares, "Taylor's been invited to compete in the Qualifying National Collegiate Chess Tournament."

"That's amazing news," Duncan beams, giving me a hearty pat on the back. "You've been dreaming about this tournament for months."

"Yeah, but..." Ryan interjects, his tone shifting the mood. "What you don't know is that Taylor's original status was downgraded from contestant to alternate."

"When was this?" Duncan asks.

"Just before our summer break started," Ryan says.

Duncan's expression softens as he places a comforting hand on my shoulder. "I'm sorry to hear that," he says gently. "I had no idea. So what's with this new invitation?"

"Taylor's status has just been upgraded—he's officially a contestant," Ryan announces, though disappointment lingers in his tone.

Duncan raises an eyebrow, clearly puzzled. "Wait, isn't this good news?"

"Well, he's expected to be in New Orleans on Wednesday," Julie replies.

"Hold on, you mean this coming Wednesday?" Duncan exclaims. "As in the day after tomorrow?"

I nod.

"You've got to go. End of discussion. And don't worry about anything here—we'll have everything under control while you're away," Duncan tells me. "It's just a couple of days, right?"

"Actually," Ryan adds, "he'll be gone for about a week."

I raise an eyebrow at Ryan.

"Wait, what? A week?" Duncan leans in with a teasing smirk. "Hold on—did I just catch a look between the two of you? Does that have anything to do with you guys being apart for a week?" He winks. "You two are practically glued together. I've never seen a couple as sickeningly in love as you two lovebirds."

Ryan takes my hand, and we exchange a warm smile that says it all.

"Alright then," Julie declares enthusiastically, her eyes sparkling. "It's settled. Taylor is going to New Orleans—no ifs, ands, or buts about it."

DAY FIFTY

Tuesday, July 3, 2018

"Come on, Taylor! Let's get a move on," Duncan's impatience echoes from the bottom of the stairs leading to the garage apartment. "You can't afford to miss your bus."

"Hurry up, sweetheart," Ryan adds from below, holding my suitcase. "Duncan's about to have an aneurysm."

"I'm coming, I'm coming!" I yell from the garage upstairs bedroom, hoping they can hear me on the ground floor.

Julie strolls into the garage, wiping her hands on a dish towel. "You guys still haven't left?" she asks, arching an eyebrow at Duncan, who's pacing like crazy.

"We're waiting for *Her Highness*," Duncan replies, impatiently glancing at his wristwatch.

"Taylor, what's taking so long?" Julie calls out, her voice echoing through the space. "Everyone's waiting for you—even Beau."

At the mention of his name, Beau perks up and lets out an excited bark, his tail wagging furiously.

"Okay, okay! I'm coming," I yell from the apartment, hurrying down the stairs as if racing against the clock—which ironically, I'm doing.

"Come on already, Duncan's about to have a stroke," Julie teases, cupping my face in her hands and planting a quick kiss on my cheek. "Good luck and give 'em hell."

"Thanks, Julie," I call over my shoulder as I dash out of the garage, a backpack slung over one arm and a fluffy bed pillow tucked under the other.

"Your suitcase is already in the SUV," Ryan assures me.

"And don't worry, I'll make sure to feed and water Beau every day."

Beau barks excitedly, his tail wagging as he trots alongside us toward Duncan's SUV. Duncan fidgets nervously behind the wheel, tapping his fingers on the steering column like a drummer waiting for the beat to drop.

As I say goodbye to my friends and step into the SUV, a wave of bittersweet emotions washes over me. I reach through the open window to squeeze Julie's hand, feeling the warmth of our connection. In a flash, Ryan leans in for a quick farewell kiss. The electronic window glides up, sealing me from them. I wave to Julie, Ryan, and Beau through the glass. Duncan revs the engine, and suddenly, reality hits me—this is really happening. Within moments, my friends fade from view in the rearview mirror, leaving behind an aching sense of separation tugging at my heart.

Duncan pulls up to the bus station—the same spot where my summer adventure began just a few weeks ago. What a transformation. Gone are the days of the occasional bus passing through Lost Creek Junction; now there's daily service bustling with tourists eager to explore this charming town.

Even though we're running late, we arrive ahead of my bus. As I tumble out of Duncan's SUV, a wave of relief washes over me. "Phew! I was worried I'd miss my bus and end up stranded —up a creek without a paddle," I smile, grateful for our timely arrival.

Duncan chuckles, shaking his head. "No way that was going to happen."

"Why not?" I ask, confused. "What do you mean?"

With a mischievous glint in his eyes, Duncan explains, "Rye set all the clocks in the apartment ahead by half an hour to make sure you wouldn't miss your bus."

"No way," I gasp in surprise.

"Yep," Duncan confirms with a wide grin. "Rye knows you all too well."

"Yes, I guess he does," I reply, chuckling at the cleverness of it all.

"Perfect timing," Duncan exclaims, glancing at his wristwatch as the bus approaches. A cloud of dust swirls as the bus screeches to a halt in front of the bus station. The bus door swings open, revealing a cheerful bus driver whose warm smile instantly puts me at ease.

"Where you headed, son?" he asks.

"N-New Orleans, sir," I stammer, feeling both excited and nervous.

"This is your bus," the driver, a friendly middle-aged man with graying temples, assures me with a nod. "You'll have an hour layover when you switch buses in Lafayette, but after that, it's a straight shot to New Orleans."

"Thank you," I reply as he expertly stows my suitcase in the cargo hold. "Well, I guess this is goodbye," I say to Duncan.

"Show 'em how Texans play chess," Duncan encourages, giving me a warm pat on the back. His support gives me the confidence boost I need for this trip. I turn to climb the steps onto the bus, but I pause for a moment to glance back at Duncan one last time. I silently promise to make him proud as I wave. As the doors close and the engine hums to life, I can't help but wonder—am I making the right decision?

You're probably wondering why I didn't drive my Jeep. Well, Duncan—the car guru—offered some wise advice. He suggested I take the bus instead. Why? Because he still needed to work out a few issues with the Jeep and wasn't confident it could handle the road trip without breaking down. With my schedule packed tighter than a suitcase on a vacation, I decided it was best to heed his suggestion and take the bus.

Anyway, back on the bus, I find myself among a small group of about six passengers. Among them is an elderly couple sitting comfortably together, while solo riders occupy various seats in the front half of the vehicle. Feeling a surge of excitement, I walk down the aisle to claim a window seat toward the back of the bus. This spot offers solitude and a unique perspective on the upcoming journey. The back of the bus serves as an ideal retreat from distractions and other passengers, allowing me to enjoy the books I brought along.

With a collection of paperback novels tucked away in my backpack, I eagerly look forward to the next twelve or more hours before reaching New Orleans—an ideal opportunity to immerse myself in these books.

Once I'm comfortably settled in my seat, I unpack my novels and arrange them neatly on the empty aisle seat beside me. I insert my earplugs to enhance my reading experience and maintain my focus. These unassuming devices create the illusion that I'm listening to music, when in reality, the plug is buried inside my backpack and not connected to any device—my secret weapon against distractions and intrusive fellow passengers. Clever, don't you think?

"Attention, passengers, this is our last stop until morning," crackles the bus driver's voice through the overhead speakers, abruptly waking me from my nap. Fortunately, I followed Julie's advice and brought a bed pillow for the trip—without it, I'd definitely be struggling with a painfully stiff neck.

As I sit up and stretch, I sense a familiar sensation—hunger. It's amazing how quickly time passes on a long trip—I finished the snacks Julie packed within the first hour on the road.

As I peer out the window, the fading light of the setting sun casts a warm glow over our surroundings, revealing our arrival at a truck stop diner. A vibrant red neon sign atop the building pulsates with alternating words *FOOD—GAS*, serving as a beacon for weary travelers seeking nourishment and fuel along the desolate highway. This raises an intriguing question—does this establishment offer meals that gives one gas, or is it merely a convenient pit stop for those needing sustenance while refueling their vehicle?

Regardless, my stomach growls audibly—a powerful

reminder hunger is an undeniable force. Since this diner represents our last opportunity for a meal until morning, I feel a surge of anticipation for a satisfying dining experience. Additionally, I look forward to replenishing my snack stash to hold me over until breakfast.

Dale Thele

DAY FIFTY-ONE

Wednesday, July 4, 2018

The bus driver's voice crackles to life over the overhead speakers, announcing the start of a new day on the open road. "Good morning and Happy Independence Day, travelers. This is our breakfast stop. We'll be here for approximately 40 minutes."

As I rub the remnants of sleep from my eyes, I stretch my limbs to ease the stiffness that's settled in after an uncomfortable night's rest. It's becoming increasingly clear I dozed off not long after our supper stop last evening—a clear indication of how exhausted I truly was.

As I step off the bus and form a single-file line with my fellow travelers, I'm immediately struck by the surrounding darkness of the early morning. However, a gentle blush of soft pink is beginning to spread across the eastern sky—a promise of the sun's imminent rise. On the roof of the truck stop, a large neon sign blazes the word *FOOD*, serving as a beacon for hungry travelers and weary truckers alike as they approach this comforting roadside oasis.

The allure of a truck stop is undeniable, drawing travelers in like moths to a flame. What is it about these roadside havens offering not just sustenance but also an experience? As my fellow travelers and I step inside, we're wrapped in the rich aroma of sizzling bacon and fresh brewing coffee, awakening our senses and inviting us into the comforting ambiance of the diner. The sounds of clattering dishes mix with lively conversations, creating a warm backdrop heightening my anticipation of a hearty meal.

Stepping into the diner is like being whisked to a bygone era predating my existence. The original 1950s decor, characterized by wall-to-wall linoleum, vibrant Formica, and gleaming chrome, serves not just as an aesthetic choice but as a genuine time capsule transporting customers back to an earlier time period.

The retro ambiance is meticulously designed with chrome chairs, bar stools, Formica countertops, and linoleum flooring. This setting goes beyond mere imitation; it truly captures the essence of mid-century America. Enhancing this immersive experience is a jukebox located in the corner. Insert quarters, and it plays popular tunes from the past. The diner remains all original, just as it was on opening day in the 1950s.

However, one can't help but notice the missing poodle skirts swirling with every dance step, bobby socks peeking out from beneath playful hems, and saddle oxfords tapping rhythmically on the floor.

I take a seat at the counter, wedged between two burly truck drivers who are eagerly devouring their breakfast. As a solo diner, I believe there's no need to occupy an entire table or booth meant for four or more people. I respect others' space, and sitting at the counter allows me to enjoy my meal in peace, free from interruptions from my fellow bus companions who might want to join me.

A slender, middle-aged waitress in her forties, with voluminous, bleached-blond hair styled in a beehive updo, navigates the diner with a pot of coffee cradled in one hand, her striking emerald green eyes glisten with a mischievous sparkle, inviting curiosity and warmth. "Coffee?" she inquires. Her engaging demeanor is warm and welcoming, making me feel at home.

"Yes, please," I reply, flipping the hefty ceramic mug upright from its saucer—a signal to the waitress I'm ready to indulge in my morning ritual. The warmth of the recently washed mug radiates and envelopes my palm in a comforting embrace.

"Check out this classy gentleman," the waitress nods in my direction while remarking playfully toward the truckers sitting on either side of me. Her words carry both amusement and admiration. "He's polite and appreciative. You guys could certainly take a page out of his playbook."

I feel my cheeks grow warm, a sure sign of embarrassment. I'm not used to being the center of attention, especially in a place like this. Yet, the waitress's words, while making me blush, also fill me with a strange sense of pride.

The gritty and unrefined truckers enjoy their breakfasts with the same enthusiasm as Hereford cows grazing in a pasture.

With its red vinyl booths and the mouthwatering aroma of food sizzling on the grill, this diner stands in stark contrast to the rugged expanse of the open road that the truckers usually travel. As they eat, their attention remains firmly focused on their plates, responding to the waitress's friendly banter with simple grunts—a testament to their unwavering concentration. Are they afraid their meal might scamper off their plates if they divert their gaze, even for a moment?

"Men," the waitress sighs, expressing her frustration over the two truckers who ignore her. "What can I get for you, hun?" she inquires, poised with her pad and pencil, ready to take my order.

As I consider the menu options, I feel a sense of empathy for this weary waitress. It's clear she's had a challenging morning, especially with the influx of truckers filling the seats around me. Such an environment can be overwhelming.

"I'll have two eggs over hard—call me crazy, but I can't stand runny yolks—along with sausage and toast, please," I respond. My intention is to communicate my order clearly while remaining as courteous as possible, fully aware of the obstacles she faces during her shift.

The waitress casts a disapproving glance at the truckers seated on either side of me. What fuels her frustration? Their apparent oblivion to her silent cues, as they remain absorbed in their meals. With pieces of toast in hand, they sop up the remnants of runny egg yolks from their plates. Ew!

"Yer breakfast will be out shortly, hun," she assures me with a playful wink, her warmth cutting through the chilly, air-conditioned atmosphere of the diner. The apron she wears—composed of a patchwork of stains and stories—whispers tales of countless meals served with love and care. Her bleached hair is piled high, framing a face displaying the signs of years spent toiling in this bustling, thankless diner. As she brushes a wild strand of hair behind her ear, the costume jewelry ring on her finger catches the light, sparkling and shimmering. The stones can't be genuine; no woman in her right mind would wear such expensive jewelry without being surrounded by a private security detail. Still, it's a nice touch, even if the gaudy stones are nothing more than cheap colored glass.

Turning away with a flourish, she tears my paper order from her notepad and hangs it on a shiny metal spinner mounted on the wall separating the diner from the kitchen. With a quick spin of the doohickey, she ensures the cook can easily see what I've ordered. "Order in," she announces, punctuating her declaration by ringing a bell in the wall opening.

As I take a sip, the hot coffee dances on my tongue, releasing a wave of intense aroma to fill the air. Can you smell it? The rich, earthy notes swirl around me, wrapping me in a comforting warmth that feels like a cozy hug from the inside out.

But wait—there's something special about this brew. A hint of chicory tickles my taste buds, whispering secrets of Louisiana.

The two truckers abruptly rise from their stools, their heavy boots thudding against the linoleum floor like a drumbeat signaling the end of a long day. They toss crumpled bills onto the counter and head for the exit. One of them, the burlier of the two with a weathered face that seems to tell stories of countless miles traveled, shoots me a quick, disapproving glance before grunting and following his companion out of the diner.

For a fleeting moment, I feel as if I'm staring into the ghostly face of Ezekiel or Abrahim from Lost Creek Junction. Have you ever experienced one of those moments when someone's face feels eerily familiar? It's as if time folds in on itself, unexpectedly connecting the past and present.

A momentary shiver runs down my back.

"Order up," a faceless male voice booms from the kitchen, punctuating the air with the sharp slap of a spatula against the window bell.

The waitress glides over to scoop a steaming plate from the kitchen window and, with a simple gesture, sets it down in front of me. "Hun, ya all set? Need anythin' else?" Her voice slices through the din of clattering dishes and lively chatter, her hands resting confidently on her hips. I can only imagine the stories she could tell—of countless meals served and whispered secrets shared in this wide spot beside the highway.

"Thanks, I'm good," I reply, grateful for her attentiveness.

With a nod, she quickly scoops up the trucker's cash left on the counter and sashays to the cash register as if it's part of her daily dance.

Savoring my coffee, I notice the bus driver standing up from his table. I gulp the last of my chicory coffee, settle my bill, and board my bus.

Settled comfortably on the bus, I wonder what's happening in Lost Creek Junction right now. How are my friends celebrating the holiday?

For the past couple of years, Ryan and I have made it a tradition to pack a quilt and a picnic basket, joining hundreds of fellow picnickers on the lawn of a local park in Austin. Kids run around laughing while adults relax, savoring crispy fried chicken and creamy potato salad. As the sun dips below the horizon, families gather closer together, to watch the breathtaking aerial fireworks display light up the night sky. The air fills with gasps of delight—*Ahh!* and *Ooh!*—as each dazzling explosion paints vibrant colors across the heavens. Thunderous applause erupts from the crowd when the final explosive burst fades away, echoing our shared joy. That's when Ryan and I roll up our quilt and pack away our picnic basket for the journey home. I wonder—will my friends create similar memories in Lost Creek Junction tonight?

"Lafayette," the bus driver announces over the overhead speakers as we come to a gentle stop. Did I doze off dreaming about a fireworks show? Half-asleep and slightly disoriented, I scramble to gather my belongings, eager not to miss my transfer.

As I step off the bus, the driver opens the luggage compartment beneath, revealing a collection of bags. "Is this yours?" he asks with a friendly grin, handing me my suitcase as if it's a precious gift. I smile back—his warmth made this leg of my trip feel special.

With my bag in hand and excitement bubbling inside me for what lies ahead, I take a deep breath of fresh Lafayette air.

"You've got about an hour before the New Orleans bus arrives," the driver informs me, his voice cutting through the noisy terminal.

"Thank you, sir," I nod appreciatively.

"There's a little cafe just up ahead that won't break the bank," he gestures up the street with a friendly smile. "They make great coffee and fresh pastries—much better than waiting around here in this lonely bus station."

"Thanks. I'll definitely check it out," I reply, shaking his hand and feeling grateful for his advice.

As the driver boards his bus and closes the door behind him, I watch it slowly back out of its bay. The fading glow of the taillights sparks a wave of nostalgia within me. So far, this trip has given me plenty to think about—where I've been and where I'm headed next.

As I step into *Café Vendre*, a charming little bakery and coffeehouse recommended by the friendly bus driver, I'm immediately drawn into its warm atmosphere. The delightful aroma of fresh baking bread mingles with the rich scent of brewing coffee. Behind the counter stands a friendly guy who appears to be around my age, wearing an apron dusted with flour like a badge of honor. Although he's the only person working, he effortlessly creates a welcoming vibe. It's hard not to smile back at him as customers sip their coffees and share laughter. The place feels like a neighborhood hub.

"Did I come at a quiet time?" I ask, glancing around the nearly empty shop with curiosity.

"Ouais," he replies, his charming French accent flowing through the air. "It's the quiet time between the morning and lunch rush."

I'm digging the french accent, and how it comes so naturally to him. Now I wish I'd paid more attention in high school french class.

"So, handsome," he continues with a playful grin, "what can I get for you?"

I feel a warm flush creeping up my neck—this guy is adorable. Wait a minute, did he honestly call me *handsome*?

"I didn't mean to embarrass you," he says, flashing a smile that instantly puts me at ease. "I couldn't help but notice."

"No, it's just I'm not used to being called *handsome*," I admit, feeling a mix of surprise and flattery.

"Someone as attractive as you should be told that every day," he replies, his bright smile radiating genuine warmth. His words send a delightful surge of appreciation through me, if you know what I mean.

It's been ages since someone flirted with me, and honestly, I'm out of practice regarding how to respond.

"Would you like something to drink?" he asks, his warm grin lighting up the space between us.

"I'll have a coffee," I reply, trying to sound casual while my heart dances.

"Anything else?" he prompts, leaning in slightly as if eager to know more.

"How about one of those pastries?" I suggest, pointing at an intriguing treat that catches my eye. It's a delicate, golden-brown pastry, deep-fried and dusted with a generous sprinkle of powdered sugar. What could it taste like? Is it crispy or soft? The curiosity bubbles up inside me. I feel butterflies over something as simple as ordering coffee.

"A coffee and a beignet?" he asks, confirming my order.

"What did you call that pastry?" I inquire.

"Ah, it's called a *beignet*. They're our specialty," he replies.

"I've never had a beignet before," I admit, feeling a mix of curiosity and excitement.

"They are quite popular around here," he informs, eyes sparkling. "By the way, I hope you don't mind me saying this, but you have an interesting accent. Where are you from?"

"I'm from Texas—Austin, to be exact," I reply, a hint of pride in my voice.

"What brings you to Lafayette?" he asks, handing me a steaming cup of coffee and a warm beignet wrapped in a paper napkin. The aroma of hot coffee mingles with the rich scent of the warm pastry, making my mouth water.

"I'm on my way to New Orleans," I explain, taking a sip and savoring the delicious flavor. "I'm transferring buses here and have a little time to kill before my next bus."

"Oh," he responds, his tone tinged with disappointment. "You'll be leaving soon?" His eyes reflect an unmistakable longing—a silent wish as if I might linger just a little longer.

"Yeah, unfortunately," I say, gazing at the attractive guy behind the counter. There's something magnetic about him that makes it hard for me to want to create any distance between us.

"I hope I've made your visit to Lafayette a memorable one," he says, flashing a warm smile that lights up the room.

"You definitely have," I reply, my cheeks warming with a slight blush.

As I settle into a table, ready to indulge in my pastry and sip my coffee, I can't help but steal another glance at the guy behind the counter. His effortless charm and infectious smile linger in my thoughts, making me wish I could stay a little longer.

The New Orleans bus finally pulled into the Lafayette terminal, running behind schedule. A nagging thought crept in—could this be a bad omen for what lies ahead? Thankfully, everything else went smoothly during the final leg of my trip. Although the ride from Lafayette to New Orleans was uneventful, my mind was anything but calm.

I found myself lost in a whirlwind of emotions. Why was I flirting with that guy at the cafe when I have a boyfriend waiting for me back in Lost Creek Junction? I'm happy with Ryan—we were best friends before we started dating. Flirting with other guys has never been on my radar—I'm committed to Ryan and not looking for anyone else. So why do I suddenly feel this way?

It's confusing because I truly value my relationship with Ryan. He means the world to me, and that should be what matters most, right? But then again, why does it feel like there's an itch I can't scratch?

Stepping off the bus in New Orleans, I feel the city's energy buzzing around me. As I grab my suitcase from the luggage compartment, a sense of adventure washes over me.

Navigating through and out of the bustling terminal, I search for a taxi when suddenly, a cab screeches to a halt in front of me. The energetic driver hops out with a friendly grin, eager to help with my suitcase. He opens the trunk and carefully loads my bag as if it's made of glass. Then, he courteously holds the back door open for me—talk about feeling like royalty.

I slide into the backseat. When he settles into the drivers seat, I catch his eye in the rearview mirror. His warm brown eyes sparkle with friendliness, instantly creating a connection.

"Where to, good-looking?" the cab driver asks.

"The Excelsior," I reply, momentarily lost in the depths of his dreamy eyes. Did he just call me *good-looking*?

"Are you a chess fan?" he asks, navigating traffic while glancing at me through the rearview mirror with genuine curiosity.

"Uh, yeah, how did you know?" I respond, my jaw dropping in surprise, as if he'd revealed a well-kept secret.

"Everyone knows the Excelsior is hosting the National Qualifying Collegiate Chess Championship," he says, his eyes sparkling with excitement as they meet mine in the reflection.

I momentarily break away from his mesmerizing gaze and find my eyes landing on the driver's license attached to the dashboard. It boldly declares: Giles Broussard.

"So, your name is Giles?" I inquire.

"My friends call me *Gilly*," he replies.

"Nice to meet you, Giles," I say, trying to keep my composure.

"Please, call me *Gilly*," he insists playfully. "And what about you? Do you have a name?"

"Oh, um, I'm Taylor," I stammer, suddenly feeling shy in front of this charming stranger.

"Does Taylor have a last name?" Giles asks with an inviting twinkle in his eye.

"Yes, it's Greene with an *e*," I say.

"So, Taylor Greene with an *e*," Giles echoes. "Are you in town for the big chess tournament?"

"Yep," I reply, excitement bubbling up inside me. "Do you play chess?" I ask, eager to find a shared interest.

"Just for fun," Giles admits with a casual shrug. "How about you?"

"Well, I suppose you could say I dabble a bit," I respond, feeling a spark of camaraderie forming between us.

"I have a sneaking suspicion you're a much more dedicated player than you're letting on," Giles says, his eyes sparkling with mischief.

"What makes you say that?" I ask.

"I know for a fact most spectators won't arrive until Friday since the tournament doesn't start until Saturday morning," he grins, clearly enjoying this game of cat and mouse.

"Okay, you caught me," I admit, surprised at how easily he saw through me.

"So, you *are* a contestant in the tournament, aren't you?" Giles presses further.

"Guilty as charged," I reply.

"So, you traveled all the way from Texas by bus to compete

in the chess tournament," Giles observes.

"How do you know I'm from Texas?" I reply, raising an eyebrow in surprise.

"Your luggage tag says so," Giles chuckles.

"You don't miss a thing, do you?" I say, shaking my head in amusement.

"We're here," Giles announces with a grin as he pulls the taxi up to the entrance of a stunningly luxurious hotel. As I gaze out the taxi window at the opulent building, it hits me—how on earth did I end up here? Of all people, why am I staying in such a fancy place?

I hand Giles his fare along with a generous tip, and his smile widens in appreciation. With a cheerful nod, he hops out of the cab to open the trunk.

As he hands me my suitcase, our fingers touch, and in that brief moment, something electric occurs. It's as if time pauses just for us—the busy world blurs. We lock eyes, and a rush of warmth spreads through me—like a spark igniting a flame. I wish this feeling could last forever, like a scene straight out of a romance movie, where every second is filled with magic and the background music swells with emotion. My heart skips a beat, and I sigh softly.

Giles breaks the spell with a crooked smile and says, "You're right." His words linger in the air like a challenge. "To answer your question, I don't miss a thing. Can I call on you while you're here? I'd like to see you again," he adds, sliding a card into my shirt pocket with casual confidence.

I stand, frozen in place, engulfed in the whirlwind of everything that's happening. It feels as though time is speeding up to a dizzying pace—too fast for me to keep up.

As I watch Giles's taxi merge into the bustling New Orleans traffic, I shake off the remnants of my daze and regain my footing in this vibrant city. A voice cuts through my thoughts like a warm breeze: "Sir, may I assist you with your luggage?" A striking bellboy reaches for my suitcase, his charm as captivating as the city itself.

He escorts me to the front desk, where I'm greeted by yet another eye-catching clerk. Seriously, are all the men in New Orleans this good-looking? It feels like I've stumbled into a city of gorgeous male models.

After settling into my hotel room, I take a shower and put on my outfit for the eat-and-greet soirée being hosted in the ballroom for all the contestants. To be honest, I'm not what you would call a social butterfly. In fact, back in elementary school, I was more of a *wallflower*, and not much has changed since. I'd much rather fade into the background than engage in small talk with strangers.

Then there's Ryan—my complete opposite. He thrives on being the life of the party, effortlessly striking up conversations with everyone he meets. It's moments like this when I miss having him by my side. When I'm surrounded by unfamiliar faces and feel out of place, his energy helps ease my discomfort.

As I step into the ballroom, I feel a rush of excitement mixed with a twinge of anxiety. Here I am, wearing my trusty sports jacket and slacks, while all around me, the guys are decked out in sharp tailored suits. It feels like I've walked into a fancy dress party and I'm the only guest who didn't get the dress code memo.

A wave of inadequacy washes over me as I look at the sea of polished shoes, starched shirts, and crisp ties. Am I ready for this? The atmosphere buzzes with confidence and style, and I feel expected to blend in, even though I have no idea how.

I suppose now is as good a time as any to confess—I don't ever remember owning a suit. Sure, I've seen those old, yellowed Polaroids of me in kindergarten, all gussied up in a tiny suit, but the memory is as hazy as the photographs themselves. In later years, a suit was simply beyond our family budget.

Don't get me wrong—we weren't poor by any means, but we certainly weren't rolling in money either. My parents were both dedicated school teachers—Mom shaping young minds in elementary school and Dad bringing history alive to unappreciative high school students. They took on summer jobs to make ends meet, but let's be honest—the pay wasn't exactly impressive.

I never went hungry or lacked the essentials, and I'm genuinely grateful for that. However, those little luxuries—the ones that made life feel special—often slipped through our fingers like fine sand.

Growing up, my family's wardrobe consisted of treasures from thrift shops. I wasn't particularly focused on brand names, but I noticed the top brands I wore were always a couple of seasons behind current trends. My shoes came from the Shoe Warehouse, which meant I wore budget-friendly, off-brand footwear.

My wardrobe was simple yet functional, consisting of three sets of clothes: one for church, one for school, and one for play. I also had two pairs of shoes—a dressy pair suitable for church and a sturdy pair for all my outdoor adventures.

During birthdays and Christmas, instead of receiving toys, games, or shiny new outfits from big-name stores, I excitedly unwrapped clothes that were new to me, all from the thrift store. I was aware of our financial situation, and I was taught a gift is about the thought behind it, not its price tag.

Because of my family's financial situation, I learned to appreciate the value of money. This lesson has remained with me to this day. Generally, I'm not self-conscious about my clothing, but tonight, I'm overwhelmed with insecurities and feeling out of place.

As a kid, Ryan was the friend who truly stood out in my memories. Regardless of our families' differing financial situations, he always made sure I felt included and valued. He'd surprise me with ice cream or candy, sharing it without a second thought. His generosity didn't stop there. He often treated me to movies, always buying my ticket and ensuring we shared a giant bucket of popcorn. What struck me most about Ryan was his selflessness—he never asked for anything in return. Our friendship was built on genuine kindness and mutual respect. In his eyes, I was never inferior. He treated me as an equal every step of the way.

After my parents passed away, I moved in with my grandma, and our financial situation took a turn for the worse. Grandma's monthly Social Security check became our lifeline. I was eager to get a part-time job to lighten her burden, but she insisted I should *enjoy this time of life with your friends and focus on your studies*.

Her words carried the wisdom of a lifetime, and I heeded them. I found inspiration in her advice, I balanced my studies and friendships while cherishing every moment with Grandma. We faced the challenges together, supporting each other through thick and thin.

Anyway, I got side tracked with my reminiscing.

As I enter the hotel ballroom, I can't shake the feeling of being out of place in my well-worn sports coat and slacks. The atmosphere is buzzing with energy, and I immediately spot the three main social cliques. First, there are the *snobs* huddled together, their laughter echoing as if they're in a world of their own. Then, the *social butterflies* flitting from one group to another, effortlessly engaging everyone in conversation. Finally, there are people like me—*the wallflowers*—too shy to initiate a chat but hoping to see a friendly face.

A few of those outgoing types approach me with bright smiles and eager chatter, but honestly, my mind goes blank. Before long, they float away to find someone more engaging. It feels like the event is destined for disaster—until I discover the food.

Oh my goodness! Every bite is an explosion of flavor that dances on my taste buds. I think I've just experienced my first authentic Cajun cuisine—a delightful surprise to say the least.

As the party comes to a close, I hurry back to my hotel room and change into something more comfortable. Sinking into the plush California King bed, I relish the tranquility of my temporary sanctuary. I start to think about how I'll occupy my time until Saturday. While there will be orientation and some planned activities for the contestants, none of those will fill up all my time. Being in an unfamiliar town, the only person I know is Giles. But what do I really know about him? Should I err on the side of caution and take a chance by calling him? After all, he's quite attractive. But what could someone like him possibly see in someone like me?

As I weigh my options, the room phone suddenly buzzes to life.

"Hello?" I answer, curious who's calling me at this hour.

"Do you have plans for tonight?" a familiar voice asks, laced with excitement.

"Not that I know of," I reply.

"Meet me in the lobby right now," he insists, urgency crackling through his tone. "We're hitting the town."

Even without saying his name, I know it's Giles on the other end of the line. The memory of that electric moment when our fingers brushed as he dropped me off at the hotel still sends shivers down my spine. With my heart racing and a flutter of excitement in my stomach, I dart out of my room, making a beeline for the elevator, each step fueled by anticipation. I can't get to the lobby fast enough.

Dale Thele

DAY FIFTY-TWO

Thursday, July 5, 2018

Slowly opening my eyes, bright sunlight floods the room, forcing me to blink against its intensity. Rubbing the sleep from my eyes, I realize it's morning. But wait—something feels off. What happened last night?

I sit up in bed and scan my surroundings, only to find clothes scattered everywhere. My heart skips a beat when I spot micro briefs dangling from the chandelier. Panic rises within me as it registers: Those aren't my underwear. I wear boxers.

I bolt upright, my heart pounding as I shake off the remnants of sleep. A low groan escapes from the tangled mass of bed covers beside me. With a mix of curiosity and dread, I cautiously peel back the layers—only to find Giles sleeping soundly and completely naked in my bed.

The sight jolts me into a whirlwind of confusion. My pulse quickens as the realization dawns: I'm naked too! What on earth have I done? The question reverberates through my mind like an alarm bell.

Suddenly, a knock at the door shatters the silence, sending panic coursing through my veins. What should I do? My thoughts race as I glance at Giles, who remains oblivious to the chaos around us.

"Giles," I whisper urgently, shaking him gently to wake him.

"Five more minutes," he mumbles, burrowing deeper under the bed covers.

"Giles," I urge, "please wake up. There's someone at the door."

"Housekeeping," a muffled voice calls from the other side of the locked door, intensifying the tension in the room.

"Giles!" I shake him insistently. "Please, wake up!"

He pops up from beneath the covers like a startled zombie, his eyes wide and glassy. "What's going on? Where's the fire?" he demands, scanning the room, still caught in that dreamy haze.

"There's no fire," I say, trying to steady my voice. "But we have a bit of a situation—there's a housekeeper at the door. What are we going to do? She can't see this room in its current state."

In a daze, Giles, completely naked and utterly oblivious, stumbles out of bed and toward the door. With a dramatic flair, he flings open the door, revealing his bare self to the unsuspecting housekeeper.

Her eyes widen in shock, and her mouth forms a perfect *O* of disbelief as she instinctively takes a step back.

Giles stands facing the maid, her expression a confusing mix of shock and disbelief. He speaks to her in a foreign language. After their brief exchange, he closes the door with a soft click and flops back onto the bed, face down, surrendering to sleep almost instantly. Unmistakable snoring soon fills the room, proof he's drifted off into dreamland.

The whole scene is so absurd it could be straight out of a comedy sketch. Yet here I am, too stunned to even chuckle at the ridiculousness unfolding before me. I find it both hilarious and baffling.

Eventually, I manage to wake Giles from his sleep. "So, um... did we, like, do anything last night?" I ask as I pull on my pants, feeling a wave of embarrassment wash over me at the awkwardness of the moment.

"Are you asking if we... you know, *did it* last night?" Giles replies with a playful, crooked smile making my heart race.

"Yes," I admit, unsure if I'm ready for the answer that may come next.

"Have you seen my briefs?" Giles asks, rummaging through

the mess on the floor.

"Look up," I suggest with a smirk.

He glances at the ceiling, and there they are—his briefs proudly hanging from the chandelier like a quirky flag of victory. "Oops," he chuckles, his eyes sparkling with mischief. "Guess I'm going commando today."

"Will you stop changing the subject," I insist. "I asked you a question, and I want an answer—did we *do it* last night?"

"To clarify, we were both tipsy and ended up crashing for the night. What kind of person do you think I am? I would never take advantage of anyone—especially not in the state you were in. Honestly, I doubt Gilly Junior would have even stirred. He was just as out of it as I was". He looks down at his lap and gives Gilly Junior a playful pat, as if it's a loyal pet.

"But wait," I protest, my cheeks flushing with embarrassment. "We were completely naked."

"Doesn't everyone sleep in the buff?" Giles replies with a cheeky grin. "I undressed you to make you comfortable while you slept. And just so you know, you're quite impressive down there—if you catch my drift." He winks suggestively, making my face heat up even more.

I haven't even had breakfast yet, and here he is, making me squirm. I shift uncomfortably in my chair, wishing for a distraction—maybe a sudden earthquake or a flock of pigeons crashing through the window. At this point I'll take anything.

"By the way, what time is it?" Giles asks with a hint of urgency.

I check my cell phone and reply, "A little before 11."

"Perfect, we've still got time," he exclaims, quickly putting on his clothes. "I know a place that serves the best brunch. Let's go—we don't want to miss out."

About twenty minutes later, Giles and I arrive at our destination, exhausted from running the whole way. As I step inside, the place is a delightful restaurant that surprises me with its elegant interior. I'm greeted by crisp white linen tablecloths, stunning crystal glassware, and delicate china glimmering under the soft glow of grand chandeliers above. It's truly breathtaking. However, what captivates me is the magnificent buffet at the heart of the dining room, featuring a dazzling ice sculpture embodying the grandeur of ancient Rome or Greece. It feels like stepping into a scene from a historical epic movie, and I can't help but feel a sense of awe as I take it all in.

A striking male figure, impeccably dressed in luxurious evening wear, leads us to a secluded table tucked away from the bustling crowd. As I glance around at the elegantly dressed diners, a wave of self-consciousness washes over me. Here I am in my everyday clothes, feeling like an outsider in this sea of sophistication. Again, my insecurity surfaces.

"Am I underdressed?" I ask Giles, my voice tinged with uncertainty. "Everyone here seems to be—"

"Don't sweat it," Giles replies with a casual wave of his hand. "They'll think we're tourists who wandered in by mistake."

Just when I think things can't get any better, an incredibly charming waiter glides over to our table. His polished demeanor perfectly matches the upscale vibe of the restaurant, adding a touch of elegance to our experience. He pours a splash of vibrant orange juice into our exquisite crystal flutes, and then, with a smooth motion impressing any sommelier, he pops the cork from a champagne bottle to top off our glasses with fizzy delight.

The waiter places the opened bottle into a nearby ice bucket, his movements polished and confident. As he walks away, I can't help but admire how those snug-fitting slacks accentuate his cute butt cheeks.

"Did I just see you checking out the competition?" Giles teases, a playful smirk dancing across his lips.

"Oh, um, no—I mean, well, okay, you caught me red-handed," I admit, feeling my cheeks flush with embarrassment.

"He's attractive," Giles exclaims, a grin spreading across his face as he nods in agreement.

"We came here to eat, not to cruise," I reply. "Shall we check out the buffet?"

"Absolutely," Giles responds, springing from his chair. "I'm famished."

After enjoying the rich, velvety goodness of Eggs Benedict alongside a refreshing melon medley, I experienced pure bliss. The sweetness of the strawberries and the delightful burst of flavor from the grapes still dance on my palate, making this brunch unforgettable. Giles and I have opened our third bottle of champagne—cheers to us. We originally started with mimosas but somewhere along the way we switched to straight champagne.

Our hunky stud waiter, Luc, who introduced himself earlier, saunters over to our table. "Is there anything else I can get for you?" he asks, his tone friendly and inviting.

With a playful glint in his eye, Giles gestures for Luc to lean in closer to whisper into Luc's ear. What secret could Giles be sharing? As they exchange whispers, the atmosphere buzzes with anticipation. Luc's gaze flickers toward me, and suddenly, a broad smile lights up his face as he nods knowingly at Giles.

I have no idea what those two are scheming. As I try to figure it out, Luc shoots me a playful wink and saunters away from our table.

"What did you say to him?" I ask Giles, narrowing my eyes in suspicion.

"Earlier, didn't you tell me you thought he was cute?" he replies, a teasing smirk spreading across his face.

"Yeah, I suppose I did," I admit reluctantly, feeling a mix of embarrassment and excitement.

"Well then, it's settled," Giles proclaims as he slides his credit card onto the small tray cradling the brunch bill.

"Settled? What do you mean?" I ask. "What are you getting at?"

With a cheeky grin, he leans in close and poses the question hanging in the air: "What are your thoughts on threesomes?"

Threesome? Wait, what?! I can't believe it. Did Giles actually suggest a three-way with him, Luc, and me? This proposal hits me like a bolt from the blue. I must be feeling the effects of the champagne because, shockingly, I'm actually considering it. Usually, I pride myself on being a private person. This isn't something I'd normally entertain. Yet here I am, grappling with disbelief and somehow saying *yes*. My mind is a whirlwind of thoughts and emotions. On one hand, the idea of diving into something new and thrilling is undeniably enticing. But then there's that nagging voice reminding me that sharing such an intimate experience with anyone other than Ryan—my partner for years—feels deeply wrong.

The thought of indulging in a three-way both thrills and terrifies me. It's completely new territory, as I've only been with one partner, Ryan, who has been my rock throughout our committed relationship. I've never felt the urge to explore beyond what we have—until now.

Has something changed in me since I hopped on that bus at Lost Creek Junction? It's like something inside me has flipped, making me feel more desirable than ever before. Honestly, I'm not sure how this transformation happened—especially for someone like me—but I'm starting to embrace this exciting new version of myself.

I won't go into the sordid details, but if you've ever experienced intimacy and have the slightest bit of imagination, you can probably picture how our afternoon and evening played out. The three of us enjoyed each other's company in my hotel bed, in the tub, and even on the balcony. You get the idea?

DAY SIXTY

Friday, July 13, 2018

With the chess tournament behind me, I'm relieved it wrapped up yesterday. Who in their right mind would want to compete on Friday the 13th? I'm not saying I'm overly superstitious, but really? I'm glad it's over. Now, I'm looking forward to returning to Lost Creek Junction to resume my summer college break.

The thought of reuniting with my boyfriend, my dog, and my friends fills me with pure joy. I can already picture the laughter and the comfort of familiar faces.

There's a knock at my hotel door, and I know who's waiting on the other side.

"Morning, Taylor," Giles says as I open the door. Are you ready?" His smile is tinged with sadness.

I take a deep breath and glance around the hotel room one last time. This space is filled with both sweet and bittersweet memories, and I'm not quite ready to let them go.

"Are you sure you haven't forgotten anything?" Giles asks concern etched on his face.

"Yep, I'm sure," I reply, though my voice wavers slightly, and my eyes betray the storm of emotions brewing inside me. I fight back tears with fierce determination, unwilling to show my vulnerability.

Giles takes hold of my suitcase while I toss my backpack over my shoulder and tuck my pillow under my arm. As I close the hotel room door behind me, it feels like I'm closing a chapter of my life—one I'm not entirely ready to end.

While Giles navigates the bustling streets in his taxi on our way to the bus terminal, a wave of sadness washes over me. How can I say goodbye to such an incredible place? My time in the Big Easy has been magical, filled with vibrant music, delicious food, and unforgettable moments. But deep down, I know it's time to return to my life in Lost Creek Junction.

Stepping out of the taxi at the bus terminal, emotions come over me. Can you believe it? Just a week ago, Giles and I were strangers, and now it feels like we've shared a lifetime together. We've created memories stretching far beyond those fleeting days. Standing side by side in the busy terminal—a place that's seen countless goodbyes and tearful reunions—we wait for my bus to arrive. The air is thick with anticipation, and I can't help but wonder how Giles and I became so deeply connected in such a brief time.

When the bus finally arrives, I'm overwhelmed by a flurry of emotions. Do I really have to leave? My heart pleads to stay, but responsibility calls.

With a heavy sigh, I settle into my bus seat, my eyes fixed on Giles as I wave goodbye from the window. My hand hovers in the air, silently urging him to join me or hold me just a little longer. As the bus pulls away, I feel the emotional distance between us widening—it's like being in the final scene of a tearjerking Hallmark movie.

Giles fades into the distance, to become a tiny speck on the horizon. I fight back tears, but his image begins to blur, swallowed by a wave of overwhelming emotions. How can something so beautiful feel so heavy? I promised myself I wouldn't cry, yet the weight of this goodbye is almost unbearable.

As I snuggle into my pillow, hot salty tears roll down my cheeks. The bus trip home has begun, and I look forward to the layover in Lafayette. I can hardly wait to see the charming barista at the coffee shop. It'll be a brief yet delightful interlude before I hop on the next bus to Lost Creek Junction.

The excitement of reuniting with Beau and Ryan after a week apart sends butterflies fluttering in my stomach. What have I missed in Lost Creek Junction? What stories and adventures have unfolded while I've been away?

Yet, amid all this joy, memories of Giles linger in my mind—haunting me in a wonderfully bittersweet way.

You won't believe what I just found out—there's no bus layover in Lafayette. It's such a disappointment, especially since I was looking forward to seeing that adorable coffee shop guy one last time. You know, the one who called me *handsome*? I guess that won't be happening.

I'm cutting it close with my bus transfer. If I don't hustle, I might miss my bus to Lost Creek Junction. And let's be honest—spending the night in Lafayette isn't exactly on my bucket list of things to do. If I miss this bus, I'll have to wait until tomorrow for the next one. The thought of possibly readjusting my plans adds a layer of stress, especially since Duncan is counting on meeting me at the Lost Creek Junction bus station tomorrow afternoon.

As I settle into my seat after transferring buses, I feel a wave of relief. Fluffing my pillow, I wedge it snugly between the window and my seat, determined to create a cozy nest for this homeward bound journey. With only a handful of fellow travelers on board, the entire back of the bus feels like my personal retreat.

The gentle rocking motion, combined with the soothing hum of the engine, lulls me into a state of blissful relaxation. Is there anything better than finding that sweet spot where comfort meets tranquility? As my eyelids grow heavy, I reflect on how these quiet moments on the road are often the most precious.

As I drift off into a nap, my thoughts wander back to New Orleans and the unforgettable moments I shared with Giles. It all began when I stepped off the bus, weary from my travels, and was greeted by Giles and his taxi, ready to whisk me to my hotel.

The evening began with an eat-and-greet dinner for the chess tournament players, which was much fancier than my simple tastes. Afterward, Giles took me to a gay dance club where we danced as if nobody was watching, fully embracing the vibrant energy of the city's nightlife. We even watched fireworks from the rooftop of a building.

The following day, I opened my eyes to the unexpected sight of Giles nestled beside me in my bed. What a surprise to wake up to. From that moment on, he became my constant companion.

Giles didn't just show me around town; he transformed my experience of the city into something unforgettable. He guided me through must-see tourist spots—the iconic landmarks everyone raves about—and introduced me to mouthwatering local delicacies making my taste buds dance with joy. But that wasn't all; he even orchestrated my first thrilling three-way experience, adding an exciting twist to our escapades.

During tournament week, one thing consistently filled my heart with joy: Giles. Always seated in the front row of the gallery, he was my silent cheerleader, and his unwavering support shone through every smile and nod. Whenever I wasn't competing, we'd sit together in the gallery, hands intertwined, sharing quiet moments as we watched the competition unfold on the arena floor.

Wow, what a whirlwind of a week. It flew by much too fast for my liking, but let me tell you—it was nothing short of transformative. I earned a third-place title, which filled me with immense pride. While it feels incredible to have accomplished that, it doesn't qualify me for the national competition—only the top two winners receive that honor.

Still, the entire experience felt surreal, as if I were living in a dream. For perhaps the first time in my life, I felt like I was genuinely myself—without filters or reservations holding me back. The reserved person I used to see in the mirror is gone. Instead, I embraced everything and everyone around me without hesitation. Can you imagine what it's like to shed those self-imposed expectations? It's liberating.

This journey taught me something invaluable: the power of self-acceptance and the importance of embracing who I truly am. Who knows? Maybe this trip changed me for good. Only time will reveal how deep those changes may go.

Dale Thele

DAY SIXTY-ONE

Saturday, July 14, 2018

The bus screeches to a halt, kicking up a cloud of dust swirling about the bus like a tornado—what a rude awakening. I rub my eyes, shaking off the remnants of sleep, to peer out the window. As the dust settles, it hits me—I'm back at Lost Creek Junction. Excitement bubbles inside me as I quickly gather my belongings and leap off the bus.

Stepping into the blistering heat, I squint against the relentless sun. Shielding my eyes with one hand, I spot Duncan standing beside his SUV, waving like he's guiding an airplane in for a landing. As I make my way over, he greets me with a warm, one-armed hug that feels like home after what seems like an eternity away.

"I've missed you more than words can express," I say, pulling him into a tight embrace. It's incredible how every second apart seems to melt away in this moment. Yet, the weight of our separation lingers in the air like an unspoken truth.

"Things haven't been the same without you," he replies, his eyes reflecting a mix of relief and longing as he gently releases me. "Toss your gear in the back seat and let's go home."

A few moments later, Duncan pulls his SUV to the curb outside my house. I can't deny that I'm relieved to be home. As I step out into the shade of the sprawling live oak trees, the summer heat hits me like a wall—I don't recall the heat being this intense. The cicadas screech so loudly it feels like they're having a party in my ears, drowning out any coherent thoughts I have.

"Hey, when I left, we were putting up the Fourth of July

decorations," I say, glancing around and noticing the house is bare. "Where's all the festive bunting"?

"We took it down, the celebration is over," Duncan replies. "But we had a blast over the Fourth of July weekend. Oh, and guess what? Rye totally crushed it in the hot dog eating contest."

"My Rye?" I ask. "You've got to be kidding. I know he loves hot dogs, but this takes his dedication to a whole new level."

"He won the contest fair and square," Duncan confirms with a grin. "But he kept us up all night, throwing them back up. I doubt he'll be craving hot dogs anytime soon."

"I can't even imagine Rye in a hot dog eating contest," I chuckle, shaking my head at the thought.

As Duncan swings open the door to the garage apartment, Beau comes barreling toward me, barking with pure excitement. I brace myself for the inevitable onslaught of puppy love.

Julie trails behind Beau, her arms outstretched. As she embraces me, I ask, "Where's Rye?" My eyes dart around the apartment, searching for him.

"He'll be along," Julie replies, her voice carrying an odd tone, making me pause. I give her a questioning glance but quickly shake it off—maybe I'm just overthinking things.

"I'm really happy to be home," I say.

"We're thrilled you're back," Julie exclaims as she pulls away from our embrace. "We missed you." Her words wrap around me like a fluffy blanket on a chilly evening, instantly filling me with a sense of belonging and warmth.

"Congratulations, old man, we heard the fantastic news—you placed in the tournament. This definitely calls for a celebration," Duncan beams. "We've made reservations for supper at the Hungry Man Cafe downtown. Trust me, it'll be a night you won't forget."

"Guys, you shouldn't have gone to all this trouble," I respond, my voice trembling as tears of joy start to well up in my eyes. Just then, I notice Ryan leaning against the doorframe in the hall, and his expression tells a different story—he doesn't appear to be happy.

"Rye," I say as I walk over and wrap my arms around him.

Oddly, he remains rigid and doesn't return the embrace.

"What's the matter?" I ask.

"That's our cue to leave," Julie announces softly, taking Duncan's hand and leading him out of the apartment.

"What's the deal?" I ask.

He shoots me an angry glare, his silence heavy with unspoken words.

"I seriously have no idea what's going on," I admit, feeling the unexplained tension rising between us.

"Explain this," Ryan demands, jabbing a rigid finger at a grainy newspaper photo which seems to hold secrets I'm not privy to.

"What is that?" I ask, struggling to make out the image.

"Really? You thought I wouldn't find out?" Ryan shoots back, his tone sharp and challenging.

"I honestly have no idea what you're referring to," I reply as I reach for the newspaper.

"Go on—explain this," he demands, frustration evident as he flings the paper at me.

I pick up the paper from the floor. Unfolding the crinkled pages, I see a photo of two chess players locked in an intense duel at the New Orleans chess tournament. They sit across from each other at a polished table, game pieces meticulously arranged in perfect order. Their eyes are fixed on one another, each lost in their own world of strategy and concentration.

"What's the big deal?" I ask. "It's two competitors playing chess."

Ryan's eyes shimmer with frustration and emotion. "Really? Look closer."

I squint at the photo, trying to identify what he wants me to see. "Okay, it's two players deep in thought over their chessboard," I reply. "And in the background, there's an audience watching from the gallery—"

Suddenly, it dawns on me like a flash of lightning cutting through a stormy sky. The intensity of the moment hits me. I finally see what Ryan wants me to see.

"Well?" Ryan presses, his eyes narrowing. "What do you have to say for yourself?"

I'm speechless. How can I convey the unexpected context behind this photo? The photographer accidentally captured an intimate moment between Giles and me while we were sitting in the gallery. It was completely unplanned—his arm draped over me while my head rests on his shoulder. It's hard to believe the photographer intended to capture us that way—it was a surprising coincidence. The caption under the photo mentions the chess competition, but fails to convey the overlooked context of our intimate moment in the background.

I'm at a breaking point and desperately want to make things right. Yes, I've been caught red-handed cheating on Ryan, and the weight of my actions are crushing me. I've never strayed before, but Ryan now has undeniable proof I've betrayed his trust—at least once. I completely understand why he's furious with me—honestly, who wouldn't be? But here I am, at a complete loss on how to mend this mess other than to come clean.

"Rye," I plead, "it's not what it looks like. Okay, I know it looks bad, but think about everything we've been through together. We can work through this."

"I don't see how," Ryan says, his voice devoid of emotion.

"Please, Rye," I plead.

"It's over," he replies, his words heavy with disappointment. "I've packed my bags and I'm going back to Austin. I can't stay here after everything that's happened."

"No, Rye," I plead again, my heart racing.

"We're done," he snaps, turning his back on me as if slamming a door shut.

I genuinely messed up. Never in a million years did I think I would end up here, facing the consequences of my actions. Ryan is leaving, and honestly, I can't blame him. It's hard to watch someone you care about walk away because of your stupid mistakes.

I wish there were a way to make things right, but time has run out. My heart aches under the weight of my mistake, and I can't help but wonder if I'll ever be able to forgive myself.

Ryan keeps his promise, and Duncan drives him to the bus station for the morning bus back to Austin. I can't shake the gnawing sense of dread I feel at the thought of Ryan spending the night at that lonely station. Can I honestly blame him for being upset with me? After all, I made a huge mistake, and now we're both left to deal with the consequences.

I feel a deep sense of sadness about how everything has unfolded between Ryan and me. It feels like we're not just closing a chapter; we're shutting the cover on the entire book of our shared story. Almost twenty years of mutual laughter, tears, and unforgettable memories have vanished in an instant.

Isn't it wild how one mistake in New Orleans unraveled everything? I often wonder if I genuinely deserved Ryan after what happened. Maybe I didn't, but part of me wishes he would've given us another chance. Despite all the hurt I caused, my heart still holds onto hope for reconciliation because, at the end of the day, I still love him deeply. Our relationship wasn't just a part of my life; it was my *entire* life.

"I'm sorry, Taylor," Julie says, her voice warm and empathetic as she messages my shoulders. "Duncan and I tried to talk to Rye, but ever since he saw that newspaper article, he's not been himself."

"Julie," I reply, the weight of guilt heavy on my chest, "this is all my fault. I should have seen this coming. For a week, I felt this incredible happiness that someone like me probably didn't deserve."

"Hey, don't be so hard on yourself," Julie assures me, her eyes sparkling with sincerity. "If he truly wanted to make things work, he would have stayed and fought for your relationship. Instead, he tucked tail and ran."

"I totally agree," Duncan says as he strides into the room. "Honestly, I think Rye was looking for an excuse to call it quits. That newspaper article? It was his golden ticket out."

"Duncan," Julie interjects, her brow furrowing. "Don't you think that's a bit harsh?"

"Harsh? Not really," Duncan replies with a shrug. "When a guy wants to bail on a relationship but doesn't want to come off looking like the bad guy, he'll seize any opportunity he can to make the other party look guilty."

Julie raises an eyebrow, clearly taken aback. "Would you do that to me?"

Duncan hesitates, dodging her question like a curveball, and instead turns to me with a grin. "So, are you ready to put on the ol' proverbial feed bag for your homecoming celebration?"

"Honestly, I'm not in the mood," I reply. "I mean, I'm not exactly feeling festive."

"Come on, it's your first night back home, and we're excited to celebrate with you," Julie urges.

"I think I'll pass," I say, trying to keep my tone light despite the heaviness in my heart.

"Alright, we'll respect your wishes," Julie says.

"Don't wait up for us," Duncan says with a casual wave as he and Julie go out the door.

Now it's just Beau and me in the apartment, and it feels eerily quiet—too quiet for my liking. My mind drifts back to when Julie asked Duncan, *Would you do that to me?* What an odd question. It makes me wonder if something more is going on between them that I don't know about.

"Hey, Beau," I ask. "Is there something going on between Julie and Duncan? You can spill the tea with me—what's the deal?"

Beau flops his head onto my lap with a heavy sigh, as if he's carrying the weight of the world.

"Thanks a lot, buddy," I say, gently scratching behind his ears. "That's not the straightforward answer I was hoping for. You're just too darned loyal to your friends."

DAY SIXTY-THREE

Monday, July 16, 2018

Julie finally came clean—admitting she and Duncan started dating while I was away at the chess competition. Can you believe it? On the third night of my trip, Duncan moved into Julie's bedroom, and at first, everything was going fine. However, as the days and nights went on, their relationship began to lose its spark and excitement.

What should have been an unforgettable adventure in New Orleans turned into a whirlwind of emotions, shifting the dynamics between me and my three friends.

Ever since returning from New Orleans, the atmosphere has shifted dramatically. Julie and Duncan's arguments have become more frequent and increasingly intense, leaving me caught in the middle as an unwilling mediator. It's difficult to watch either of them storm out of the room or sit in silence, giving each other the cold shoulder. Duncan spends his nights alone on the sofa, which Beau doesn't understand. He doesn't comprehend why he has to give up his bed for Duncan.

At lunch today, with Duncan sitting across from her, Julie said to me, "Please tell Duncan that I'm not talking to him."

"Tell Miss Priss, I have nothing to say to her," Duncan instructs me, his tone sharp and dismissive.

"Good," Julie replies, her arms crossed defiantly over her chest.

"Good," Duncan echoes, shooting a glare in Julie's direction that could cut glass.

Their ongoing feud is like a tense game of tug-of-war, and

here I am—stuck in the middle, feeling emotionally torn by their relentless conflict. How did things escalate to this point? I grapple with the complexity of their situation, desperately searching for a way to mend the rift between them. But honestly? It's proving to be far more complicated than I imagined—a troubling scenario that has turned my homecoming into an unexpected battlefield.

That afternoon, things between Julie and Duncan reached a boiling point. I drove Julie to the bus station, her luggage piled in the back of my Jeep—a tangible reminder of her decision to leave. With a heavy heart, she purchased a one-way ticket to Dallas. Despite my best efforts to convince her to stay—after all, who wants to see a friend walk away? She had reached her limit with Duncan's *endless drama* (her words, not mine).

As I drove back home, I felt a whirlwind of emotions inside me. It was tough watching someone I care about make such a difficult choice. However, at the end of the day, what mattered most was respecting her decision.

It's just Duncan, Beau, and me left in the big ol' house. I hope Beau is blissfully unaware of the craziness around us. Lucky him. But let's be honest—he's not stupid.

Returning home from dropping Julie off at the bus station, I'm surprised to find Duncan frantically shoving his suitcases into his SUV.

"Hey, what's going on?" I ask, genuinely puzzled.

"I'm going back to Charleston, South Carolina," he replies. "There's nothing keeping me here."

I can't believe it—three untimely farewells in just one week. I've said goodbye to three incredible friends in just a matter of days: first Ryan, then Julie, and now Duncan. It feels surreal. The group of college friends who arrived here just months ago, laughing and looking forward to making memories during our summer getaway, has suddenly splintered.

Reflecting on the past few weeks, I can't help but wonder:

What if I'd chosen not to go to New Orleans and instead stayed in Lost Creek Junction? Would things have turned out differently? The sweltering summer heat and cramped quarters may have contributed to the strain on our friendships. Additionally, the added stress of running the bed-and-breakfast —could that have been a tipping point?

Regardless of the reasons, Beau and I are now solely responsible for running the bed-and-breakfast.

Wallowing in self-pity, I'm suddenly jolted back to reality by the sharp ring of my phone. I scramble to pull the cell from my pocket and am surprised to see Mr. Andrews's name displayed on the screen. It turns out he wants me to drop everything and come to his office right away for something urgent. But what could it be?

His vague request sends a wave of curiosity and anxiety twisting in my stomach. Is it good news or bad? Am I about to face a life-changing decision or just another hurdle? My mind races with questions, each one more pressing than the last.

"Oh, just fantastic. What else can possibly go wrong?" I mutter, my heart racing and my palms slick with sweat. The phone in my hand feels like a lead weight dragging me down. Isn't it true bad things come in threes? Haven't I already hit my limit? First, Ryan left. Then Julie followed suit. And now Duncan? Seriously, what more can life throw at me?

As I step into the reception area of Mr. Andrews's law office, the atmosphere is charged with anticipation. His secretary looks up from her desk and says, "Go on in. He's expecting you."

I take a deep breath and push open the door to his office. My heart skips a beat when I spot a woman dressed entirely in black, sitting in a chair with her back turned to me. "Excuse me," I say softly, not wanting to interrupt whatever serious discussion they might be having. "I didn't realize you were with someone." I turn to slip back out.

"No, my boy. Please come in," Mr. Andrews says with a warm smile, gesturing toward the empty chair across from the mystery woman. I feel a mix of surprise and curiosity at this unexpected invitation.

As I settle into my seat, I'm immediately surrounded by a delicate fragrance—the unmistakable scent of rosewater. This perfume doesn't just linger in the air; it evokes a whirlwind of memories within me. This rare and feminine aroma feels like a warm embrace from the past, reminiscent of the special occasions when Grandma got gussied up and wore her favorite scent. I long for the time I spent with her. Suddenly, I'm transported to an afternoon not long ago when I discovered Ol' Lady Blackburn's hat boxes tucked away on a dusty shelf in the bedroom closet. As I moved one aside, I caught a whiff of that enchanting fragrance drifting through the air.

"Taylor, I invited you here today because I want you to meet someone very special," Mr. Andrews says, glancing at the elderly woman beside him. "Allow me to introduce Mrs. Mabel June MacAllister-Blackburn."

Wait, what? My jaw drops in disbelief as I struggle to find my voice. It feels like the world has fallen out of rotation. All I can do is stare at her with wide eyes, completely overwhelmed by this unexpected revelation.

She offers a fleeting smile—a quick flash of warmth—before her expression hardens again, returning to its icy demeanor.

"Wait, you're dead," I blurt out, my eyes darting nervously between Mr. Andrews and the woman sitting across from me.

"Actually, yes and no," Mr. Andrews replies, his tone steady yet cryptic. "Mrs. Blackburn was never truly dead. She staged her death for personal reasons."

His revelation hits me like a baseball bat to the head, shattering my understanding of reality into countless fragments, each reflecting a different version of the truth.

"But wait a minute—what about the last will and testament? What about the money, the house, and the Jeep?" I ask, feeling confused.

Mr. Andrews looks at me calmly. "The money is yours to keep," he explains matter-of-factly. "However, the widow wishes to buy back the house."

"But if she's still alive, doesn't that mean the house rightfully belongs to her?" I ask, confused.

"Legally speaking," Mr. Andrews replies with a reassuring nod, "you signed all the paperwork making you the rightful owner of the house."

"I can't accept money for something I never truly owned," I say, feeling the weight of the situation pressing heavily on my shoulders. It's a difficult position to be in—caught between legal ownership and moral responsibility.

"Mr. Greene," the widow pleads, her words trembling with urgency. "Would you please consider selling the house for one dollar? You have no idea how much I need to have that house back." Her request hangs in the air like a fragile thread, pulling at my heartstrings.

I glance at Mr. Andrews, searching for a sign of his thoughts. To my relief, he nods in agreement. "Alright," I say to the widow, "you can buy your house back for one dollar."

Mr. Andrews promptly hands me some papers to sign, making everything official, transferring ownership of the house back to her. In exchange, the widow hands me an uncirculated, crisp one-dollar bill, her arthritic fingers trembling slightly as she clutches the deed to her cherished home to her bosom.

"Simon," the widow says to Mr. Andrews, her voice firm yet urgent, "could you please give Mr. Greene and me a moment alone? It's very important."

"Of course, take all the time you need," Mr. Andrews replies, rising from his chair with a nod. He strides toward the closed door but pauses briefly, turns to us, furrows his brow in thought, before stepping into the reception area and gently pulling the door shut.

The widow pauses, takes a deep breath, then says, "I can only imagine how overwhelming all of this must feel for you," the widow continues, her tone revealing something deeper beneath the surface. "What would you like to ask me?"

"Where do I even begin with all these questions?" I exclaim, feeling a mix of curiosity and confusion.

"Take your time, dear. I'm in no rush," she replies with a reassuring nod.

"I guess my first question has to be: why did you leave your house and money to me when you were pretending to be dead?" I ask, my heart racing.

She chuckles, as if my question was expected. "How could I not see that coming? Let me break it down for you in two parts." Her eyes twinkle with mischief. "First off—why did I leave the house to you? How can I say this without sounding too blunt?"

"Just say it. I'm not a kid. I can handle the truth," I insist, eager for answers.

"Brace yourself. I'm about to drop a bombshell on you. You see, what you probably aren't aware of is that you were adopted."

"Adopted?" I gasp. The words hit me like a ton of bricks. The idea is utterly unfathomable. "No way, that can't be true."

"Oh, but it is," the widow replies gently, her voice laced with a mix of compassion and resolve.

"If I'm adopted, as you say," I press on, my mind racing with questions, "then who was my birth mother?"

"Your birth mother couldn't care for you," the widow gently explains, her voice filled with a mix of sadness and understanding. "She realized early on in the pregnancy she wasn't in a position to provide the life you deserved, so she made the incredibly difficult choice to give you up at birth to the loving parents who raised you."

"How do you know about any of this?" I ask.

"Because your birth mother was my sister," she reveals with a soft sigh.

"What?" I gasp, my heart racing.

"My dear boy," the widow says gently, her eyes filled with sorrow and warmth. "Your birth mother—my sister—passed away while bringing you into this world." She pauses for a moment, allowing the weight of her words to sink in. "She had a premonition something might go wrong during your birth. In her wisdom, she made arrangements for you long before you took your first breath."

"This can't be true," I mutter, struggling to comprehend this shocking revelation. Why am I only hearing about this now?"

As the widow's words sink in, a wave of anger and confusion overwhelms me. "How could my parents keep such a monumental part of my life a secret?"

"I suppose your adoptive parents thought there was no real benefit in telling you," she replies gently. "Since your birth mother was no longer alive, they probably believed you didn't need to know where you came from. After all, you would never have the chance to meet her. Or maybe they just hadn't found the right moment to share this information with you before the car accident. I wish I had more answers for you."

"How do you know about the accident?" I ask.

"I know a lot about you," she replies, implying she holds secrets about my past I can only begin to understand.

"But what about my grandma?" I ask, curiosity bubbling within me. "She could have told me everything at anytime."

"Adoption details are not typically something a grandparent feels comfortable discussing with their grandchild," the widow responds, her voice full of understanding and deep empathy. "I've watched you from a distance all these years. I made sure you had a loving home and someone to care for you—it was my way of honoring the love your birth mother would have wanted for you."

"Wait, hold on a second," I exclaim, my mind racing. "How does my adoption relate to faking your death and putting me in your will?"

"Bear with me—I'm getting to that," she says, her voice trembling with emotion. "You see, I don't have children of my own. It's not that I didn't dream of having a family—life took an unexpected turn when my husband passed away too soon. But you—oh, you are the light in my life—you are my nephew.

"Because of the adoption terms, I had to stay out of the picture until after your twentieth birthday. Can you imagine how hard that was? Watching from a distance as you grew up without knowing who I was? When your parents left this world, my heart ached to hold and comfort you. I was there when you went to live with your grandmother, silently cheering you on every step of the way.

"I attended all your school plays and recitals, bursting with pride as I watched you shine on stage. And oh, your high school graduation—what a moment that was. Tears of joy streamed down my face as I celebrated the incredible person you'd become. You are the child I never had but have cherished from afar."

"Wait, are you telling me I'm your only living relative?" I ask.

The widow nods slowly. "When Simon drafted my Last Will and Testament, you were my only blood relative. Since then, I've discovered a distant great-niece, but that's a story for another time."

I lean in closer, intrigued. "But why did you fake your death and leave this town behind?"

Her expression shifts to one of somber reflection. "I was diagnosed with a terminal illness and given a few months to live. The thought of dying here haunted me. Have you heard about the ghost curse that plagues this town? It's chilling. The idea of my spirit being trapped here forever, unable to cross over... I couldn't bear the thought of becoming one of those restless souls doomed to wander these streets for eternity," she explains, her voice heavy with emotion.

I nod in understanding.

"Believe it or not," she begins, her eyes sparkling with a mix of excitement and relief, "I faked my death to escape this town and the curse which would haunt me. During my travels, I sought out medical experts and learned I had been misdiagnosed all along. Now, I have many healthy years ahead of me."

"That's great news," I reply, genuinely thrilled for her.

"But there's something else you need to know," the widow continues, her tone shifting to one of urgency. "There's another curse you are not aware of. I didn't discover it until recently, which prompted my immediate return to town."

"Another curse?" I ask.

"I recently discovered a curse associated with the house on the hill, which was once owned by the wife of General Samuel T. Scruggs. According to legend, only female descendants of the widow can claim ownership of the property." She leans in closer, her voice dropping to an urgent whisper. "You see, any male heir who attempts to gain full ownership faces a fate so horrifying it makes death seem like a walk in the park." She looks at me and pauses for dramatic effect, allowing the weight of her words to sink in. "I had to come back. I needed to purchase the house from you to save you from this dreadful curse."

"How do you know about all these curses?" I ask, curiosity bubbling within me.

"I, like the other female descendants of Mrs. Scruggs's line, am a witch," the widow replies with a knowing smile. "I possess knowledge of all the curses that have plagued our family for generations."

"So, if you're a witch, does that make me a warlock?" I question, my mind racing with possibilities.

"No, my dear," she says gently. "You are not a warlock. You are an extraordinarily talented young man in your own right. The witch bloodline flows solely through the females of the Scruggs ancestral line."

Wait a minute—is she serious? Is she joking, or is she a card-carrying witch from some secret coven? I'll play along for now, but I can't shake my skepticism. Since arriving in Lost Creek Junction, I've witnessed some truly bizarre things that make her wild story seem almost believable. Yet, there's a nagging doubt in my mind—could it all just be one big prank? For the moment, I'll keep my thoughts to myself. The last thing I want is to end up transformed into a toad or frog by someone who claims to have magical powers.

"Earlier, you mentioned finding a long-lost great-niece?" I

ask.

"Yes," the widow replies. "Her name is Rachael, and she's around your age. When I pass on, she'll inherit my house. You see, she's a descendant of the original Scruggs family line. I'm leaving the house to her. I hope you're not too disappointed?"

"I have no intention of meeting a horrible death, you can have the house. But when do I need to pack my bags and move out?" I ask. "Currently, I'm staying in the garage apartment because the bedrooms in the main house are occupied by bed-and-breakfast guests."

"My dear boy," she says, her voice filled with heartfelt gratitude, "you are welcome to stay for as long as you wish. I want to commend you and your friends for saving Lost Creek Junction. You four are like guardian angels, swooping in to protect our town from the brink of ruin during its darkest hour. We will forever be ingratiated to you for everything you've done for the citizens and the hundreds of ghosts trapped here."

"Will the ghosts always be trapped?" I ask.

"While I was away," the widow says, a twinkle in her eye, "I came upon a spell that I believe can break the two-hundred-year-old curse."

"Are you telling me the ghosts might finally find peace and move on?" I ask.

"Absolutely," she nods confidently. "I truly believe many of those ghostly souls will choose to stay right here in Lost Creek Junction. After all, this was their home when they were alive, and they've formed deep connections with the living residents." She pauses for a moment, allowing her words to sink in. "But we'll have to wait and see what the spirits decide for themselves, won't we?"

"What's going to happen to the bed-and-breakfast?" I ask. "It's fully booked for another year."

"Don't you worry your little head about that," the widow assures with a warm smile. "All reservations will be honored, and the bed-and-breakfast you established will continue to welcome tourists for years to come."

"Will you be taking over the operation?" I inquire.

"No, my dear boy," she replies gently, shaking her head. "I'm much too old for that now. But there is one individual who can definitely step in and keep things running smoothly."

"Who?" I ask.

"My newly discovered great-niece," she exclaims, her eyes sparkling with excitement. "She's on her way here to take over as both the bed-and-breakfast proprietor and the lady of the house."

"What will happen to you?" I ask.

With a knowing smile, she replies, "It's time for me to step aside and let the younger generation take the reigns. I'll stay in Lost Creek Junction long enough to ensure the bed and breakfast transition goes smoothly. After that? I'm off to an exotic island paradise where tanned, shirtless, muscular waiters serve up tropical drinks garnished with colorful chunks of fruit and those cute fancy paper umbrellas."

Dale Thele

DAY SIXTY-FIVE

Wednesday, July 18, 2018

To say the least, my summer break spent in Lost Creek Junction has been truly an adventure. When I first arrived in May, I had no idea what to expect. Little did I know this summer would become one of the most impactful experiences of my life.

Have you ever had a summer that completely changed your perspective? That's exactly what happened to me. This summer has been unlike any other, filled with unforgettable moments and lessons I'll carry with me forever. Although there were challenges along the way, I wouldn't trade this experience for anything. It's a chapter of my life I'll always cherish.

As I'm about to say goodbye to Lost Creek Junction, I feel how much I've grown during my time here. It's bittersweet, but I'm leaving as a different person than when I arrived—and for that, I'm incredibly grateful.

Tossing my suitcase into the back of the Jeep—a generous gift from my new aunt, the widow—I sense the excitement as I embark on a whole new chapter of my life. As I press the accelerator, I leave Lost Creek Junction behind in a swirling cloud of dust. Will I ever return for an extended visit? Who knows. Beau is staying here in Lost Creek Junction with my aunt for the rest of my summer vacation, and I've promised to come back before school starts in the fall to pick him up.

It's heartwarming to see how close he and my aunt have become; they're inseparable. While a twinge of jealousy creeps in, it's quickly overshadowed by the thrill of exploration that lies ahead. The open road beckons—where will it take me?

As I drive out of Lost Creek Junction, I'm reminded of when I first arrived in town, a dramatic cloud of dust trailed behind me. Now, with each turn of the wheel, my Jeep kicks up a plume of dust, creating a fitting farewell to the fleeting memories I'm leaving behind.

Looking into the rearview mirror, I see those sun-soaked memories fading into the haze—adventures that now feel like whispers in the wind.

END OF SUMMER BREAK

Sunday, August 26, 2018

After leaving Lost Creek Junction, I returned to the apartment in Austin where Ryan and I once called home. The place felt empty without him. Although he wasn't there, my belongings were packed neatly in boxes, waiting for a new story. As I loaded everything into my Jeep, a wave of sentimentality washed over me. It was hard to say goodbye—not just to the city but to all the memories Ryan and I had created together over all those years.

I wish I could've told Ryan how much he meant to me face-to-face. Instead, I left him a note with my heart racing as I wrote it, unsure if he'd read it or how he might respond. Did he know hurting him was never my intention? I wanted him to understand that our time together was invaluable, and no matter what happened next, I genuinely wished him all the best in life.

With nearly a month left before classes resumed, I felt the urge to hit the road and see where it would take me. As you might have guessed, I ended up in New Orleans. The journey was nothing short of magical, filled with breathtaking scenery, quirky roadside attractions, and unforgettable conversations making every mile worthwhile.

As I rolled into the Big Easy, I couldn't wait to reconnect with Giles.

Last week, Giles and I returned to Lost Creek Junction for a quick visit to pick up Beau on my birthday, which made the day even more special. The joy in Beau's eyes when he spotted me was absolutely priceless.

What surprised me most was how quickly he bonded with Giles. It seems I'll be sharing my life with both of them now— talk about an unexpected twist in our family dynamic. It looks as if I'm destined for yet another three-way relationship, but this time it's a heartwarming blend of Giles, Beau, and me. And you know what? It feels right.

You won't believe what happened next. Instead of returning to Austin for school in the fall, I boldly decided to transfer to Xavier University in New Orleans on a full chess scholarship. After securing a third-place finish in the collegiate chess tournament in July, I realized I wanted to make a change. The scholarship I received as my prize became the ticket to my future.

Now, I'm sharing an apartment with Giles and Beau, located just a short distance from campus. Let me tell you, we're living our best lives.

The summer of '98 was an unforgettable adventure that stands out in my memory like a vibrant splash of color on a gray canvas. If someone offered me the chance to swap out that exhilarating summer for a quiet, uneventful one, I'd decline without a moment's thought. Why settle for the ordinary when you can dive into the extraordinary?

In life, we often face choices between taking the easy road or venturing into the thrilling unknown. What wonders might be waiting just around the corner if we dare to explore? I took that leap into the uncharted territory of summer adventures, and let me tell you—I've never looked back.

When you reflect back on your life, what do you think you'll wish you'd have done differently? It might be time to step off the beaten path and embrace the adventures that await you on the path less traveled. Life is fleeting, and it's essential to approach each day with determination and an open heart.

Looking back on my unforgettable summer, one lesson

stands out above all others: sometimes, what you're searching for finds its way to you when you least expect it. Trust your instincts and follow your heart—you never know what delightful surprises await just around the bend.

The End?

All your favorites, Julie, Duncan, Ryan, Taylor, Giles, and introducing Beauregard Winston Churchill Greene II, return to Lost Creek Junction by invitation of ol' lady Blackburn's great-niece Rachael. Strange things are happening at the Blackburn house, and Rachael can't handle things alone. Curses, witches, skeletons, and ghosts complicate matters, challenging our friends to solve the mysteries at the Blackburn house.

Coming in late 2025

About The Author

Most of Dale Thele's life has been a lengthy series of compulsions strung together by atrocious acts of stupidity due to boredom. After raising heck in a sleepy oil town in north-central Oklahoma for eighteen years, he ventured to Oklahoma City University on a quest for higher education. He quickly learned "higher" education meant to "elevate" one's mind with the aid of either a reefer or a bong, and ample amounts of alcohol. Some years later destiny dragged him to Austin, Texas, where he currently lives vicariously through the fictional characters he conjures up, and the far-fetched adventures he writes.

Visit the Official Website:
www.DaleThele.com

"corrupting readers since 2008"
with LGBTQIA+ themed fiction

LGBTQIA+ RESOURCES

The Trevor Project – www.thetrevorproject.org
TrevorLifeline – 1-866-488-7386
A non-profit organization focusing on suicide prevention efforts among lesbian, gay, bisexual, transgender, queer, and questioning (LGBTQ) youth. They also operate The Trevor Lifeline, a confidential service that offers trained counselors.

National Suicide Prevention Lifeline –
www.suicidepreventionlifeline.org
National Suicide Prevention Lifeline – 1-800-273-8255
A suicide prevention network of over 160 crisis centers providing 24/7 service via a toll-free hotline:
1-800-273-8255 (TALK)
It is available to anyone in suicidal crisis or emotional distress.

It Gets Better Project – www.itgetsbetter.org
An Internet-based nonprofit founded in response to the suicides of teenagers who were bullied because they were gay or because their peers suspected that they were gay. Its goal is to prevent suicide among LGBT youth by having gay adults convey the message that these teens' lives will improve.

PFLAG – www.pflag.org
The United States' first and largest organization uniting parents, families, and allies with people who are lesbian, gay, bisexual, transgender, and queer. PFLAG National is the national organization, which provides support to the PFLAG network of local chapters.

Other Titles by Dale Thele

Chasing Unicorns

Masked Identities

Roadhouse Friday

Harvest Moon

Naughty Gay Adult Bedtime Stories

Clipped Wings

Blurred Lines

Find these titles at

www.dalethele.com